Fifty Psalms

FIFTY PSALMS

a New Translation

Huub Oosterhuis

Michel van der Plas

Pius Drijvers

Han Renckens

Frans Jozef van Beeck

David Smith

Forrest Ingram

A CROSSROAD BOOK
THE SEABURY PRESS · NEW YORK

1973
The Seabury Press
815 Second Avenue
New York, N.Y. 10017

Library of Congress Catalog Card Number: 71–80273
Manufactured in the United States
ISBN: 0–8164–2581–7

The priests and the levites had to bring up the Ark of the Lord, Israel's God. David set apart for the service a number of men from the clans of Asaph, Heman, and Jeduthun ; they all sang in the house of the Lord under the king's orders and under the direction of their fathers, to the accompaniment of cymbals, harps, and lyres. All of them were trained in singing to the Lord, two hundred aud eighty-eight skilful musicians. Benaiah and Jahaziel, the priests, had to blow the trumpets all the time.

It was on that day that David had the praise of the Lord sung for the first time by Asaph and his brethren :

> *"Give thanks to God, for he is good,*
> *his love endures in eternity."*

And the whole people cried : "Amen ! Halleluiah !"

And when Solomon had finished building the house of the Lord, a song was raised, with trumpets and cymbals and other instruments :

> *"Give thanks to God, for he is good,*
> *his love endures in eternity."*

Then the Lord's house was filled with a dark cloud, so that the priests could not go on with the service, for the glory of the Lord filled the house of the Lord. And Solomon said : "The Lord has chosen to live in clouds and darkness. I have built a lofty house for you, a house to live in for ever. Now,

my God, look down and listen to the prayers heard in this place." At last he let the people go home with joy and gladness in their hearts because they knew that God was good.

Thus, ever since the days of David, the Man of God, long ago, there have been guilds of singers with their songs of praise and thanksgiving to God.

Contents

Introduction

An attempt is an experiment, a beginning made with a minimum of fixed rules.

When work was first started on the Dutch original of this book, not everything was completely clear, and much more time could have been spent in preliminary discussion. Yet it seemed preferable to get down to business with a provisional method of work, and to try to reach greater clarity while actually working. This clarity in fact came in this way. Thanks to this lack of previous discussion the effort to translate the psalms was not directed against anything or anybody—the collaborators were concerned only with the psalms themselves.

At first many more people were involved in the project and an even wider sphere of collaboration was envisaged. But the need for efficient work and frequent meetings spontaneously led to the formation of a small group of collaborators. The result is that basically only two poets and two scripture-scholars are responsible for the texts in this collection. It is not difficult to guess how the undertaking came about—there was an existing situation and a holy conviction, and the two interacted on each other.

The introduction of the liturgy in the language of the people exposed the painful lack of good texts both for speaking and for singing. The urgent liturgical need was for a strong vernacular that would be both fairly durable and carefully considered by experts from the point of view of sound and rhythm. The content was, of course, even more important, but this was readily available—the psalms express man's existence and his religious experience in such a pure and im-

pressive way that they provide irreplaceable material both for liturgical singing and for personal prayer.

Although the first intention of the collaborators was to provide psalms that could be used in the new liturgy, they also aimed consciously at a much wider sphere of interest and hoped that their fifty psalms would prove suitable in all kinds of situations, including the field of education. This meant that their selection had also to reflect something of the rich variety of the psalter, with the result that at least one typical example was chosen to represent each of the most important kinds of psalm. Weak passages in the translation cannot therefore in themselves and in all cases be attributed to lack of ability on the part of the translators—the original poetry is sometimes itself weak.

In spite of all the initial lack of clarity, then, there was a clear aim at the very outset: the language had to be as good as possible, but not at the expense of the psalms themselves, which had to remain authentically the psalms. This explains why the poets and the exegetes always worked so closely together. Older and more recent translations, both Dutch and foreign, were constantly consulted. These clarified and confirmed the special purpose of the undertaking—after all, why simply do again what has already been done so often and so well? In other words, this attempt at a translation of fifty of the psalms does not make the slightest claim to replace any of the existing translations. After all, it comprises no more than one-third of the psalter. Those who have collaborated in it believe that the result of their work may be of use at an opportune time and place, and that it may possibly also serve as a contribution to a more authentic understanding of the already existing translations.

Within the group of collaborators, the task of the two exegetes was to make clear what the whole range of meaning and expression was in each psalm selected for translation, word

by word, verse by verse, and finally in the psalm as a whole. Wherever the text was disputed or corrupt, they had to make a responsible choice or else leave the choice between several possibilities open after giving their reasons for and against. In this way the poets knew the sphere within which they could move, and within this sphere they had then to track down and exploit all the possibilities of form, vocabulary, and idiom in their own language. Their first draft, often very uneven and full of provisional translations and unanswered questions, was then thoroughly discussed together with the exegetes, and a combined search was afterwards made for any possibilities of new meanings in the Hebrew and of new expressions in the vernacular. In this way, an increasing number of psalms came very gradually on the stocks, each psalm, however, in a different stage of construction—some hardly looked at and others entirely or almost completed.

The most difficult aspect of this task, which was at the same time its most fascinating aspect, was that of "translating" the psalmist's world of ideas and experience in such a way that the human and religious content of the psalms could really come across to people of today, and be recognized, prayed, and realized by them. To achieve this, it was impossible simply to translate one word by another. "Words are not coins, dead things whose value can be mathematically computed", as Ronald Knox warns in that delightful by-product of his translation of the Bible, *On Englishing the Bible*. So one association had rather to be "translated" by another. The translators had therefore not only to enter into the psalmist's human situation and religious experience—they had also, and above all, to penetrate into what the psalmist's real intention was within this human and religious experience. In other words, his experience had to be understood simply as the expression of human religiosity determined by conditions of time and place. Once this had been achieved, it was possible to go further and

look for a more contemporary expression of the same basic fact.

There was, then, a constant interaction between the exegetes, who looked for indications in the psalms of the Hebrew mode of feeling and expressing human and religious experience with all its echoes and overtones, and the poets, who explored the possibilities of man's contemporary sensibility and modern ways of expressing this. This often led to a common level of contact which really gave access for the first time to a certain word in the psalms.

When the psalms had been published and were being used it occurred to a Dutch theologian who is also an English scholar that the gap between the Hebrew psalms and the Dutch translation had been far more difficult to bridge than the gap between the Dutch translation and an English one would be, not only at the level of meaning and sensibility, but also at the level of poetical form and diction. The translation into English on the basis of the Dutch text actually proved a minor enterprise, compared to the previous process of transformation from Hebrew into Dutch, which the translator was in a position to retrace with the help of the notes made by the exegetes and the drafts made by the poets. Yet, the English translation, whose final text was established in collaboration with an Englishman and an American, both of whom are modern-language scholars who know Dutch, is a translation from the Dutch only in so far as a straightforward rendering of the Dutch text could result in an English text with the same qualities as the Dutch. In many cases, a recourse to the Hebrew text and other English translations was necessary to arrive at an English text which would do justice to the intentions of the authors of the Dutch translation.

It is, of course, to be expected that some people will think that the translations in this collection are not literal enough,

and in certain cases they may be right. The translators have probably not always succeeded in replacing a wooden or unintelligible literal version that is no longer meaningful by a freer text which at the same time still goes to the very heart of the matter. Within the framework of their set purpose they had, in these cases, either to translate creatively and therefore fairly audaciously or else not to translate at all. These fifty psalms can justify their existence only in so far as they have been able to avoid the blemishes which are inevitably associated with literal prose translations. What are these blemishes? They are that literal translation not only presents us with a rendering that is, in many cases, open to question, but also that it does not really fulfil its own special purpose. If it is true, in Ronald Knox's words, that "what the reader wants, I insist, is to get the illusion that he is reading, not a translation, but an original work in his own language", then it must be said that *a too literal translation does not do sufficient justice to the original text precisely because it is too literal*. This point deserves to be illustrated by two comments, which, it is hoped, will throw light on the whole situation.

1. The linguistic and stylistic means of ancient Hebrew are different from those of modern European languages such as Dutch or English. Anyone who simply takes over a Hebrew expression is being unfaithful to the datum of the text if the effect of this expression is not conveyed in his own language. The translation is only faithful when the translator uses a vernacular expression which has a similar effect. Thus, parallelism ("the subtlest irritant of all"—Ronald Knox) is a "law" of Hebrew verse, but not of English poetry. If it is reproduced in English, it can have a disturbing and enfeebling effect, whereas, in the original, it was used to strengthen the effect of what was being said. A quotation from the Revised Standard Version reflects very well this Hebrew habit of parallelism. A strong pair of lines is weakened in the modern version, because

the two halves of the verse simply have the effect of pure repetition:

> *I cry with my voice to the Lord,*
> *with my voice I make supplication to the Lord* (Ps. 142. 1).

The repetition, especially that of the name of God, has the effect of simply marking time. The translators of *Fifty Psalms*, on the other hand, making use of all the Hebrew terms and using their fundamental meaning as their inspiration, build up an English climax which very closely approximates the urgency and the fierceness of the original Hebrew:

> *I am crying out, I cry to God—*
> *o God, I implore you and beg for mercy.*

In this way, the parallel elements of this Semitic turn of phrase are linked to each other in a more English manner. In the same way, the well-known phrase from the Revised Standard Version:

> *... let the earth rejoice;*
> *let the many coastlands be glad!* (Ps. 97. 1)

has become in this new translation:

> *all the shores on earth*
> *are laughing and shouting for joy.*

Similarly, all the data of:

> *He makes peace in your borders.*
> *he fills you with the finest of the wheat* (Ps. 147. 14)

are contained in:

> *He gives you bread and peace—*
> *you live a life of abundance*

in which the sacrifice of a genuinely Hebrew expression is

compensated by a terse phrase which yet evokes the whole of human life and human aspirations. Leaving certain hebraisms out of the translation does not therefore imply an impoverishment. An example of this can be found at the beginning of Psalm 139. In the older translation, the three hebraisms are reproduced thus:

> *Thou knowest when I sit down and when I rise up, . . .*
> *Thou searchest out my path and my lying down,*
> *and art acquainted with all my ways.*

In the present translation, they appear as follows:

> *My God, you know where I am, where I go. . . .*
> *you have decided my roaming and resting,*
> *and you are familiar with all that I do.*

The "law" of parallelism imposes on Hebrew verse an excessive use of closely synonymous words such as God and Yahweh, soul and spirit, praise and bless, rejoice and exult, sea and water, ways and paths, and so on. These regularly recurring tautologies do not by any means always arise from poetic necessity, with the result that they frequently occur in places where the inner tension of the poem does not require them at all. The collection of *Fifty Psalms* had therefore to be sometimes more concise and sometimes more detailed. It is, for example, more concise in Psalms 8. 3; 22. 24, 26; 24. 1, 5, and elsewhere, and more detailed, by means of a kind of resolution into factors, for example, in Psalms 23. 5 and 97. 4. In this latter psalm, the older versions had

> *the earth sees and trembles*

or a similar phrase. But this really does not express any of the strength of the description, in Hebrew, of the theophany—it just does not make it. The original Hebrew, however, is very powerful, because "tremble" is the technical term for "labour", the pangs of childbirth, and a favourite image for

eschatological terror (cf. Is. 13. 8; 26. 17; Jer. 4. 31; 6. 24; Ps. 48. 7; 1 Thess. 5. 3). The translators therefore felt that it was necessary to charge the word "tremble" with special meaning, not by trying to make something of it, but by drawing on the biblical echo contained in it—that of the pain of a woman in childbirth. Their version thus reads:

> *The whole of the world has seen it.*
> *The earth was writhing and groaning*
> *like a woman in labour.*

This is, of course, an extreme example. It does not lend itself to systematic application, but it does illustrate what was involved in the translation.

2. Many Hebrew terms have a different range of meaning and evoke associations which are quite different from, and often much richer than, those evoked by the traditional translations of these terms. Biblicisms such as "justice" (also one of Ronald Knox's cruxes: cf. *On Englishing the Bible*, pp. 11, 30–4) and "fearing the Lord" certainly evoke a mistaken image, unless one has learnt to understand them precisely as biblicisms. But the whole purpose of the translation was to make the psalms accessible to those who do not belong to the elect group of those who are familiar with biblical language. It was here especially that the translators had to seek out new paths if they were to avoid doing essentially superfluous work. Terms, images, and expressions which have a different function or which do not function at all in modern English or in contemporary human experience had to be fathomed for their full range of meaning and their actual meaning in the text, before an equivalent that does function now could be sought.

How far-reaching that task was can be gathered from a summary and incomplete list of such words. Firstly, some which relate to God: holiness, glory, face, Yahweh (Lord), name, justice, mercy, peace, salvation, right hand, law, ways, judg-

ment. Secondly, some relating to man: the saints, the godly, those who fear God, the upright in heart, the righteous, the blameless, the pure, the poor, the humble, the lowly, the afflicted, the sinners, the wicked, the scoffers, those who do violence, the strangers. And thirdly, some that are of a more psychological nature: heart, soul, spirit, "reins", truth, vanity, deceit, knowing, confessing, praising, exalting, extolling, and putting to shame. The beginning of Ps. 103 in the Revised Standard Version may serve as an example:

> *Bless the Lord, O my soul;*
> *and all that is within me,*
> *bless his holy name!*
> *Bless the Lord, O my soul,*
> *and forget not all his benefits.*

The very first word, "bless", already presents us with a difficulty, because it is no longer very much alive in modern English. What is more, its real meaning is: to pronounce a blessing, which to Hebrew ears means: to state and enumerate in detail and to extol—hence "to praise", which is what the psalm in fact goes on to do.

The word "soul" is also very difficult. In Hebrew it is intense and meaningful, but it hardly needs to be said that it is weak in English. The word "soul", however, still continues to function in such expressions as "heart and soul" and "deep down in my soul". The translators have therefore tried to find a solution in this direction. How the rest of the opening of this psalm came about will be sufficiently clear from the result. Every line has a metre of four stressed syllables:

> *I want to call him by his Name,*
> *the holy God, as truly as I live.*
> *I thank him from the bottom of my heart,*
> *and I will forget none of his benefits.*

This is, of course, in no sense a literal translation, but it is

better than the older translations in two ways—the pathos of the original Hebrew is conveyed more clearly and the idiom is better. Just imagine the first two lines being sung as a refrain, and then compare the two versions.

The original Dutch edition of these fifty psalms does not contain a single word of comment or explanation. The psalms can indeed be left to speak for themselves, but the book was still felt to be a bit merciless. Moreover, if the book of psalms is really—to quote St Thomas Aquinas—the whole of the Old Testament in the form of prayer, it was felt that a collection of psalms like the present one could be turned into a prayerful (and therefore unsystematical) introduction to the Old Testament, offering knowledge in the only framework in which knowledge can be fruitful—experience. The commentaries, various as they are, are designed to give this extra purpose to the book, which means that they must be ignored if they are felt to be in the way of the psalms themselves.

For the psalms speak for themselves, reveal what the collaborators have done with the text, and, on closer comparison, give some indication of the frequently laborious paths and detours which had to be followed before a given text acquired its present form. It is an attempt. This presupposes the possibility of better discoveries. Note them down.

Fifty Psalms

Psalm 1

Happy is the man
who does not seek advice from godlessness,
who does not set his foot in the ways of evil,
who will not sit in circles where they laugh
at God and at his law.
Happy is that man—
he seeks with all his heart the word of God,
and savours words of wisdom night and day.

He is a tree, planted near living water,
he always bears good fruit.
And he will never wilt before his time—
whatever he undertakes will thrive.

But unhappy those people who despise God's word;
they are like chaff, blown away on the wind.
They will not keep their foothold in the judgment,
when he assembles all his righteous friends.

God knows his people and he keeps their ways.
Whoever despises him loses himself.

[Psalm 1] When the different collections of psalms were finally brought together and edited around 300 or 250 B.C., Psalm 1 was added to the collection by way of a general preface. What with its emphasis on the Law and its oracular tone in the vein of the Jewish wisdom-tradition, it is a typically Jewish meditation, impersonal, moralistic, and a bit conventional. The prophetic tone of Joshua 1. 7–9 and especially Jeremiah 17. 5–8 has been formalized to suit the demands of "organized religion". Yet, for the Jew the word *torah* continued to convey more than our present concept of "Law". It also represented "instruction", an introduction to a personal awareness of the fundamental risks and demands of life.—"Go in through the narrow doorway. For the road to perdition is wide and easy, and there are many who take it. But the road to life is narrow and the way to it difficult, and there are only few that discover it" (Matt. 7. 13–14).

Psalm 4

Give me an answer,
God, when I call to you.

You are my truth,
you give me freedom
when I am oppressed—
have mercy on me,
hear my prayer.

Man, how long
will your heart remain hardened,
will you go for appearances
and run after lies?

Do you not know
that God has a friend,
that he makes him great,
and so—that he listens
if I call to him?

Admit defeat
and sin no more,
brand it on your mind
before you sleep,
come to yourself.

Bring your gifts
just as you are,
put your trust
in our God.

Many are asking:
"Who makes us happy?"
Bless us with
the light of your eyes,
Lord our God.

You have given me
greater joy
than all those others
with their riches,
wheat and wine.

In peace I lie down
and I sleep at once.
You make me live
safe and sound, Lord
God, you alone.

[Psalm 4] An evening prayer for reliance and assurance in the form
of a quasi-dialogue, taking into account an audience of people who
also experience the struggle for faith. The background of this type
of self-encouragement lies in the ancient administration of justice
in a sacral and cultic setting (cf., e.g., 1 Kings 8. 31 ff.). Here, this
background has been given new life by casting it into the form of an
invitation, addressed to the believer by the Wise Man, to appeal to
God and surrender to him, as a man would surrender to sleep after
the day's struggles are over.—"Make yourselves humble under
God's powerful hand: He will relieve you in his own good time.
Confide all your anguish to him, for he cares for you" (1 Peter 5.
6–7).

Psalm 8

Lord our Lord, how powerful is your Name
everywhere on earth.

You show your majesty in the heavens,
yet you open the mouths of helpless children,
and there rises a song that bewilders your enemy—
all your opponents are put to silence.

If I look at the heavens, the work of your fingers,
the moon and the stars which you set in place—
what, then, is Man, that you remember him,
the son of Adam, that he touches your heart.

Yet you have made him almost a god,
and you have crowned him with glory and splendour.
You make him lord of the work of your hands,
and you have laid the whole world at his feet,

sheep and cattle, all, all things,
even the animals in the open plain,
the birds of the air, the fish of the sea,
all that wanders on the paths of the water.

Lord our Lord, how powerful is your Name
everywhere on earth.

[Psalm 8] Israel has always marvelled at the humanity of her God. All the gods of her neighbours were associated with the irresistible forces of Nature and the World, which left to Man no attitudes but those of cowering fear or arrogant collusion. But from the first chapter of Genesis onward the Bible presents Adam and his children, in spite of all their weakness, as never at the mercy of "the powers", but on the contrary, always above them. God is not the Lord of creation at the expense of Man. He is not a Moloch, but the God of Mankind, and "serving him is reigning" (St Leo the Great). At the basis of Israel's belief in God is the conviction that power is not the key to life, but service and love, which are stronger than the powers, even the powers of death and destruction. Our God has displayed the height of his power in the faithful and humble Servant (cf. Is. 42), "in Christ, by raising him up from the dead and by making him sit at his right hand in the heavens, high above all authorities, powers, forces and dominions, and above all that deserves a name both in this world and beyond it; and 'he has laid the whole world at his feet'. And God has made him the Head of the Church, his body; and thus he is the full realization of all creation" (Eph. 1. 20–23).

Psalm 11

My shelter is with him.

Why, then, say to me:
"Bird, flee into the mountains.
There, that man without God
bends his bow and takes aim,
shoots in the night, will strike
the heart of innocence.
If the foundations are crumbling,
what is the use of goodness?"

God, in his holy house,
he, on his throne in heaven,
seeks the world with his eyes,
tests the children of Adam.

He sees through the good and the wicked,
and whole-heartedly, he
detests those who breed terror.
He rains on their kind
showers of fire and sulphur;
a scorching desert-wind is
what they get for their thirst.

He, the true God himself,
he loves justice and truth.
Innocence will live to see him.

[Psalm 11] The social world of Israel offered two alternatives to somebody who was persecuted: he could either make use of the right of asylum, or he had to leave everything behind and go into hiding in the mountains, the abode of the outlaws and the victims of power. But where is the just man to go if he finds that "the whole earth is filled with violence" (Gen. 6. 13)? The psalmist says: ultimately we are faced with the choice between a panicky flight from the world and the surrender of faith. Faith and trust are in the end the only cure for the uncertainty brought about by the kind of demoralization described, for example, in Isaiah 59. 3–8. The psalmist does not believe in violence against violence, no more than the suffering Servant, who "had done no violence" (Is. 53. 9). Again, the key to life is not grabbing for power, but the faithful distinction between "the Lord loves" and "the Lord detests", the anticipations of the later concepts of Heaven and Hell.—"What, then, shall we say? If God is for us, who will be against us? Will the God who did not spare his own Son but gave him up for us all not also give us everything with him? Who shall bring any charge against God's chosen people? If God gives justice, who can condemn?" (Rom. 8. 31–34).

Psalm 19

1

The heavens unfold the glory of God,
the firmament boasts of the work of his hands.
The day hands it on to the following day,
the nights tell each other of what they know.
There is no speaking, there are no words,
and their voices are not to be heard—
and yet their rhythm is everywhere felt,
their echo reaches the edge of the earth.

There he has pitched a tent for the sun—
a bridegroom leaving the bridal chamber,
a hero that shouts for joy on his way,
that is the sun—he climbs along the skies
and goes down again at the farthest horizon,
and nothing can hide itself from his heat.

II

The word of the Lord is perfect,
source of life.
Our God's witness is trustworthy—
unwisdom grows wise.

Limpid water is his law,
refreshing our hearts.
His commandments: right and reason,
light to our eyes.

What he promises is pure truth,
only peace.
What he does is all done well,
everlasting.

And as exquisite as honey,
no, still more—
far more precious than pure gold
is the Lord's own word.

III

You will be worth all our trouble
if we keep your word, o Lord.
But who knows the ways of his heart?
Free us from our secret evil.

Let us not be the slaves of pride,
preserve your people from conceit.
Let us not break with you, God,
but go to meet you without fear.

All the words we speak to you,
all we think within our hearts
may find grace with you, my God,
with you, my rock and my redeemer.

[Psalm 19] This magnificent psalm is a liturgical composition, consisting of a hymn to God the Creator, a meditative praise of the Law, and a prayer for purity of heart and faith in God. It may have been used in the Temple at the time of the morning sacrifice, which celebrated the rising sun as the symbol of justice and the giving of the Law on Mount Sinai. Israel, conscious of having God's eternal mercy and wisdom dwelling in her midst in the shape of the *Torah*, the Law (cf. Sirach 24. 3–12), does not cower under "the frightening silence of those infinite spaces" (Pascal); on the contrary, their very silence has become eloquent to the People of God.—"In the beginning was the Word, and the Word was with God, and the Word was God. He was in the beginning with God; all things were made through him, and nothing of all that was made was made without him. (. . .) And the Word became flesh and dwelt among us, full of mercy and faithfulness, and we have seen his glory. (. . .) And from his fulness we have all received, mercy after mercy. For the Law was given through Moses; mercy and faithfulness have come through Jesus, the Christ. No one has ever seen God, but the only Son, who is in the bosom of the Father, he has been our guide" (John 1. 1–3, 14, 16–18).

Psalm 22

1

God, my God, why have you abandoned me?
I cry out, and you stay far away.
"My God", I call all day—you are silent,
I call through the night, and you just let me call.

O you, most holy God, enthroned
in the place where Israel's songs are sung,
our fathers put all their trust in you,
they trusted and you have been their rescue.
They called for you and you were their way out,
and never have you disappointed their trust.

But I am no longer a man but a worm,
scorned by men, despised by my neighbours.
I am a mockery in everyone's eyes,
all of them laugh at me, shaking their heads—
"He held on to the Lord, then let him deliver him,
let the God that so loves him come to his rescue."

Was it not you who drew me from the womb
and made me rest at the breast of my mother?
At birth I was put in the hollow of your hands,
you are my God from my mother's womb onward.
And why should you now be so far away?
I am close to despair, there is no one to help.

II

A savage crowd bears down upon me,
lumbering bulls press in from all sides,
they open wide their jaws to me,
ravenous lions are roaring for prey.

I am poured out, wasted like water,
and my bones are out of joint.
My soul in me is melted away,
my heart is torn from within me.

Dry as burnt clay is my throat
and my tongue sticks to my palate.
They force me down into the dust of death,
they are unleashing their hounds at me.

The mob has gathered all around me
and they have pierced my hands and feet.
One by one, I can count my ribs.
They are looking on and enjoying it.

They divide my clothes among each other,
and they gamble for my cloak.
And you, my God, you are so far away—
will you not help me, are you not my strength?

Do not surrender me to the sword,
do not give me up to the power of those dogs.
Save my life from the jaws of the lion,
me, poor man, from the horns of the bulls.

III

I will tell my brothers about him,
hold up his Name in the midst of the gathering—
"Sons of Israel, people of God,
you must worship him full of awe.
Never has he scorned the poor for being poor,
never has he turned his back upon me,
nor avoided me, but heard my cries."

This is my song in the heart of the gathering,
and there I shall fulfil my promise.
The poor, they shall eat and have their fill,
and all who look for him bless his Name.
They will come to life for ever and ever.

The ends of the earth will remember it,
and turn round to meet this God.
And all generations of all mankind
will one day bend their knees before him.
For to him belong the power and the kingdom,
he is the Lord of races and nations.
And even those who lie down in the dust
and no longer live shall worship him.

But I will live with heart and soul.
My children will also be there to serve him,
and speak about him to their children, too.
All who are yet to be born after us
will come to hear it: our God is faithful.
It is the Lord who has done all this.

[Psalm 22] The basic structure of this psalm is that of a complaint of someone wrongly persecuted, followed by a hymn of thanksgiving for the hoped-for deliverance. But the violence of the complaint as well as the large scope of the thanksgiving have given this psalm a much broader significance. Thus it became, together with chapters 52–53 in Isaiah, to which it bears a strong resemblance, one of the classical texts used by the Christian tradition to bear witness to the redeeming passion of Jesus. The synoptic Gospels have Jesus say the first line of this psalm on the cross, and the synoptic accounts of the passion allude to the first two sections several times. The last section, with its liturgical overtones, puts the past sufferings of the just man in a universalist perspective, so that the Christian tradition has also come to look upon this psalm as a prophetic witness to the resurrection of Christ and to the offer of salvation to all mankind.—"It was fitting that God, the Creator and End of all things, should bring the pioneer of all his children that were to be saved to perfection through suffering. For those who are sanctified by Christ have the same common origin as Christ, who is the source of their sanctification. And that is why he is not ashamed of calling them his brothers: "I will tell my brothers about him, hold up his Name in the midst of the gathering'" (Heb. 2. 10–12).

Psalm 23

My shepherd is the Lord,
I shall never want for anything.

He takes me to an oasis of green—
there I stretch out at the edge of the water,
where I find rest.
I come to life again, then we go forward
along trusted roads—he leads the way.
For God is his Name.

Although I must enter the darkness of death,
I am not anxious since you are with me—
in your keeping I dare to do it.

You invite me to sit at your table,
and all my enemies, with envious eyes,
have to look on while you wait upon me,
while you anoint me, my skin and my hair,
while you fill up my cup to the brim.

Happiness and mercy are coming to meet me
everywhere, every day of my life.
And always I go back to the house
of the Lord, as long as I live.

[Psalm 23] Ever since Abraham set out on his journey (Gen. 12. 1-4), faith in God, according to Scripture, has been, not an entrenched position, but a "Way" (Acts 9. 2). And for the "wandering Arameans" (Deut. 26. 5) the notion of journeying was inextricably bound up with the life of the nomadic shepherd, leading his family and his flock with unremitting faithfulness (Hebrew: *emet*, truth) from one oasis to another, from one pasture to another. No wonder, then, that these straying people, always strangers wherever they were, developed a nostalgia for a promised land where life would be without any further travelling. It is against this background that this beautiful psalm was composed, and that, for example, the prophet Ezechiel (34) came to describe God as the shepherd, faithfully leading his people to Life along his own ways. The mention of the table also points to a cultic background, also suggested by the meal on Mount Sinai (Exod. 24. 11) during Israel's journey through the desert; this has been taken up by the Christian tradition, which has applied this psalm to Baptism and the Eucharist.—"I am the good shepherd. The good shepherd gives up his life for his sheep." "I am the Way, the Truth, and the Life. Nobody comes to the Father except through me" (John 10. 11; 14. 6).

Psalm 24

The earth is the Lord's, his is this world
and those who live in it. He by himself
built it on the streams and anchored it safely.

Who may climb to the height of God,
who has the run of his holy city?
People with no guilt on their hands.

People with hearts that have been cleansed,
who do not build their lives on appearances,
who will not forge lies against others.

They find comfort and blessing with him,
they are the kind that look for God,
that want to see him, with their own eyes.

Gates, lift up and raise your heads,
reach up higher, you everlasting doors—
here comes the king of glory.

Who is the king of glory?
It is the Lord, the powerful and strong One,
it is the Lord, the strong One in battle.

Gates, lift up and raise your heads,
reach up higher, you everlasting doors—
here comes the king of glory.

Who is he, the king of glory?
He is our God, the Lord of the powers,
he is the king of glory.

[Psalm 24] This psalm is a liturgical composition consisting of several elements. The end is formed by an old processional hymn, celebrating God as the protector of his people in the holy war (*Yahweh Sebaot*, Lord of the powers, the armies); this part may go back to the days when the Ark as the symbol of God's presence accompanied the people on its expeditions, to be victoriously carried back to the sanctuary after the battle (cf. 2 Sam. 6. 1–19 for a prototypical description of this). The middle part is a liturgy at the gates of the Temple, incorporating an instruction, in the mouth of the priest, about the virtues required to take part in the cult, whereas the opening lines declare that the God of Israel's rescue and of personal salvation is also the Creator of the world. From these very different elements the psalm builds up a meditation on the discovery of God's presence through a humble search and purity of heart.—"Blessed are the pure in heart, for they will see God" (Matt. 5. 8).

Psalm 25

My desire goes out to you.

Lord, my God, I am certain of you—
and would you ever let me down,
will my enemies carry the day?
No, you will never put us to shame,
all those people who wait for you.
But those who recklessly break with you,
they will be put to shame.

Make me, Lord, at home in your ways,
lead me, put me on the track of your truth.
Guide me, you are the God who saves me,
I am waiting for you as long as I live.
Have you not always been good to me,
merciful love, from the very beginning?
Forget then, Lord, the sins of my youth,
and if I broke faith, do not remember.
Think of me only with love and mercy.

God is good and no deceiver,
He shows straight ways to those who are lost.
And to poor and humble people
he gives the strength to go his way.
All he does is love and trust,
for all who keep his covenant alive,
for all who hold on to his word.

For the sake of your Name, forgive me—
you alone can forgive my guilt.

Let a man hold God in honour—
he will know what ways to go.
He will find happiness and life,
his sons will receive the earth to themselves.
God will take him into his trust
and guide him into his covenant.
My eyes are always looking for him,
he lifts me up when I have fallen.

Take notice of me and show your mercy,
for I am lonely, with no one to help.
My heart is anxious and oppressed—
open me, give me space and freedom.

Do not turn away from my misery,
take my sins away from me.
Surely you know that I have enemies
who hate me with a deadly hatred?
Rescue me from their hands, Lord God,
or will you put my trust to shame?

May simple uprightness always keep me,
for I wait for you as long as I live.

Come and free us from our anguish.

[Psalm 25] In the Hebrew original this psalm is an alphabetic poem: the first letters of the lines follow the Hebrew alphabet. The result is a patchwork of standard formulas adding up to a prayer interrupted by lines of Jewish wisdom and covering a number of concepts and attitudes going back to very different layers of the Old Testament tradition: the Covenant, the sufferings at the hands of (pagan) enemies, awareness of sin and prayer for repentance and salvation, "the way" after the fashion of Deuteronomy and the Wisdom books, and the frame of mind of the *anawim*, the poor of the Lord, who await their rescue from oppression from God alone. The surprising feature of this psalm, however, is its unity of atmosphere, which shows how all the major elements of the variegated tradition of the Old Testament were eventually fused in the spirituality, at once simple and full of ardour, of the pious Jews after the period of exile, a few centuries B.C.—"This is also the witness of the holy Spirit to us. For first he says: 'This is the covenant I will make with them one day, says the Lord; I put my laws in their hearts, I stamp them on their minds.' And then: 'I will no longer remember their sins and their evil acts.' But where these are forgiven there is no need for a propitiating sacrifice any more. Therefore, brothers and sisters, we may confidently go up to God's holy place in virtue of the blood of Jesus, by the new and living way which he inaugurated for us through the temple-veil of his own body" (Heb. 10. 15–20).

Psalm 30

I will speak of you, God,
and everyone may hear it:
You have drawn me up,
You have spared me the unholy
glee of all my enemies.
I called to you: "God, help me"—
and you came to heal me.
It was you who brought me back
from the deepest pit—already
I was numbered among the dead—
you have given me life again.

Sing to the Lord our God,
all you that share in his love.
Keep it alive in your songs
that he is the holy One.
His anger is but for a moment,
his friendship lasts a lifetime—
the evening comes with sorrow,
the daybreak brings you gladness.

I was carefree and happy,
I thought: it will ever be so,
I stand, and I will not fall.
And I was not aware
that nothing but your mercy
keeps me alive, Lord God.
And so, when you turned away
from me, I was nowhere.

Then I called out to you, God,
and I begged you for mercy—

"What use is it to you if I die,
if I am laid in the grave?
Can you be praised by the dust,
can a dead man sing of your faithfulness?
So in your goodness hear me, Lord,
be merciful to me and help me."

Then you changed my sorrow
into joy—I was in mourning
and you clothed me with gladness.
And now, with all my heart,
I sing this song to you,
I may no more be silent,
and therefore, God, my God,
I give you endless thanks.

[Psalm 30] Psalm 30 is a classical example of the psalm of praise as a literary kind: the praise of God consists in elaborately and repeatedly recounting, for everybody to hear, the former distress and the rescue from it, accompanied by an appeal to join the psalmist in recognizing God's saving presence. The poet of Psalm 30 has come to realize what it means to come to life and to exist. As the Hebrew title of this psalm indicates, this psalm was sung during the annual feast of the dedication of the Temple: Israel as a whole then celebrated her coming to life as a religious community. The Christian tradition has always prayed this psalm as a confession of Christ's resurrection from the dead.—"We, too, believe, and that is why we speak up. For we know that God, who raised the Lord Jesus from the dead, will also raise us up together with Jesus and bring us with you into his presence. For all this is done for your sake, so that God's grace extends to more and more people, and thanksgiving abounds to the glory of God. No, we do not lose heart. Even though we perish outwardly, our inner life is being renewed every day" (2 Cor. 4. 13–16).

Psalm 32

1

Happy is the man
whose unfaithfulness is forgiven,
whose evil is forgotten.
What a blessing for him if his sins
do not count any more with God,
if he dares admit:
I have sinned.

As long as I was deaf to
the voice of my own conscience,
I was inwardly eaten up,
I took refuge in self-pity.
Your hand weighed heavily on me,
long days and nights.
My strength was wasting away,
just as a man wastes away
under the heat of summer.

But then I could no longer
hide my evil from you.
I thought: I will go to him
and tell him what I have done—
and you forgave my sin.

And therefore every man
who puts faith in your Name
may go to you with trust
while you let yourself be found.
And should a flood break loose,
he will come to no harm—
as you have allayed my fears,
as you have been yourself
the ark of my salvation.
The song of your redemption
surrounds me everywhere.

II

Word of the Lord your God:
"I will show you the way,
my counsel is for the taking,
I follow you with my eyes.
Man, do not be senseless
and headstrong like a mule,
a horse that has to be
curbed with bit and bridle—
it would go hard with you."

Avoid your God and find
misery where you go;
but admit defeat
and he is merciful.
People of good will,
he is a source of joy—
rejoice, then, be glad in him
with hearts that have been cleansed.

[Psalm 32] Psalm 32, traditionally listed as one of the so-called penitential psalms, was the favourite psalm of St Augustine. It is not so much a penitential prayer as a hymn of thanksgiving, looking back on penance and forgiveness, and turning a personal experience into a passionate appeal to others. A person who tries to run away from his conscience—which means that he is trying to hide from God—will suffer grave distress of conscience, until he stops deluding himself and admits the truth. Relieved and thankful and certain that all is forgiven, the poet warns others that resisting the grace of conscience is a dead end.—"The younger son gathered all he had and left for a distant country, where he squandered his property in loose living. (. . .) But when he came to himself he thought: 'All my father's day-labourers have food enough and to spare, and I am starving. I will go back to my father and say to him: Father, I have sinned against heaven and against you; I am no longer worthy of being called your son.' (. . .) But while he was still at a distance his father saw him; he was moved by pity and came running to meet him. (. . .) 'My son was dead and he has come to life again; he was lost and he has been found again'" (Luke 15. 13, 17–18, 20, 24).

Psalms 42-43

I

As a deer yearns for living water, God,
so do I long with all my heart to go to you.
I thirst for God, the living God—
when will I be at last face to face with my God?
I have no bread but tears, night and day,
and always I hear them saying: "Where is your God?"

I cannot help remembering—and my heart is moved again—
how I went among the throng, to the house of the Lord our God—
then I hear them singing again, all that festive band of people.

But why so discouraged,
why rebellious?
I will wait for God
and one day I shall thank him—
you are my safety, Lord,
you are my God.

II

I am broken-hearted, I think of you
here in the highlands of Jordan and Hermon,
far away from your holy mountain.

Waterfall roars on waterfall here,
voice of your streams—
all your breakers are dashing against me,
waves are sweeping over me.

God, give me to-day and every day
a sign of love, then I will sing to you
till far into the night, as long as I live.

Why, living God, have you forgotten me?
My rock, why do I go about in rags,
harassed and abased?
My enemies drive me to death, body and bones,
I hear them calling: "Where is this God of yours?"

But why so discouraged,
why rebellious?
I will wait for God
and one day I shall thank him—
you are my safety, Lord,
you are my God.

III

God, take up my cause and fight for me
against a godless people that knows no mercy,
save me from the grip of cunning and lies.

For you are my God and my strength—
why did you ever throw me out,
why do I go about in rags,
harassed and abased?

Send out your light and your trust to meet me.
They lead the way to your holy mountain,
they will take me into your house.

Then I may go to the altar of God,
to him, my joy from my earliest years.
Then I shall thank you singing to the harp,
my Lord and my God.

But why then so discouraged,
why rebellious?
I will wait for God
and one day I shall thank him—
you are my safety, Lord,
you are my God.

[Psalms 42–43] Psalms 42 and 43 are looked upon by a long tradition as one psalm, which marks the beginning of a fresh group of psalms, covering books two and three of the present psalter. The first seven (42–49) of this second group are attributed by the Hebrew original to the "sons of Korah", as are Psalms 84, 85, 87, and 88; they may have been a school of singers and poets who considered themselves the heirs of a particular tradition going back to the temple cult of the days of David (cf. 1 Chron. 6. 31, 37). The psalms of the Korah tradition are in any case among the finest literary products of the psalter.—Ostensibly, this psalm is the complaint of a Jew, perhaps a Levite, in exile, who feels that his faith is shaken because he misses the experience of God's presence in the common worship in the Temple at Jerusalem now destroyed by foreign and pagan invaders. But the fact that the third part of the psalm uses the literary convention of the complaint of the man wrongly persecuted suggests that in the last resort this prayer reflects the hankering after God of every believer: "We are always full of courage and aware that while we are at home in the body we are far away from the Lord. (For we lead our lives in faith, and we do not see.) We are, I say, full of courage, and we would rather be away from the body to be at home with the Lord. And thus our only ambition, whether at home or away, is to please him" (2 Cor. 2. 6–9).

Psalm 46

God is our refuge and our strength,
always in adversity he is our help.
Therefore—though the earth should change,
we shall not fear. And let the mountains
tumble and fall deep into the sea,
and let the water foam and rage,
assault the cliffs to set them rocking—

He is for us the God of the powers,
a safe stronghold, a God of men.

I saw a stream of living water,
a stream of joy that branches out
through the city of the Most High.
There he lives—it will stand firm.
His rescue dawns like the morning light.
Kingdoms are tottering, they will fall,
nations are scared and filled with panic,
and the whole world comes crashing down,
when he raises his powerful voice.

He is for us the God of the powers,
a safe stronghold, a God of men.

Come and see, you will stand in awe
of the powerful things he will do on earth:
he puts an end to all war in the world,
shatters the bow, breaks spears into splinters,
throws our weapons into the fire.
He says: "Stop, for I am your God,
I will show myself to all nations,
I will make my Name felt on earth."

He is for us the God of the powers,
a safe stronghold, a God of men.

[Psalm 46] This psalm, the first of three Korahitic ones celebrating God's presence among his people on Mount Zion (46–48), is a solemn liturgical proclamation of the ultimate power of God, who is at the same time "the God of Jacob", i.e. of Israel, "of men", as the present translation puts it. The first part evokes a kind of inverted creation: the separation of the inhabitable earth from the waters of chaos (Gen. 1. 9) is cancelled again. The third part evokes a totally different perspective: the perfection of creation, the perfection of order, not only in Nature, but also among men. And wedged in between these two extremes stands the experience that leads the celebrating community to hope for the latter perspective in the teeth of the possibility of the former: the experience of the life-giving presence of God in the midst of his people, symbolized by the stream (cf. the powerful evocation in Ezech. 47. 1–12; Is. 8. 3), in which the waters of chaos have been turned into a source of life, just as the streams of Eden watered Paradise (Gen. 2. 10) and the circuit brought the water from the Gihon spring into Jerusalem, the city of peace (cf. 2 Kings 20. 20; Is. 22. 11).—"On the last day of the feast, the great day, Jesus stood up and proclaimed: 'If anyone is thirsty, let him come to me; he may drink, if he believes in me.' As the Scripture says: 'Streams of living water will flow out of his heart.' And in saying this he was referring to the Spirit, which those who were to believe in him would receive" (John 7. 37–39; cf. Apoc. 22. 1).

Psalm 51

Be merciful to me, you who are mercy,
wipe out my guilt, in your compassion.
Wash me, I am dirty with sin—
who can forgive but you alone?

I see the evil that I have done,
it is all around me on every side.
Against your holiness I have sinned,
I have done what is hateful to you.
Your word justly sentences me,
you are righteous.

In unrighteousness I was born,
I was conceived and carried in sin.
Now you want me to come to the truth,
I hear your voice, God, in my conscience.

Cover my sins and wash me clean,
and I shall be as white as snow.
Speak your saving word to me,
you have broken me, you can heal me.
Close your eyes, then, to my sins,
let them no longer exist for you.

Give me a different heart, my God,
make me new and make me firm.
Do not turn away, do not reject me,
never take your holy spirit from me.
Save me, and I can again be happy,
and I dare to live freely again.
Let me be a sign of your mercy,
and all who have disowned you, God,
will find the courage to go back to you.

Hold me no longer a captive of dumbness,
or must I be silent about your mercy?
Put the right words into my mind
to bear witness to your forgiveness.

You want no gifts and sacrifices.
If only, broken and made humble,
if only I open my heart to you,
that is my sacrifice. Lord, accept it.

[In your mercy be good to Zion,
build Jerusalem up again.
Then you will again be pleased with our gifts,
bulls will be offered and burnt on your altar.]

[Psalm 51] Although the formal structure of this famous psalm is that of the prayer for rescue addressed to God by an innocent man (cf. Ps. 22), its novelty is in the fact that the usual protestations of innocence have been replaced by a confession of sinfulness. In this way, the fundamental inspirations of the great prophets, notably Isaiah and Ezechiel, are brought to bear on the problem of persecution and suffering: the loss of peace and worship and prestige can lead the believer to search his own heart. There he may discover the enemy inside (cf. Is. 59. 1–12), and he will wish to be inwardly renewed, to be given a new heart (cf. Ezech. 11. 9), to discover the truth inside so that cult and prestige will no longer rank first as signs of God's blessing. No wonder, then, that the Hebrew Bible attributes this psalm to David at the height of his splendour, and yet repenting of having taken Uriah's wife and driven Uriah himself to death (2 Sam. 11–12). The final lines between brackets, which somehow contradict the passage immediately preceding, were added to justify the cult restored in Jerusalem after the period of the great captivity.—"The woman said to Jesus: 'Lord, I see that you are a prophet. But our fathers used to worship on this mountain, and you Jews say that Jerusalem is the place where people should worship.' Jesus said to her: 'Woman, believe me, the hour comes when neither on this mountain nor in Jerusalem you will worship the Father. (. . . .) The hour comes, and it has already come, when the true worshippers will worship the Father in spirit and truth. God is spirit, and those who worship him must worship in spirit and truth'" (John 4. 19–24).

Psalm 63

God, my God, I look for you.
All I am is thirst for you.
My body is a land without water,
exhausted with desire for you.

I have seen you in your holy house,
with my own eyes, your power and your light.
I know it—your love is more than life.
I wish to praise you as long as I live.

I stretch out my hands to you,
I call your Name—you are my God,
my daily bread, life in abundance—
I will never tire of singing of you.

Night after night you keep me awake,
waking and dreaming I think of you—
always till now you have been my help,
close to you is where I am happy.

You have bound me on your back,
you hold me tight with both your hands.
All those who seek to take my life
perish in the hollow of the earth.

They will fall, die by the sword,
they will be a prey to wild animals.
But I will live and be glad in you,
those who recognize you may speak—

liars will have their big mouths stopped.

[Psalm 63] This is what the experience of a real liturgy can do for a man. The Temple liturgy has brought home to the poet of this psalm who God is, and who he is himself. The experiences of emptiness and fullness, distance and closeness, exhaustion and life, near-despair and profound trust go hand in hand if a man, carried on the waves of common worship, discovers his deepest and most fundamental aspirations, expresses them in words at once too big and too vulnerable, and finally comes out with the Name for it: "You are my God".

> "Thou art lightning and love, I found it, a winter and warm;
>   Father and fondler of heart Thou hast wrung:
> Hast thy dark descending and most art merciful then."
> (G. M. Hopkins, *The Wreck of the Deutschland*)

The psalm has a classical *finale*: a prophetic verdict on those who are the enemies of the psalmist's craving for faith, and a prophetic proclamation of the happiness of the king. (The Hebrew text reads: "The king will be glad in God", etc.; the psalmist here identifies himself with the happiness of the king, who is the representative of the entire people. The present translation replaces this piece of ancient sensibility with a straightforward first person singular.)—"I heard from the throne a loud voice, which said: 'See, this is where God is present among men. He will be in their midst, and they will be his people, and he, God-with-them, will be their God. And he will wipe all tears from their eyes, and there will be no more death nor mourning nor crying nor pain, for the old world is over'" (Apoc. 21. 3-4).

Psalm 69

Save me, God, I am up to my neck in the water,
I am sinking, the mud is sucking me down,
my feet can no longer find firm ground anywhere—
water, only water, the current drags me along.
I am tired with crying, my throat is a burning wound,
my eyes are dead with staring, with waiting for God.

I have more enemies than I have hairs on my head
and I am no match for their hatred and lies.
They demand the return of things which I never stole—
Lord, you would know if I had done any wrong,
for who can hide from you, o powerful God?
No, do not shame those who are waiting for you—
if they see me, what are they to think of you?

Because I have trusted in you they are laughing at me,
yes, I have lost my face and become a stranger,
even my brothers do not recognize me.
My passion for your house has eaten me up,
the names they are calling you are falling on me.
I am crying, I will not eat—they are mocking at it.
I go about in rags—they are saying: that fool!
My name's in the gutter—I feel they are talking about me,
they are making up songs about me in their drunken talk.

Will there be ever an hour of grace for me,
Lord, will your love give an answer, your truth come to save me?
Then pull me up from the mud, or am I to drown
in this contempt, in this abysmal water?
Let the flood, the precipice never devour me,
let the mouth of the grave not close over me.
In your love, God, I would be secure,
as in a mother's womb—after all, I am yours.
Do not turn away, do not be such a silent God,
speak and have mercy upon my anxious soul,
claim me back, set me free from the clutch of my enemies.

You know them by name, all those who rise up against me,
you know how they trample on me, how abased I am.
Shame has broken me down, I am past recovery.
I waited for comfort, but no; I hoped for some one
to bring me relief, but I found no one at all.
They gave me bread—it was bread that had been poisoned,
they gave me drink—I found that it was vinegar.

I wish they would eat till they were ready to burst,
yes, let them choke in their plenty, the whole lot of them.
Strike them with blindness, cripple their loins for ever,
pour out your curses upon them like so many flames,
just let them burn in the blazing fire of your anger.
Turn their city into waste land, drive all life out of it—
when I was beaten by you, they were bold enough then,
when I was wounded by you, they beat me still harder.

Just let them pile up sin upon sin, my God,
and find no grace in your eyes in the hour of your coming.
Lord, wipe out their names from the book of life,
and they will not be recorded among your friends.

But me—you will save me, tormented and poor as I am.
Then I will thank you, sing in praise of your Name—
that will make you happy rather than sacrifices.

The poor and the humble, all who are looking for God,
they may know it, they will come to life in joy.
People in anguish and misery find a hearing—
people in chains, God does not let you down.
Heaven and earth will praise and proclaim his Name,
and also the sea, with all living creatures in it.

He will come to rescue his people, rebuild their cities,
and their children will also live there in peace.
And so his Name will be known and loved, for ever.

[Psalm 69] The psalms are not perfect prayers in the sense that they only express the so-called higher, purer, or more "perfect" emotions. Their perfection lies in their being immersed in the human situation with all its fears, doubts, and crudities, while at the same time bringing God's presence to bear on all this. Chaos, disintegration, injustice, vulgarity, and abuse are real, and as such they can be the stuff of the experience of faith, and in cases even its mainspring. Psalm 69 affords a classical example of the complaint, in which the experience of undeserved suffering is not glossed over but fathomed. A first level of desolation consists in the discovery of loneliness and chaos when friends turn into enemies. But then comes a far worse disillusion: faith in God, no matter how passionate, carries no prestige among these people; on the contrary, it is an occasion for further slights. And it is precisely at this point, when the psalmist realizes that his very faith makes him vulnerable, that he can turn his complaint into a prophetic hymn of thanksgiving, and call upon the poor in spirit and the humble and the whole world to share in his experience.—"Did not the Messiah have to go through all this suffering in order to come to his glory?" (Luke 24. 26).

Psalm 72

Give your wisdom, God, to the king,
lay your kingdom in his hands,
that he may be a shepherd for your people,
for your poor people a righteous judge.
And the mountains will yield sheaves of peace
and the hills will bear a harvest of justice.

He will stand up for the poor and the needy,
do justice to the least of his brothers.
He will break and bind the powers
which are holding us—he will live
and never fail, like the sun,
like the moon, generation after generation.

Like the rain descending on the fields,
like the dew that waters the earth—
thus he will come, and in those days
faithfulness and truth will flourish
and there will be peace in abundance,
until the light of the moon is put out.

He will rule from sea to sea,
from the great River to the end of the earth.
Foreign nations will be forced to stoop,
all his enemies will bite the dust.

Faraway kings, faraway coastlands
come to offer their gifts to him.
Wealthy princes, the richest of lands
lay down their treasures in front of him,
and one day all the great ones on earth
and all nations will kneel before him.

He will be the deliverer of the poor,
a friend to those who have no one.
For humble people he is within reach,
he gives hope to those without rights.
Their blood is precious in his eyes,
he ransoms them from the house of slavery.

And they will live, a golden age,
call him happy day after day,
and pray that it may ever be so:
a flood of wheat, fields that wave,
trees full of fruit, high on the mountains—
a city arises from a sea of green.

His name is in eternity,
as long as the sun is in the heavens.
His name goes round, all over the earth—
a word of peace, from man to man.

[Psalm 72] The idea of royal government in the ancient Near East was so bound up with the risk of idolatry (cf. 1 Sam. 10. 17–19) that Israel was for a long time loath to adopt it. The story of Saul's election and anointing shows Israel's struggle between secularization at the expense of the sole worship of Yahweh, and the desire for national and religious unity after the destruction of the national shrine at Shiloh (1 Sam. 4). When Saul was finally chosen by Samuel he was told that it was the Lord who anointed him and that it was the Lord's people he was going to lead. This conception of the king as "the Lord's Anointed One" was gradually deepened in the course of David's and Solomon's reigns. But when after Solomon's death in 931 B.C. the kingdom fell apart and many of the subsequent kings proved traitors to the God of Israel, Israel's former fears proved to have been only too well grounded. To culminate the disaster, the split kingdom came under continual attacks from the side of Assyria and Babylon. It was then that the prophets began to give expression to Israel's craving for deliverance by projecting the image of the ideal king, who as the Lord's Anointed One (Hebrew: *Mashiah*, Messiah) would bring about God's kingdom. This psalm, attributed by the original text to Solomon, the just and glorious king of peace (*Shelomoh—Shalom*), evokes this eschatological kingdom in the wake of Isaiah (e.g., 11. 1–5) and Zechariah (e.g., 9. 9–10). The oldest Christian traditions have recited this psalm with Jesus Christ in mind, and Matthew's legend of the magi offering their gifts to Jesus must have been inspired by this psalm.

Psalm 73

Yes, surely God
is good for us,
for a man
who has been cleansed.

As for me,
I had almost lost
my foothold, I
had nearly fallen.
I was envious
of that boaster,
I saw his peace
without God.

He has no cares—
excellent health,
no worries about
the sorrows of men,
and never harassed
like everyone else.
Pride is for him
a signet-ring,
craving for power
fits him like a glove.

His eyes are bulging
from his fat face,
his heart brims over
with basest thoughts,
mockery, cynicism,
menace and threats,
and his big mouth
is raised against heaven,
his tongue is spoiling
the whole of the earth.

Of course he carries
the mob with him.
They lap up his words
like so much water—
"What has God
to do with us,
if, that is,
he is still there?"
So he goes his own godless
way with a will.
He is getting on fine
always doing better.

Why did I ever
have faith in you,
why did I keep
my hands clean?
Every day
is punishment to me,
every morning
I am beaten.
I have often thought:
do like those others.
But then I would have
to break with you,
have to deny
the faith of my father.
So I was tossed
backwards and forwards,
harassed, desperate,
without any prospect.

Until I found
peace in your mystery,
and learned to see life
in the light of your future—
the whole of their life
is built on quicksand,
it falls to ruins,
they are in one
fell moment destroyed.
Like an evil dream—
you wipe them out
of the world of men.

I was embittered
and rebellious,
I was hurt
deep in my soul.
I was like a senseless
animal with you.

With you, I am
always with you.
You hold me tight,
your hand in mine.
You will bring all things
to a good end,
you lead me on
in your good pleasure.
What is heaven
to me without you,
where am I on earth
if you are not there?
Though my body
is broken down,
though my heart dies,
You are my Rock,
my God, the future
that waits for me.

Far away from you
life is not life.
To break faith with you
is to be no one.

With you, my highest
good, my God,
with you I am
secure.

[Psalm 73] Psalm 73 is a problem-psalm like Psalms 37 and 49, and in many ways recalls the book of Job. It fathoms in a passionate, and almost rigorous way the power of faith in God by comparing it with unbelief. Rhetorically, the psalm opens with the conclusion: when all is said and told, a man can say that God is good; but he will only be able to say so after he has gone through the experience that faith has not a leg to stand on. Psalm 37 offers the simple solution: the wicked will be destroyed, the just will possess the land. Psalm 49 admits that arrogance is power, but also that it does not last beyond the grave. Both these psalms, however, fail to reach the mystery which lies at the bottom of the problem. In Psalm 73 the fullest possible allowance is made for human prosperity for its own sake, and it is precisely in this way that the poet succeeds in subjecting it to radical criticism: human prestige becomes essentially relative. And his prayer becomes: No matter what happens, You are there. It is this faith that carries him through and beyond all the theories about what will be the lot of power and arrogance. In this way Psalm 73 articulates faith in God as a process of purification, as an inner growth towards communion with God, ultimately in the resurrection.—"Brethren, I may say with all assurance that David, our patriarch, is dead and buried, since we have his tomb among us down to this day. But being a prophet he knew that God had promised him under oath that a descendant of his would sit on his throne. This means that he foresaw and announced the resurrection of Christ, who indeed has not fallen a prey to the Pit, and who has not lived to see corruption. God has raised him up, this Jesus; this is what we bear witness to" (Acts 2. 29–32).

Psalm 80

Shepherd of Israel, hear our prayer.
You, leading Joseph like a flock,
you, enthroned on the winged animals,
guide and blessing of Benjamin,
God of Ephraim and Manasseh,
show your glory for us to see,
stir up your power and come to our rescue.

Be here among us,
light in the midst of us,
be our saviour,
bring us to life.

O Lord, God of the powers, how long yet
will you turn angrily away when we pray?
We have had to eat the bread of tears,
a flood of tears you made us drink.
We are the plaything of our neighbours,
we are the laughing-stock of our enemies.

God of the powers,
light in the midst of us,
be our saviour,
bring us to life.

There was a vine in the land of Egypt,
with tender care you dug it out;
then you drove away other nations
in order to plant it in their land.
You tilled the soil to make it grow,
to let it take root in every place
and spread itself over all the country—
and with its shadow it covers the mountains,
and with its twigs the divine cedars;
it stretches its branches out to the sea,
its tendrils down to the great River.

Why, then, were its fences destroyed?
Why can every passer-by
plunder and loot it, why do the boars
break loose from the forest to trample it down,
why are the vermin stripping it bare?

God of the powers,
be our saviour,
be here among us,
bring us to life.

From your heaven look down on this vine,
go out, recover it, cherish the stock
which you planted with your own hand.
May those who once burnt it like firewood
be consumed in the fire of your anger.
But never again take away your hand,
away from the one whom you have chosen,
away from Man, the son of your mercy.

We will never turn from you again.
Make us new and we call your Name:

God of the powers,
be here among us,
light in the midst of us,
bring us to life.

[Psalm 80] This powerful psalm can be looked upon as the prayerful counterpart of the prophecy addressed to Israel, the Northern kingdom, by Jeremiah's "Book of Comfort" (Jer. 30. 1–31. 22; the references to Judah, the Southern kingdom, are insertions and additions of a later date). Both Jeremiah's "Book of Comfort" and Psalm 80 bear witness to the religious and national revival in Jerusalem under Josiah, king of Judah (640–609 B.C.), who took advantage of the weakness of the Assyrian invaders. He conquered again the lands of the former kingdom of Israel, defeated and deported in 721 B.C., and restored the cult of Yahweh, adulterated for political reasons by a whole series of kings before him. At the heart of this so-called "deuteronomistic" revival (cf. 2 Kings 22. 3–23. 24) was the inspiration of the prophetic movement, which men like Elijah, Elisha, Amos, and Hosea had inaugurated in the North. This was the territory occupied for the most part by the tribes that traced their origin to Jacob's (Jacob = Israel: cf. Gen. 32. 23–31) favourite wife, Rachel: Ephraim and Manasseh, the sons of Joseph (cf. Jer. 31. 15 ff.). There were visions of a restoration of God's own kingdom, which were shattered again when the kingdom of Judah was finally defeated by Nebuchadnezzar in 586 B.C., but which were revived when Cyrus' edict of 538 B.C. allowed the Jews to go back to Jerusalem and rebuild the temple. Thus Psalm 80 has become a passionate appeal to God's faithfulness in terms which recall not only the past glories of the militant theocracy around the Ark, but especially also the prophetic proclamation of Israel's election and rejection, expressed by means of the image of the vine, first used by Hosea (10. 1), and expanded later on, notably in the famous allegories by Isaiah (5. 1–7) and Ezechiel (15. 1–8; 17. 3–10; 19. 10–14).—"I am the true vine, and my Father is the vinedresser. He cuts off every branch of mine that bears no fruit, and he prunes and cleans every branch of mine that does bear fruit, so that it may come to bear more fruit. You are already cleaned thanks to the word which I have spoken to you. Remain in me, as I remain in you" (John 15. 1–4).

Psalm 84

I am eaten up with the love of your house,
o God of all the powers.
I am longing heart and soul
for the fore-courts of the Lord,
my whole body is crying and yearning
for the living God.

Every bird will find a home—
even the swallow builds a nest
in the shadow of your altar,
where she may lay down her young
close to you, Lord of all the powers,
to you, my king, my God.

And happy is the man
who may live under your roof—
he will praise you day by day.
Happy are those people,
who will find their strength in you—
your ways are in their hearts.

Are they to pass through a barren valley,
they will make it a valley of springs.
Spring showers will bless the land.
And so they go on as if they had wings,
to find you in your holy city.

Lord of the powers, hear my prayer,
God of Jacob, listen to me:
protect the people whom you have called,
bless us—we are here before you.

One day in your court is better
than a thousand days outside.
And to wait upon the threshold
of the house of our Lord God,
is far better than to waste
away my life in the tents of sin.

The Lord is a sun, the Lord is a shield.
He makes us respected, he makes us loved.
The man who goes on the path of life
upright, without lies, will find
mercy in the eyes of God.

Happy is the man
who will put his trust in you,
o Lord God of all the powers.

[Psalm 84] If Psalm 46 celebrates Yahweh, present on Mount Zion, by enlarging his function as God of the Powers (cf. Ps. 24) to eschatological proportions, this psalm follows a different path: the God of the Armies becomes the God who gives inner safety and reliance, and his Temple is no longer the centre of a military stronghold, but the symbol of the inner strength of the believing community, the faithful "Remnant of Israel", which would survive the disillusions of the captivity thanks to a deepened sense of faith. In this way Psalm 84 also reflects the mood of the period of the Second Temple, built between 520 and 515 B.C., which became the spiritual home, not only of the Jews that had come back to Jerusalem, but also of those many Jews who in the course of the centuries of disintegration had settled elsewhere, for example, in Egypt or Babylon, and become the pilgrim Jews regularly going up to Jerusalem. Psalm 84 can therefore be looked upon, together with Psalms 42–43, as the background of the collection of the "Songs of Ascents" (Pss. 120–134).—"No one can be the servant of two masters, for he will either dislike the one and love the other, or be devoted to the one and despise the other. You cannot be the servants of God and of Vested Interest. That is why I am telling you: do not worry about your lives, about what you will eat or drink or put on. Is not life more than food, and is not the body more than clothes? Look at the birds in the sky: they neither sow nor reap nor store up food, and yet your heavenly Father feeds them" (Matt. 6. 24–26).

Psalm 85

Again and again you have favoured your land,
o God, and changed our lives for the better.
You have covered all our sins,
taken away all guilt from your people,
again and again revoked your threats
and quenched the burning fire of your anger.

Now be merciful to us again
and no longer embittered, or would you be angry
for ever with us, throughout all generations?
Would you not rather see us alive
so that we may be glad in you?
Give us a sign of your covenant, then,
God of love, restore us to honour.

I want to hear the word of the Lord.
Peace—that is the word of the Lord.
For his people, for his followers,
for whoever turns back to him,
the Lord holds out a word of peace.
Yes, his rescue is close for them,
his glory will be at home in their land.

Mercy and faithful love will meet,
truth and peace will embrace one another.
Faithfulness sprouts like a seed in the earth,
truth is like a sun in the sky.
Our Lord God will lavish blessing,
and the land will bear its fruit.
Truth, like a messenger, runs on ahead of him,
peace follows him wherever he goes.

[Psalm 85] Psalm 85 is a prayer for a second Exodus experience: the People comes back from exile, and God returns to the Land of Jacob—the Hebrew word for "turn round", "come back" occurs no less than five times in the original. Its scene, like that of Psalm 84, is the return to Jerusalem after the great captivity and the building of the Second Temple. Its spiritual background is formed by the famous "Book of Israel's Comfort" by the anonymous author of Isaiah 40–55 and by the prophecies of Zechariah 1–8, both of which date from the same period. Its characteristic attitudes are those which gradually developed through the activities of the prophets: dispositions of the heart have become the basis of the experience of God's "glory" in the midst of the community rather than national and ritual assurances.—"The fruit of the Spirit is: love, joy, patience, kindness, goodness, faithfulness and mutual trust, gentleness and recollection—no law can touch people who are such. Those who belong to Jesus, the Christ, have crucified their selfish nature with its passions and desires. If we live by the Spirit, let us then also act according to the Spirit" (Gal. 5. 22–25).

Psalm 90

You have been a safe place to live in,
for us, o Lord, throughout all generations.
Even before the mountains were born
and the whole of this world was brought forth,
within living memory you are God,
and in all ages to come.

You make people crumble into dust,
you say: it's all over, ah children of Adam.
In your sight, a thousand years
are like yesterday, a day that has passed,
are like an hour of watching by night.
You sweep us out like a dream in the morning,
we are like the vigorous grass that grows—
it comes up at daybreak and flourishes,
at dusk it is mown down and dead.

Yes, we are perishing with your rage,
eaten up with anxiety when you are angry.
For you remember all our sins,
our innermost secrets are before your eyes—
that is why our days are so trivial,
our years as fleeting as a sigh.

The life of a man lasts seventy years,
or eighty, if we are strong.
Most of that is hardship and sorrow—
all at once it is over and we are gone.
Who can fathom the power of your rage,
and who is aware how fearful you are?
Teach us, then, so to value our days
that we may learn to cherish wisdom.

How long must we still wait for you?
O God, come back, and make peace with us.
Do not hold back your grace any longer
and we will from now on be glad in you.
And give us as many happy days
as we have suffered days of misery.

Show us that you are at work for us,
and let our children see your glory.
Be all around us with your mildness,
o Lord, and let the work of our hands be lasting,
let the work of our hands be lasting.

[Psalm 90] This psalm, which the Hebrew Bible calls "The Prayer of Moses, the Man of God", is a meditation on the question: What is Man? The poem is entirely in the vein of the wisdom-tradition, one of the classical elements in the Bible, although its incorporation into it is of a relatively late date. Besides the Law with its many cultic prescriptions and the inspired word of hope and fear, the utterances of the priests and the prophets respectively, there had always been a kind of culture of human wisdom in Israel as well as in the Ancient Near East as a whole. This experience found expression, not so much in formalized philosophy as in endless collections of *meshalim*, short, pithy proverbs and sayings, which could be expanded into parables, allegories, symbolic fables, and suchlike. Its practitioners were the "wise men" (cf. Jer. 8. 9–10; 18. 18). And just as Moses and Aaron passed for the prophet and priest *par excellence*, and David was considered the original mind behind the psalms, so the schools of wise men liked to point to Solomon as to their prime example, and even attributed their collected sayings to him (cf. Prov. 1. 1; 25. 1; 1 Kings 4. 29–34). But Jewish wisdom always distinguished itself from the wisdom of its neighbours by its being related to the awe of Israel's God. True human wisdom is only achieved by putting it to the test of God's eternal and inscrutable wisdom, shown in Creation and in the Law. Psalm 90 is a fine example of this "ecstatic humanism", and was composed on the basis of the same experiences that went into the making of the stories of the Fall and the Deluge (Gen. 3; 6) and the Book of Job. The experience of the contrast between human frailty and God's eternal reliability is deepened to an awareness of the contrast between sinfulness and holiness, and then turned into a prayer for "wisdom"— the ability to feel strengthened by God's faithfulness, even to the point of death.—"God has chosen what is foolish in the eyes of the world to put the wise to shame; God has chosen what is weak in the eyes of the world to put the strong to shame; God has chosen what is of low birth and insignificant; he has chosen what is nothing, in order to bring to nothingness what is something. Thus no human being can afford to boast in the presence of God. It is thanks to him that you are now alive in Jesus, the Christ, who on God's behalf has become all our wisdom" (1 Cor. 1. 27–30).

Psalm 91

Whoever lives in the shelter of the most high God
and spends the night in the shadow of God almighty—
he says to the Lord: my refuge, my stronghold,
my God, in you I put all my trust.

He sets you free from the nets of the bird-catcher,
he keeps the plague of evil from you,
he will cover you with his feathers,
under his wings you will find safety.

In the dead of night you have nothing to fear;
neither dread in the daytime a stab in the back,
nor fear the plague that stalks in the darkness—
no fever will ruin you in the heat of day.

Although a thousand fall at your side,
ten thousand go down before your eyes,
it will not touch you, your God is faithful,
he is a shield, a wall round about you.

You have only to lift up your eyes
to see how wickedness is avenged.
Then you say: "The Most High is my refuge",
and you will be at home with him.

No disasters will happen to you,
no pestilence will come close to your tent.
He has sent his angels out,
to guard you at every step you take.

They will bear you up on their hands—
no stone will hurt your feet on your way.
You plant your foot on the head of the lion,
you will trample on the snake, you will kill the dragon.

"Yes, if he clings to me I will rescue him,
I will make him great, for he holds on to my Name.
If he calls, I will answer. In anguish and need: I with him,
I will make him free and clothe him with glory.

He shall live to be full of years.
He shall live to see my rescue."

[Psalm 91] This impressive psalm shows how the different traditions of Old Testament religious experience were fused when the priestly class and the schools of wise men in Jerusalem set about collecting, editing, commenting on, and adding to, the existing oral and written literary deposits of Israel at the time of the Second Temple. The psalm opens with four traditional divine names. *Elyon* (Most High God) is originally a name derived from the Phoenician pantheon and used for the deity at the Canaanite sanctuary at Jerusalem (cf. Gen. 14. 17-19). *El Shadday* (Almighty God, or perhaps: God of the Mountains) is the ancient divine name going back to the days of the patriarchs (cf. Gen. 17, 1). *Yahweh* (in reading the Bible aloud always substituted by *Adonay*, Lord) was used mostly in the tradition of the Southern kingdom of Judah, whereas *Elohim* (God) was used mostly in the Northern kingdom of Israel. The spirituality of Psalm 91 harks back to the desert experience of the Exodus, which under the influence of the prophetic and wisdom traditions is presented as the model of the life of every believer. Priestly influence is noticeable in the cultic setting of the psalm: a liturgical proclamation of the assurance with which the man who believes can make his way through life, clinched by a divine oracle to confirm the proclamation. The oldest layers of the Christian tradition have presented Jesus as fulfilling this psalm: the strongly symbolic accounts of Jesus' Baptism and Temptations have been composed with, among other things, this psalm in mind (cf. Matt. 3. 16; 4, 6. 11). And in the wake of Jesus the messengers of the kingdom will lead their lives strengthened by the same assurance (cf. Luke 10. 18).—"Let us not put the Lord to the test, as some of them did, only to be destroyed by the serpents. Do not grumble as some of them did, only to be destroyed by the Destroyer. What happened to them is a warning to us, and it was recorded for our instruction, since we are the witnesses of the fulfilment of time. Let therefore everyone who thinks that he stands take care not to fall. You are not exposed to any temptation that exceeds your human limits. And God is faithful: he will not let you be put to the test above your strength. With the temptation he provides the way out of it, so that you may endure it" (1 Cor. 10. 9-13).

Psalm 93

The Lord our God is king,
majesty is his robe,
strength he wears for a garment.

Unshakeable is the earth,
unshakeably firm is your throne,
you are from everlasting.

The seas are raising, o Lord,
the seas are raising their voices,
their floods of thundering breakers.

More powerful than the voice of that water,
more powerful than the waves of the sea,
are you, the God of the heavens.

Your word is unfailing and faithful,
may your house be holy,
Lord God, for ever and ever.

[Psalm 93] Psalms 93–100, the so-called "royal psalms", form, like Psalms 46–48, a collection of hymns celebrating God's presence in the Temple. There he manifests himself to the cultic community, not only as the giver of the faith-inspiring word of the law, but also as the king of the awe-inspiring order of the world (cf. Ps. 19). It was in the atmosphere of common worship in the Temple that the *kebod Jahweh*, the Glory of the Lord, was evoked and revealed: Psalm 150 provides an eloquent inventory of liturgical expedients used to express and actualize the common faith. And the content of the experience was: God is present among us, he will make his word come true, he will also be faithful to his own creation. The latter conviction is amply elaborated in psalms like 104; Psalm 93 only expresses the experience of God's presence: "The Lord of the earth has shown himself" (Ps. 114).—"Jesus woke up and rebuked the wind, and said to the sea: 'Silence! Be quiet!' And the wind ceased, and a great calm ensued. He said to them: 'Why are you afraid? Have you no faith?' And they became full of awe, and said to each other: 'Who is then this man, that even the wind and the sea obey him?'" (Mark 4. 39–41).

Psalm 95

I

We must sing at the top of our voices,
rejoice before God, the rock of our safety,
appear before him, giving thanks and playing,
and shout: "He is a powerful God,
a king far greater than all the gods."

The depths of the earth belong to him,
the highest mountains, they are his.
The sea is his, it is he who made it,
the land was modelled by his hands.

Come and bow before him in worship,
kneel to the God who created us all.
He is our God, he is our Shepherd,
and we are the people, the flock of his hand.

II

Listen, then, to his voice to-day:

"Do not become hard, as once you did
in that place of discord, that day of your Testing,
when your fathers defied me in the desert,
and yet they had seen what I had done.
For forty years I loathed that generation.
I said: that people with their hearts gone astray,
they neither know nor want my ways.
So, in my anger, I took an oath—
never will they come into my Rest."

[Psalm 95] This psalm, a dramatic liturgical invitation to worship followed by a prophetic oracle, has for centuries been sung as the *invitatorium*, the beginning of the daily Office in the Latin Church. It is again an exploration into the divine names—God, King, Rock, Shepherd, *Yahweh*. The last of these names, rendered here by "he" and "him" at the example of Martin Buber's translation, is the key to understanding Israel's attitude towards God. When according to the tradition of Exodus 3. 13–15 Moses heard the ineffable Name in the desert, it was after a common literary convention explained by popular etymology, and taken to mean: "I am who I am". Translated into modern idiom this Hebrew locution would run: "I am with you, so do not ask any questions". For all his closeness, the God of Israel remains infinitely transcendent, and for all his transcendence, he remains infinitely close. Thus he is the faithful and gracious Shepherd of Psalm 23, but also the King of Glory of Psalms 24 and 93. Thus he is the "ground of being, and granite of it" (G. M. Hopkins), the Rock of salvation and safety, from which the water flowed when Israel was at a loss in the desert. It is from this last point that the prophetic warning of the second part of the psalm takes its start. It was in the desert, near Kadesh, the "holy place", or—according to a different tradition—near Sinai, the mountain that was looked upon as the prototype of the later Temple (cf. Exod. 25. 40), that the faith of the People of God did not stand up to the test: they in their turn tested Yahweh's reliability by defying him, so that the names of that place became known as *Meribah* (discord) and *Massah* (test) (cf. Num. 20. 1–13; Exod. 17. 1–7).—"Everyone who hears these words of mine and acts upon them will be like a wise man who built his house on the rock. And the rain fell, and the floods came, and the winds blew and threw themselves upon that house, but it did not collapse because it had been founded on the rock" (Matt. 7. 24–25).

Psalm 97

The Lord our God is king,
all the shores on earth
are laughing and shouting for joy.
He lives in clouds and darkness,
righteousness and truth
support his royal throne.

Fire sweeps on before him,
it burns his enemies away.
It flashes across the earth.
The whole of the world has seen it.
The earth was writhing and groaning
like a woman in labour.

Mountains melt like wax
wherever our God appears,
lord and master on earth.
The heavens have proclaimed,
the pagans have come to see
his love in all its splendour.

Shame upon the man
who bows down before statues,
who prides himself on nothing.
Must not all the gods
bow to the ground before him,
kneel down before our God?

Zion has heard it, the cities
of Judah shout for joy
because you are their saviour.
O Lord, most high God,
you are much more, much greater
than all the gods of the earth.

All those who hate what is evil
are loved by the Lord our God;

he has their hearts in his keeping.
And he will one day
set all his loved ones free
from the grasp of evil for ever.

Light is sown like seed
for God's own righteous friends,
gladness will be flourishing.
Friends, rejoice, be glad,
and proclaim his Name
high above all names.

[Psalm 97] This hymn is a patchwork composition of many standard idioms from the book of psalms. It first expresses the experience of God's presence in a series of cosmic images, and then goes on to face the believing community with a final option: they will either be subject to the powers of the world and live according to their norms, or they will experience the joy of relying on the king of all the gods of the earth. This fundamental connection between God's kingship and the simple justice of God's friends is also the subject of a passage in Isaiah, which in many ways is comparable to Psalm 96: the first of the four so-called "Songs of the Servant of Yahweh" (Is.42. 1–9; the other three: 49. 1–6; 50. 4–11; 52. 13–53. 12, cf. Ps. 22). The poet of this Song, however, puts rather more emphasis on the unobtrusive righteousness of the mysterious servant of Yahweh by first presenting him as the manifestation of God's goodness, which is then celebrated as God's royal victory afterwards.—"Jesus withdrew, but there were many who followed him. He healed them all, but also told them not to make him known. Thus the word of the prophet Isaiah was fulfilled: 'Behold, my servant, whom I have chosen, my beloved one, the man of all my favour. I will make my Spirit rest upon him, and he will bring the message of true faith in God to the nations. He will not quarrel or shout, and his voice will not be heard in the streets. He will not break a bruised reed or quench a smouldering wick before he has led the true faith in God to its triumph—all the nations will put their trust in his name'" (Matt. 12. 15–21; cf. Is. 42. 1–4).

Psalm 103

I want to call him by his Name,
the holy God, as truly as I live.
I thank him from the bottom of my heart,
and I will forget none of his benefits.

He is the forgiveness of my sins,
he will heal me, time after time.
He calls my life away from the grave,
surrounds me with goodness and tender love.
He fills my days with happiness,
and like an eagle my youth revives.

He makes good whatever he has promised,
he takes the part of all the oppressed.
He made known his Name to Moses,
and all the people saw his works—
merciful Lord, God full of grace,

faithful, endlessly patient love.
He does not quarrel with us to the end,
he does not haunt us with our sins,
he will not repay evil with evil,
he is greater than our sins.

Yes, what the heavens are for the earth,
that is his love for those who believe.
As far as the east is away from the west,
so far away from us he throws our sins.
Just as a man is merciful to his sons,
so is he a merciful father to us,
because he knows us—he has not forgotten
that we are made of the dust of the earth.

People—their days are like the grass,
they bloom like flowers in the open field;

then the wind blows, and they are gone
and no one can tell where they once stood.
Only the love of God will be lasting,
and age after age he will do justice
to all who hold on to his covenant,
who take his word to heart and fulfil it.

He is king, his throne is the heavens,
he is powerful all over the earth.
Bless him, then, you angels of God,
strong men, carrying out his word.
Powers and authorities, you must praise him,
faithful servants, who do his will.
Bless him, all you works of God,
all over the world—he is your king.

I want to call him by his Name,
the holy God, as truly as I live.

[Psalm 103] This psalm, a confession of divine forgiveness and patience supporting and guiding human frailty and sinfulness, shows very well how Israel could be creative in lending fresh vigour to the old, rugged traditions about her own origin. The evocation of the presence of a God who is merciful rather than unflinchingly just, and whose reliability extends beyond the grave, is firmly referred to Exodus 33–34. After the breach of the Covenant around the golden calf and Moses' dramatic intercession (Exod. 32), God continues the journey with Israel: he passes before Moses, exclaiming his Name and professing his mercy (Exod. 34. 4–9), renews the Covenant and gives the Law. This is how God deals with frail and sinful people; their sins are no obstacle to his abiding presence. This basic conviction, the core of the Exodus message, is here orchestrated by means of a subtle chain of images and metaphors, which actualize and give new depth to the old story of human sin and divine rescue. And so this very poetical expression of faith finally returns to a new recognition of God's kingship, now no longer a reason to cower, but a challenge to be confident and face the future.—"Children, let our love not consist in thoughts or words, but in acts and in truth. By this we will know that we are the children of truth, and then we may also reassure our own hearts in God's presence whenever our hearts accuse us. For God is greater than our hearts, and he knows everything" (1 John 3. 18–20).

Psalm 104

I want to call you, God, by your Name,
as truly as I live.

My Lord and my God, you are great and tremendous,
clothed with splendour and majesty,
and with a mantle of light wrapped around you.
You stretch out the heavens like a tent,
you build your lofty halls on the water,
you ride the clouds, they are your chariot,
and high up on the wings of the wind
you make your way, and the storm is your messenger,
burning fires, they are your servants.
You have firmly founded the earth,
in eternity it will not be shaken;
the sea once covered it like a cloak,
the water was still above the mountains—
then it took to flight when you threatened it,
it was gone at the voice of your thunder.
The mountains stand up, the valleys spread out,
and all things find the place you intended.
You have set limits to the flood,
never again will it conquer the earth.

You make the springs well up in the valleys,
and the streams are flowing between the mountains.
They water all the beasts of the field,
the wild ass quenches his thirst from them.
There the birds of the sky are living,
high among the branches they sing their songs.
The mountains are watered by the clouds,

the whole earth drinks its fill from your rain.
You just let the grass grow for the cattle,
and green crops for man to look after.
And so he produces corn from the earth,
and harvests the wine that makes his heart glad,
and also the oil that makes his skin glisten,
and the bread too that keeps him alive.
God's own trees are in full flower,
the cedars of Lebanon, which he has planted.
The birds have begun their nests in them,
high up in the tops the storks have their homes.
The high mountains are for the wild goats,
badgers take shelter among the rocks.

You are the creator of moon and time,
you, the creator of sun and of sunset.
You darken the world—at once it is night,
and the whole of the forest begins to stir:
the young lions are roaring for prey,
they are asking God for their food.
The sun rises and they slink back,
and in their dens they lie down again.
Now man goes out to do his work,
he labours until darkness falls.
And all this, God, is your own work—
your wisdom speaks from so many things,
your power of creation fills our earth.

And then the sea, so wide and enormous,
teeming with animals, great and small—
there the ships sail to and fro,

there is Leviathan, the monster,
made by you, for you to play with.

Everything waits for you full of hope,
all the living ask you for food.
You give it to them, always in time,
you open your hand and they eat their fill.
If you turn away they are frightened,
if you take their breath they die,
and they fall back into the dust.
But send your spirit, and they come to life,
you give the earth the freshness of youth.

Thus the world is full of him,
glory to God and lasting joy.

If he looks at the earth it trembles,
if he touches the mountains they burn.
As long as I am I will sing to him,
a song to my God while I am alive.
I hope that this song will make him happy,
I am happy myself with you, my God.
And let there be upon earth an end
to all evil, to every sin.

I want to call you, God, by your Name,
as truly as I live.

[Psalm 104] Israel experienced the glory and the faithful love of her God in the rescue from Egypt and the introduction, by Covenant and Promise, into Canaan. As Israel's faith was widened and deepened, she came to realize that the God of her rescue was also the God who made the world. The first chapter of Genesis was composed to bear witness to this faithful realization, and Psalm 104, which has its parallels in other literatures of the Ancient Near East, orchestrates this even more abundantly: the man who has the eyes of faith can interpret the marvels of creation as manifestations of God's glory and reliability. "From the creation of the world his invisible being has been perceived by human reason in his works" (Rom. 1. 20). The conclusion of this psalm is therefore the same as that of the psalms that deal with Israel's salvation: the People of God have to be faithful to the Word of God, of which it is the depositary.—It is from this concrete, lyrical and in a way very "secular" prayer that the Christian tradition has taken one of its strongest liturgical formulas to express its belief in the life-giving power of God's holy Spirit.

Psalm 105

Proclaim the Name of the Lord,
proclaim his wonderful acts.
Let it be known to the world
that he does wonders for us.
Let all who look for him
be glad with all their hearts—
for who would fail to glory
in his holy Name?
Turn to him, he is powerful,
do not give up looking for him.
Remember, then, his promise,
the signs he gave to us,
you, sons of his servant Abraham,
you, sons of Jacob, his friend.
He is our God, he alone,
his wisdom fills the whole earth.
He always remembers his covenant,
for a thousand generations—
that word which he gave to Abraham,
that oath which he swore to Isaac,
renewed and sealed before Jacob,
a covenant forever with his people—
"I will give you Canaan,
there you will live for good."

They were just a handful of people,
a little group of strangers,
homeless, in the midst of pagans,
wanderers, now here, now there.
But he allowed no one
to tyrannize over them,
he even punished kings
for their sake, and he said:

"Do not touch my anointed,
do no harm to my prophets."

Famine struck the country,
and they ran out of all bread.
Then he sent a man ahead of them,
Joseph, sold as a slave,
accused and thrown into prison—
his feet were painfully fettered
and chains put around his neck—
until he interpreted dreams
and what he foretold came true.
Then the king gave him his freedom,
the Pharao of the Egyptians,
and put everything in his hands,
his house and all his possessions—
he became the adviser of wise men,
the court was subject to him.

And Israel went into Egypt,
Jacob was a welcome guest,
there, in the land of Ham.
There the Lord made them fertile,
more numerous than the Egyptians,
and that annoyed the Egyptians,
they began to hate Israel,
they dared to torment Israel,
with violence and with cunning.
But the Lord called Moses, his servant,
and chose his brother Aaron—
he made them accomplish wonders
there, in the land of Ham.
And he sent darkness down,
it became as dark as the earth,
water was changed into blood,

and all the fish were killed.
The country was swarming with frogs—
they overran the king's palace.
He spoke, and there were the gnats,
mosquitoes throughout their country.
Hail and fire rained down—
the figtree and the vine
lay stretched out on the ground
and all the trees were shattered
everywhere round about.
He spoke, and there were the locusts,
swarms of teeming vermin—
not a blade of grass was left,
they stripped the country bare.
Then he struck their first-born,
the first-fruits of their strength.
Then he led his people to freedom:
there were the tribes, setting out,
loaded with silver and gold,
and nobody tried to harm them.
Egypt, crippled with terror,
Egypt was glad that they went.

He sent a cloud along
to cover them in the rear,
and a fire to give light in the dark.
They asked him: "Give us food"—
and he made quails come down.
He gave them bread from heaven,
and they were no longer hungry.
He tore the rocks apart,
and there was water gushing out,
streams of living water
in the very heart of the desert.
And he did all these things

because he had once made a promise
to Abraham, his servant.

He gave his people freedom,
and shouting for joy we went out.
He gave us the lands of the pagans,
he gave us the works of their hands,
so that we might keep his words,
and live in the light of his covenant,
and praise and give thanks to him,
now and for ever and ever.

[Psalm 105] The body of this "catechetical" psalm recites again
the old story of Israel's rescue from Egypt, the creed which the Jews
have never tired of telling down to our own day (cf., e.g., Deut. 6.
20–25; 26. 5–10): a handful of straying nomads, "wandering
Arameans", made into a people, brought to Egypt and rescued
from it again. But the story in itself is not the only, nor perhaps
even the main, concern of the psalm: the story is bracketed by
references to the "Promise". Israel has to "remember" that her
God was as good as his word, and thus the remembrance, the
anamnesis, becomes a pledge of God's continuing reliability.—
This is also the message of this psalm "to all who imitate the faith
of the father of us all, Abraham. Of him it is written: 'I have made
you the father of many peoples.' And this he is in the sight of God,
in whom he believed, who makes the dead come to life and calls
into existence what does not exist. Hoping against all hope he
believed (. . .). And these words were written down, not only for his
sake, but also for our sake (. . .) since we believe in him who has
raised Jesus, who is our Lord, from the dead" (Rom. 4. 16–18,
23–24).

Psalm 110

Word of God
to my king and lord:
"Take your seat
at my right hand.
I make your enemy
the step of your throne.
I put in your hand
the sceptre of my power.
Rule from Zion
over your enemy.
You are king
on the day of your birth,
light from light,
I have begotten you—
dew from the womb
of the break of day."

Word of God,
inviolable oath:
"You are a priest
in eternity,
just as once
Melchizedek was."

He is your God,
he is at your side.
When the day
of his anger has come
you will crush
the heads of kings;
you summon nations
to come to judgment,

heads are falling
throughout the land.
You drink from the brook,
and, victorious,
you go your way,
head held high.

[Psalm 110] The literary form of this psalm is a congratulation addressed to the king on the day of his accession to the throne. The king of Israel is the personification of the people as a whole, and as such he is God's chosen one *par excellence*, the priestly mediator of his people with God, and God's agent in bringing about his kingdom.—The oldest layers of the Christian tradition, following Jewish traditions about the Messiah, have already used this psalm to articulate the Christian faith in Christ's pre-eminence: cf. Mark 12. 35–37; Heb. 1. 13; 5. 6; 7. 17, 21; 10. 13.—"We give thanks to the Father, for he has enabled us to have a share in the inheritance of the saints in the light. He has rescued us from the powers of darkness and transferred us to the kingdom of his beloved Son" (Col. 1. 12–13).

Psalm 114

When Israel came away from Egypt,
the children of Jacob,
away from a strange and gabbling people,
then the Lord made
of Judah his holy dwelling-place,
his kingdom of Israel.
When the sea saw it, it took to flight,
and the Jordan shrank back,
the mountains and hills, like rams, like sheep,
like lambs, they were jumping.
Sea, what is wrong, that you take to flight?
Why creep away, Jordan?
And mountains, why like rams, like lambs,
why are you jumping?

The Lord of the earth has shown himself,
the God of Jacob,
who changes rocks into springs and pools,
stones into water.

[Psalm 114] An old popular hymn to celebrate the dramatic experience of Israel's election to be God's own people. The rescue from Egypt is described in terms that bear out Israel's triumphant disdain of the pagans. But also the elements of Nature are held up to ridicule by the people of the Covenant: it marches through the water—symbol of chaos—of the Red Sea (Exod. 14) and—according to a different tradition of the Exodus story—the Jordan (Jos. 3); the mountains—the traditional habitats of local deities—are startled like a flock of sheep. Thus Israel again expresses its faith in a God who can save men ("God of Jacob") because he is greater than the powers of the world ("God of the earth").—"I tell you, if your faith is like a mustard-seed, you will say to this mountain: 'Move from here to there'" (Matt. 17. 20).

Psalm 115

Not to us is the honour due, God, not to us,
but to you alone.
For you are reliable mercy and love,
God here among us.

How, then, can there be people who ask:
"Where is that God of yours?"
Our God is above everything,
what he wants he makes.

Pagans make their gods for themselves,
out of silver and gold;
they have mouths, but they cannot speak,
eyes, and they cannot see;
they have ears, but they cannot hear,
and noses, but they cannot smell;
and their hands—they do not feel,
and their feet—they do not walk,
and from their throats, and from their throats
no sound will ever come.
And the man who relies on gods of that kind
is quite as worthless as they are.

Israel, keep on trusting your God,
he is your help and your shield.
All of you, who in the house of God
perform your services, continue to trust him,
he is your help and your shield.
People of God, always keep trusting,
he is your help and your shield.

The Lord God keeps us in his heart
and gives us his blessing.
Happiness and blessing for Israel,

and much happiness for all who serve him,
nothing but mercy for all his people,
great and small.

He will make us great and numerous,
and also our children.
We are the favourites of God,
he has created heaven and earth.
The heaven is the Lord's own heaven,
he has given the earth to men.

Not the dead will speak of him,
not the dead in their dead silence.
But living men—we make him happy,
now and for ever.
Halleluiah.

[Psalm 115] Ever since the first important Greek version of the Old Testament, the so-called Septuagint, was made a few centuries B.C., there has been a tradition to consider this psalm as forming a unity with Psalm 114. The memory of Israel's rescue from Egypt does indeed act as the basis on which this liturgical psalm encourages the whole people, Israelites, priests, and non-Jewish worshippers, to go on relying on their God, who is still with them. The mockery of the idols, which reminds of the famous satire in Isaiah 44. 9–20, is used to strengthen this trust, and the psalm ends with the assurance that Man is not subject to the powers of this world: "He has given the earth to men" (cf. also 1 John 5. 4)—"In all these things we are more than victorious through him who has loved us. For I am sure that neither death nor life, neither angels nor authorities, neither the present nor the future, neither powers nor height nor depth nor any other creature will be able to separate us from the faithful love of God, which is present in Christ Jesus, our Lord" (Rom. 8. 38–39).

Psalm 118

Give thanks to God, for he is good,
his love endures in eternity.
All of Israel must proclaim:
his love endures in eternity—
and all the priests in the house of God:
his love endures in eternity—
all who put their faith in our God:
his love endures in eternity.

I was imprisoned, I called:
"God"—and he gave me an answer,
he gave great freedom to me.

He stands up for me, I am safe,
who will be able to touch me?
He stands up for me like a friend,
and my enemies count for nothing.
Better to shelter with God
than to rely on people;
better to shelter with God
than to rely on power.

All nations surrounded me,
I beat them down with the Name of God.
They closed in on me from every side,

I beat them down with the name of God.
They set upon me like a swarm of wasps,
a buzzing straw-fire round about me,
I beat them down with the Name of God.

I was beaten, I had fallen,
God has helped me to my feet.
He is my pride, he is my song,
my God has become my victory.

Shouts of gladness and triumph are
ringing out from the tents of the righteous:
"The powerful hand of the Lord does wonders,
raised up high, ready to bless us,
the powerful hand of the Lord does wonders."

I shall not die, no, I shall live,
bear witness to his powerful works—
it is true, the Lord has beaten me hard,
but he did not give me up to death.

Open to me
the door of his house,
I want to enter,
I want to thank him.

This door opens
the way to God;
men of good will
may go inside.

I give you thanks, for you have heard me,
you have become my victory.
The stone the builders could not use
has become the cornerstone.
This way God has let it happen—
we see, but fail to understand.
This is the day which the Lord has made,
a day of gladness for all of us.
Come and save us, you, our God,
bring us to a happy end.

You are blessed if you come in the Name of the Lord.
From his house we wish you blessing.
His light has risen over us.
Form a festive procession, then,
and come close around the altar,
wave palm-branches and sing to him:
You are my God, I want to thank you,
my God, and praise you to the skies.

Give thanks to God, for he is good,
his love endures in eternity.

[Psalm 118] A hymn of thanksgiving in the form of an elaborate liturgy at the gates of the Temple. After an introductory hymn that repeats the standard ritual chorus in praise of God's Covenant, an important person, perhaps the king, recounts his rescue from distress, enlarging it to national proportions and thus referring his personal salvation to the salvation of Israel as a people. After a dialogue at the gates of the Temple comes the thanksgiving proper, followed by acclamations, a blessing pronounced by the priests, and an invitation to a ritual procession. The psalm closes with a repetition of the chorus of praise. This liturgical setting is at least partly also a literary convention, as is suggested by the very general terms of the account of the distress and the rescue from it. In this way the psalm has come to acquire a much more general significance.—The Christian tradition spontaneously interpreted this psalm as an Easter hymn. The stone rejected by the builders is one of the oldest images for Jesus (cf., e.g., Mark 12. 10–11; 1 Peter 2. 7), who was received into Jerusalem by the crowd using the blessing taken from this psalm (cf. Mark 11. 9–10).—"In the days of his mortal life Jesus prayed with loud cries and with tears, imploring God, who could save him from death. He was heard on account of his righteousness: although he was Son of God, he learned obedience through suffering, and thus God brought him to perfect glory" (Heb. 5. 7–9).

Psalm 121

I raise my eyes up to the mountains—
will anyone come to help me?
Yes, my God comes to help me,
the maker of heaven and earth.

He will not allow you to stumble,
he will not sleep, he keeps watch over you.
No, he will not slumber or sleep,
he watches over all of his people.

Our God is keeping watch,
like a shadow spread over you.
The sun will not strike you by day,
and by night the moon will not harm you.

He keeps all evil away,
he takes you under his care.
And whether you are coming or going,
God will keep you for ever.

[Psalm 121] Each of the Psalms 120–134 bears the title: "Song of Ascents", in the original. They are all hymns used by pilgrims "going up" to the Temple in Jerusalem, the house of God, "the Maker of Heaven and Earth". Psalm 121 has the literary form of a dialogue between the pilgrim and the priest. Instead of looking for help to the mountains, the traditional places of idolatrous worship, the pilgrim puts his trust in the Creator. The priest confirms his trust by proclaiming that the Maker of heaven and earth is also the God who keeps people on their ways and who cares for their personal well-being. The pilgrimage, of course, is the image for the life of the believer: ever since Abraham felt the call to leave his certainties behind (cf. Gen. 12. 1), this has been one of the most telling images of the Jewish and Christian traditions.—"We do not have a lasting city here, but seek the city that is to come" (Heb. 13. 14).

Psalm 122

It was a joy for me to hear:
"We are on our way to the house of the Lord."
And now we are here in front of your gates,
on your ground, Jerusalem.

City of my heart, Jerusalem,
with your houses shoulder to shoulder.
All the tribes of Israel
are going there, caravans of people,

to celebrate the Name of the Lord,
for this is our sacred duty.
There the seats of judgment are,
there is the royal throne of David.

Pray for peace, for peace on this city,
wish its children every blessing—
city of peace, within your walls
a man may be safely happy.

I wish you all prosperity,
dearest home of all my friends,
city of God, I wish you peace,
peace for evermore.

[Psalm 122] The pilgrims have arrived in Jerusalem: they burst out into a hymn of praise and prayer. The Hebrew text exploits the name *Yerushalayim*, as in some other psalms, for a number of significant word-plays: sh*a'alu*, (pray), sh*alom* (peace), *yi*shl*ayu* (have rest), sh*alwah* (happiness); these strongly emotional overtones have been made explicit in the translation.—"According to God's promise we expect a new heaven and a new earth, where justice will prevail" (2 Peter 3. 14). "And I saw a new heaven and a new earth. The first heaven and the first earth were vanished and there was no sea any more. And I saw the holy city, Jerusalem, coming down from the heavens, from God" (Apoc. 21. 1–2).

Psalm 123

I raise up my eyes to you,
my God, to you in heaven.

Just as the eyes of a servant will
turn to the hand of his master,
just as the eyes of a slave-girl will
turn to the hand of her mistress,
so our eyes turn to the Lord our God,
until he will show mercy.

Have mercy, Lord, have mercy on us,
God, we are tired of this contempt.

We are sick and tired to death
with the way they have trampled on us and scorned us,
in their recklessness,
in their self-conceit.

[Psalm 123] It took centuries before Israel learned how to pray with a naked faith like this. For centuries there had been visible blessings as signs of God's mercy: the rescue from Egypt, the successful tribal settlements in Canaan, the political power of David's kingdom. As Israel was gradually stripped from these and became a dispersed people, the problem of the happiness of power and arrogance became an ever more pressing challenge to faith, and even the restored community in Jerusalem immediately after the great captivity and in Nehemiah's days saw many of its high-strung hopes defeated by the contempt of the pagan world. Many psalms (e.g. 11, 25, 32, and especially 73) bear witness to the struggle which was the result of this painful challenge. The struggle came at last to rest in the *anawim*, the poor, who discovered that ultimately the future was God's; ultimately there was "no reason to worry about the question: what shall we eat, or what shall we drink, or what shall we have for clothing? For the pagans pursue all these things. Your Father in heaven knows that you need them. So look for his kingdom and its righteousness first, and all these things will be yours as well" (Matt. 6, 31–33).

Psalm 124

Israel may say with justice:

If God had not been for us,
when people were against us—
if God had not been for us,
we would have been eaten alive,
we would have been burnt in their rage,
the water would have sprung upon us,
the flood would have swept us away,
and in those seething waves
we would all have been lost.

But God—thanks be to him—
has saved us from their teeth.
We have escaped, like a bird
from the net of the bird-catcher.
The net is torn,
and we are flown—

Our help is the Name of the Lord,
who made the heavens and the earth.

[Psalm 124] A short hymn of thanksgiving with a liturgical beginning and using traditional imagery to express chaos and rescue. Like so many passages in the Bible, this little psalm insists on describing the attitude of faith by starting from the worst possible hypothesis: "when people were against us", a condition which in the experience of the Jews had only too often been true. In the agelong experience of Israel, however, God's help had never been conceived or proclaimed as a facile reassurance or an easy way out—from time immemorial Yahweh was known as a difficult friend. If, therefore, this psalm proclaims the freedom of Israel's Remnant from the oppression of the pagan world, it does so by alleging the Name of a God who is not only the Rock of Rescue, but also the demanding God of the patriarchs, Moses, and the prophets.—"I am convinced that the suffering of the present day is in no way comparable to the glory which is waiting to be revealed in us. For the creation, too, is yearning for the revelation of the glory of God's children. For the creation is subjected to a futile existence, not because it has wanted to, but because it was God's will that it should be so subjected. But this situation is not without hope, for the creation, too, will be delivered from its slavish subjection to destruction, to have its share in the glorious freedom of God's children" (Rom. 8. 18–21).

Psalm 126

When from our exile
God takes us home again,
that will be dreamlike.

We shall be singing,
laughing for happiness.
The world will say:
"Their God does wonders."
Yes, you do wonders,
God here among us,
you, our gladness.

Then take us home,
bring us to life,
just like the rivers
which, in the desert,
when the first rain falls
start flowing again.

Sow seed in sadness,
harvest in gladness.
A man goes his way
and sows seed with tears.
Back he comes, singing,
sheaves on his shoulder.

[Psalm 126] The history of Israel's salvation through the rescue from Egypt, her painful journey through the desert, and her occupation of the Promised Land acted as the pledges of God's continuing faithfulness. But experiences of the past, no matter how tenaciously handed on and believed, tend to harden into tales too good to be true and too far distant to be believable, unless they tally with valid experiences in the present. This is what tradition did for the great stories of Israel—it remoulded them into models of experience. The rescue from the house of slavery became the model of the life of the believer; the biblical short story (Daniel 1–6; Esther; Judith), the narrative psalms, and large portions of the wisdom-books reinforced the validity of the Exodus. This psalm, with its sapiential ending, is an example of this fusion of wisdom and generalized Exodus-spirituality.—"Amen, amen, I tell you: if the grain of wheat does not fall into the earth it remains alone; but if it dies it yields much fruit. The man who loves his life will lose it; but the man who disregards his life in this world will keep it into life eternal. If somebody wants to serve me he will have to follow me, and wherever I am, my servant will be there also. If somebody serves me, the Father will crown him with honour" (John 12. 24–26).

Psalm 127

Purify our hearts, O Lord

If the Lord does not build the house,
poor builder, why go on working?
If the Lord does not guard the town,
poor watchman, your watch is in vain.

Why, then, should you get up early,—
and toil on into the night.
Your bread will still taste of sorrow.
Happiness can never be made—
the Lord gives it to his friends,
just like that, in their sleep.

Children come from God,
a son is a precious gift.
Like arrows on a man's bow
are sons born to him in his youth.
Happy is the man who has them—
he has no need to worry,
he can face up to his enemy,
he can take on the world.

[Psalms 127 and 128] These two pilgrimage hymns express the same feeling. Yahweh is present to the man who believes, and consequently he experiences the world that surrounds him not as a bare reality, but as "given", as a promise and as a challenge. Believing in God means: taking him seriously according as he can be found in the concrete situations of life—cherishing ordinary things and ordinary experiences—looking for the mystery in what you have, not in what you do not have. Happiness, in this way, comes to the believer as blessing. He experiences God's presence in a house, in a town, in labour, in strength, in a wife and children. The images of the defeat of the enemies, the olive and the vine enhance the dynamism of this experience by evoking the great themes of the Exodus.

Psalm 128

Happy is the man who
may lead his life with God.
You are that man if only
you keep his words alive.

Your hands—they will be working,
your land—it will bear fruit,
enough for you to live on.
You will be more than rich.

Your wife is a fruitful vine
that blooms in the heart of your house.
Sons, like olive branches,
are standing around your table.
In this way a man of God
knows blessing after blessing.

Receive as long as you live
all blessing from God's house,
enjoy to your heart's content
the peace of his holy city.

Be fruitful in your sons,
find blessing in their children—
thus the Lord saves his people
and gives all peace to us.

By these overtones the modest experience of human happiness is
linked up with the Covenant: the God of the Rescue gives depth to
happiness, which becomes safety, reliance, peace, trust, faith.
Psalm 128 also refers the happiness of each family to the national
happiness around the cult in the Temple.—"Is there any father
among you, who will give his son a stone when he asks for bread?
Or, if he asks for a fish, will he give him a snake instead? Or, if he
asks for an egg, will give him a scorpion? If you then, although you
are evil, are capable of giving good gifts to your children, how much
more will your Father in heaven give the holy Spirit to those who
ask him!" (Luke 11. 11–13).

Psalm 130

From the depths I am calling you, God,
Lord God, do you hear me?
Open your heart to me,
I am begging for mercy.

If you keep count of sins,
my God, who can hold his own?
But there is forgiveness
with you—your way is our life.

I expect the Lord,
I wait with all my heart—
and I hope for his word.

I look out for him,
just as a man on guard
looks out for the morning,

looks out for the morning.

Keep on trusting in God,
for there is mercy with him,
he is your redemption.

He will make us free
from the power of evil.

[Psalm 130] This intensely personal psalm sets to sound the depths of human existence in terms of guilt and forgiveness. The experience of life going on in the teeth of the destructive forces of human inadequacy and sinfulness has led the poet of this psalm to the conviction that God must be a God of forgiveness, and thus he can turn his complaint into a profession of reliance, with faith in God acting as the pivot. But faith in God is not a facile attitude—it affords no easy assurance. It is an attitude of waiting in the midst of darkness, a precarious balance between hope and fear, with hope ultimately prevailing.—"Joseph, son of David, do not fear to take Mary as your wife. The child in her womb is of the holy Spirit. She will give birth to a son whom you must call Jesus [which means: God saves], for he will make his people free from their sins" (Matt. 1. 20-21).

Psalm 131

God I am not haughty
I do not look down on others

do not imagine that I am great
do not dream enormous dreams

yes I have tamed my desires
my soul has come to rest

like a little child that has drunk
and lies at the breast of his mother

a little child that has drunk
so is my soul in me

expect everything from him
now and for evermore

[Psalm 131] This beautiful short lyric sums up the attitude of the *anawim*, the "poor". Freed from the passion for achievement and self-affirmation, reconciled to the insignificant shape of Israel after the Exile, without regrets and without disillusion, the poet of this psalm has surrendered his own limited capabilities as well as Israel's destiny to God, in the conviction that God will take care of all things, and that all things are to be found with God. "Our hearts are restless until they come to rest in You" (St Augustine).—"At that time Jesus said: 'I bless you, Father, Lord of heaven and earth, for having hidden these things from the wise and the knowing, and revealed them to children. Yes, Father, this has been your good pleasure. All things have been surrendered to me by my Father, and no one but the Father knows the Son, and no one knows the Father but the Son and any one to whom the Son chooses to reveal him. Come to me, all you who are exhausted and bent down under your burdens, and I will give you relief and rest'" (Matt. 11. 25–28).

Psalm 133

Yes, that is comfort—to live
in one house together as brothers.
It is like precious balsam,
poured out over the head
and flowing down into the beard,
the beard of Aaron, down
into the collar of his garment.
It is like the dew of Hermon,
descending on Zion's mountains.
There the Lord gives his blessing,
life in eternity.

[Psalm 133] A "Scene from Clerical Life" in the Temple at Jerusalem: the common joy of the priests and levites is expressed in the common pride in the attributes of their office: the oil, the garments, the name of Aaron, and especially the height of Zion, inconspicuous in comparison with the holy mountain of Hermon, and yet the place of God's life-giving presence.—"All who had come to believe formed a close unity and had everything in common. They used to sell their property and their goods to distribute the money among all as they needed. And day after day they met in the Temple, faithfully and of one accord. They had the breaking of the bread in one or other home. They enjoyed their food in joy and simplicity of heart. They praised God. They were held in esteem by all the people. And day after day the Lord added to their number more people to be saved" (Acts 2. 44–47).

Psalm 137

By the streams of Babylon we sat down,
mourning at the thought of Zion.
And on the branches of the willows
that stood there we hung up our harps.

For those who had carried us away
called on us to sing a song;
our tormentors wanted something cheerful—
"Sing us one of your songs from Zion."

Ah, how should we be able to sing
of our God in a foreign land.
Jerusalem, should I ever forget you,
let me lose my right hand first.

Let my tongue turn to stone in my mouth,
if I no longer remember you,
if I do not find my greatest joy
in you, my city, Jerusalem.

O God, repay the sons of Edom
for that day when disaster came to our city—
repay those who cried: "Away with it,
let not one stone remain on another."

O city of Babylon, destroying fury,
my blessing on the man who will repay you.
My blessing on the man who seizes your children
and smashes them against the rocks.

[Psalm 137] To sing a liturgical hymn to Zion, a hymn like Psalm 46, in Babylon would be a self-defeating gesture, because the destruction of Jerusalem would seem to imply that Yahweh was no longer capable of bringing peace and prosperity to Israel. Besides, to celebrate God's presence in the territory of foreign gods would imply that after the defeat Israel's God had become one of the minor deities in the Babylonian pantheon (cf. Sennacherib's words in Is. 36. 18 ff.). And this, in turn, would be tantamount to writing off the entire history of Israel, centred around the sanctuary on Mount Zion—the playing hand and the singing tongue would be the instruments of unbelief. In this way Psalm 137 shows Israel tenaciously clinging to her faith in the teeth of an ever more meaningless *impasse*, cursing Babylon, the city of injustice and evil, and Edom, its accomplice (cf. Ezech. 35. 5–15; Obadiah 8–14), and blessing the City of God that has disappeared from sight.—"It is in faith that they all died, without having received what had been promised. But they had seen it and greeted it from afar, recognizing that they were strangers and wanderers on the earth. For people who speak thus make it clear that they are in quest of a homeland. And if in so speaking they had been thinking of the land they had left, they would have had an opportunity to return there. But actually their desire went out to a better, a heavenly country. And therefore God is not ashamed to be called their God, for he has indeed built a city for them" (Heb. 11. 13–16).

Psalm 139

My God, you fathom my heart and you know me,
my God, you know where I am, where I go.
You see through my thoughts from afar,
you have decided my roaming and resting,
and you are familiar with all that I do,
yes, and no word comes to my lips
but, my God, you have already heard it.
You are before me and you are behind me,
you have laid your hand upon me—
marvel of wisdom, far above me,
I cannot reach it, you are beyond me.

How should I ever run away from your spirit,
and where should I seek refuge—you see me everywhere.
If I climb to the heavens, you are in the heavens,
if I go into the earth, I find you there too.
And if I should fly with the day-break
down to the uttermost shore of the sea,
there also your hand will help me on,

there also your powerful hand holds me tight.
If I should cry: "Darkness, cover me,
let the night come down round about me"—
for you the darkness does not exist,
for you the night is as bright as the day,
the darkness is as clear as the light.
I am your creation in my bones and tissues,
you have woven me in the womb of my mother.
I thank you, you have so wonderfully made me,
awesome wonders are all your works.
I am known by you, to the core, to my soul—
nothing in me was hidden from your eyes
when I was fashioned in deepest secrecy,
beautifully twined in the womb of the earth.
I was still unborn—you had already seen me,
and all of my life was in your book
before one day of it had been shaped.

How difficult are your thoughts to me,
my God, what a world of wisdom!
Were I to count them, they are as numerous
as the sand on the seashore, and yet—
I still know nothing at all about you.

God, kill the man with wicked plans—
away from me, people with blood on your hands.
They speak of you, but mean to discredit you,
they use your name, but only to betray you.
Should I not hate, God, those who hate you,
not be sick at heart over those who oppose you?
I hate them as fiercely as I can hate,
from now on they are my own enemies.

Now fathom my heart, o God, and know me,
test me and know what is happening in me.
I shall not come to a dead end, shall I?
Lead me forward on the way of my fathers.

[Psalm 139] One of the classical elements of supplication is a profession of innocence, often accompanied by an indignant denunciation of the unrighteous; a prayer like Psalm 26 is even wholly based on this pattern. As, however, the awareness of God's transcendence was more explicitly explored, Israel became ever more sensitive to the precariousness of protestations of innocence: who can fathom the depths of his own heart, and who knows his own secret evil (cf. Ps. 19. 11-13)? For the poet of Psalm 139 this question leads to a dreadful ambiguity. He is faced with a God whose fearful presence does not even let a man swallow his own spittle in peace (cf. Job 7. 19), but who is also the God of Psalm 8, the God whose heart is touched by the thought of Man. No wonder, then, that his protestation of innocence sticks in his throat, and that the close of his impressive poem is not the simple affirmation: "Your mercy is before my eyes, and I lead my life in your truth" (Ps. 26. 3). On the contrary, it is a surrender to the inscrutable scrutiny of a God whose faithfulness is as reliable as it is mysterious.—"The word of God is alive and active, sharper than any two-edged sword. It penetrates to the point of contact of soul and spirit, of joints and marrow, and discerns the deepest thoughts and intentions of man. No creature is hidden from him, but everything is open and laid bare before his eyes. It is with him that we have to do" (Heb. 4. 12-13).

Psalm 142

I am crying out, I cry to God—
o God, I implore you and beg for mercy.

I pour out my troubles before his eyes,
I pour out my whole heart to him.

I can go no further, I am out of breath—
but you, you know a way out for me.

They have set traps and snares on my way,
whichever way I turn, no friend,

no friend for me, no refuge any more,
no one who cares for me in the least.

I cried out to you, o God, I called:
my refuge, you, my all in this life.

But listen then, I am almost dead,
save me then, they are after me, they are too much for me.

They are hemming me in, God, get me out of this,
and I will show you how grateful I am.

And all your friends will wish me joy,
because you have been good to me.

[Psalm 142] This psalm is a classical specimen of the complaint. Starting from a description of the situation of someone wrongly persecuted, it turns into a desperate prayer, and looks forward to the atmosphere of relief and gladness around the thanksgiving sacrifice when the trial is over. The Hebrew Bible attributes this psalm "to David, when he was in the cave", the prototypical situation of the just man called by God and hounded down by his enemies (cf. 1 Sam. 22. 1; 24. 1–7), whom he refuses to attack because he trusts in God.—"You have heard that the Law says: 'An eye for an eye, and a tooth for a tooth.' But I tell you not to resist injustice. But if anyone strikes you on the right cheek, turn to him the other also. And if anyone wants to take you to court in order to get your coat, let him have your cloak as well. And if anyone forces you to go one mile, go with him two miles"(Matt. 5. 38–41).

Psalm 147

1

A song of praise to the Lord,
singing makes you happy,
singing to our God,
for he is pleased with psalms.

He builds a city of peace
for the people of his covenant.
However far we are scattered,
he calls us together again.

Broken people are healed,
and he binds up their wounds,
our God, who defines again,
every night, the number of the stars,

who calls them all by name—
a powerful God is he,
this God of ours—and his wisdom
is great beyond all measure.

He helps the poor man up,
he brings pride to a fall.
We must sing in praise of his Name,
we have to make music for him,

who covers the heavens with clouds
and makes the rain for the earth,
who clothes the mountains in green
and gives the animals their food—

and even the fledgling raven
gets what he cries out for.
No, he does not care
for horsepower or iron muscles,

his heart goes out to those
who are waiting for his love,
his friends in hope and fear—
and so he is our God.

II

Jerusalem, city of God,
people, glorify him.
He has safely barred your gates,
he has given your children his blessing.

He gives you bread and peace—
you live a life of abundance.
He sends his word to the earth,
and it runs, it spreads like wildfire.

And sometimes he makes it snow,
a white and woolly fur,
he scatters hoar-frost like ashes,
and hail-showers, stones of ice.

Who can endure his cold?
But then he speaks a word—
it thaws, the wind is blowing,
the waters are flowing again.

To Jacob and to his house
he has entrusted his word,
his law, his revelation,
his covenant and promise.

There is no other people
that may so experience him,
that may so keep his words—
our song rings to high heaven.

[Psalm 147] This psalm, which the Vulgate divides into two separate psalms, is a very poetical summary of the discoveries which Israel was led to make in the course of its history. It is full of memories and quotations from the prophetic writings before, during, and after the Exile, and from the book of Job. God is the Rescuer of Israel who is also the Creator of the world. He is the God of the poor, the friend of the helpless, whom he gathers around his city of peace in order to make himself known to them. The peculiar charm of this poem lies in the fact that the awe of God, the Creator, has been interiorized and incorporated into the modest joy of the believing community that feels at home with its God.—"Life is more than food, and the body is more than clothing. Look at the ravens—they neither sow nor mow, they have neither storehouse nor barn, and yet God feeds them. How much more are you than the birds! And for that matter, who among you can add one cubit to his span of life by worrying? If, then, you are powerless in such a small matter, why do you worry about the rest? Think of the flowers, how they grow—they neither spin nor weave. Yet I tell you, even Solomon in all his splendour was not arrayed like any one of them. But if God so clothes the plants in the fields, alive today and thrown into the oven tomorrow, how much more will be clothe you, men of little faith!" (Luke 12. 23–28).

Psalm 149

Halleluiah,
a new song for the Lord our God.
Sing to him,
he has called you all together.
Israel
must be glad for the sake of her maker,
Zion's children
must revel and shout for joy for their King.
Dance to him
as a tribute to his Name,
strike up music
on your kettledrums and harps.
Our God
has chosen a people for himself.
He redeems,
he brings to greatness humble people.
All his friends
may glory and take a pride in him,
nights on end
they may acclaim and worship him.

From their mouths
comes a hymn of praise to the Lord,
in their hands
the two-edged sword is eagerly flashing.
So they will
execute his revenge on the peoples,
punishment
across the shoulders of the nations.
And their rulers—
they will tie them fast and shackle them,
powers that be—
they will put them in chains and fetters.

So they will
carry out his law and his sentence.
So God gives
glory and honour to all his friends.
Halleluiah.

[Psalm 149] As the Jews had to cope with the problem of oppression they came to reassert their faith in God's rescue in terms of a belief in the ultimate victory of God's chosen people over their enemies, just as the decline of the monarchy produced the image of the ideal king at the end of time (cf. Ps. 72). During the last few centuries B.C. the proclamation of this ultimate victory, rooted in the prophetic tradition (cf., e.g., Is. 60–66; Ezech. 25–28), took the shape of apocalyptic literature: the book of Daniel (which the Greek Bible was to expand and count as one of the great prophets) is a brilliant effort to come to terms with the disintegration of the Jewish nation under the oppression of the pagan world, by pointing to the final restoration of justice and righteousness on the ruins of the powers that be. In the dream-world of the apocalyptic writings historic personages and events loom large in and out of context, imaginary characters and hosts of angels join in a cosmic struggle between light and darkness, God's hidden plans are revealed by means of allusion, symbolic numbers, oracles and meaningful events—all with the purpose of encouraging the humiliated believers not to give up faith and hope. This holy conviction about the victory of the righteous, however, also found a rather more down-to-earth and realistic expression in stories such as the rescue of Daniel from the lions' den (Dan. 6), and above all in the penny novels of Judith and Esther, with their strong appeal to popular chauvinism. Psalm 149, militant, chauvinistic, and visionary, illustrates the fervour as well as the ambiguity of Jewish eschatology.—"Halleluiah! Salvation and glory and power belong to our God, for his judgments are true and just. He has condemned the great harlot who ruined the earth with her harlotry. He has avenged on her the blood of his servants. Halleluiah!" (Apoc. 19. 1–3).

Psalm 150

Praise the Lord in his holy house,
the firmament of his majesty.
Praise him for his powerful works,
praise him, he is immeasurably great.

Praise him with your resounding horns,
and with your lutes and harps and guitars.
Praise him with dancing and tambourines,
tune your strings and play the flute.

Praise him with kettledrums and cymbals,
brass and woodwind, a choir of voices,
halleluiah, shouts of joy,
all the living are praising the Lord.

[Psalm 150] Psalm 150 is the final doxology, the epilogue of the book of psalms. It sums up its character by summing up the character of the cult: the liturgical evocation of God's glory, present in the midst of the community. It was in the liturgy that Israel celebrated her coming to life as the community whose faith in God was founded upon the rescue from Egypt, the social and religious experiences in the desert, and the entry into Canaan (cf., e.g., the liturgical prayers in Deut. 26). It was in the liturgy, too, that this original core was developed: the repeated proclamation of the Covenant permitted Israel to view her subsequent history as well as the traditions about what lay before the Exodus as ever so many manifestations of God's abiding faithfulness, and thus, as being vitally connected with the Exodus. In this way the history and sensibility of Israel was accompanied by a steady flow of liturgy, which articulated and interpreted the present by re-enacting the past. It is not surprising, then, that—when the fullest available traditions about Israel's desert experiences were recorded (Exod. 1–Num. 24)–they were clustered around a highly dramatic, "prototypical" account of the most solemn moments of the Temple liturgy, set on Mount Sinai (Exod. 19. 9–25), with the blast of the horn evoking the presence of God as its culminating point. Psalm 150 expresses Israel's faith in a liturgy feeding into life and fed into by life, just as the account of the Sinai liturgy served as a literary expedient to lend present relevance to past facts.—"Let your hearts be ruled by the peace of Christ, to which you were indeed called as members of the one body. And be grateful. Let the word of Christ live among you abundantly. Teach and admonish one another with all wisdom. And with grateful heart sing to God psalms, hymns, and songs inspired by the Spirit. And whatever you do, in word or deed, do everything in the name of Jesus, the Lord, giving thanks to God the Father through him" (Col. 3. 15–17).

Index to First Lines

A NOTE ON THE AUTHORSHIP OF THIS BOOK

In the course of 1967 the model, and in many ways the original, of the present book appeared in the Netherlands under the title *Vijftig Psalmen, Proeve van een nieuwe vertaling.* It was the result of a close collaboration of two poets, Huub Oosterhuis and Michel van der Plas, with two exegetes, Pius Drijvers and Han Renckens. The psalms in that collection were translated into English by Frans Jozef van Beeck in collaboration with David Smith and Forrest Ingram. The introduction is largely based on an article by Han Renckens, published in the catechetical review *Verbum* under the title "Vijftig Psalmen", translated by David Smith, and adapted for the present book by Frans Jozef van Beeck, who also wrote the commentaries on the psalms.

ROGUE LIES

Web of Lies, Book #2

KATHLEEN BROOKS

An original work of Kathleen Brooks. *Rogue Lies* copyright © 2017 by Kathleen Brooks

Cover art by Sunni Chapman at The Salty Olive

Dedication

This is my 25th book so I have a lot of people I want to thank. It starts with you, my reader. I wouldn't be able to write these books without you. I draw support and encouragement from every email, post, and tweet you all send. To my Facebook group, Kathleen's Blossom Café, for making me laugh every day and for letting me tease you relentlessly about upcoming books. You all know I love you. To every person who has picked up one of my books, THANK YOU.

To my husband, for like the 25th time, but he's seriously the best man I know. He's the one who told me I should publish my first book. He's there every day with encouragement, praise, and then has the courage to edit the book first. But then he also says sexy things like, "Honey, you need a new laptop." I love you, Chris.

To my daughter who types THE END to every book. Mommy loves you and couldn't be prouder of the young lady you are becoming.

To my mom, Marcia, who tells everyone about my books, sometimes holding them hostage to do so. To my dad, Milo, who goes into the Lexington Public Library and moves my books to the front display – I'm so lucky you're my parents, and I love you both so much.

A big thank you to my friend and fellow author, Heather Sunseri, for the hours of talks we have about our books, storylines, writing sprints, and for being a great friend who can make the best martinis. And to all the great authors I have met and am now happy to call friends.

To my in-laws, Mike and Pat, for the crazy support you've shown and for never bringing up the sex scenes I write, because that would be embarrassing.

To my Uncle Craig for helping with every book. It means the world to me that my family is involved with my books, and I appreciate each nitpick you send me.

To Melissa and Katie, thank you for being the best friends a girl could have. From our epic senior night in college to not thinking I was crazy when I told you I wanted to be an author instead of a lawyer. You all have been with me every step of the way and I love you!

PROLOGUE

J oel Davidson sat in his tiny cubicle at *The Washington Leader* newspaper. It was the biggest newspaper in the DC area, and he was one of their top reporters. Joel stared unseeingly at his desk piled high with papers. Notecards had been tacked onto the tan, rough material blanketing the walls of his cubicle. He didn't see the people walking by his small space. He didn't hear the phones ringing or people shouting over the cubicles at each other for information on pieces they were running. He couldn't because all of his attention was focused on the anonymous email he'd just received.

I know what you're investigating. Stop now or you'll die.

Joel still hadn't breathed as he read the email for the eighth time. No one knew what he was working on. One of his sources must have talked. Now thirty-six and a reporter since college, Joel had received his fair share of threats. And he sure as hell wasn't going to let this one bother him.

Joel printed the threat and took the long walk out of the pits to the senior editor's office. He knocked, and Jeff Sargent waved him in. Jeff's tie

was crumpled on the desk and his coffee-stained, white button-up shirt was open at the neck. "You got something for me, Joel?"

Joel set the paper on his desk. "I went a whole two months without getting a threat," Joel joked. "But this one is a little different. No one knows what I'm working on."

Jeff read the note and leaned back in his chair. "Shit, son, I don't even know what you're working on. Maybe it's time you told me."

Joel looked around before closing the office door. "I'm looking into that FBI agent's death in Africa. Agent Phylicia Claymore."

Jeff shrugged. "So? Every reporter under the sun is looking into her and the rest of the FBI."

"I know, but I think I have a good lead on something. Something big." Joel started to pace the office. This was the story of a lifetime—Pulitzer material, book deal material, major motion picture type of material. "I'll know more tomorrow. I'm meeting with a source tonight."

"I bet Sheila loves that. Another night at work," Jeff tried to joke. Joel had been married for five years. Jeff had been married for seventeen. "But seriously, what's the scoop?"

"I'll fill you in tomorrow morning. It's big, Jeff. Front page material that will have *The Washington Leader* crushing our competition."

Jeff smiled at the thought of his newspaper being the top in town. "I've learned to trust your feelings, Joel. I look forward to hearing what you have tomorrow."

Joel gave a nod and opened the door. It was six o'clock, and he was meeting his source an hour outside of DC. He needed to hurry or he'd miss his chance.

★ ★ ★

Joel pulled up at Manassas National Park and parked his car. It was dark, and the park was deserted. He opened his car door and got out to look down the empty road leading into the park — the same park that was once the site of the Battle of Bull Run, the first major battle in the American Civil War. Soldiers from the North and South clashed fighting. Brothers fought against brothers, fathers against sons, and cousins against cousins. It truly was a country torn in half.

The sound of a car reached Joel's ears before he saw it. He pressed Record on his phone and set it on the roof of his car so that it was hidden by the luggage racks. The car was driving up the lane with its lights off as it pulled next to Joel.

The door opened and a man stepped out. His brown hair was military short and a tattoo covered the inside of his wrist. "Mr. Davidson?"

"Yes. And you are . . .?"

"I need to check you for a wire," the man said, coming around the car.

"Of course," Joel untucked his shirt and lifted it up. The man patted him down and then closed the door to Joel's car. Joel had left his work phone sitting on the passenger's seat, and so far his source was

doing exactly what Joel had hoped — thinking no one was listening. Joel wasn't going to share the recording, but he would use it all the same to get direct quotes and to try to ferret out any information leading to this man's identity so he could guarantee the story's authenticity.

"You said you have something about Agent Claymore's death." Joel nudged the man back a step.

"It's bigger than Claymore. The FBI is compromised by enemies of the United States."

Joel raised his eyebrow. "What kind of enemies?"

The man shook his head. "I don't know. But things are happening that aren't being ordered, or at least there is no record of the orders. Phylicia Claymore was a power-hungry bitch who would never have gotten a job at the FBI in the first place if it weren't for her senator father. But what's interesting isn't what happened in Africa, it's what happened before Africa. There have been items disappearing from the FBI laboratory at Quantico over the past year. Items such as the biometrics identifying who set off certain bombs and even a chemical weapon that had been defused at an investigated site of a terrorist attack. Director Kirby has kept it quiet. But don't you think it's strange that the biometrics we thought showed proof the rebel leader had touched it suddenly disappeared two weeks before that same rebel leader allegedly used that exact type of weapon on a small town that refused to bow to his power? It would have been the proof needed to bring in the UN to support the

leadership and, hopefully, help quell the rebellion. Instead, now there's a missing bomb, and he got away scot-free until he was found dead with Phylicia Claymore of all people."

Joel sucked in a deep breath. "But you had the proof at the lab . . ."

"The proof was wiped away as if it never existed. Now, who has the power to do that?"

"You think it was Claymore?" Joel asked.

"I do."

"Was her name on the list of visitors for that day?"

The man nodded his head. "Yes. There's evidence she was there for twenty minutes but then left in the company of Director Kirby, who was at the FBI Academy giving a speech to new recruits. However, there are ways into and out of the base that she could have used undetected."

The man handed a log to Joel showing that Agent Claymore had signed into the labs at 16:36, right before they closed for the day. "Or she scoped out the location of what she wanted and passed it along to someone else to steal," Joel suggested.

"Look into it more. None of the reporters are looking into anything other than her involvement in Africa. Look at her movements here in Washington. Talk to people at Quantico. Shit, she got our bartender fired because she was threatened by Elizabeth's climb up the FBI ladder."

"Elizabeth who?"

"Elizabeth James. She was under Phylicia, and they did not like each other."

"Anything else?" Joel asked. He was itching to find Elizabeth James.

"There's still a missing chemical weapon out there. I hope you can find it because I've been shut down." The man turned and got back into his car. Joel watched as he drove away before moving to turn off the recording. Stolen weapons ending up in the hands of United States enemies all because of a rogue FBI agent. This was the story of a lifetime.

Joel pumped his fist as he jerked open his door. He couldn't wait to get home to start his research.

★   ★   ★

"Honey! I'm home!" Joel shouted as he tossed his keys on the side table. He rushed in, opening his laptop as he headed toward the light from the kitchen's open window, looking out into the living room. "Did you keep dinner warm?"

Joel pushed the swinging door to kitchen open and took a deep breath as he smelled dinner warming in the oven. He powered up his laptop before looking up to kiss his wife.

"Sheila," Joel gasped. His wife wasn't alone. A man wearing black gloves and a suit stood behind his wife with a knife to her throat. He was just under six feet with blond hair, blue eyes, and a pink paisley necktie. His face was handsome, but his eyes . . . they were empty.

"Joel," Sheila gave a strangled cry before the man jabbed the point of the knife harder into her neck. Blood pooled around the sharp edge of the

knife and began to trickle down her throat.

"I'll do whatever you want, just let my wife go," Joel begged.

"I warned you, didn't I?"

Joel's mind couldn't compute the man's words. "Warned? The email from today?"

"Haven't you learned that reporters do what we tell them to? What were you told to do?"

"You told me to leave the story. I will. I'll burn everything I have," Joel swore as he looked into the pleading eyes of his wife.

"No, before I warned you. What were you supposed to be writing a story on? The one that came down from corporate. The one that you thought you could ignore."

Joel's eyes flashed up to the man's. "The story about President Stratton secretly supporting a coup in Zambia in order to steal the mineral rights of the country?"

"They even gave you the source's name, and you just ignored it."

"The story was completely fabricated. The source has no direct knowledge or contact to the so-called rebels, which I couldn't prove existed in the first place. No one would believe it."

The man dug deeper into Sheila's neck as tears and blood mixed. "People will believe it because we tell them to. The media and the people are entangled in a beautiful dance. The stories don't have to be real because before they're found to be fake, folks are already up in arms. *How dare the president support a coup! It's a violation of human rights!* It will be all over

social media in hours. When the paper later finds the story to be false, they'll print a short retraction and not a single person will see it. How do I know this? Because we will have moved on to the next dance that enrages or scares the people, just as we have been successfully doing for years."

"I'll write it!" Joel promised. "Right now. Just let my wife go, please!"

"Dance, puppet," the man laughed as he slid the blade across Sheila's neck.

"No!" Joel yelled. He ran to his wife as the man dropped her to the floor. The sound of his newborn son crying echoed in the house, mixing with his unintelligible sounds of grief. Sheila gurgled and tears fell from her eyes as Joel held her. It was over in seconds. Her beautiful green eyes faded closed.

"You didn't think I'd let her live, did you?"

Joel looked up in despair at the man who was now kneeling down in front of him. "Go to hell."

The man smiled and Joel knew the man had no empathy. He'd never seen anything as bone-chilling as the way this man looked amused at the death upon his hands.

"Where are all your notes on the piece you've been writing?" the man asked, cocking his head to one side and staring at Joel.

"How did you know what I was writing?"

"You saved it to the newspaper's cloud. Now, give them to me."

Joel made a sound of disbelief. "I'm not going to give them to you. You're going to kill me anyway."

The man smiled again, only this time bigger.

"Yes, I am. The question is, will I also kill your baby?"

Joel's whole life flashed before him. Every thought was focused on keeping his son safe as he deleted his story from the cloud, handed over his cell phone, and told the intruder where to find his notes in his home office. Sheila's mother and father would raise him. What would he look like grown up? Would he know how much Joel and Sheila had loved him? And when the bullet ripped into his brain, he died remembering the way Sheila looked while she held their son for the first time.

CHAPTER ONE

Tate Carlisle sat in the chair at her hair salon and scrolled through her phone, reading the news. Her hair was growing longer, and she had decided instead of cutting it, she was going to get some blonde highlights. In the short time she'd been working as President Stratton's press secretary and involved in the shadow group he'd formed headed up by former FBI Agent Elizabeth James, Tate had changed. And she needed a new look to show that change.

The past was the past. While she'd always been a strong, independent woman, she realized she hadn't been as strong as she thought. Not when she watched Elizabeth James work. As a television journalist, Tate had been able to keep her face flawless and emit the perfect emotional response at the appropriate times. She had reported for KNS News's smaller lifestyles division after her reign as Miss Georgia. Then she'd moved up to weekend reporting. Four years ago, at thirty-two, she'd been given an hourly show at seven o'clock on Saturday night. It wasn't a big-time slot like media darling Claudia Hughes had, but she received excellent ratings on her in-depth investigations.

Then BBN Nightly News offered Tate an investigative show right before *The Claudia Hughes News Hour*. Tate had eagerly taken it, but it was clear Claudia didn't want to share the limelight. Tate was constantly battling Claudia over who got to report on stories, even when it was a story that Tate had uncovered and investigated. She had been given freedom to continue her investigative pieces as part of her package for moving to BBN. However, between Claudia and pressure from her editors, agent, and even the other journalists, Tate felt suffocated. And then it had happened. She had a source who wanted to present her with evidence that media outlets were working together with certain Hollywood and political heavy hitters to assert a certain agenda. People were being manipulated, and the press was being biased. When she brought the investigation up with her boss, she'd been fired on the spot.

As she sat in the hair salon, she reflected on the changes in her life over the last several weeks. In the past month, she'd been filled in on a group trying to influence world events from the shadows. They went by the name *Mollia Domini*, or *Puppet Masters* in English. Tate had gone from asking questions to answering them from her former colleagues during presidential press conferences, all the while making sure not a hint of what she knew about this evil group escaped her lips.

In the time since she'd started working for the president, she had broken the law and had seen death and compassion in their most basic forms. It

had only been a week since that horrific night at Jason Wolski's camp for military veterans up in the woods of northern Virginia. The memory of a man as big and strong as he was, trying to save his wife— it broke her heart. The sight of President Stratton, or Birch, as the group knew him, hugging Jason and whispering private words in a way only a fellow widower could do, turned her frozen heart soft.

During her years of investigating the worst of the worst, Tate had turned into a cold person. Oh, yes, she was bubbly, energetic, and everything a prime-time reporter should be. But to continually report on these truly evil deeds done to innocents, Tate had closed her heart and her feelings from the world. It was the only way she could sleep at night.

As the hair stylist pulled the foil from her hair and washed it, Tate felt empathy. She thought when facing the people out to destroy the world, the ones who had murdered Elizabeth's father and countless others, she could compartmentalize them as she had when reporting crimes against children. But with that one hug, the president had taken her frozen heart, thawed it, and handed it back to her. Now she was fully engaged in the mission. She knew in her heart she would do anything to stop *Mollia Domini* and protect her small group working to defeat them.

"How do you like it?" the stylist asked, turning Tate's chair to face the mirror. Tate looked at the new version of herself. Her hair had a slight wave to it, and the blonde highlights made her violet eyes seem brighter and livelier. Today she was going to embrace the new her.

"I love it," Tate smiled.

★   ★   ★

"Now you really look like Little Miss Sunshine," Valeria McGregor said dryly when Tate walked into their newly acquired gym. Valeria was a couple inches shorter than Tate. She stood with her hands on her hips, her long, rich, walnut brown hair streaked with highlander red tied back into a ponytail. Valeria was ex-DEA in the same way Tate was an ex-reporter and Elizabeth was an ex-FBI agent. One thing Valeria had that the others in the group didn't was the ability to curse creatively in multiple languages. Valeria had tan skin inherited from her Puerto Rican mother and bright blue eyes from her Scottish father. She spoke both English and Spanish well, especially the cuss words.

"I like it," Elizabeth smiled as she hit a punching bag. Her long blonde hair swayed with every punch she delivered.

"Thanks. I feel as if I've changed somehow and needed to reflect that." Tate looked around the small, former mechanic's garage down the road from Quantico in Dumfries. There were no windows, and the only way in was a small door by the garage door. They had placed rubber matting on the floor and added punching bags, weights, and cardio equipment. After the president saw what Elizabeth had gone through during her last mission in the South China Sea, he figured a private place for them to keep in military condition would be a good

idea.

"I understand that. It's like we've taken off the rose-colored glasses," Elizabeth said, slamming her knuckles into the bag, sending it swinging with the force of her punch.

"And on that note, I was hoping y'all would help me with the more physical aspect of our job," Tate said a little nervously. She was the last to join the team and still felt as if she were an outsider.

The shadow group the president had formed was comprised of their leader, Elizabeth, or Lizzy, to most of them now. Then he'd brought in a techie in young Alex Santos, who helped forge documents, hack into computer systems, and anything else that involved a computer. Next came Dalton Cage. He was a former Air Force Pararescueman, basically Superman in camo. Valeria came next, and Tate filled in the last spot. The president worked with his childhood best friend, Sebastian Abel, who had surpassed nearly every billionaire's worth by the time he was thirty. Abel was privately bankrolling the operation.

"You want to get your hands dirty?" Valeria asked as she dropped the weights and wiped her sweaty hands on the short black elastic shorts she was wearing.

"I do. I can outshoot all of you. I know because Alex showed me your DEA and FBI files. Hand-to-hand is something completely different," Tate said defensively. She may be a former Miss Georgia, but she was also an Olympic sharpshooting medalist.

"You don't break a nail firing a gun," Valeria

pointed as she looked at Tate's perfectly manicured nails.

"Val," Lizzy warned as she stopped punching the bag, "I'll be happy to help you. It's probably a good idea for you to learn some moves. Valeria is right, though. You need to cut your nails or you could potentially tear one off and that hurts like a motherfucker. Just ask Phylicia."

"Asking Phylicia anything will be hard since she's dead," Dalton said as he strode into the garage with a duffle bag over his shoulder.

"We were talking about fingernails," Lizzy said in a familiar way. They weren't overly affectionate, but there was definitely something going on between Dalton and Lizzy, even if they didn't know what exactly it was.

Dalton cringed. "Yeah, I saw Lizzy rip Phylicia's off. You don't want that."

Tate swallowed hard at the mental image. Phylicia deserved it. She'd been Lizzy's boss at the FBI and was part of *Mollia Domini*. She'd ordered Lizzy's father's death, embassy bombings, assassinations, and she'd killed Jason Wolski's wife.

"Little Miss Sunshine wants to learn how to fight," Valeria taunted.

"Good," Dalton said with a shrug as he turned the treadmill on and started to jog.

Tate turned away from Dalton and faced Valeria. "What is it? Why don't you like me?" All the snide remarks from the past weeks culminated as Tate lost her temper. "What have I ever done to you?"

Valeria put her hands on her hips, and Tate nearly regretted her outburst. But she was tired of being considered the weak link in the group. Even Alex got more respect, and he couldn't form a sentence without saying the word *dude* in it.

"It's not what you've done, it's what you won't do. You won't be protecting any of us. You won't be on any missions with us. You won't be putting your life on the line," Valeria responded as she ticked off each point on her fingers.

Tate shook her head in frustration. "I know. But that doesn't mean I can't be useful. We know there's someone *in* the White House. What if they go after President Stratton? I may need to defend him. Goodness knows Orville won't." Humphrey Orville was a former professor of military history turned chief of staff. He was a little man with a shaved head and black wire-rimmed glasses that he kept pushing up his nose.

"She's got a point," Dalton called out, not even breathing heavily as he ran.

Val cocked her head and looked at Tate. "Fine. I'll help you, but no girly shit. No whining about sweating or your muscles hurting or your manicure scuffing."

Tate held out her hand. "Deal."

Valeria shook it and with a flick of her head indicated for Tate to follow her.

Tate had never felt so alive. She slammed her hand into the pad Dalton held for her and then rammed her knee up and into the pad.

Valeria shook her head. "You know what? I might have been wrong about you. Tate, I'm sorry. Under that Little Miss Sunshine smile is a girl who likes to kick ass," Valeria grinned as she slapped Tate's sweaty back.

"Thank you for showing me. I can't wait to learn more." Tate said as she took a towel from her bag and wiped her face off.

"You've created a monster," Lizzy laughed as she looked down at her watch. "I have to go. I have to open Lancy's soon," she said. Lancy's was the bar her father owned and ran in downtown Quantico until he was killed by members of *Mollia Domini*. The team now spent nights at the bar as part of their cover story.

"I'll see you down there tonight," Tate said, picking up her phone to check messages. "I'm meeting my brother for a drink."

Tate had missed multiple calls from an old classmate from journalism school. Like, five of them in the past two hours. "I'll be right back," Tate mumbled as she walked outside to return the call.

The phone rang once and was picked up immediately. "Oh my God," Brenda gasped into the phone. "Where have you been? Have you heard the news?"

Tate blinked at the rush of words. She hadn't talked to Brenda in three years, maybe more. "What news?"

"Joel Davidson killed his wife, Sheila, and then committed suicide."

"What?" Tate asked shocked. Joel had been in

their class, and they went through school with him. He was the nicest man. Tate even remembered when he had first met Sheila and how during finals she would cook for them all. "Didn't they just have a baby?" She remembered receiving the announcement a couple months before.

"They did. A little boy. Sheila's mother came over to take Sheila and the baby to go to the zoo. She discovered Joel and Sheila in the kitchen and the baby upstairs crying in his crib," Brenda told her.

Tate felt her heart break for them. They hadn't been in constant contact, just Christmas cards and social media, but the thought of their poor son tore at her. "They seemed so happy," Tate said, sounding like every neighbor ever interviewed after someone committed a crime.

"I know. I thought they were, too. The funeral is tomorrow. I thought you'd want to know."

Tate nodded even though Brenda couldn't see her. "Yes, I want to go. Thanks."

After getting the information on the funeral, Tate headed back inside. Lizzy was pulling her shirt on over her sports bra, and Valeria was taking a turn at the punching bag as Dalton reached for his duffle bag.

"Everything okay?" Lizzy asked.

"A friend was involved in a murder-suicide with his wife. The funeral is tomorrow. They had a newborn son." Tate was still trying to process it as Dalton gave her an awkward pat on the shoulder.

"Sorry, Tate. Let me know if you need anything."

"That goes for me, too," Lizzy added.

"Want to get drunk? I'm your girl," Valeria offered.

"Thanks. I have some calls I need to make. I have to tell Birch, and I'll have to miss a meeting tomorrow for the funeral. I'll see you all tonight." Tate grabbed her stuff and numbly headed to her car to get to work on reorganizing her schedule.

CHAPTER TWO

Tate hung up the phone just as she walked into Lancy's bar. Valeria was off that night, and Dalton and Lizzy were pouring beers behind the old wooden bar to the left. The rest of the bar Lizzy's father had started was filled with a couple pool tables in the back and some small tables with wood chairs up front. It wasn't fancy, but then again the people who drank at Lancy's weren't the fancy type. They were military men and women from the surrounding Quantico Military Base. They were FBI, DEA, and even foreign soldiers and government agents who were training on the grounds.

Tate scanned the crowd for her brother, Tucker. He was sitting at a table with a bunch of his colleagues from the FBI crime lab. From the hard set of their faces, they had had a tough day as well.

"What's up, dude?"

Tate turned a managed a soft smile for Alex Santos. At twenty-two, he was the youngest person on their team. They were certainly an odd mix of people. Lizzy owned the bar and had hired Alex as a busboy. Dalton and Valeria were part-time bartenders. Tate's excuse to come to the bar was to see her brother. Sometimes it really was, and other

times it was to talk about their mission in the clean room Alex had set up in the storage closet.

"Hi, Alex. Have you enjoyed the past couple of days off?"

Alex's eyebrows shot up into his shaggy hair. "Days off? Dude, some shit's about to go down. I'm just trying to figure out what it is."

Tate looked at the young kid and felt like rolling her eyes. She didn't know if she should take him seriously or not. "Why do you say that?"

"It's quiet. It's never good when it's quiet. I mean, the dark boards that we hackers hang out in have been jumpy. No one wants to say anything all of a sudden. I think there's someone in there who shouldn't be."

"A hacker hacked the hackers?" Tate asked, shaking her head. Going off a quiet illegal hacker message board on the dark net didn't seem to be a reliable source.

"Exactly," Alex drew out, wide-eyed.

"Well, keep us updated." Tate patted Alex on the shoulder and headed for the bar. Buzz and Snip, the two old former military barbers sat in their usual places, plotting to hogtie Alex and shave his mop of a head. Tate smiled at them as she took a seat by herself and let her thoughts turn back to Joel. What would drive a man to do that?

"Hey, Tate. How are things in DC?" Lizzy asked from across the bar.

"Quiet. How are things here?" Tate asked.

"Same ol', same ol'. You want your regular?" Lizzy asked as Tucker caught sight of his sister and

made his way to the bar.

"Yes, please. Large and strong."

"You know," Alex said with a wink as he wiped down the bar, "the type of drink a lady likes is the type of man she's looking for."

"Sound advice," Tate chuckled. "Guess we know you're not in the running then."

Alex pretended to be wounded as he moved along to a young FBI agent from the academy. Tucker took the seat next to her, slinging his arm around her shoulder and giving it a squeeze before getting Dalton's attention and tapping his empty beer mug.

"Long day?" Tate asked, worried. Her brother looked upset as Dalton refilled his beer.

"A friend of mine died," Tucker said, running a hand over his short hair in frustration.

"I'm so sorry. What happened?" Tate asked as she took her younger brother's hand in hers.

"Car accident. The thing is, I even called him when he was late for work and didn't think about it again until the sheriff stopped by the lab so one of us could make identification. He crashed on Route 619 close to Independence Hill."

Tate paused as Lizzy set down a gigantic margarita on the rocks. Lizzy looked between the two of them with concern. "Is everything okay, Tucker?"

Tucker nodded and then gave a weak smile to Dalton, who handed him his beer. "I was just telling Tate that a friend and colleague of mine, Caleb Brown, died in a car accident two nights ago. I had

to identify his body today."

Tate sat quietly while Lizzy and Dalton offered their condolences. "Wait, two nights ago?"

"Yeah."

Tate shook her head slowly. No, it couldn't be . . . "My friend died two nights ago. A journalist by the name of Joel Davidson."

Lizzy and Dalton showed no outward signs of recognition, but she knew they were thinking the same thing she was.

"What a horrible coincidence," Lizzy muttered as she looked at Tate. They were learning quickly that nothing was ever a coincidence.

"Did your friend Caleb know this reporter friend of Tate's?" Dalton asked casually.

Tucker shrugged as he took a deep drink of his beer. "I don't think so. Although Caleb was quite the conspiracy theorist."

"Really? What was his theory?" Tate asked, trying to hide the interest from her voice.

"Some things have been disappearing from the lab. I think they're in the warehouse and were just misfiled, but Caleb was sure they were stolen," Tucker told them before going back to his beer.

Tate tried to laugh it off. "Who would want blood and hair samples? Gross."

Tucker shook his head and then leaned forward and dropped his voice. "It was biometric samples proving the rebel leader killed with Phylicia Claymore had set off a chemical bomb in that small village six months ago. It's proof of mass genocide. And," he said, dropping his voice even lower, "a

diffused chemical weapon."

Tate's eyes shot to Lizzy's. Concern was clearly written there. "Well, if it was diffused, it couldn't hurt anyone, right?" Tate asked.

Tucker shook his head. "It could become active with the right part in under a minute. Caleb thought someone stole it, but a cart of things that were supposed to go in storage was near the cart the bomb and lab samples were on. The warehouse cart was left behind and this cart was taken by accident. Simple mistake. It's just somewhere in the warehouse. People are looking for them now."

"Probably. That place is huge if I remember correctly," Lizzy smiled as she poured a round of beers. "Here, for your table. It's on me."

"Go ahead," Tate told her brother. "I want to tell Lizzy about this man I think is perfect for her."

"Are you sure you don't mind?" Tucker asked.

"Not at all. Go be with your friends."

"Thanks, Sis." Tucker gave her a quick peck on the cheek before grasping the beer mugs and heading to his table.

"No way they're connected, right?" Tate whispered to Lizzy and Dalton the second her brother was out of earshot.

"Alex, take over for a sec," Lizzy called out.

Without saying a word, Lizzy, Dalton, and Tate headed for the clean room. They pushed through the hanging 1970s beaded door, which was really a jammer for listening devices, and headed into the storage closet filled with beer, liquor, cleaning supplies, and countless hidden devices that made

the room impenetrable.

"I wouldn't think so, but stranger things have happened recently. If Caleb believed there was a cover-up at the FBI, he could have got Joel to write a story on it," Lizzy said, thinking out loud.

Dalton shook his head. "But why would Joel kill his wife and then himself? It doesn't make sense."

"I agree," Tate said, "but I think I'll ask around at the funeral tomorrow just to be sure."

"I can ask Alex to look into it at the same time," Lizzy told her. "We'll meet back here tomorrow night to discuss."

Tate nodded and Lizzy watched her head out of the clean room. Lizzy closed her eyes and let out a breath as she leaned against the shelves. This was just one more thing to factor into the web she was filling in of *Mollia Domini's* network of terror.

Lizzy opened her eyes and found Dalton studying her. They had had days together to explore who they were to each other. Lovers, yes. More than that, maybe. How much more? She didn't know, and now she didn't have time to find out.

"What are you thinking about?" Dalton asked as he came over to rub his hands down her arms.

"I've decided to do what Sebastian asked and question Trip Kameron." Lizzy thought about her last meeting with billionaire Sebastian Abel. He had arrogantly kept her waiting. When he finally graced her with his presence, he demanded she either sleep with, spank, or drug Trip into giving information about one of the many women he was having an

affair with, Vivian Geofferies. Why Vivian? Because Sebastian wanted to know about her husband, Rupert, who insisted on being called Bertie because it made him more relatable to the common man. Although the nickname was speculated that it was chosen because he wanted to be likened to the king of England who had made that nickname famous.

Bertie Geofferies was Sebastian's main rival. He's old British money, old British ways, and has a young American wife. Surprise, surprise, Vivian was screwing playboy Trip, who similarly was old money, old family, but he wasn't seventy some years old like Bertie. In fact, Trip, or John Kameron III, was only in his thirties and quite handsome, which was why he was able to get gorgeous women like Vivian, heiress Blythe Stanworth, reality star Kerra Ruby, and news anchor Claudia Hughes into his bed.

"Corporate espionage seems kinda low, doesn't it?" Dalton asked. It was clear from the set of his lips he was not happy with this decision. She couldn't blame him. Trip was a womanizer who believed himself above the law because of his family name.

"I don't care about whatever Bertie Geofferies is up to. That idiot Trip has some information on *Mollia Domini* somewhere in his drugged mind that I need to learn."

"Or maybe he was really talking about BDSM, in which case . . ." Dalton's hands tightened on her arms at the idea of Trip pushing Lizzy for sex before he yanked them away from her body. They were on uneven ground as they balanced their desire for

each other with the knowledge they could be killed at any moment.

"I can handle myself," Lizzy reminded him.

Dalton clenched his square jaw and then released it. "I don't like the idea of another man touching you," he finally admitted.

Lizzy smiled. "Don't worry, he won't lay a finger on me."

★ ★ ★

It had taken two minutes on Brent Eller's popular gossip site, TinselGossip.com, to find out that Trip was in the Hamptons at a party. The hostess, Blythe Stanworth, was of the old-money Stanworth family, whose mom and grandfather ran a media empire called Fourth Estate Media Trust, among a multitude of other investments. According to TinselGossip.com, Blythe was best friends with Kerra Ruby and was trying to break into acting. So far Mommy was buying her way into films produced by Stanworth Motion Pictures to horrendously bad reviews.

Sebastian Abel was happy to loan Lizzy one of his private planes for the night. Dalton hadn't spoken to her except for briefly muttering for her to "be safe" as she left the bar at one in the morning with a bag of goodies slung over her shoulder.

That's how she found herself dressed in a trench coat walking up to private security in front of a mansion in the Hamptons at three in the morning. The mountain of a man, who Lizzy was sure she

could disarm in second, looked down his nose at her as she stopped in front of him.

"Sorry, this is a private party." Lizzy wanted to shake her head. Why did celebrities or celebrity wannabes think the bigger the bodyguard, the better? They were slow to react and easy to outmaneuver.

"I know," Lizzy smiled. "I'm a gift for Trip." Lizzy opened the trench coat and the bodyguard smiled.

He lifted his phone to his ear and waited. "Tell Mr. Kameron he has a gift out front, and I need to know whether he wants it returned or not."

Lizzy cocked her head and acted bored as she let her coat close. She waited with her heavy purse slung over her shoulder for some nameless guard inside to drag Trip out of whatever trouble he was involved in.

Finally the door opened and Trip Kameron stumbled out. His shirt was unbuttoned and his shorts were slung low over his hips so he could show off his impressive muscles. "I love gifts. What is it?" Trip called out as he swaggered closer.

"Me," Lizzy purred as she opened her coat. "Courtesy of Mr. Abel."

"Sebastian always has good taste," Trip grinned as he took in the blood-red leather corset that made the top of her breasts swell over, and then his eyes traveled down to the tight black leather miniskirt and thigh-high spiked stiletto boots.

Lizzy leaned closer so her leather-encased breasts pushed against Trip's bare chest and

whispered, "Mr. Abel said you've been naughty and need to be spanked. Now you're going to accept this gift and lead me to a private room." Trip put his hand on her waist and Lizzy slapped it away as she clucked her tongue. "No touching without me telling you where and how to touch me. You'll have to be punished for that."

When Lizzy stepped back, the answer to her invitation into the party was clearly seen in Trip's shorts. Too easy.

"Right this way," Trip said as if he were an excited puppy about to pee on the floor. He was practically wiggling with excitement.

Lizzy shot a wink to the guard and followed Trip into a smaller pool house where he locked the door behind him. Small was an understatement. It was easily five thousand square feet. But compared to the mansion out front, it appeared small. The party outside the pool house was raging. People were swimming, dancing, drinking, and the drugs flowed freely. It was quieter inside the pool house. Apparently this was Trip's "room" when he stayed with Blythe.

"Will Blythe be joining us?" Lizzy asked as she followed Trip upstairs and into the master bedroom at the end of the hall.

"Maybe later," Trip grinned as he rubbed his hands together. "Now, take off your coat."

Lizzy reached into her bag and with a quick move slapped a leather crop against Trip's chest. "You don't get a say, Trip. I tell you what to do, and you do it or you'll be punished. Understand?"

"Yes," Trip said breathlessly.

"Good boy," Lizzy said as she shrugged out of her coat. "Now strip."

"Yes, ma'am," Trip eagerly and somewhat clumsily shed his clothes.

"Now, bend over the bed," Lizzy said, reaching into her bag for a small leather spanking paddle. "Am I going to have to punish you further?"

Trip moaned when he saw the paddle and quickly turned, placed his hands on the bed, and stuck his ass up in the air. Lizzy grimaced at the sight, and, with a roll of her eyes, began spanking him until she was pretty sure his ass was numb. She reached between her cleavage and pulled out the needle full of sodium pentothal. Lizzy jabbed it quickly into Trip's red ass cheek. Trip jumped at the pinch.

"What was that?" he asked, looking over his shoulder at her.

"I just had to pinch that sexy ass of yours. Now, let's have some fun." Lizzy smiled as she pulled out some silk ropes, and Trip's eyes went in and out of focus.

"I want to fuck," Trip said and then giggled.

"Good. Then let me tie you up so we can get started. It enhances your pleasure," Lizzy purred as she quickly tied his arms and legs to the head and footboard. "Now, Trip, why don't you tell me how you are feeling?"

"Like I want to fuck."

"Are you feeling anything else?" Lizzy asked with the kind of patience she reserved for young children.

"I'm afraid you'll think my dick is too small."

"No worries, Trip," Lizzy comforted even as she lied to him. "Have you heard the term *Mollia Domini* before?"

"Uh-huh. Can we fuck now?" Trip asked as if asking for dessert after cleaning his dinner plate.

"Not yet, Trip. Where did you hear *Mollia Domini* before?"

"When I was fucking."

Dear lord, this man was trying her patience. "Who were you fucking when you heard it?"

"A blonde, Kerra, Claudia, Viv . . ." Trip laughed. "They're all blonde. You're blonde. Let's fu —,"

Lizzy slapped his face hard, and it only caused Trip's erection to jump with anticipation. "What did the blonde say about it?"

"That it was a secret group I should join. But I'm too busy to join some group that tells you what to do and say. They told the blonde what to say. Who was it? I don't think it was Vivian. She only complains about her husband. Do you know he's like seventy something years old?" Trip shivered and so did Lizzy.

Okay, so it was either Kerra or Claudia who talked to Trip. At least she'd narrowed it down. "What else did the blonde say about the group?"

Trip shrugged his shoulder and his penis wiggled. "Just that if I joined I would be rich and powerful, but I already am. Shit, my younger brother killed his maid during rough sex and dumped her in a river and no one said a thing. I don't need a group to make me untouchable. Even if

they said they were about to . . . about to . . . what was it? I think it was blow something up. I don't remember."

"Is that all you can remember about this group or the person who told you?" Lizzy asked one more time.

Trip closed his eyes and a second later nodded. "Yup."

"One last thing before I bring you pleasure unlike any other," Lizzy said, reaching into her bag. "What has Vivian told you about her husband, his family, and his company?"

Trip giggled. "Vivian is pregnant, but don't tell anyone. I'm the daddy."

Lizzy raised her eyebrows as she uncapped the second needle, keeping it hidden in her hand.

"Bertie has slow swimmers so every night they have sex, we have sex. Do you know that Vivian is twenty-six years of prime yoga sex on a stick? She's prostituting herself with that old man just so she doesn't have to work again, and she's going to pop out as many of my babies as possible so when Bertie bites the dust, she'll get a large part of the estate since he only has one child, Geofferies the VII. And for helping her, I'll get a nice reward from the estate, too. Plus that woman is a freak in bed."

"What about Bertie's business? Any big business deals coming up soon?"

"I don't know what, but he's excited about the launch of something new. Viv said he's hardly home, and he's sure he'll put Sebastian out of business. I hope not. I like Sebastian. He sends me

things like you and drugs."

This got Lizzy's attention. "Sebastian has sent you gifts before?"

"Oh, yeah. You should have seen the twins he sent me when I stayed at his Pacific Hotel. And no one can get better drugs than Sebastian. He rewards me with it when I tell him the things I hear from my part of society, because no matter how hard Sebastian tries, he's not part of our group."

"Who is?" Lizzy asked.

"You know, old money. The Kamerons, the Stanworths, and the Geofferies — together our wealth makes up most of the wealth of the entire world. Has for generations, and that's what Sebastian wants. But there's one thing he'll never have — breeding. He's just some poor boy who grew up moving from town to town."

"Do you know what Geofferies has planned to put Sebastian out of business?"

Trip shook his head. "Nope. Can we fuck now?"

"Yes, now just close your eyes," Lizzy ordered as she tied a blindfold on before she jabbed the second needle into his hip. The mixture of dopamine and a host of drugs that Valeria had mixed up shot into Trip's body, causing him to moan and gyrate on the bed.

"I'll be damned," Lizzy muttered as she gathered her things. Valeria had sworn this mix would make Trip think he was having the best night of his life. And by the way he was reacting, it appeared to be true. Lizzy headed out the back door, cautiously avoiding any interaction with security.

CHAPTER THREE

Tate stood quietly in her black sheath dress as she watched the clergyman bless Joel's casket. No one from either Joel's or Sheila's family was there. The police ruled the official cause of death a murder-suicide and closed the case. Joel's son was now being raised by Sheila's parents and would grow up believing his father was the worst sort of villain unless Tate could prove otherwise.

Three of Joel's coworkers, two classmates from journalism school, and one person from his church were at the funeral. In total, six people, including Tate.

"This is so sad," Brenda whispered as the ceremony concluded. "Thanks for coming. I still don't believe it."

"Me neither," Tate said with a sigh.

"Want to have a drink to Joel?" Brenda asked.

"Sorry, I have to get back to work. But it was really great seeing you again." Tate smiled at her old friend. So many nights they had stayed up to the wee hours studying or writing articles for school — Brenda, Joel, herself — and now Joel was gone. It was surreal.

"I understand. I still can't believe you're press

secretary to the president!" Brenda lowered her voice. "Is he as hot as I think he is up close?"

Tate closed her mouth so she wouldn't laugh out loud.

"Come on, spill," Brenda said, opening her car door but waiting to get in.

"More than you can imagine," Tate whispered conspiratorially before her friend gave her one last hug and headed out.

Tate looked back at the casket being lowered into the ground. If it hadn't been for a burial policy Joel had gotten before he headed to Iraq a couple of years ago, he'd be in the paupers' section of the public cemetery. Sheila's parents had refused to lay their daughter to rest next to the man who had allegedly killed her, so Joel was alone with no one wanting to claim association with him.

"Tate Carlisle?"

Tate looked up for the casket to see a frazzled-looking man in his early fifties walking toward her. His shirt was wrinkled with a mustard stain on it.

"Yes?"

"I'm Jeff Sargent. I'm, um, I was Joel's senior editor at *The Washington Leader*. Can I have a word in private?" Jeff ran a hand through his tousled hair and looked around.

"Of course. Would you like to meet at my office or would you like to talk here?"

Jeff shook his head. "I can't be seen at the White House. Let's take a short walk."

Suddenly nervous, Tate looked around. There were only the two men working on burying Joel.

Everyone else had left, and the cemetery appeared empty.

"I'm not going to hurt you. We'll stay in sight of those men if it will make you feel better," Jeff said, picking up on her nervousness.

"How about that bench by the pond?" Tate asked. Jeff looked around once again and gave a slight nod before starting off in that direction. "What can I do for you, Mr. Sargent?"

"Jeff, please. Joel talked about you quite often. He was really proud of your accomplishments. He said you were one of the smartest people he'd ever known. He was working on something big," Jeff told her, suddenly dropping his voice. "He was collecting more evidence, and then he was going to take it to you after we ran the story."

"To me? Why?" Tate asked in a hushed voice.

"Because it was about FBI Agent Phylicia Claymore. You may think I'm crazy, but I don't think Joel killed himself or Sheila. He'd received a threat the day he died to drop the story he was working on. He didn't tell me much. Only that he was meeting a witness to gather evidence that night. He said everyone was focused on Africa, but it was what happened before Africa that was the big news."

"Do you know who he was meeting?" Tate asked, trying to hide the urgency from her voice.

Jeff nodded and reached into his inside coat pocket. "Joel kept everything backed up to the company cloud. I swore I would never look at it, but curiosity got the better of me after he left the office.

See, corporate sent down an assignment he was supposed to be working on, an assignment about your boss helping a coup in Zambia. Joel took one look at the assignment and deemed it false news and trashed it. He said he was working on something bigger than a fake story. Well, after he left that night to meet his source, I got a call from corporate demanding the piece. I got chewed out for not publishing it. I was told it was the story or my job. So I swore the piece would be in the paper the next day."

Jeff took a deep breath and looked around again before handing her the papers from inside his coat pocket. "I admit I didn't want to stay late so I logged onto Joel's cloud account to find his research on the coup assignment. Joel isn't anything if not predictable. You could probably guess his password."

"Sheila," Tate said softly.

Jeff nodded. "Then I admit, curiosity got to me and I printed off what Joel had been secretly working on. I was going to read it at home that night. Instead, I fell asleep and forgot about it. We heard about Joel at work the next morning. I had left the story at home so I logged on to print the story off again only to find it gone. Someone had permanently deleted it from the cloud last night after seven o'clock, which was when I printed it off."

Tate nervously opened the folded papers and scanned them. She felt the blood drain from her face. "Oh shit," she cursed.

"There's something big going on, Miss Carlisle,

and I think it got Joel killed," Jeff said solemnly.

Not think. It did. Tate folded the papers and slid them into her purse. "Tell no one about this or your life will be in danger."

"Is there anything you can do?" Jeff asked.

Tate wanted to say yes. She wanted to say she knew who was behind this. She wanted to tell him she would get revenge for her friend's death. Instead, all she could say was, "I don't know, but I do know this is dangerous. Let the authorities handle it." Jeff nodded, and she could tell he was fighting his reporter instincts. "Give me your card, and I'll let you know the second anything happens but only if you promise to not say a word about it. Deal?"

"Deal," Jeff said, handing her his card.

Tate put the card in her purse and headed to her car. Her team needed to meet tonight, the sooner the better.

★   ★   ★

Lizzy smiled at Coco, the exquisite young twenty-something who curated the lobby of SA Tech. "Hiya, Coco. How are you today?" Lizzy asked as she breezed through the lobby.

"I am amaze. Totally obsessing the boots, Miss James," Coco said in her own youthful way.

"Thanks, Coco. Is Judith in today? I'm hoping I can slip by to see Mr. Abel without her yelling at me for not having an appointment."

Coco cringed. "She's a *B*. Sadly, she's the first

one here every morning."

"Then I'll just have to surprise her." Lizzy grinned, knowing it would drive Sebastian's stick-up-her-ass secretary crazy. She had a thing for appointments.

Lizzy rode the elevator up to the penthouse. Judith and her tight silver hair bun met her as the elevator doors opened. "You don't have an appointment."

Lizzy smiled and reached into her bag. "I brought you a bran muffin." Lizzy handed it to Judith and wondered whether Valeria's magic little formula worked if it was eaten as opposed to injected. Guess she'd find out soon enough if Judith ate the muffin.

"You can't bribe your way into Mr. Abel's office. Go home and make an appointment, Miss James."

"Bite me, Judith." Lizzy snickered before pushing her way past the secretary who she guessed was in her sixties. "Sebastian, I need to see you now!" Lizzy yelled out as she stalked down the hall toward the large, thick double doors of Sebastian's office.

The doors opened and Sebastian, in all his handsomeness, stood glaring at her. "Miss James, back so soon?"

"Men always think they can last longer than they really can." Lizzy smirked as she walked by him and into his office as Judith hurried as fast as her chunky heels could go.

"I told her she had to make an appointment," Judith huffed.

"It's okay this time," Sebastian said before closing the doors. "Can I take your coat, Lizzy?"

"Sure." Lizzy shrugged out of the overcoat and watched as all six feet two inches of Sebastian Abel, one of the richest and most powerful men in the country, suddenly went rigid. His black hair was gelled back, and his gray eyes were focused on her body taking in her outfit. "You told me you didn't care how I got the information."

Sebastian's eyes snapped up to hers. "And I don't. I have ten minutes if you're in the mood for a real man instead of some man-child."

"Sorry, not interested."

"I know, and that's what makes you very desirable," his deep voice rumbled as he made his way to his desk.

Lizzy took a seat and waited for Sebastian to sit behind his massive desk. It was his power position. "Vivian is pregnant with Trip's baby, and Bertie is planning something that will put you out of business. Trip didn't know the specifics."

"Didn't know or isn't saying?" Sebastian asked, and the only sign of how he took that news was the way his fist clenched on the desk.

"Doesn't know. I did my job and did it well. Trip doesn't know what Bertie has planned. I don't think Vivian does either, for what it's worth. She just seems set on her pregnancy securing her share in Bertie's future estate."

Sebastian relaxed his hand and leaned back. "What does he expect when he's seventy and marries a twenty-year-old bimbo? Serves him right."

Sebastian took a deep breath. "Thank you for finding out something is in the works. I'll handle it from here. How is Birch doing?"

Lizzy didn't know what to make of Sebastian. He was ruthless, he was cunning, and he fought dirty. There was a war brewing, and it wasn't the one she was trying to fight. It was a war of two industry titans determined to obliterate all competition. It was only now that she realized what a strain Birch put on his friend by asking him to provide funding for this secret group of theirs. Sebastian was fighting his own war.

"He's well enough. Unfortunately, we have a new coincidence that may not be a coincidence and needs to be looked into. But, I think you have enough to worry about," Lizzy said as she realized being Sebastian Abel wasn't necessarily a good thing. The man was a walking contradiction. He gave money to fund their group, yet he bugged their computers and demanded to know what was happening and then bullied her into being a corporate spy for him. Right now she couldn't get a read on Sebastian, but she was pretty sure he was about to become too busy trying to fend off Bertie's attack to care what their little group was up to.

"Yes, I do. I'll be in touch." It sounded more like a threat than an offer to help.

★   ★   ★

Tate waited patiently outside the Oval Office. The phones rang constantly. Preparations for the Fourth

of July celebration were in full swing. All the while, there were assistants filing papers, stacking documents to be reviewed, and making coffee with the skill of a barista. At least the drink one of the new girls had handed her was a work of art. It didn't matter it was hot outside, Tate needed the coffee to warm her insides after reading the papers Jeff had given her.

The phone of President Stratton's chief assistant rang and a second later the man stood to escort Tate through the thick door and into the Oval Office as members of the president's inner circle stood to leave.

Humphrey Orville stood behind the president, so small he almost disappeared, but behind those little glasses was a man who never missed a thing. Secretary of State Sandra Cummings stood and pressed a wrinkle from her skirt with one hand and picked up her briefcase with the other. Her short, dirty-blonde hair was styled reminiscent of Doris Day, though the hard lines on her face proved she wasn't America's sweetheart. Instead, Sandra had the reputation of a bulldog. She wasn't President Stratton's pick. Actually, no one in the room except Tate and Humphrey Orville were President Stratton's picks. They were still carry-overs from President Mitchell's administration—something Tate personally thought needed to be rectified.

"Mr. President, I'll let you know as soon as we have verifiable evidence," FBI Director Conrad Kirby said.

"And then the CIA will work with State to offer

any assistance," CIA Director Kevin Milward added as he and Sandra shared a brief nod. "We'll get back to you as soon as we have something."

The rest of the men and women filed out the room, except Humphrey and Sandra, who looked impatiently between the president and Tate.

President Stratton waved Tate to have a seat on the couch and then turned to Sandra. "Go ahead. Miss Carlisle has all necessary clearances, and if this is what I think it is about, she may be able to help."

Sandra didn't look convinced but nodded anyway. "Senator Epps is creating problems on the foreign affairs front." Sandra turned to Tate. "We are gathering evidence that China is overstepping in the South Sea. It's thought they have been blowing up fishermen's ships from countries that don't support their claim to the waters. Anyway," Sandra said, turning back to the president, "Senator Epps agrees with China's claim. You know he's going to run against you in two years, and he's setting up the differences now. He's *working* with our allies while you are working against him. He's even threatened that China could call in all their loans if you don't handle the situation to China's liking."

"The stock market took a hit right after Epps said it, too," Humphrey added.

Tate let all the scenarios run through her head on how to handle Epps. "We need more time to look into him and his actions these past couple of months before we address his comments. I'll have my office start investigating immediately."

President Stratton drummed his fingers on his

knee as he sat quietly for another moment. "Thank you for bringing this to me, Sandra. Epps certainly isn't making your job any easier. Set up an appointment with the Chinese ambassador for next week. I'll have a plan of action by then."

"Yes, Mr. President," Sandra said, standing.

"And I'll get you anything I think will help from the research I do," Tate offered.

"Thank you. We'll be in touch. I'll see you both for the July Fourth celebration as well."

Tate stood and shook Sandra's hand as Humphrey escorted her from the office. A moment later, the door closed and Humphrey took a seat across from Tate. "Ironic that we killed the bastard who is responsible for the South China Sea troubles, and he's still causing problems."

"That's not our only problem," Tate said, pulling copies of Joel's notes from her bag. "There's a chemical weapon missing, and Director Kirby has covered it up."

"What?" President Stratton asked, quickly reading the notes. "Who wrote this? We need to talk to him."

"The person who wrote this died in an apparent murder-suicide the same night his potential source died in a single-car accident driving back to Quantico. We are investigating that coincidence now. However, the senior editor of *The Washington Leader* gave this to me at the journalist's funeral this morning," Tate explained. "Mr. President—"

"Birch," Birch Stratton said as he rubbed his hand over his face in frustration.

"Birch, this is a lot deeper than Dan March and some assassins. We're talking a major threat to the public."

"Does Elizabeth know?" Birch asked.

"Not the full scope. We are worried there may be a connection between the deaths."

"Humphrey, call a meeting for tonight for the entire group. Tate, I know we looked into Epps, but dig deeper. Shit, I can't even go to Kirby to have him investigate the bomb. Maybe the team will have an idea tonight."

"I'll get to work on Epps and Kirby, right away," Tate said as she stood.

"Thank you. I'll see you tonight at our usual time."

President Bircham Stratton watched his press secretary hurry from the room. She was on a mission, and he hoped her investigative instincts could ferret out not only who had the bomb, but also who on the Hill was manipulating things against him.

His old professor closed the door behind Tate and let out a long breath. "We have to expand our group."

Birch shook his head. He was already operating so far over the line that he'd be impeached if anyone found out about his shadow group of agents working without Congress's knowledge and approval. Not to mention they were funded solely with private money.

"I can't risk it. It's already a group of five and

now my Marine One pilot knows who the group is, along with Jason Wolski," Birch said, sitting back in the chair, watching Humphrey walk toward him.

"Then bring them into the loop. You need protection. We don't know if we can even trust the Secret Service."

Shit. Humphrey had a point. "Not Jason. He's already lost his wife to this cause. Order Crew Dixon to join our meeting tonight. Blindfold him, though."

Humphrey's bald little head bobbed as he left Birch alone. Alone is what he felt, but he wasn't. Birch had allies, and tonight he would add one more. The feeling of being held underwater washed over him. One wouldn't be enough. Humphrey was right. He needed someone on his detail whom he could trust with his life. Because if Birch died, his whole team would be left unprotected. He had promised Lizzy she'd have her life back at the FBI, Valeria would be back at the DEA, and Dalton would return to the PJs. What they didn't know was that Birch didn't want them to go back. They were the only people he could trust.

CHAPTER FOUR

"**W**e *have* a lead already," Lizzy said as her voice rose in frustration. "Phylicia gave us a clue before she took her header off the cliff. 'They always keep an eye on the world' were her exact words. Clearly something is going on at BBN, and Claudia Hughes was one of the names Trip Kameron gave me as possibly trying to recruit his sorry ass for *Mollia Domini*."

"You're right," Tate said finally. "But how can we investigate her?"

"Well, something needs to be done," Humphrey complained. "Did you see Claudia tonight? She's killing us with talks of instability and danger to the United States. She even wondered if President Stratton's actions with China would lead them to declare war on the United States. The stock market went down in after-hours trading because of it." Humphrey looked at his watch. "I'll be right back."

"Why don't you have Tate set up an interview with Claudia? It would give Tate a reason to go to BBN to talk with Claudia about the interview and maybe have her *assistant* go with her and hack into Claudia's electronics," Valeria suggested.

"Who, me?" Alex asked.

Valeria rolled her eyes. "I could do it if Alex is scared."

"Dude, I've been to prison," Alex reminded her.

"Then stop being a wimp and get all the electronics you need to ghost her phone and computer," Valeria challenged. Alex rolled his eyes under his shaggy hair.

Birch cleared his throat and everyone immediately stopped talking. "I need some help. We realized today that I don't have any protection I can fully trust to bring into the loop. It's hard to ditch Secret Service constantly, and it would be easier if I had someone working with me I knew would be looking to stop a bullet as opposed to hurling me into its path. Do any of you have any contacts in the Secret Service that I could pull into my presidential detail?"

"I might," Valeria said as she pulled up her contact list. "The last I talked to him he was assigned to the L.A. office, but that was probably five years ago."

"How do you know him?" Birch asked.

"He was my college boyfriend. We broke up when I went to the DEA and he went into the Secret Service," Valeria said after shooting off a quick text.

Everyone blinked as they stared at Valeria.

"And you would want to work with him?" Birch asked slowly.

"Yeah. He's the best, and we're totally cool. No hard feelings. And if there's one thing about Brock, he hates when innocents are wronged. This time everyone in the entire world are the innocents."

Valeria looked back at her phone. "Oh. He just messaged me back. It's morning in France. He's been stationed in Lyon at the INTERPOL office for the past four years."

"I'll have him vetted when Humphrey gets back. Speaking of Humphrey, he went to get Crew Dixon. It's time we brought him in," Birch told the group.

"Shit," Dalton cursed under his breath.

"What's the problem?" Birch asked, keeping his gaze on Dalton.

"Nothing we can't work out between ourselves," Dalton answered with clenched teeth as Lizzy discreetly moved closer to his side.

Tate saw the tension in the room and moved to divert it. "So, you will now have guards while in the air and on land."

"I guess I'm the air?" Crew drawled as he stepped into their meeting room in the residence.

"If you want to be," Birch told him as he stood up and shook Crew's hand. Crew's black hair was cut with military precision around his brown skin. His grandfather, Buzz, would be proud. Tonight he was in running shorts and a T-shirt. Humphrey must have waylaid him like he had the others.

Crew looked around, his eyes taking in everything, including the way Dalton stood protectively next to Lizzy. "I decided the night I helped you sneak out of Camp David that I wanted in."

Birch slapped Crew on the back and the next hour was spent filling him in. Tate waited until they

were done explaining the events of the past couple of months before she cut in. "And now we have a bigger problem. My brother thought the FBI agent killed in the single-car accident was just a conspiracy theorist." Tate handed out copies of the papers she'd shown Birch and Humphrey earlier. "There really is a chemical bomb missing, and no one knows where it is."

Crew sucked in air and slowly exhaled. "This is real? Not a joke?"

"Very real," Birch reassured him.

"Why isn't the media covering this?" Crew asked as all eyes turned to Tate.

"They will be," Tate swore. Tomorrow she would be paying a visit to BBN, and she also had an idea on how to start combating the agenda the media were pushing.

Two hours later, everyone had their assignments. Humphrey was looking into Brock Loyde and would be on a plane by morning if everything checked out. One of these days he was going to break into the wrong person's house and get shot while trying to recruit them to the cause.

Valeria was trying to find a connection to FBI Director Kirby and Phylicia Claymore, in hopes of finding the chemical bomb. Lizzy was looking into Senator Epps, while Dalton was trying to find out what he could about this coup Birch was supposedly supporting, while Birch worked to calm the situation in the South China Sea. Meanwhile, Tate and Alex would meet up at noon to head to BBN for

a surprise visit.

Tate said goodbye to the group as they entered the underground parking garage of the hotel down the street from the White House. No one knew of the hidden tunnels that connected the hotel to the White House, and even Tate wondered where the other tunnels led. She knew the path to the White House, but the main tunnel branched off in multiple directions as they made their way to the White House.

The drive into Alexandria was quick this early in the morning. She would get three hours of sleep if she were lucky, but who had time to sleep when she was saving the world? Flint Scott, Snip's grandson, had been a big help in pushing public opinion against Phylicia Claymore. Flint didn't know who had sent him the evidence, and Tate thought that might be a good resource to counter the media spin against Birch. If she heard one more story about how Birch was bringing the United States to war or how the country needed to be more like China or Cuba, Tate would scream. The media was making the case that these dictatorships provided stability. They left out the human rights violations, lack of democracy, abuse of power, and everything people had forgotten that Americans had fought wars to achieve.

Tate pulled into her small one-car garage and started to formulate her anonymous email to Flint as she walked into her kitchen and froze. Fear's icy hand had reached down to choke her before her brain could even register what she saw. Her house

was trashed. There wasn't a single thing left in her cabinets, dishes were broken, her table was overturned, her chairs broken.

Tate's shaky hands reached into her shoulder bag and pulled out her phone. Relief so strong it made her want to cry washed over her when Lizzy answered the phone on the first ring.

"Some . . . some . . . someone has been in my house," Tate stammered as she finally forced herself to move her feet. She ran back into the garage, jumped in her car, locked the doors, and started to drive away from her house as fast as she could.

"Was anyone there?" Lizzy asked as she heard Lizzy telling Dalton to turn around.

"I don't know. I only walked into the kitchen before leaving. I can't go in there alone. Valeria hasn't taught me enough," Tate rambled.

"Shh. Tate, it's okay. We'll meet you at that strip mall under construction three blocks from your house, okay? We'll be there in ten minutes."

"Okay," Tate managed as she relinquished her death grip on her phone.

Eight minutes later, Dalton instructed her to park in the back behind the large dumpsters. He parked his car next to hers and the two hurried over to Tate. Lizzy wrapped her arms around Tate, and finally Tate felt able to breathe.

"How did they find me?"

"We don't know if they did. We need to look around first to see what's missing. However, you can bet they watched you leave. We circled the block numerous times and didn't see anyone tail you. This

is what we're going to do," Dalton explained. "You two wait here. I need to find a cop car to borrow, then I'll be back. We can drive home together, and Lizzy and I can look around freely. If someone's watching, it'll look like you went to call the cops. There's nothing suspicious about that. I'll be back."

Dalton took his car and drove off while Lizzy looked at Tate. "Are you okay?"

"My house wasn't simply burgled, it was destroyed. Someone has a lot of anger toward me. But I'm more worried about our mission. How did they know I was looking into them? It had to be Jeff Sargent, Joel's editor. He's the one who gave me the story Joel was working on," Tate told her as she rubbed her arms to chase the goose bumps away.

"Okay, good. You have an idea then. Let me call Valeria and have her check on Jeff." Lizzy placed the call, and Tate pulled out her phone to make notes. Work would keep her mind off the devastation at her home.

"What are you working on?" Lizzy asked after hanging up with Valeria.

"I'm putting together some leads to send to Flint. Anonymously, of course. It'll start as a whisper, but by the time I'm done, I'm going to squash Claudia and whoever else is dictating this biased news like a bug," Tate said with passion. She may quake when faced with the possibility of an intruder still in her house, but putting pen to paper to tell a news story, well, she was fearless with that. Every line would be backed with evidence. Every implication, every name, every fact would be

researched and undeniable. With pen and paper or a television camera pointed at her, she was a warrior.

"What are you thinking?" Lizzy asked, moving to look over her shoulder.

"I'm going to start discrediting the Zambia coup. It doesn't even exist. Zambia is a peaceful country that we are allied with. Joel was told by his higher-ups to write the piece, and I have his research that discredits it. I am verifying it now and will send all of it, along with everything Claudia has said, to Flint so he can connect the dots," Tate said as she worked with her thumbs flying on her phone.

"Should we let them know we're onto them?" Lizzy asked, sounding a little worried.

"They already found me. I refuse to back down for a story."

Lizzy took a deep breath. "At least wait until we look through your house before you hit Send. You're like a girl sending drunk booty-call texts with that thing, except evil assassins will show up at your door instead."

"I'll wait. There may be clues at my house," Tate agreed, never taking her eyes from her phone.

"You won't have to wait much longer. Dalton's here."

Tate finally looked up to see Dalton driving an unmarked cruiser. "Hop in, Lizzy. Tate, go home, and we'll follow right behind you."

★　★　★

Destruction. Total destruction. Tate fought back

tears. Everything in her house was ruined. Her mattresses and furniture were shredded. Stuffing from cushions was strewn about the house. Each drawer was pulled out and turned upside-down on the floor. Her closet emptied. Paintings sliced and tossed on the floor.

"This is actually good news," Dalton said sympathetically.

"How is this good?" Tate asked, trying to keep her voice from turning shrill.

"It tells us a lot about who did this. One, nothing was stolen so it wasn't burglars. Two, you've said there's absolutely no evidence of our group or any of our investigations here, and it's obvious they were looking for something. My guess is they were looking to see if you knew something and had evidence, but they didn't find any. Three, they didn't think you warranted surveillance. There're no bugs or video feeds in the house," Dalton explained.

Lizzy cocked her head as she took in the destruction and what Dalton had said. "Could you have been seen talking with Jeff Sargent at the funeral? If *Mollia Domini* did kill Joel, someone was probably watching the funeral and saw him approach you."

Tate closed her eyes as she thought about the funeral. "I didn't see anyone, but Jeff was constantly on the lookout." Tate opened her eyes back to the destruction of what had been her sanctuary. "I guess it's possible."

Lizzy's phone vibrated and they all turned to

her. "It's Val," Lizzy said as she put it on speaker. "We're all here."

"Good," Valeria said as there was noise in the background.

"Is everything okay?" Lizzy asked.

"Yeah, all good. Just getting out of my disguise. I didn't know if anyone would be watching the house. I can tell they are. Not physically, but when I carried in the morning muffin delivery for Mrs. Sargent, my scan found one bug in the living room and another in the kitchen. I couldn't make it to the bedroom, but I'm guessing they're all over the place. She said she thought they had a break-in last night. That's why she asked for my identification, and thanks to Alex, I had a fake one to give her. But she said it was strange since nothing was missing. It was just a feeling as if something had been misplaced. Although, she said, her husband was really anxious about it and has now installed security alarms and cameras."

"Wow, you learned a lot," Tate said, impressed.

"I can be nice when I want to be," Valeria snapped. Yeah, she was an angel, Tate thought. "I hate to tell them they're a little too late. Someone wants to know what Jeff knows. For now though, he's alive. If he keeps his mouth shut and doesn't say anything about that article Joel was writing, maybe he has a chance of staying that way. Tate, want to meet at the gym tonight after work?"

Well, maybe Valeria wasn't all bad. "I'll see you there. Thank you."

Lizzy hung up the phone and looked to Tate.

"What are you going to do now?"

"I'm going to grab whatever I can and check into a hotel so I can sleep for an hour or two. It's almost eight a.m., but I don't think I can stay here. I don't feel safe." Tate looked around her home that was barely recognizable and shivered.

"We'll wait for you to grab whatever you need. We can all leave at the same time," Dalton told her as he stepped around the overturned bench at the foot of the bed and picked up one of her suitcases. "What can we do to help?"

Tate took a deep breath. She would not cry. She had friends helping her. She wasn't alone. It was just stuff. "Just find as many bags as you can. Thanks."

As Dalton took off on a mission to find luggage, or as a last resort, garbage bags, Lizzy and Tate quickly went through the clothes strewn about, trying to find the ones that weren't destroyed. In the end, it only took ten minutes to gather everything Tate could. Dalton carried the belongings and loaded her car up as Tate took one last look around.

"Anything else?" Dalton asked gently as he came back into the house.

"That's it. Let me walk you out, in case someone is watching." Tate opened the front door and Lizzy and Dalton walked out.

"Good luck today," Lizzy said in reference to Tate's plan to go to BBN and see Claudia.

"Thank you. For everything." Tate watched as her two friends left in the police cruiser they had *borrowed*. Within two minutes, Tate was pulling out of her garage and heading for downtown DC.

Thirty minutes later, Tate had checked in at the hotel close to the White House. It was comforting knowing that the secret tunnel was beneath her. That was the only thing that gave her enough peace to be able to fall asleep.

CHAPTER FIVE

"**W**ho the hell are you, and what the are you doing in my apartment?" Secret Service Agent Brock Loyde asked as he held his gun to the bald head of the tiny man asleep in the recliner.

The little man snorted and startled himself awake. He blinked as he turned to look at Brock and wipe a dribble of drool from the corner of his mouth. Brock had just come home for the evening when he'd heard snoring coming from his small living room. He'd pulled his gun and crept into his apartment only to find a middle-aged bald man with black wire-rimmed glasses asleep in his favorite chair.

"Oh, so sorry. I tried not to fall asleep this time. Brock Loyde, I presume?" the little man asked, not looking at all concerned by the fact a gun was pointed inches from his head.

"I asked who the hell you are and how did you get into my apartment?" Brock repeated, his voice cold and hard as he looked at the intruder.

The man chuckled, seemingly amused. "You would think after doing this three times I would remember to introduce myself. But, I've got to tell you, when I picked my first lock after watching how

to on the Internet, it seemed to take forever. Now it's a cinch."

Brock felt his mouth drop open. "Who *are* you?"

"Humphrey Orville, and I need to have a word with you if you don't mind putting down the gun. Although you're nicer than the person who recommended you to me. She about killed me. The other one with the umbrella was unnerving, but she was my first so I was pretty nervous already."

Brock blinked. He had no idea what to think of this . . . wait a second. "Humphrey Orville? The chief of staff for President Stratton?" No, that couldn't be right. Brock would have been notified if a dignitary such as Orville were in town.

"That's me. You were personally recommended for guarding the president."

Keeping the gun aimed at the little man, Brock pulled out his cell phone. Using voice command, he searched Humphrey Orville's name and sure enough a picture of the man sitting in his recliner was the same man pictured standing next to President Stratton in the Oval Office.

"But I haven't asked for a presidential detail, and I do a lot more here. I'm not made for standing around," Brock told him as he wondered how the man got into the country without him knowing. Someone was going to get his ass chewed out when he got to work tomorrow. "When did you arrive?"

Orville smiled. "Not two hours ago."

"How did you get past customs without being flagged?" Brock asked. The second Orville swiped his passport when he arrived, a message would have

been sent to Brock's office.

"I used a fake passport. No one can know I was here. As I said, I need to interview you for a job with the president. There will be standing around, but so much more."

"You committed a crime."

Orville held up his hand to cut Brock off. "*So much more.* No one can know I'm here because there's an elite group you were recommended for that operates outside the law and at the president's discretion. Now, have you ever heard of *Mollia Domini*?"

Brock stood quietly as Orville talked. Puzzle pieces of things he'd seen during his time working in the same offices as INTERPOL began to click into place. As the picture came into focus, it became frighteningly clear that Orville was telling the truth.

Brock collapsed onto his couch as he looked in disbelief at Orville. "I knew something was going on, but this? You know it sounds crazy, right? A group of powerful people banding together to force the world's hand from behind the scenes?"

"Is it really crazy? There's been a yearly meeting of the world's most powerful players as part of the Bilderberg Group for the past sixty plus years. Now *Mollia Domini* has taken it one step further. We don't know exactly what they want, but we know they are manipulating world events, including assassinations, elections, arming rebels, and causing trouble in the South China Sea. Now, are you ready to do what's right and help us fight them?" Mr. Orville asked with more seriousness and backbone

than Brock thought the little man had.

"Who recommended me?" Brock asked before answering Mr. Orville. He supposed it didn't matter, this was the whole reason he joined the Secret Service. He already knew he'd take the job protecting the president from this group and help in any other way he could.

"Um," the little man said, suddenly looking flustered, "Valeria McGregor."

Brock wasn't expecting that name. Val had been his college sweetheart. They broke up when he went into the Secret Service and she went into the DEA. "Country first" had been their motto.

"If it makes your decision any easier, she recommended you because she said you were the best, and she wanted me to tell you she has no interest in a relationship with you." Mr. Orville then turned a deeper shade red. "Then she might have said something, um, very colorful about you being an idiot if you didn't join the group."

Brock chuckled. He could imagine the colorful language Val used. Some Puerto Rican and Gaelic cuss words were probably thrown in for good measure. "I'm in. What now?"

"Oh good!" Mr. Orville smiled. "Not a thing. You never talked to me. I'll take care of everything, and you'll be stateside in a matter of days."

Brock stood as the chief of staff scrambled from the recliner and held out his hand. "It's great to have you aboard. You will report to the president, but a woman by the name of Elizabeth James is the leader of the small group. She'll be your point. We're an

interesting bunch, Agent Loyde, and I'm sure Dalton will be thrilled to have another man around to help. Right now he's trying to protect our three agents: Elizabeth, Valeria, though she doesn't need much protecting, and Tate Carlisle."

Brock shook his head. "The press secretary is the third agent?"

"Don't underestimate her. She doesn't know her own strength yet, but she holds a different sort of power than you and I do. She'll discover it soon." Mr. Orville looked at his watch. "Any minute, in fact. And call me Humphrey, they all do."

Humphrey held out his hand and Brock shook it. "I'll see you soon," Humphrey said before showing himself out the door. Brock looked around the small apartment. Well, he might as well start packing. He wanted to be ready for the States, and for Valeria.

Tate wanted to collapse onto the bed in her corner-room suite, but instead she popped two ibuprofens and waited for the knock at her door. She'd gotten two hours of sleep before she'd hurried to slap on more concealer than any one person should wear. She was about to stand in front of the firing squad that consisted of her former colleagues. Freaking BBN had been pushing the story of the dollar weakening due to President Stratton's support of a nonexistent coup overseas.

Tired, pissed, and having spent a ton of money

to pay someone to put her house back together since she was too afraid to go back there herself, Tate had lost her temper. Well, as much as any Southern belle from Georgia did. A slow smile had spread across her face and suddenly her accent, which had been beaten out of her at the networks, started to come through as she blessed their hearts and told them to get their facts straight.

Then she'd had to explain her behavior from the press conference to Birch. While he'd understood, he reminded Tate that she still had to be professional. Right now being professional was exhausting. And now, instead of crawling into bed and forgetting this horrendous day, Tate had to go see Claudia at BBN. She had to face the viper and get the bitch to agree to an interview with the president, all the while giving Alex time to bug her electronics. It would make her day to take Claudia down. But to be fair, if Claudia hadn't gotten Tate fired, she wouldn't be working with the president and the team.

The sound of a knock had her groaning as she slid her feet back into her heels. When Tate opened the door, she gasped. "Alex? Is that you?"

Tate walked to the front door of BBN's international headquarters in Washington, DC, unnerved by Alex walking slightly behind her shoulder. Gone was the shaggy hair, it was gelled back into a hipster half-ponytail. Normally clean-shaven, his scruff had grown into the beginnings of a beard. He was wearing thick bright-green-framed glasses with a hot pink bowtie. Gone were the baggy clothes and in

their place were fitted slacks, loafers, and a paisley dress shirt. What really had weirded Tate out was the fact that Alex hadn't said *dude* since he picked her up.

Tate took one last deep breath as Alex moved to open the glass door leading into the lobby. Plastering on her best happy smile, she walked through the open door and into the busy lobby. She strode straight toward the welcome center and let her smile widen as she saw Marge, the gatekeeper.

"Marge! It's so good to see you again. How is the family? Did your son get that football scholarship?" Tate asked as if she were still working there.

Marge looked up and blinked in recognition before a genuine smile broke out. "Tate! Oh, it's good to see you again. That's so kind of you to ask. He did, and he'll be starting college this fall. We're very proud. But what about you, Miss Press Secretary?"

Marge stood up and leaned across the counter to give Tate a hug.

Tate chuckled as Alex kept behind her. "I'm good. Thanks. I'm actually here to see Larry. Is he in the studio?"

"Let me check. Is this business or personal?" Marge asked, slipping back into her chair and reaching for her headset.

"Business."

"Give me one sec," Marge said as she dialed an extension.

So far, so good.

"Buzz me through, will you?"

Tate sucked in a breath as she heard that deep voice walking toward her from behind. What was *he* doing here? Tate turned and saw Fitz Houlihan's overstyled hair bent over the cell phone he rarely put down. Not that the most powerful talent agent out of Los Angeles would ever put down his lifeline to his clients, or more specifically, to his clients' money. Fitz was rude, ruthless, and everything mothers warned their daughters about. He was a flashy, money-hungry agent whom Tate had fallen madly in love with when she had met with him to see if he would represent her.

What could Tate say; she had been young and dumb. Fitz had been the older, wiser, sexy man who'd promised her fame and fortune. And he'd delivered, until she was fired by BBN. When Tate was fired, she not only lost her job, but also her agent and lover. Not that they were exclusive. He lived on the West Coast after all. But that was the only kind of relationship she had time for. She wasn't so naïve to think that she was the only client he was sleeping with, but it hurt all the same when he dumped her as a client and a lover via text.

"What's taking so long—Tate?" Fitz asked, finally looking up from his phone. It was hard to tell if he blushed under his tan as his fake blue eyes focused on her. Yup, he had laser treatments to turn his brown eyes blue. He thought he would look more irresistible with his black hair if he had blue eyes. Unfortunately, it worked. Fitz was still as handsome as ever.

"Hello, Fitzy," Tate said, purposely using the nickname she knew he hated. "What are you doing here?"

Fitz's tight lips spread into a smile. "Seeing my client. You might know her, Claudia Hughes. You know," Fitz paused, "I feel horrible about how we ended things. Now that you and Claudia aren't competition" — Fitz moved in closer as he looked down at her with his bedroom eyes — "I can take you on as a client again. I'm sure I could get you a seven-figure book deal for a tell-all after Stratton is voted out of office."

"I'll think about it," Tate said in the sugary voice that Fitz would realize really meant "eat shit and die" had he ever paid attention to her outside of the bedroom.

Marge hung up her call. "You're all set, Mr. Houlihan," she said, pressing the button that allowed him through to the elevators.

Before leaving, he smiled sweetly at Tate. "Call me and we'll work out a deal. You have my number." He winked before he walked away with a cocky swagger that he unfortunately lived up to.

"Larry is in the studio. They're live so you know what to do," Marge said with a smile. "Best wishes at the White House."

"Thank you, Marge," Tate said as she signed herself and her assistant in before she and Alex were buzzed through.

"Who was that guy and why do I get the feeling he was picturing you naked?" Alex whispered as they waited for the elevator.

"Because he knows what I look like naked. He's my ex-agent and my ex . . . well, just ex."

"You dated him? He seems like an asshole," Alex said as the doors opened.

"I wouldn't call it dating," Tate said, trying to hide her embarrassment. "When I got fired from BBN he dumped me in all aspects and picked up Claudia."

"You think they're—?" Alex did a quick hand gesture that left Tate rolling her eyes.

"Probably. Okay, you know the plan, right?" Tate asked, happy to get away from the topic of Fitz and Claudia.

"Yeah. Stand by the refreshments with the other interns. Wait until Claudia approaches you during commercial break. Grab some water bottles to serve to the people sitting behind the desk. Reach down to the shelf next to Claudia's seat to place a water bottle and connect the electronics to my devices to download and plant my software, giving me access. While I wait for the downloads to complete, I just stand back and play on my phone like all the interns. Got it."

"Then let's do this," Tate said as the doors opened.

Tate quietly opened the thick doors leading to the studio. With a nod, she sent Alex scurrying to the refreshment area where a boy and girl around Alex's age sat playing on their phones as Claudia read off the monitor.

Tate looked around at the staff and crew and felt

a longing for her old job. She missed being in front of the camera, delivering her investigative stories. But now she was living one giant investigation. Larry Wilkinson, BBN's managing senior editor, started toward her as soon as he saw her enter the studio. With a nod of his head, he directed her to meet him at the back of the studio.

The smile on Larry's face made Tate's smile turn real. She had really liked Larry. He was a good boss who had fought for her when the higher-ups had fired her. His hair was bright white, his outfit wrinkled, and he was the best in the news business at his job.

"Tate, it's damn good to see you," Larry whispered as he stopped close to her.

"You too, Larry. I haven't had time to thank you, but I heard that you gave the White House a glowing recommendation for me. I appreciate that," Tate said sincerely.

"I was happy to. I hated to see you leave BBN. I've been watching the press conferences. You've been doing well. How do you like it on the other side of things?"

Tate looked around the studio one more time. "I miss it some, but I really love working in the heart of it all. The White House is constant commotion, and I really feel as if I'm making a difference."

"Well, I've missed you. But Marge said this was a business visit?" Larry prodded as the quick buzzer indicated the station was now on commercial break. Tate tried not to look, but since she was facing the media desk it was easy to see Claudia was on her

way over to investigate. As soon as Claudia stepped from behind the desk, Alex was walking over with a handful of water bottles.

"Tate Carlisle, is that you?" Claudia asked as if she didn't know the answer. She stopped directly in front of Tate with her back to the desk and smiled insincerely at her.

"Sure is," Tate answered with her appropriate *fuck you* smile.

"What are you up to now?" Claudia asked, again, as if she didn't know. Tate took a deep breath to stop herself from choking the woman. She saw Alex bend over and place the water bottle by Claudia's electronics. Her phone and tablet would be there so she could look at them during commercial.

"I'm the press secretary for President Stratton now," Tate smiled before turning slightly to her left to look at Larry. "That's why I'm here. President Stratton wants to do a sit-down about his first couple months in office. You know, a lifestyle piece so the citizens can get to know him better. He feels he should let them into a day at the White House since they didn't get a good chance to know him during the election. After all, who pays attention to the vice president?"

"What a great idea," Claudia gasped as if she already was interviewing the president.

"Yes, well, we thought Kimber would be a good fit. She does great human interest pieces on your weekend slot."

Claudia's smile slipped, and Tate tried not to

laugh. "Kimber? She hasn't interviewed a celebrity yet. Nonsense, I'll interview President Stratton. We'll do it prime time, and the viewers will love it. Isn't that right, Larry?"

"Well, Kimber is new, and it would help our ratings if we could make a big production out of it. President Stratton has been very private. I take it this was your idea? It's a good one," Larry said, sending a pleading look to Tate. She knew that look. It conveyed that he didn't feel like fighting with Claudia over who got the interview, and it was exactly what she had planned.

"That's not what the president and I agreed on, but I'm sure I can convince him to do the interview with Claudia. Especially if you submit your questions ahead of time and pretape the segment earlier in the day. That's okay, right?" Tate asked.

"Perfect," Claudia said victoriously.

"Then I'll be in touch," Tate said to Claudia as she saw Alex pull the attached cords from Claudia's devices and move back to rejoin the other interns staring like zombies at their phones.

"Thirty seconds," the producer called out of the loudspeaker, sending Claudia scurrying to her chair to be swarmed by makeup.

"You'll come, too, won't you? How's Monday night? I'd love to see you again and you can keep Claudia on task. President Stratton doesn't like surprises," Tate chuckled, knowing Claudia always had something up her sleeve.

"Ten seconds," the producer called.

Larry smiled at Tate and nodded. "I'll be happy

to."

Tate didn't stay to watch Claudia smack the hand of the makeup artist or the silent countdown until they went live. She walked straight out of the room, barely pausing for Alex to fall in line behind her.

Tate waved to Marge on her way out as Alex hurried ahead to get the car. A minute later, Alex pulled to a stop in front of the building and double-parked for Tate to get in.

"The car's clean," Alex told her as he pulled into traffic. "Dude, she had two phones and a tablet. That's why it took so long. Luckily I came prepared. Dalton's constant state of preparedness from being a PJ is rubbing off on me," he joked as he ripped off his bowtie, throwing it along with his fake glasses into the backseat.

"And there he is." Tate laughed, feeling the relief from being able to pull off her manipulation.

"Seriously, dude, Claudia must save everything because it took forever to download. I'll work on it tonight. It's going to take a long time to go through everything. While I was waiting for the clones to finish, the other dudes were talking about Claudia. They're jealous that she's been getting a lot of new *sources* for her stories on the economy and the White House. They're wondering where they are coming from."

"Hopefully, you'll be able to find that out because if you do, I think it could lead us to someone within *Mollia Domini*." Tate looked out over DC as Alex drove back toward the hotel. Her

blood was pumping just as it did when she was onto a new story. She had been feeling out of place in the shadow group until now. But now she had a purpose. She knew how every aspect of the news worked and it was her turn to manipulate it, only this time she was going to manipulate the news like no one else was doing—by telling the truth.

CHAPTER SIX

"We're talking to experts who are worried that you, the citizens of our great country, are unknowingly about to lose everything. Make sure you tune in at eight to *The Claudia Hughes News Hour* to find out how to protect yourself."

Tate stopped hitting the punching bag Valeria was holding and shook her head. Claudia's teaser for tonight's episode was just what she expected from her—fear-mongering. But that was what made ratings pop.

"What is she talking about?" Valeria asked as she motioned for Tate to get back to work on the bag.

"Who knows? I'm sure it's something completely blown out of proportion. The way it works, she'll have decided broccoli can kill you, and she'll put experts up on TV who say 'Whatever you do, don't eat broccoli. Eat carrots instead.' Then you'll have high ratings and the carrot company that just bought a ton of advertising will see a spike in sales and happily continue to advertise," Tate explained as she slammed her fist into the bag.

"And I thought I was cynical," Valeria joked.

"It's not cynical if it's the truth." Tate stopped

punching the bag and wiped the sweat from her forehead.

"So you think Claudia is working with *Mollia Domini* to push their agenda?" Valeria asked as she pulled a pad onto her arm to hold in front of her. The pad stretched from her chest to mid-thigh. "Now I want you to grab my shoulders, bend me forward while kicking your knee as hard as you can into my stomach—or groin if your attacker is male. Go."

"I guess we'll find out soon," Tate said, out of breath as she worked her knee strikes. "Claudia comes on air in a couple of minutes. But I've been thinking about this since I left the studio. With all of the bad press Birch has gotten, and the complete lack of reporting on some major news stories, I think *Mollia Domini* is waging part of their war through the media. The question is whether Claudia is behind it or someone higher up is."

"Change legs," Valeria instructed. "Who is higher up? Do you know them?"

"Larry Wilkinson is BBN's senior managing editor for the US segment of the company. He was my boss's boss. He's very hands-on, but today I got the feeling he was being pressured. I invited him to the White House when Claudia films with Birch."

"So, who's above him?" Valeria asked as Tate grabbed her shoulders and slammed her knee into the pad covering Valeria's stomach.

"Lots of people. You have all of the executives of BBN, not to mention the parent company," Tate grunted as she practiced her self-defense.

"Parent company? You mean BBN doesn't own itself?" Val asked as she dropped the pad and went to get a drink of water.

"No. Most newspapers, news stations, magazines, and book publishers all have parent companies, and there are only a few parent companies out there that encompass almost the entire market. Each outlet is run as its own company, but Big Brother has final say, if you know what I mean."

"So, BBN is owned by someone else who may also own newspapers? What's stopping them from colluding to pass the agenda of their parent company?"

"Not a thing. Here's a harmless example," Tate said as she wiped a towel over her face. "BBN News is owned by the Stanworth family under their massive Fourth Estate Media Trust. In that trust, they also own *The Washington Leader, NYC Tribune*, SFT Publishing, Silver Television, and Stanworth Motion Pictures," Tate explained. "They can make anything happen and have it look true, when it's all manufactured. Say they make a movie at Stanworth Motion Pictures, then have BBN report that it's the best movie of the year. Next the parent company will have the *NYC Tribune* list it on their supposedly unbiased Top Watch list, all the while they are publishing the accompanying book through their publishing company and running ads on their television station saying this movie has MOVIE AWARD written all over it. And that's only part of the Stanworth family holdings."

Valeria thought for a moment. "They can do all of that just for a movie or a book. What can they do for some nefarious purpose?"

"Exactly," Tate nodded in agreement. The idea gave her chills as she looked up at Claudia's intro.

"Americans beware, your money may not be yours much longer," Claudia warned into the camera. "We have the *NYC Tribune's* leading financial analyst with us to explain how President Stratton's involvement with corrupt Prince Noah and the unsuccessful coup the president supported have put you in danger of losing everything. Stocks have taken a hit, consumer confidence is dipping, and the dollar is weakening. Now, let's hear what the expert has to say."

"And this is the person you want Birch to do an interview with?" Valeria asked, disgusted as the supposedly unbiased financial analyst spouted doom and gloom.

"Definitely." Tate slammed her hand into the punching bag, sending it flying backward.

Tate pulled into the underground parking garage of her temporary home at the hotel and felt tired to her core. She parked and grabbed her duffle bag from the front seat of her sedan before hauling her sore and tired body out of the car.

The parking garage was well lit with valets coming and going constantly. It was one of the reasons Tate had picked the hotel. She felt safe as

she saw a valet drive by in an expensive car. Tate's sneakers didn't make a sound as she made her way toward the elevators. She heard the valet turn off the car and get out. The door closed behind her and the car's horn honked as it was locked.

Tate pulled out her phone and pulled up Tinselgossip.com. She had a weakness for celebrity gossip, plus she wanted to learn as much as she could about Trip and Kerra, who appeared to be loosely connected through an affair. Maybe she could find the link between them and *Mollia Domini*.

The gossip site loaded and there was a picture front and center of Kerra Ruby's long blonde hair pulled back into a sleek ponytail and a cut-off shirt that showed the underside of her breasts. The headline was her quote claiming that it's a good thing she is rich or else she'd be worried about becoming homeless because of President Stratton's foreign policies killing Americans' dreams and finances.

"What the—?" Tate stopped quickly as she scrolled down to see the story. There were already over a thousand comments and twenty thousand shares on social media.

Tate was so absorbed in reading she blindly reached out and pressed the elevator button. If it weren't for the ding when the doors opened, she wouldn't have known when to step forward due to being so engrossed in reading the story.

As she entered the elevator, she was knocked hard from behind. Tate went to scream but a hand clamped over her mouth. The arm that locked

around her shoulder and shoved her into the elevator was clad in red, the same color as the valet's uniform. Tate dropped her phone and fought. She stomped her foot. She slammed her head backward, but all it did was bring the man closer to her. He shoved her against the side of the elevator, her face smashed against the wall as she heard the emergency stop activated. Hot breath on her neck and the feel of solid muscle against her back rocked panic throughout her body.

"Hand over everything you have," he whispered against her ear, his voice an unidentifiable accent.

"I . . . I . . . I just have my bag," Tate said, trying to muster courage.

"You don't have anything on your body? I don't believe you." The voice was deep as his lips tickled her ear as he spoke.

"Are you the one who broke into my house? What are you looking for? If you just tell me, then I can help you find it." Tate took as deep a breath as she could. Her burning lungs reminded her she had been holding her breath since she'd been shoved into the elevator.

The man didn't answer. Instead he ran his hand down her sides, felt inside her pockets, and ripped the thin gold chain from her neck. "Look, lady, all I want is what you have on you. Now stop squirming or I'll take even more. Understand?"

"I understand," Tate whispered back as she stopped struggling.

"I enjoyed our time together, Tate." The

emergency button was turned off, the doors slid open, and then he was gone.

Tate turned to look after him to see if she could get a better look, but all she could see was the retreating form of a man who seemed to blend into every valet coming and going from the property. Tate — he'd known her name after all.

As the doors slid closed and the elevator ascended, Tate fought to feel safe once again. The elevator opened on the ground floor and security stood waiting for her. "We saw on the monitors that you were in trouble. Are you all right, Miss Carlisle?"

"I am now," Tate sighed. "Did you catch him?"

"I'm sorry, we didn't. By the time our men got down to the parking garage, he was gone and out of range of our cameras. The police have been called, though." The head security guard stepped into the elevator and pressed her floor. "Let me accompany you to your room."

"Thank you. Lewis, would you do me a favor?" She asked as she read the nametag on the large man who looked as if he had played offensive line in the NFL at some point. His dark brown head was shaved, his dark brown eyes held both confidence and concern. Tate instantly liked him. He had to be well over six feet five inches and about three hundred thirty pounds of muscle.

"Of course, Miss Carlisle," Lewis answered.

"First, call me Tate. Second, can you get me a copy of the video footage you have, ASAP?" Tate asked.

"Right away, Tate," Lewis said as he stepped off the elevator and led her down the hall. "Would you like a DVD or for me to email it to you?"

"DVD would be best. Thank you." Tate needed to get that DVD into Alex's hands. Sure, she could have emailed it quicker, but right now all her electronics were in the hands of who she suspected was *Mollia Domini*.

"Your room is all clear. We'll be increasing patrols in the area to make sure he doesn't come back. I'll be back in a couple of minutes with that DVD for you. I'm sorry this has occurred, and your room will be comped for your stay."

"Thank you, Lewis. That's very kind." Tate smiled at the big man as he left her room. Tate rushed to the phone and called her brother's cell phone.

"Hello?" Tucker asked hesitantly.

"It's Tate."

"Oh, what number are you calling from?"

"I was robbed! Someone took my phone. I'm all right, don't worry, but I'm going to be staying at a hotel and this is the number."

"I'll be right there. Which hotel?"

"I'm at The Knox, the one across from the White House. I'm fine. Please don't trouble yourself. By any chance are you at Lancy's?" Tate asked.

"I just walked in. I'm at the bar, and Valeria is staring at me. You think she's into me?" Tucker whispered.

Tate shook her head. "I had told Valeria I was going to get something for her and bring it tonight,

but now I just feel exhausted. The adrenaline is wearing off. Would you mind passing her the phone so I can say my excuses."

"Sure, but I think I should come see you." Her brother sounded determined, but Tate knew he didn't really want to drive the forty-five minutes to DC.

"Really, Tucker, I promise. I am completely unharmed. The police have been called and the hotel security is on top of it. I'm going to go to bed early, so I'd probably be asleep by the time you arrived anyway."

"Fine. But I want you to call me in the morning."

"Thanks for being such a good brother."

Tate listened as Tucker held out the phone and called for Valeria.

"Yeah?" Valeria said, her voice tight, knowing something was wrong.

"I was robbed in the parking garage of my hotel. They took my electronics. I need Alex to wipe everything."

"When did that happen?" Valeria asked, her voice clearly worried.

"Five minutes ago, so we need to hurry. I'm unhurt, but I think it was the same person who went through my house. I told Tucker I was supposed to bring you something tonight. I'll come to the bar tomorrow, okay?"

"No problem. As long as you're unharmed."

"I am. I don't have a phone, so can you notify everyone? Also, I'll have a DVD of security footage."

"I'll handle it. See you soon." The phone went

dead, and Tate hung up her hotel phone, feeling completely lost without her connection to the group. She had said she didn't want her brother visiting, but when Lewis came with the DVD she found herself talking to the security guard so he'd stay longer. But, eventually, he left and Tate was alone.

Tate moved to the window and looked out as people in suits walked in groups to the local bars and restaurants. In the distance, she could see the sights and sounds of DC, including the White House and the Washington Monument. Tate cracked the window and closed her eyes. The sounds of the city were comforting and even though she was way above the people on the street, she didn't feel quite so alone.

Tate's thoughts drifted to Birch. He was a good man doing an impossible job. The media were tearing him to shreds. He had spies in the White House and knew very well that if he took one wrong step, there would be a bullet with his name on it. It didn't stop him from checking on her when he'd heard someone had broken into her house. He had even offered her a room at the White House, but Tate knew what kind of damage that could do. The media were already trying to find anything, whether true or not, to make him look bad. Having a single woman spending the night at the White House was definitely one of those hot ticket items the press was looking for. They would question his focus on the country and call her names. It wouldn't matter that Birch had never looked at her in that way, even if she couldn't help but admire him. The press didn't

care who they hurt with their lies if it sold copies and won ratings. Tate would be dragged through the mud, and the president would be accused of all sorts of sordid things.

Tate blinked her eyes open when her stomach rumbled. She didn't feel like going to the famous bar the hotel had or even to their more casual restaurant. Room service it was. Tate placed her order, and when she hung up there was a knock on the door. Lewis filled her vision when she looked through the peephole.

Tate opened the door "Hey, Lew—" Lewis wasn't alone.

"I caught this man lurking in the hallway. He says you know him."

"I wasn't lurking. I just need a new prescription in my glasses, and I was having trouble seeing the numbers. I told you that."

Tate almost laughed at the way Lewis was holding Alex by the scruff of the neck. "Yes, he's my assistant. Thank you for looking out for me, Lewis. I just ordered room service and in light of the fake valet—"

"Say no more. I'll bring your food up. And keep an eye on this one," Lewis stared Alex down, and Tate saw Alex's Adam's apple bob as he swallowed hard.

"Thank you, Lewis," Tate called as the large security guard strode off down the hall.

Alex slipped into the hotel room. "Dude, that man is scary."

"Isn't he great?" Tate smiled. "Is something

wrong? I wasn't expecting anyone tonight." Alex shook his head and some tendrils of hair escaped his half-ponytail. "You remind me of someone."

"Flint Scott, the reporter from the bar. I've fashioned my preppy hipster look after him," Alex said as he began to open his bag. Ah, yes, that was exactly who Alex reminded her of. "I brought you a new phone. It's all programmed. I remotely wiped your phone as well. From what I could see on my end, no one had logged in to our secure network. But to be safe, I moved it all around and changed all the passwords. If they manage to even recover anything from your phone to the secure site, it'll show as a fitness forum."

Tate took the phone and practically hugged it. Her lifeline to her friends was back.

"I also backed up all of your files before I wiped your phone. You shouldn't be missing a thing. This is your new tablet. And Dalton thought you should have this."

Alex handed Tate a pretty watch. It looked like one of those designer watches that tracked your steps. "Does he want me to work out more?"

"Nope, it was his idea and pretty badass if I may say so. It's a GPS tracker. He took the exercise band and, with a little help from yours truly, made it so it reported directly to our secure site. We can log in and see exactly where everyone is. Works just like a normal step counter in case anyone checks." Alex held it down for a second and the number of steps appeared.

"This makes me feel so much better, thank you."

"Anything for my girls," Alex smirked. He was the baby of the group and all the women thought of him that way. It didn't stop him from loving working with them, though. "Val said you had something for me?"

"Oh, yes." Tate handed him the DVD Lewis had made for her. "Here's the security footage. I thought you could track him through some hacking and whatever other wonders you do."

"No problem-o. I'll get to work on it as soon as I get back to the bar. Valeria and I are on duty tonight. I've started going through Claudia's things, but there's just too much. I'm running a program I designed to read it for me. I'll have the report later tonight."

Tate watched Alex put the DVD into his backpack and head for the door. "Call if you need anything," he said before closing the door after him.

Tate looked down at her new tablet. She had wanted to counter the media with the truth, and tonight she was going to do just that. Flint Scott was going to get the story of his life.

CHAPTER SEVEN

D alton closed the door to Lizzy's house behind
them and locked the door. The white powder-
puff dog, Dave, had just pissed all over the
neighbor's garden gnome. The little Bichon Frise
hated that thing along with hating Crew Dixon,
which showed the lap dog had good taste, and that
was something Dalton could respect.

Dave darted up the stairs to where Dalton knew
Lizzy was waiting for him. He let out a long breath
and shoved his hand through his hair. What the hell
was going on with him? He had practically moved
in with Lizzy after the first time they slept together,
and he hadn't really gone home since. It wasn't like
him. It was clouding his judgment, and as a
pararescueman, he lived and breathed by his
judgment. It's what saved lives in split seconds
during rescue operations.

Dalton was here to protect the group. He was
the one who pulled them out of dangerous
situations and made sure no one was left behind. In
return, when this operation was over, he would be
reinstated as commander for his unit of PJs. He'd
run into Grant Macay, his former pilot, during an
operation with Lizzy in the South China Sea and

had learned the unit had been split up and scattered to the four corners of the world.

When this assignment had started, it was solely a means to an end. But now, Dalton looked up the stairs . . . now it had changed. Shoving the feelings he didn't want to explore back down, Dalton climbed the stairs and headed to the bedroom. Lizzy was stepping out from the bathroom. She was wet from her shower and wrapped in a towel that didn't seem to want to stay on as she brushed her wet hair.

"Thanks for taking Dave out," Lizzy said as she took her hair and wrapped it into some sort of twisty up-do thingy. Dalton let his eyes travel down her bare shoulders and to the swell of her breasts straining the towel that was barely hanging on. Dalton knew he had a problem. The sex was mind-blowing, but it wasn't just the sex. It was this. The ability to work as a team was the best way he could put it. Damn, he was in over his head and sinking fast.

"You know how you can pay me back for taking him out in the middle of the night?" Dalton asked as the left corner of his lips turned up into smirk and his eyes willed the towel to fall.

"It's our first night off from the bar all week. I know exactly what we're going to do," Lizzy grinned. "We're going to binge-watch that show I've been telling you about."

Dalton growled and launched himself at her. Lizzy's laughter turned to a squeal as he chased her around the bed. When he caught her, he tore the damned towel from her body before lowering her to

the bed with his mouth latched onto her nipple and his fingers between her thighs. He knew he was in deep trouble. When the time came for him to go, he didn't know if he'd be able to.

"What the hell?" Dalton murmured hours later. Lizzy was sprawled naked with half her body across his and her face buried in his chest when the knock at the back door woke him.

"Hmm?" Lizzy mumbled as she snuggled closer to him.

"Someone's at the door," Dalton told her as he was already grabbing for his gun and leaping from the bed. Dave dashed down the stairs. His high-pitched bark was louder than any alarm.

Dalton hunched over and ran into the kitchen. He pressed himself against the wall and used the barrel of his Glock to pull the blinds away from the window enough to see who was there. With a roll of his eyes, he let the blinds fall back as he unlocked and flung open the door.

"Dude, you're like, naked. Cover that shit up," Alex said, pushing past him and into the kitchen. He set a laptop on the kitchen table and opened it.

"What's going on?" Lizzy asked as she entered the kitchen with Dalton's T-shirt on and a gun in each hand. Damn, she'd never looked sexier. "What time is it?"

"It's five-thirty in the morning. Look." Alex stepped back. Dalton and Lizzy stepped forward to read what was on the glowing screen.

Shooting at The Knox tomorrow.

"That's where Tate is," Lizzy said. "Have you called her?"

"I came straight to you. What should we do?" Alex looked worriedly between them.

"Call the president. We need to evacuate Tate if the email is verified and have it look completely normal. We don't want them knowing we have this information," Dalton ordered as Alex pulled out his phone.

"Yes?" the sleepy voice said over the phone.

"Sir, it's Dalton. Alex just came over. He discovered an email from an unknown source that says *Shooting at The Knox tomorrow.* Alex is working on finding out who sent the email."

"Get Tate out of there!" the president yelled as all trace of sleepiness fell from his voice.

"I think we should verify —" Dalton began before the president cut him off.

"No, I want her out now!"

"I was thinking of evacuating her at seven-thirty. We could walk her right through the front door of the White House and no one would think twice about it," Dalton said calmly. "And it would give us more time to determine who sent this email."

"I want you there now. Alex can keep you informed. And tell Tate that she's moving in here temporarily. I don't care how much she protests," the president said sternly.

"Birch," Lizzy said gently but strongly, "she

can't stay there. You know that. You know someone will find out. The media shitstorm that will follow will hurt both you and our cause."

The president sighed over the phone, and Dalton could sense his agitation. "One night. She can stay here for one night and sleep in her office. By then, we can surely find a safe place for her to stay. But, Dalton, I want you there now."

"Yes, sir."

The line went dead and the three of them looked at each other. "I think he could be overreacting," Lizzy finally said.

"Dude, they're going to shoot someone at the same hotel where Tate is staying. This email came through just minutes after I cloned the phone. It can't be a coincidence," Alex said, shutting his laptop.

"I don't know, but I have my orders." Dalton turned and walked bare-assed out of the kitchen. "Someone call Tate and tell her I'm on my way."

Birch paced the private quarters in the White House. He had banished the Secret Service to outside all exits, and his staff was gone for the night so he could roam freely until the butlers, ushers, and maids appeared in the early morning hours. He walked the Center Hall, leaving the East Sitting Hall. He passed the Lincoln Bedroom, the hidden staircase near the Treaty Room where the entrance to the tunnels were located, guest rooms, the Yellow Oval Room, his

room, and stopped at the window in the West Sitting Hall. From there, if he craned his neck, he could see The Knox Hotel and the corner room Alex told him was Tate's. Here he was, the most powerful man in the world, just blocks from her, and he couldn't do anything to protect her.

Birch's immediate reaction to the news of what had been found on Claudia's phone had been to rush through the tunnels and storm into Tate's room with his Army-issued gun in hand. Birch looked at the weapon on the coffee table and still had to tell himself not to do it. Dalton was there. He would keep her safe.

Birch rested his forehead against the bulletproof glass window of his gilded cage. What had he done? When he had approached Lizzy's father, Birch was just the senator from Virginia with an idea that someone was selling classified information. He never envisioned this. He never imagined a secret organization like *Mollia Domini*, an organization with enough power to convince him to accept the vice presidency and then disappear quietly into the night. But when President Mitchell, who was a member of *Mollia Domini,* died from cancer, Birch's eyes were opened. Asking around led to Lizzy's father's death. When Lizzy and Dalton had shown him the video of Dan March, an assassin for *Mollia Domini* who Lizzy had killed, Birch had wanted to call an end to this mission. These people were playing not only with lives but countries. They called themselves the puppet masters, and they were making the world dance by pulling invisible strings.

He was putting his group at risk.

Lizzy had been forced to cross lines she'd never be able to come back from. She and Dalton had almost lost their lives, and now Tate was in danger. While they had taken down two assassins, Dan March and Bram Schmit, and their commanders, FBI Agent Phylicia Claymore and President Mitchell's senior policy advisor, Harriett Hills, they still hadn't found who comprised the inner circle of this organization.

Birch was still looking into Sandra Cummings, the secretary of state appointed by President Mitchell, and Senator Epps. It had to be someone with enough power and inside information to give orders to Hills and Claymore, who in turn passed them to the assassins. Epps was the most powerful senator on all the top-secret congressional committees. And Sandra was privy to the most intimate White House discussions and had powerful contacts all over the world.

But now Tate was in the crosshairs because she'd met with the editor of a newspaper. A paper that had been against Birch's presidency since it became public knowledge that President Mitchell was dying. All this time, Birch had been quiet. He hadn't wanted to rock the boat. Now, though, he wanted to return to his roots. Birch wasn't some silver-spoon brat like Trip Kameron. No, Birch had been career military. As an Army military intelligence officer, he had been on the ground in some of the most dangerous locations in the world. He'd interviewed terrorists responsible for mass

genocide. Now he was here, hiding in the cloak of the presidency.

Something about Tate brought out his protective side. Something he hadn't felt since leaving the service. It had been twelve years since he lost his wife in an armed robbery. While Tate didn't remind him at all of his wife, the natural reaction to protect her was strong. It wasn't because she was weak. In fact, Tate was strong in a way Lizzy and Valeria weren't. She had a positive never-give-up attitude and a dogged determination to dig at a story until she had the whole picture.

As Birch pondered Tate and the situation his group was in, the sun broke through the horizon. The first rays of light spread out over the city, and Birch knew it was time to stop playing politics. Some things were more important than winning a future election. If he only had this small amount of time in office, he was going to use it as best he could. He wasn't going to hide behind his team. He was going to challenge *Mollia Domini* to a type of warfare he doubted they knew existed.

Birch looked at his watch. Tate should be getting here soon. He headed to his room and splashed water on his face. He had just finished shaving when his phone rang.

"Let her up," Birch ordered the Secret Service agent at the check-in point for the residence. Birch stripped off his athletic shorts and stepped into his black suit pants. He pulled off the *ARMY* T-shirt and tossed it onto the bed. He was reaching for his light blue dress shirt when he heard Tate's voice.

"I'm in my room," Birch called out. He started walking toward the hall as he slipped his shirt on. "How are you?" Birch asked. He looked up from buttoning the first buttons when Tate didn't reply. Instead she was staring at his exposed torso.

"Oh," Tate said, blinking rapidly. "Tired. Sorry, I zoned out for a second. I didn't get much sleep after Alex called me."

"Where is Dalton?" Birch asked.

"He drove the town car to the door and dropped me off. He's heading back to the hotel to take down Claudia. I just can't figure out how they are onto me."

"Come in. Sit down before you fall over." Birch clasped Tate's elbow and escorted her into his room. She took a seat on the couch, and he walked into his dressing room to get his tie.

Tate watched as Birch walked across his room and disappeared into his dressing room. No man had the right to look so good, certainly not a president who was off limits. Tate had been off and on with Fitz for years and Fitz was Hollywood idealism personified, but Birch was something more. Something real. And when she saw the light sprinkling of hair on his sculpted chest leading in a little arrow downward, well . . . her mind just refused to think of anything else except that damn little arrow. Tate shook her head. She had a job to do, and she was going to do it regardless of how she felt about the president.

"I've decided I'm not sitting passively anymore. I know you don't want to draw attention, but I think

it's time to fight back in the press. I have a plan for your interview with Claudia, and I also have information on Epps. Secretary Cummings has been a little more difficult to find dirt on that hadn't already been discussed at her confirmation hearings," Tate called out as Birch walked out with a bright red tie draped over his neck.

Tate refused to let her eyes travel to the buttons he was finishing. Instead, she looked around the bedroom. Well, *bedroom* didn't really describe it. It was larger than her small house. There were two bathrooms, a dressing room, a sitting area, and then the actual bed.

"Funny, I've been thinking the same thing. What do you have in mind?" Birch asked as he moved to a mirror and started to tie his tie.

"I want to use Flint Scott to push stories with our point of view. We have to be careful, though. I don't want anything at my press conference to be worded the same. I was thinking of sending him snippets of facts, documents, and so on, but not tell him what they're for. It's better for him to research and write it in his own words," Tate explained.

"Do you think it will cause Flint to be in the crosshairs of *Mollia Domini*?" Birch asked.

"Yes. I do. But I think we should give him the first round and see what he does with it. Then I can slip information to all major news sources of a complete story. If they don't run it, someone else will, and they'll look as if they're not on top of the story. Then the third thing is to change up my press conferences. I'm going to run the narration, and the

White House will issue press releases to rebut every false story out there. We will use the truth to show the biased and purposeful manipulation of some members of the press. I just don't want to sit quietly by anymore," Tate said vehemently as she stood and walked over to Birch who was struggling with his knot. "What do you think?"

Tate stopped in front of Birch and reached up to his tie. Their hands met and her eyes shot up to find him looking down at her. "Let me. I had to help my brother all the time with his."

Birch slowly lowered his hands but kept looking at her. "I think that's a good idea. I've decided it's time to wield the power of the presidency as well. I believe a joint press conference will be good after I make some calls. Plan it for right after Claudia's interview airs. We won't tell the press until an hour before." He winked at her.

Tate pulled the knot tight and worked it up to his collar. "There." She let her hand rest for a second on his tie before dropping it. This was not the time to be thinking of what else the president could do with the tie.

"Good. And I want you to stay here tonight. You can have your pick of the rooms."

Tate blushed as her thoughts turned even more sexual. "I have a couch in my office. You know all our work would be undermined with even a hint of you having a personal life." Tate's eyes went wide. "Not that we would be, but they would assume we did—"

Birch's chuckle stopped her rambling. "I know

what you mean. I just want you safe."

"Thank you."

"Let's go downstairs and you tell me what you've found on Senator Epps." Birch placed his hand on the small of her back and escorted her to the stairs. Tate tried to banish the thought of spending the night with Birch, but the longer he kept his hand on her, the harder it was.

"Good morning, sir."

Tate watched as Secret Service flanked them as they headed for his office. Once safely inside, Tate pulled out her laptop that had thankfully been in her hotel room at the time of her robbery.

"First, I looked into Secretary Cummings. She comes from old money, but I couldn't find stories of her having dealings with any of the countries we've crossed paths with. She has a public record against the rebels in Africa that Phylicia was helping. She was an invited guest of the Netherlands' Queen Anja's thirtieth birthday celebration. She has opposed China's actions in the South China Sea. The only thing I found was her support for private military companies helping local police protect federal property." Tate closed her notes on Sandra and opened the ones on Senator Epps.

"Now, for Epps, I reached out to some of my old contacts. It's clear he's mad that he lost the election, and he fully intends to run against you. I wouldn't be surprised if *Mollia Domini* put up multiple candidates in both parties, thinking it would be a win-win for the group. Epps is known for overstepping. I found travel to Africa buried in his

office's budget. I tracked down the former African president's secretary, and she said they had no American visitors during the time Epps was in Africa. I'm guessing he met with the rebels because after that trip, he supported a bill to sell weapons to them, which Congress shot down. Further, he met with Prince Noah at the United Nations just before his arrest."

Birch leaned over her shoulder to look at her notes. "What are you going to do with all this information?"

"Release it, and let the remaining honest reporters do the job of tracing all of this for us." And with a couple of keystrokes, the material was sent. Now she needed to look into Claudia as only a reporter could. Valeria could check her bank accounts all she wanted, but there was something about hitting the phones and the streets to ferret out the truth that strummed through Tate's veins.

CHAPTER EIGHT

D alton sat in the lobby of The Knox pretending to read a newspaper. Lizzy looked on, enjoying her coffee in the lobby bar. Valeria was out jogging around the area for her morning run.

"We have trucks pulling up," Valeria said through her communication device. "Claudia just arrived with a camera crew. I'm out; they're going inside," Valeria said as Dalton heard her jog off.

Dalton answered, "I'll follow. Lizzy, you cover my back." He set down his paper and stood up as Claudia walked in with two men and a woman trailing after her and a big security guard leading the way.

"This doesn't feel right," Lizzy warned as Dalton fell into step ten feet behind the group. "There are too many people for an assassination attempt."

Dalton raised his hand and called out, "Hold the elevator, please!"

The security guard stopped the doors from closing but stared Dalton down. Shit, he didn't like being noticed. "Thanks." Dalton looked at the panel and saw the second-floor button pressed.

"Floor?" the guard asked, still looking at him as

Claudia completely ignored him.

"Three, please." Dalton kept the security guard in his line of sight as the elevator went up one floor and opened. The group filed off and Dalton hurriedly pressed the door close button.

On the third floor, Dalton darted off the elevator and dashed down the flight of stairs. Slowly he opened the second-floor door. The guard was standing by the door to the ballroom. Shit. Dalton needed to get in there.

"I need a distraction for a guard," Dalton whispered. "He's seen me, so I don't want to be the one to take him out."

"On it," Valeria said. "Give me two minutes."

Dalton kept watch as not a single person walked down the hall. The guard stood directly in front of the door, preventing anyone from entering or leaving. The stairwell at the opposite end of the hall opened and Valeria limped out with sweat dripping off her face.

"Cramp!" she called out in pain as she dropped to the ground. "Ow, ow, ow."

The guard looked down at her as Valeria sat on the floor, crying out in pain and holding her leg. He finally gave in and headed toward her. Dalton didn't waste any time slipping quietly into the ballroom with his gun in hand. But what he found wasn't an assassin shooting, but a shooting for a television show.

The ballroom was decorated to look like an old-time set filled with candles and people in period costumes. Several people mulled around behind

Claudia sitting in a chair with the famous director of those sweeping epic historical romance movies Dalton never watched. And was that Kerra Ruby? Dalton looked closer. The boobs gave Kerra away. She was dressed in a huge ball gown from the 1800s, and her trademark fake blonde locks were now dark brown. But the boobs were still on full display.

"This movie really makes a statement. It's about people who weren't afraid to stand up and protest the establishment," Kerra said seriously. "Just like today, we need to fight for what we deserve. We need to say we aren't going to take this anymore and rise up against a government who is stealing our money and getting rid of our jobs."

Dalton shoved his gun into his pants and covered it with his shirt.

"Are you talking about President Stratton's alliance with the rebels in Zambia and the traitor, Prince Noah, causing the dollar to weaken to the point of a looming economic collapse?" Claudia asked.

"Yes, it's very scary, and we should march on the White House," Kerra said as she puffed out her breasts.

"It's a very scary time for our country. It's scary that so many people don't see what we do, and they are blindly following the president to their destruction. I'm hoping that with this movie, people will wake up to what we in Hollywood have been telling them," the director said seriously.

"What are you doing here?" Dalton heard as a strong hand clamped down on his shoulder.

Dalton looked over his shoulder to find the security guard behind him. "I was hoping to get Kerra Ruby's autograph," Dalton responded. "You think you can hook a man up?"

"This is a closed set. Sorry, buddy."

Dalton shrugged and headed out the door without a fight. "It was worth a shot. Have a good day."

Dalton went to the stairs and walked to the lobby. Son of a bitch. He'd almost blown his cover over a TV interview for a movie. Now the security guard had seen him and Valeria. Dalton hoped he didn't put two and two together.

★　★　★

Back at the bar, Valeria stewed over her computer. She finally slammed her hand down. "We could have all been caught, and it would have been freaking Kerra Ruby to take us down."

Alex looked down at the floor he was mopping. "I'm sorry. I thought it was important."

"I know, Alex. It was right for you to bring it to us, but wrong for the president not to listen to our plan to observe and report," Lizzy said gently.

"It's because of Little Miss Sunshine," Valeria said with disgust. "She's a weak link."

"Birch wouldn't react the same if you or Lizzy were in that situation," Dalton said as he drank some orange juice.

"Yeah, because Tate's worthless," Valeria spat.

Dalton shook his head. "No, she's not. She's just

not like you and Lizzy. But the president reacted differently because he feels differently about her."

"What are you talking about?" Valeria asked with anger and confusion clear on her face.

Dalton tried not to lose his patience. Valeria hadn't liked Tate since she joined the team, but he thought it was getting better until this. "He likes her. It's clear as day."

"No way," Lizzy laughed.

"Seriously?" Valeria snarled at the same time.

"Yes, seriously. It's written all over his face when Tate is in the room. It also explains why he flipped out when he thought Tate was in danger," Dalton said, finding it funny that the women couldn't see it.

"Dude, totally true," Alex muttered, still looking like a whipped puppy.

Lizzy and Valeria exchanged a look, and Dalton could see them replaying every meeting between Tate and Birch. Their eyes widened and they looked back to Dalton, and he knew they realized it was true.

"Great. Now we have a leader who is being ruled by his dick," Valeria said with a roll of her eyes.

"Last I heard, I was in charge of this group, and I don't have a dick," Lizzy countered. "So, let's get back to work. Any luck on Epps?"

"I'm pulling a string. I'll let you know what I find." Valeria turned to her computer and blocked everyone else out.

"What do you want me to do?" Dalton asked.

"I don't know yet. We pulled a partial print from the orders left in the rock for Phylicia, but we haven't found a match yet. I need to get prints to compare. Want to drive around to some houses and go through the trash?" Lizzy asked sweetly.

"I'll look around, but my guess is they have a lot of security. If a man shows up on multiple cameras looking through the trash of high-level officials, they will be on to us," Dalton pointed out.

"I know. I need Tate and Humphrey in on this." Lizzy pulled out her phone and sent instructions.

A moment later Lizzy looked down at her phone. "Good. They are having a staff meeting tomorrow, and Humphrey will set down glossy folders and then pick them up before they leave. He'll put their names on the inside so they'll be marked. And in the meantime, Tate is shadowing Sandra today. I'll work on a list of all the ranking members of the Senate, House, and cabinet to determine if we need any more prints."

Dalton flipped on the television as he stocked the bar. The morning reporter for BBN filled the screen with a sad look on her face. "According to Brent Eller of Tinselgossip.com, ambulances have been called to Hollywood financier Tanswell Patton's house. Brent is reporting the investor of numerous top Hollywood hits has died from a possible drug overdose."

Valeria's head shot up. "What kind of drugs?"

Dalton shrugged and Valeria immediately went back to work. He knew the look well. She was onto something.

CHAPTER NINE

T ate had discovered three things after following Sandra Cummings all day. One, she never wanted to be secretary of state. From downright petty drama to outright terror, what Sandra had to deal with would drive anyone crazy. Second, she was positive Sandra thrived in the chaos. She never lost her cool and never backed down. And third, Sandra's right hand man, Thurmond Culpepper, was a little shit. No, he was a big stinky shit.

Thurmond had questioned Tate's every move. He spoke to her as if she were a child. Then he had the audacity to order her to leave the room during a briefing with Senator Epps and others from the Foreign Affairs Committee when Tate had come across Thurmond and Epps talking in hushed whispers as they waited for Sandra. So, Tate had sent him to bring coffee and donuts to the group.

With Thurmond and his sleazy power-climbing ways out of the room, Tate was able to observe Sandra and Epps uninterrupted. Epps was clearly into the grandeur of his status as committee head and enjoyed interrupting Sandra. Meanwhile, Sandra took every opportunity to remind Epps that he was "just a senator" and not privy to all the

intelligence and negotiations she was. The rest of the senators seemed to see this childish behavior loosely hidden under overly proper manners as annoying as Tate did. So, she had taken the opportunity to talk to the other staffers as Epps and Sandra postured.

Tate had learned that no one liked Thurmond. They thought Sandra was a good boss but gave Thurmond too much power. One swore that Epps had once been caught snooping in Sandra's office when she wasn't there.

At four o'clock, Tate excused herself from listening in on a meeting between Sandra and the Japanese ambassador. She made a quick stop at the mall and picked up a wig, glasses, and a new outfit. She wore high platform heels hidden under long, wide-legged pants. Her newly highlighted blonde hair was covered with a short-cropped black wig, and she sported large white-rimmed sunglasses that covered the majority of her face.

Tate used eyeliner to draw a cute beauty mark on her cheek before getting into her car and driving toward Claudia's posh community. She parked her car in a nearby carpool lot and began to walk. Tate didn't care what Dalton said, Claudia didn't have any sinister plan to take her out this morning. Claudia always looked out for herself and would never get her hands dirty. Tate walked around the back of Claudia's house. If Humphrey could use the Internet to learn how to pick a lock, so could she.

Tate followed the video instructions and the door swung open. The alarm sounded and she raced

to find it. She knew she had a couple of minutes before the police arrived, but she didn't want any neighbors stopping by. When she found the source of the siren, she bashed it with a lamp. Tate stood up and looked around the house. It was covered with pictures of Claudia and her various awards. She had a shrine to herself.

Tate hurried from room to room until she found the downstairs office. She opened her oversized purse and grabbed anything that looked important, including Claudia's laptop. Tate went upstairs and into the bedroom as the alarm company called the house. She opened the nightstand, found a notebook, and stuffed it into her purse. Sirens could be heard in the distance, so Tate stuffed jewelry and anything small and valuable into her bag as well, tossing everything in her path to the ground. It was shocking how little time was needed to ransack a house.

With a smile, Tate grabbed one of the awards and threw it into the flat screen with a satisfying *crash*. Tate was out the back door and slipping through the narrow driveways before the police even showed up. She stepped onto the sidewalk two blocks over and slowly walked toward her car as adrenaline raced through her system. She'd never done anything like that before in her life. As she got into her car, her clear latex-glove-covered hands were shaking.

She drove toward Claudia's house, tossing the stolen jewelry into an open trashcan before she parked in a neighbor's driveway with a *For Sale* sign

in the yard. Police were swarming the house and the neighbors who were home all huddled together. Tate slipped off her gloves and strode over to the neighbors.

"What happened?" Tate asked as she joined the small cluster of women.

"Robbery," one of them said, eyeing Tate.

Tate gasped. "Well, I'm calling my realtor right now, excuse me." Tate held the phone to her ear as she took a small step away. "Hi. I'm at the house on Lancaster. The house across the street was just robbed. Don't even bother setting up a showing. Okay, thanks."

"You were looking to buy Sue's house?" a lady who looked as if she'd just returned from the local tennis club asked as soon as Tate put her phone away.

"I was. Not anymore. I'm not moving into a dangerous neighborhood."

The women shook their heads. "This is the first robbery. It's a great neighborhood, really. It's just that, you know, there's always one neighbor." The woman with the cat-patterned leggings laughed.

"Oh, what does the owner do? Is he into drugs? Could this be a drug deal gone wrong?" Tate gasped.

"Well, I'm not one to spread gossip," the tennis player said as she lowered her voice, "but that house is owned by Claudia Hughes, the reporter. I've seen men over there at all hours of the night."

Cat Leggings nodded. "There's this one flashy guy who was there yesterday. They got into a huge

fight. It was so loud it scared my cats."

The silent mom of the sleeping baby in the stroller finally joined in. "He had to be a dealer. Who drives a flashy car like that in DC? We're all black limos and sedans. And I don't wish bad things to happen to people, but I love karma right now."

"That bad, huh?" Tate asked in a conspiratorially tone.

"She's a power-hungry slut." The mom seethed.

"You have to explain why or you just sound bitter," Cat Leggings said gently.

New Mom took a deep breath. "Sorry. See, my soon-to-be ex-husband works at the White House. He's on the Secret Service's presidential detail. As soon as Claudia found out, she was on him like—" New Mom closed her eyes and did several cleansing breaths. "Well, six weeks ago I went into labor at one in the morning. I couldn't get hold of Peter so I figured President Stratton had a late night. I called Irene"—Cat Leggings nodded, so she must be Irene—"to take me to the hospital. I came downstairs and went out the front door after leaving a note for Peter inside. I had just locked my door when I heard someone laugh. I turned around and looked across the street to find Peter coming out of that woman's house tucking in his shirt as she was draped all over him. He kissed her, and his hands disappeared under her nighty. I would have yelled his name, but my water broke right then. Irene here saw the whole thing and got me bundled into the car as she rained down curses on them both."

"It was horrible. No respect," Irene said, shaking

her head.

"Oh, my gosh, I am so sorry. She's horrible! Why would she want your husband when it sounds as if she has men over here all the time?" Tate asked as she looked down at the newborn sound asleep in the stroller. Her heart broke for the poor woman and child.

"Well, Peter used to tell me things about his job. I know he's not supposed to, but he did. And then the next night, I was in the hospital watching television as I recovered from giving birth, and Claudia was doing a story on exactly what Peter had told me was confidential — word for word. It was the story about how upset First Lady Mitchell was about President Stratton ruining her husband's legacy. Well, Peter had been on duty when Mrs. Mitchell had told President Stratton he wasn't to change a thing in the White House, including personnel. But now it doesn't matter. She can get all the stories from him she wants. I filed for divorce a week later. He didn't even fight me on it. Sometimes I still see him over there." New Mom teared up and Tate wanted to give her a hug.

"See, the neighborhood is perfectly safe," Irene said as she and Tennis Player wrapped their arms around New Mom. "It's just one bad apple. We'd love to have you here. I hope you'll still consider looking at the house."

Tate smiled at them sincerely. "Thank you for telling me this. It does make me feel better about the neighborhood."

A loud engine sounded in the quiet street as a

bright yellow luxury sports car roared around the corner.

"Here's man number two," Irene said with a roll of her eyes.

The car slid to a stop behind a police cruiser. The door opened, and Tate felt her eyes go wide behind the dark sunglasses. Fitz slid out of the car and stood to get a look around.

"He's the man Claudia got in a fight with?" Tate asked as she turned to look at the baby when Fitz looked their direction.

"He's the one. Claudia had her windows opened when we were on our walk. They were arguing about some interview she was doing. She was screaming that she was tired of doing what she was told and wanted to ask her own questions. She was the *talent* after all," Tennis Player said, nodding to New Mom.

"She said she wanted more since she was giving up her own stories," New Mom said with a roll of her eyes.

Irene nodded. "I live next door and also had my windows open. The man slammed his hand on something so hard the sound caused my poor babies to leap away from the window."

Tate watched silently as the women talked about Claudia and speculated who the man was. Fitz was stopped at the door to the house. He talked with the officers for a moment and then walked back to his car. He sent a message on his phone before driving away.

"Well, thank you so much for talking to me

today. It's always nice to know you have good neighbors looking out for you." Tate smiled at them and headed to her car.

"Alex?" Tate asked as the phone was picked up. "Did Claudia just receive a text?"

"Dude, are you like, psychic?" Alex asked as Tate put him on speaker and headed back to the White House to do more research.

"What did it say?"

"It was sent from the number that sent information about shooting at The Knox. It said that her jewelry and other small electronics had been stolen. How —?" Alex asked before Tate stopped him.

"I know who that unknown number is. It's Fitz Houlihan," Tate said, smiling. Pieces were clicking together for her. She just had a couple more things to look into.

"Her agent? Why would he go through such trouble to have a secure line that's untraceable?" Alex wondered.

"That is a good question, isn't it?"

Valeria took a deep breath as she walked into the lobby of SA Tech. An elegant young lady smiled up at her. "Good afternoon. I'm Coco, may I help you?"

"Yes, I need to see Sebastian Abel."

The woman looked at her as if she were the stupidest person on Earth. "Mr. Abel doesn't see anyone without an appointment. I'm sorry."

Valeria smiled back and her lips quirked as the girl flinched back. "He'll see me. Show him my picture." Valeria turned to the nearest security camera and flicked it off.

"I don't care who you are, you don't show up here without an appointment," the woman who would haunt Valeria's dreams as a strict librarian said the second the elevator doors opened to Sebastian's private floor.

"Will you show me how to do that?" Valeria asked, walking right by her.

"What?"

"How you've perfected that resting bitch face. I'm in awe, truly. You have a gift." Valeria thought she heard a chuckle behind her, but when she looked around the woman had a look that could make Satan apologize. "God, you're good." Valeria winked and opened the doors to the office.

"It's okay, Judith," Sebastian said coolly from behind his massive desk. He waited for the door to close before speaking to Val.

"Well, this is a surprise. What can I do for you, former DEA Agent McGregor?"

"Aw, I feel special. You've looked into me." Val took a seat on the leather chair across from Sebastian.

"You're a special woman." Valeria felt Sebastian's eyes travel over her body.

"You know what turns me on?" Valeria asked seductively as she leaned forward, allowing him a good look at her cleavage.

"I'm all ears," Sebastian said, his voice a low rumble that Valeria had to admit was sexy.

"Private jets. I need one in the next hour."

"Where are we going?" Sebastian asked.

"*We* aren't going anywhere. I need to make a quick trip to L.A. I'm sure your pilot will tell you anyway when he learns of our flight." Valeria sat back and grinned at him. She liked powerful men. She liked toying with them — seeing what it was about them that made them tick. It was why she was so good at finding and then taking down drug cartels. She didn't bother with the bottom feeders. She went straight for the top.

Sebastian kept his dark gray eyes on her as if searching for an answer. Finally he blinked, and his face relaxed. "As it happens, I am on my way to L.A. this afternoon." Before Valeria could protest, Sebastian pressed the intercom. "Judith, have my jet ready to leave for L.A. in one hour."

"Aw, you're anxious for my company. I'm flattered." Valeria tried to get a read on Sebastian. She didn't fight it because so far everything was going according to her plan. She wanted Sebastian on that plane with her because his name kept coming up in her digging, and she wanted to find out why.

★　★　★

Tate pulled up Tinselgossip.com and found the email for tips. It only took twenty minutes for the nontraceable phone Alex had gotten her to ring.

"Hello, Jane? This is Brent Eller."

Tate smiled to herself as she moved to close her office door. "Oh, my god! *The* Brent Eller?" Tate squealed.

The man chuckled. "Sure is. We received your tip on Fitz Houlihan. You know, he's a very powerful man. If we are to run a story, then we need more than just your tip that he's sleeping with a client. Shit, this is Hollywood, everyone sleeps with everyone."

"And yet you, *the* Brent Eller, are calling me," Tate said, pitching her voice higher and talking quickly.

"Yes, because it's a story we haven't had before. I may run a gossip site, but I still believe in printing the truth," Brent told her seriously.

"Then I'll make you a deal, Mr. Eller. I'll get you stories, with proof, and you get me every rumor and fact you have on a couple of people." Tate held her breath.

"Okay. Show me what you've got. If it's good, I'll get you what you want." Tate silently pumped her fist in the air as she reined in her excitement. "Let me give you my private email to send the story to."

Tate wrote down the email and took a breath. "I'll send it to you sometime in the next couple of days. In the meantime, I want you to start gathering every tip, rumor, photo, and article on Claudia Hughes, Kerra Ruby, and Fitz Houlihan. You'll be getting this information anyway on what I'll be sending you. And I want your agreement that if our

arrangement works for you, I'll continue to feed you information if you help me in return."

The line was quiet, and Tate worried she'd pushed it too far too fast. "I would ask who you are, but I have a feeling, since I already ran a trace on your number and got the result that no such number exists, that you won't tell me. I do know you're not some airhead who wants to be the next big Hollywood star like so many of these little party girls who try to sell me stories about the celebrities they sleep with. Want to give me any hints?"

"Sorry, Brent. But I believe we'll be great partners in exposing the truth. That is, if you think you can handle it," Tate challenged.

"Of course, I can handle it. I've reported the worst of the worst that Hollywood has been responsible for. I think I can handle some little story on Mr. Hot Shot Agent. Or is there more?" Brent asked, all his attention on Tate.

Tate laughed. "There's so much more. You have my number. Don't give it to anyone, or I'll be forced to cut off the flow of information to you. I'll be in touch."

Tate hung up, and with shaking hands, sat back in her chair. One contact made, one more to go. She blew out a deep breath, shook her hands out, and got to work sending the email to Flint Scott. One Pulitzer journalist, one fired television reporter, and one gossip reporter were about to take on the international media, and only one of them knew this war was about to be waged.

CHAPTER TEN

S lowly the White House began to empty out. The cleaning crew made its way through the offices, but Tate continued to work. She'd thrown herself under the bus, but it would be worth it. She waited for the shit to hit the fan. It didn't take long. At ten at night, she heard footsteps racing down the hall toward her office.

"Tate!" Humphrey panted. "Birch needs you now. I'm so sorry." Humphrey waved his hand to hurry her along.

Tate didn't ask questions about why the president needed to see her. She knew. "Welcome back, Humphrey. How was your trip?" she asked as they walked down the long hallway in the empty residence toward the informal living room where Birch liked to relax.

"Good. Brock will be here tomorrow," Humphrey said absently as he hurried along the hall.

"Fourth of July. Seems like a good time," Tate said, trying to ease the tension practically coming off Humphrey in waves.

Tate saw Birch pacing through the door. Here went nothing. This move would either save them or

get her fired. It was a fifty-fifty shot, so she'd rolled the dice and gone with it.

"Jesus, Tate. I don't know how they found this. I'm so sorry. You'd better have a seat," Birch said, taking her hand.

Tate took a seat on the couch as Birch un-paused the television. Claudia was gleefully looking into the camera. "This is not suitable for small children so I'll give you a minute to get them out of the room. President Stratton fired President Mitchell's accomplished press secretary and replaced him with former reporter Tate Carlisle. It's known that Miss Carlisle was fired from BBN, and while we don't know the reason, we can guess that this might have something to do with it."

The screen went to an old grainy photo, and Tate saw herself nude from the back straddling a man in a lounge chair. She had been at a private villa on a private beach in the Caribbean, but still someone had caught a picture of her making love to Fitz. Although, she obscured Fitz's face with her bare back, she knew who it was and soon everyone else would, too. In all honesty, it wasn't much to go on. Her face was identifiable, but the beach towel around her waist prevented anything from being seen. And since the photo was shot with a super-long lens from what looked to be a boat, the photo was also blurry. Tate was only seen from the back, so while it was bad, it could have been worse.

Tate looked back and realized Humphrey had left and closed the door behind him. Birch stood nervously by her, looking down to gauge her

reaction. "I'm so sorry, Tate, but you'll have to address it. I don't know how they got it." Birch ran his hand through his perfect politician hair, which only made him sexier. His tie was off and the top buttons on his shirt were open as he began to pace.

"I'm not fired?" Tate asked with surprise.

"Why? Because someone illegally took a photo of you in an intimate—" Birch's face got red as he let out a loud exhale. He appeared to be struggling with the next words.

"Because someone took a photo of me having sex," Tate finished for him. "Then, if you're not going to fire me, I'd better tell you the whole truth."

Tate paused as Claudia continued talking about the photo after reading off Tate's résumé. "What gets me is this woman is in on every major decision the president makes. Can we trust her to make good decisions for this country when she can't even make good ones regarding her personal life? Remember to tune in on Monday night to see my exclusive interview with the *single* President Stratton, and you can bet I'll be asking him if this photo played any role in the hiring of Tate Carlisle. Speaking of President Stratton, the economy continues to struggle as foreign investors have begun to pull out of the market."

Birch turned the television off. "What do you mean, the truth? Is that not you?"

Tate shook her head. "No, that's me. Only I know how they got it."

"How?" Birch asked as Tate pulled out her cell phone. Birch moved closer to see what she was

pulling up on the screen. She felt the couch cushion dip as he sat down to look at the photo she held up. "That's the photo, but it's on Tinselgossip.com. So—"

Birch shrugged "—Claudia pulled it from a gossip site."

Tate pulled up her photos. "And Brent Eller got it from me." Tate showed Birch the image that was now splashed all over the news.

"Why would you do that?" Birch asked in horror as he looked away from the image to Tate's face.

"Because I also have this," Tate swiped to the image of a paused video and pressed Play.

Sounds of sex seemed to echo around the room as Claudia and Fitz were clearly seen on a bed together. Claudia was on all fours as Fitz thrust into her from behind. "You'll take me as your client as soon as that bitch gets fired from BBN, won't you, Fitz?"

Fitz grunted but didn't answer.

Claudia twisted her hips and fell onto the bed, leaving Fitz flapping in the wind. "Won't you, Fitz?"

"BBN is about to offer Tate a new deal," Fitz said unhappily. "I'm just too good," he shrugged. "Now, get back up here."

Claudia slammed her hand into the mattress. "No! You don't get to finish until you promise that if I can get her fired, you'll become my agent. I want my own show. No more co-anchoring. And I want international syndication."

"If you can get her fired, then I'm all yours," Fitz said smugly.

Claudia smiled and rolled back to Fitz as the tape continued.

"Where did you get this?" Birch asked, looking slightly uncomfortable to be sitting so close to Tate while watching a sex tape.

"Claudia's tablet. She recorded many of her and Fitz's liaisons. And he's not the only one." Tate pulled up a still of one of the other recordings. From watching them, it was clear that, one, the men didn't know they were being recorded, and two, Claudia enjoyed the power trip she had over getting the men to agree by withholding sex. The men went blindly into the slaughter, dick first.

"Wait a second," Birch leaned forward to get a better look at the photo Tate had pulled up. "That's Peter. He's one of my Secret Service agents."

Tate nodded. "I met his wife today. Soon–to–be ex-wife. She didn't know who I was, but she told me Peter likes to engage in pillow talk about his work. She said as soon as Claudia found out what Peter did for a living, she was all over him. He's your leak."

"At best, he's unknowingly feeding information to *Mollia Domini*. Claudia's like a black widow spider, isn't she? She lures men into her bed and then kills them — professionally, that is. So, the first guy was your agent, and I'm guessing something else, too. Are you sure you're okay with having that out there?"

Tate looked up and saw concern in Birch's eyes. "It's for a greater cause. Claudia will come after me in her interview with you. And I'm sure she'll try to

lure you into her web as well. But while she's doing that, this video of her and Fitz will be exposed at Tinselgossip.com. Plus, Flint Scott will be running a piece on Claudia's unethical use of her position as a reporter to push her own agenda. Claudia will be on air and have no idea what hit her. The backlash will be epic from both the station and the public. It will help curb the public's opinion of you, too. *Mollia Domini* has just been caught in a massive manipulation.

"This is a huge hit to their organization since it depends on influencing the public into accepting their agenda. *Mollia Domini* wants to blame you for all of the failures in the world.

"When they get ready to revolt, *Mollia Domini* will come in to save them. The people will believe *Mollia Domini* will help give the public what it needs, not President Stratton. People will become dependent on *Mollia Domini* for everything. But as we know, *Mollia Domini* won't stop there. They'll take that power when the people give up their rights in exchange for rescue, and *Mollia Domini* will then be unstoppable. However, to do this, they need the media to push their agenda now. They need the media to manipulate public opinion of you and instill fear, which is nothing but a poison to the public," Tate said passionately.

"But, now their main conduit has been caught manipulating the system. People aren't stupid. They'll see it, now that their eyes have been opened to it. And they'll start to fight back with the simple action of questioning the news as it's presented.

Questions that *Mollia Domini* doesn't want asked,"
Birch said with understanding.

"And *Mollia Domini* will be forced off their
current plan, and that's when they'll make a
mistake. We need to find out who's up the ladder
from her in the organization," Tate said.

"I say we do that through old-fashioned
surveillance. I'm hoping Lizzy and Valeria can take
over at that point. I believe Claudia will head
straight to her handler," Birch said, standing up as
he began to pace again. Tate could see his mind
working out the problem.

Birch looked at the woman he was now standing
before. It bothered him to know she had spread that
picture of herself to the gossip site. Tate was putting
herself, her feelings, and her reputation on the line
to corner *Mollia Domini*. He'd be damned if she
hadn't done it. Now it was up to him to protect her
from the fallout.

"Stay here. With me."

Tate looked up at him, her violet eyes blinking
in confusion. "I am. I'm sleeping in my office
tonight."

"No," Birch said, shaking his head. "Stay here.
With me. Tomorrow celebrate the Fourth of July
with me. We'll stand together, knowing that, come
Monday, we have a chance at stopping this
organization once and for all. And I want you by my
side when we do."

Birch felt his heart pound. He hadn't felt like
this since his wife died. He missed her, yes, but as

the years went by, he found himself longing for a partner again. Someone for him to love and someone to love him in return. Someone who didn't care that he was a powerful member of Congress and now the most powerful man in the world. Someone who only cared about him for the man he was, not the power he wielded. He'd known Tate was that woman from the second she had walked into his office. He'd tried to keep it professional, but he found himself thinking about her more than he should. And now he was consumed with the need to keep her safe.

"I don't understand," Tate said slowly. Birch blinked. *Like his wife*. Dammit. Was he doing this because he couldn't save his wife when he was overseas in the Army or was it because he did have feelings for Tate?

Birch wanted to punch himself. He felt like an unsure teenager and that bothered him more than not knowing if what he felt for Tate was real. "You're staying here tonight. Go get your things."

"Okay," Tate said softly as she got up. "Did I do something wrong?"

"No, I did. Now go get your things. We need to discuss your statement to the press over this photo. Our next actions must be choreographed perfectly in order for this to work." Birch watched as Tate stood and took a deep breath.

"Of course. I'll be right back."

Tate left the room, and Birch finally relaxed. What an idiot he was. He might possibly be confusing his feelings for Tate with his late wife, but

that didn't mean he didn't want to see her safe. And having her under his roof would be a good way for Birch to figure out just what the hell he was feeling. He certainly knew how he felt when he saw that picture of Tate with another man — jealous. And that certainly wasn't a feeling he would have if his emotions weren't somehow engaged.

CHAPTER ELEVEN

Valeria sat back in the leather seat as she flew somewhere over Arizona. Sebastian Abel took the bottle of wine from the flight attendant and dismissed her to some hidden area on the private jet. Valeria watched as he poured two glasses of wine she was sure cost more than she made in a month.

So far Sebastian has been subtly trying to throw her off guard. He's asked questions that went from safe getting-to-know-you questions to immensely private ones. Valeria didn't mind. If Sebastian thought he could rattle her, he was wrong. Valeria had dealt with the worst of the worst drug lords. While she saw many similarities in Sebastian, he didn't have their survival instincts that made their actions cold-blooded. Right now, she could see Sebastian trying to throw her off as he prodded her for information on the shadow group. Who they were after, what leads they had, and wanting to hear about each member of the group.

Sebastian turned from pouring the wine with a seductive smile on his face. He stepped across the plane and took a seat next to her. His muscled leg pressed firmly against her thigh as he leaned in to hand her the wine.

"Here. It's the finest white wine in the world. Only the best for such an intriguing woman," Sebastian said, laying it on thick.

Valeria took a sip. "Mmm, tastes just like my favorite wine I have at home."

Sebastian's eyebrows rose. "Really? What kind?"

Valeria took another sip of the most amazing wine she'd ever tasted. "Oh, I don't remember the name of it. It comes in this pretty box that fits perfectly in the refrigerator."

Sebastian choked on his wine, and Valeria hid her smile behind her glass.

"So," Sebastian said, clearing his throat, "when we get to L.A., where do you want me to drop you off? Of course, you can stay with me." Sebastian let his hand fall to her thigh as his thumb softly rubbed a patch of her bare leg.

"Sorry, you're not my type."

"Somehow I doubt that."

"You're not enough of a badass for me. You're a little too—" Valeria's fingers wiggled as she waved at his expensive suit and clean shave "—neat. And boring."

Sebastian leaned closer and placed a kiss on the soft spot below her ear. "Trust me, I can be your worst nightmare."

"Really?" Valeria asked, tilting her head to allow Sebastian access. "How? Let's see, Bertie Geofferies is your rival, right? What have you done to Geofferies to give him nightmares?

Valeria closed her eyes as Sebastian's hot lips

trailed slowly down the curve of her neck. Damn, he was good.

"I don't need to do anything to Bertie. Everyone around him does it for him. I pay Trip to tell me what Bertie's wife tells him during sex. His own employees come to me when I announce a job opening. And I always beat him to market with new products," Sebastian said between kisses that even Valeria had to admit where causing her eyes to cross.

"Right. But sorry, corporate espionage, poaching employees, and probably some patent trolling is still pretty boring. Talk to me after you've gone skydiving, lived through a shootout, and kept your cool undercover across from a man known for skinning people alive who cross him. Then I'll let your lips travel further down my neck. And as for being bad, your white-collar crimes are nothing compared to someone like Manuel Hernandez, even if you two look similar."

Sebastian pulled away enough to look into her face. "You're comparing me with the head of the *Hermanos de Sangre* drug cartel when I've never admitted to actually committing a crime?"

"Interesting that you know who he is. Manuel likes to keep a low profile," Valeria said as she felt the plane begin its descent into L.A.

"Of course, I know who he is. And he's nothing like me. He's a good five inches shorter than I am," Sebastian sat back and downed his wine as Valeria sipped hers thoughtfully.

How did Sebastian know about Manuel — the

drug lord, who it turned out, owned the bank in Mexico where the money to Phylicia Claymore originated? The drug lord who Valeria had proof was paying off DEA agents, including her former boss, and the reason for her termination at the DEA. And the same drug lord whose name, or whose bank, kept showing up in in various people's bank records, like Senator Epps, President Mitchell, Sandra Cummings, and even Sebastian Abel.

It had been an accident finding one of SA Tech's account numbers in a wire transfer from the bank in Sinaloa, Mexico, owned by Manuel Hernandez. That was why Valeria wanted Sebastian on the plane with her. She needed to know if Sebastian was with them or against them.

"Hang out with him regularly?" Valeria asked sarcastically.

"Anyone who does business in Mexico has to deal with Manuel. He has his hand in more American pockets than the IRS." Valeria watched Sebastian regain his composure. His sexy smile slid back into place as the plane landed. The door opened and Sebastian held out his hand to her.

Valeria stood up, but Sebastian pulled her close. "Now, where can I take you? Or should we go back to my place?"

Valeria stepped closer and wove her fingers through his hair. Sebastian grinned, and Valeria yanked his head to hers. She kissed him hard, fast, and with lots of tongue. She was halfway down the steps before Sebastian realized what had hit him.

"Thanks for the lift!" she yelled with a wave of

her hand as she got into the car she had ordered. She looked through the window and saw Sebastian outlined by the plane's door watching as she left. She'd told him he wasn't her type, and he wasn't. Especially if he was in league with Manuel Hernandez. Now she just needed to prove Manuel Hernandez was helping fund members of *Mollia Domini*. And for that, Valeria was going to disappear for a while. If she got caught . . . well, if she got caught then no one would ever hear from her again. Manuel would guarantee it.

Lizzy waited quietly in the dark parking lot of the abandoned warehouse outside of DC. It was close to eleven when two headlights pierced the night air. Even though there was little chance of this being anyone other than Humphrey, Lizzy didn't take a chance. She turned off the safety on her gun and held it in her lap. Just in case.

The car stopped next to her, and the window rolled down, exposing the bald little man in round wire-rimmed glasses. "Hi, Humphrey. What's cooking at the White House?"

"You haven't seen it? Oh dear, it's not good. I thought Birch was going to kill someone," Humphrey said as he wrung the steering wheel nervously.

"Seen what?" Lizzy asked, wishing Humphrey would get to the point.

"Oh dear. Poor Tate."

"Humphrey!"

The man jumped in his seat. "Right. Tinselgossip.com. There's this—" Humphrey turned red. "You should just look."

Lizzy pulled out her phone and logged onto the gossip site. "Holy shit, that's goody-two-shoes Tate Carlisle? You go, girl." Then it hit her. "Oh no," Lizzy groaned.

"What?" Humphrey asked with concern all over his face.

"Birch likes Tate, doesn't he?"

"I think it's wonderful. Birch needs something good in his life," Humphrey blustered as he puffed himself up as if ready to fight for Birch and Tate.

"But it compromises the mission by putting every decision Birch makes into question."

"How is it any different from you and Dalton?" Humphrey asked, suddenly sounding every inch the schoolteacher he had been.

"I don't love Dalton. We just have sex," Lizzy defended.

"And if you think that, then you're even more naïve than Tate." Humphrey turned from an open-mouthed Lizzy before turning back with a large briefcase. He angled it through the window. "Here are all the folders from the meeting today. Names are on stickers on the outside of each folder. Let me know what you hear. Tomorrow is the Fourth of July celebration, and Monday is Birch's interview with Claudia. The more we know by then, the better."

Lizzy thought about what Humphrey said all the way back to the bar. Valeria and Dalton were working tonight, so she and Alex could work on the folders. It was going to be hard enough to find the right partial print without her mind thinking about love and Dalton in the same sentence. But what was there really to think about? Humphrey had called her out, and he had been right. She loved him. Now that was done, and she was going to get back to work. Lizzy didn't have time to love someone who would be leaving as soon as this assignment was over. And it was going so well as it was. She wasn't going to rock the boat by bringing up the L word. Unlike the president, she knew how to put her personal feelings aside for the benefit of the mission.

Lizzy parked behind the bar. When she opened the back door, the noise was deafening. It was a large crowd that night since many were off work for the holiday. Lizzy put the folders in an old vodka crate in the storage room and headed to see how Valeria and Dalton were doing.

Instead of finding them behind the bar, she found Dalton, Buzz, and Snip behind the bar and Alex delivering drinks as fast as he could. What the hell was going on?

"Dude!" Alex said with panic in his eyes and sweat dripping from his brow as he rushed past her to deliver a round of shots to a table.

Lizzy hurried to the bar. "Where's Valeria?"

Dalton didn't have to stop to talk. "Never showed," he called out over his shoulder as he poured more drinks. "We've tried calling but her

phone's off. Luckily Buzz and Snip are helping in exchange for free drinks."

Lizzy smiled at the old men. "Thank you. Go sit down. I'll get you a beer."

"Thank goodness. I mean, I know I have new hips, but geez Louise, it's a doozie of a night," Buzz said, patting her hand as he and Snip shuffled past her to take their seats.

"Alex," Lizzy called over. "Find her. It's not like her to drop off the map like this."

"But—" Alex looked frantically around the packed bar.

"But nothing. Our team comes first. Dalton and I can handle this."

Lizzy watched Alex head for the clean room and she felt her stomach knot. Something was seriously wrong.

CHAPTER TWELVE

Tate stared up at the canopy of her bed in the Queen's Bedroom. It was too overwhelming to stay in such a historic room as the Lincoln Bedroom so she was happy when Birch agreed she could stay in this feminine room. However, it wasn't history or even the beauty of the room keeping her awake. It was Birch. When she first started working with him, she couldn't stop thinking of him as the president. But now she couldn't stop thinking of him as a man—a man who had ordered her to spend the night with him. Sure, not in the same room, but a part of her wished it was. Okay, a large part of her wished it.

Tate reached for her tablet to study her apology speech again, but decided against it. She didn't want it to seem rehearsed when she gave it tomorrow morning. Letting out a frustrated breath, Tate shoved the covers off and quietly opened her door. Whenever she was anxious, she turned to food. It wasn't a good habit, but it didn't mean it was going to stop her from raiding the private kitchen across the hall from Birch's room.

Tate padded barefoot down the carpeted hall. She tiptoed toward the kitchen so as to not wake

Birch and then froze when she pushed open the door. The light from the refrigerator highlighted Birch's bare back as he stood reaching for something inside. Tate thought about sneaking quietly out, but the muscles rippled down his back as he moved. Before she knew it, he was turning toward her.

Birch couldn't get back to sleep. Thoughts of Tate had plagued his mind every time he closed his eyes. He saw her with that prick, Fitz, when what he really wanted was Tate straddling him. He wanted to see her toss her head back in pleasure as she moved upon him. It was a mixture of jealousy, desire, and guilt that kept him up.

He had had a moment earlier to find out if Tate felt the connection that he did, but he'd blown it. Instead he'd thought about his wife. From that time on, Birch had thought about nothing else. He'd looked at a picture of his wife as the guilt almost drowned him. But as he was drowning, a life ring had been tossed to him from the last place he'd expected — his wife.

As the guilt swamped him, the image of his wife appeared behind his closed eyes. They were laughing as they hiked the trails by their home shortly before he was deployed. They stopped at an overlook and gazed at the vast mountains dotted with a few patches of reds, oranges, and yellows as the first days of autumn made themselves known. Birch felt the pressure on his heart as he saw his wife turn to him and smile. He remembered that day so clearly. "The beauty makes my heart sing for it

inspires love. There's room in our hearts to love many, isn't there?" her figure said to him, her hand reaching for his face as she slowly disappeared. Birch had awoken with a start and now couldn't get back to sleep.

He headed to the kitchen even when his heart had wanted to lead him down the hall and into Tate's bed. He trailed his hand over the marble island and headed for the refrigerator by the small window overlooking the darkened lawns. He had just opened the door when he heard the small sound of surprise from behind him. His body was at full attention at the one soft sound Tate made. Everything in him screamed out to take hold of something good in the world and never let go.

Instead of running to her, Birch turned slowly around. Tate stood there in a fitted V-neck jersey for her hometown Georgia Vultures football team. The V-neck drew his attention to her breasts, but the short jersey danced around the upper part of her thighs. As she took a few slow steps into the kitchen, Birch's eyes moved lower, taking in her shapely legs.

"Couldn't sleep either?" Birch asked as he let the refrigerator door close behind him. He stepped over to the island and gripped the cold marble to keep from reaching for her.

"No, I couldn't." Tate stepped up to the other side of the island and paused.

Looking across the island, Birch saw her breasts rising and falling as her breathing increased. "Why couldn't you sleep, Tate?" Birch asked, his voice

deepening at the same time it softened.

"I was thinking of you. Birch, are you mad at me?" Tate asked, bringing her eyes to his.

"No, I'm mad at myself," Birch said, taking a step around the corner of the island. "I'm mad that I can't stop thinking of that picture." Her head dropped in shame as he took another step toward her.

"I know. You should see the things these people who don't even know me are writing on the Internet. I knew it would be bad. I was prepared for it, but the names they are calling me . . ."

Birch stopped next to her and placed his hands on her shoulders. "Tate, look at me." When she looked up, she didn't have tears in her eyes as he thought she might. She had determination and a look that didn't sit well with Birch — resignation.

"You don't deserve the things people say on social media. Turn it off. It doesn't matter. What matters is the person standing in front of you, not someone hiding behind a computer screen. I'm what matters, and I'm not mad because you're in the photo or that you released it. I'm mad because I'm not the man in the photo with you."

Tate was about to argue that she really wasn't a slut like everyone on the Internet was calling her when Birch's words replayed in her mind. "You're mad that I'm with Fitz?"

Birch nodded, and she felt his warm hands tighten on her shoulders, bringing her a step closer to him. The tips of her breasts brushed his bare chest

as she dragged her eyes up to his. "I'm mad because I want to be the one you share your bed with. I want my name on your lips as you cry out in pleasure. I want to be the man with you, Tate."

"But—" Tate thought of him being the president, which was more of a strike against him than for him. She thought of all the times in the meetings he had sat by her. How he had always asked for her opinion. How he worried about her safety. How he seemed to see the real her, not the televised façade she put on during conferences, but the woman who was still finding her place in their group. And as she thought about the support he'd given her and the encouragement to have confidence in her position in the group, Tate knew the feelings she felt had been returned all along.

"Tate?" Birch asked softly, and Tate realized her unseeing gaze had dropped to his chest. She looked back up, his face now filled with uncertainty, and Tate knew she'd do anything to remove that uncertainty forever.

Tate lifted her hands and tentatively put them on his chest. She felt the heat from his body and felt the beating of his heart as she rose up on her toes and tilted her head back. Words were so overrated at times like this, and talking was the last thing Tate wanted to do. Instead, she pressed her body against his and took his lips in hers.

Birch dropped his hands from her shoulders and wrapped them around her back. He lifted her from the floor as he held her tight against him. Their tongues met and did all the talking that needed to be

done. Tate felt her body catch fire. Her blood pulsed with need as Birch moved his hands to her ass, lifting her so her legs wrapped around his waist.

Tate moaned into his mouth as she felt the heat of his erection through his shorts. Her body instinctively ground against him in response. Birch turned, holding her against him before setting her on the edge of the island so he could reach for her shirt. His hands trailed up her stomach, and his thumbs brushed the underside of her breasts as his hips moved against her.

"Tate," Birch gasped as he moved his hands to the bottom of her shirt. "Tell me to stop if you want me to. If not, know this is not just for tonight, but that I'm all in."

"Don't you dare stop. I don't know what this is between us, but I've felt it, too." Tate arched her back as he stripped the jersey from her and tossed it on the floor. Tate closed her eyes and threw her head back as Birch's hand cupped her breast and his tongue circled her other nipple. She felt his hand drop from her breast as his tongue continued to wreak havoc on the other.

Birch lightly trailed his fingers up her thigh. "Please," Tate panted.

His fingers slipped around her panties at the same time he sucked her nipple hard into his mouth. Tate cried out as she felt her body begin to tighten. "Now, Birch. I want you now!"

Birch had her in his arms as her body ached for him. His mouth was on hers as he carried her out of the kitchen and across the hall to his bedroom. He

kicked the door closed behind him, but Tate didn't hear it. He lowered her onto the bed, and as he reached for a condom, Tate slipped her panties off.

"Are you sure?" Birch asked one more time. "We can try to be traditional, go on a date or something."

Tate smiled up at him. "Our situation isn't exactly traditional, but my feelings for you are. So yes, I am sure."

Birch pushed his shorts down and rolled the condom on. Her body tightened and ached all at the same time in anticipation. The mattress dipped as Birch slid onto the bed next to her. "I'll always be here for you, Tate."

"I never thought you wouldn't. Birch?" Tate asked as he propped himself up on his elbows to look down at her.

"Yes?"

"I want you. Now, tomorrow, and when things get rough. And we both know they will. I won't run," Tate said, knowing that when this got out— and she was under no illusion that it wouldn't— things would become near impossible for them.

"I know. You're stronger than that," Birch said, running a hand down her side and stopping to cup her hip as his eyes stayed locked on hers.

Birch kissed her at the same time Tate's breath caught as he entered her in one smooth thrust. She grabbed his shoulders and hung on as the world shifted. When they cried out each other's names, Tate knew they had both changed forever tonight.

Whore. Press Suck-u-tary. Slut. Bitch. I'd fuck her. Disgrace.

Tate disabled the Internet connection to the computer in her office. She wouldn't let nameless morons who sat in judgment of others when their own lives were far from perfect ruin her day. This was her honeymoon period, the beginning of a relationship when everything was perfect. This is what she and Birch were experiencing, and that's what she wanted to focus on.

They had made love multiple times through the night and once again in the shower that morning. Locked in his room, there was no press or judgment, just the passion two people shared and the freshness of a relationship both knew was something more than a casual fling. But all of that ended when she reached her office and turned on her computer.

Emails told her she was going to hell. Faceless people called her names on social media. Jokes that weren't at all funny on talk shows questioned her morality and ability to do her job. As if having sex ever prevented someone from doing a job. But Tate couldn't respond. There were simply too many to battle, and she didn't want to give them the power to admit they were getting to her. Instead, she was going to make her statement in ten minutes.

Birch had wanted to be there, but Tate had refused to let him come. This was something she had to do alone. She had to show people she wasn't ashamed, and she could stand up for herself. She

released the picture and that gave her a certain power as well.

Tate applied her lip gloss and headed for the press briefing room. The entire White House staff looked nervous as she walked by them. It was as if she were heading for the gallows. Tate lifted her chin and looked them in the eyes as she passed.

As she came around the corner of the room, the sound of reporters talking stopped for a brief second before erupting into a barrage of questions.

"Are you having a sexual relationship with the president?"

"Did you hear the joke on *Late Night* about you being a slut?"

"Are you going to resign?"

"Are you and Fitz Houlihan still together?"

Tate grabbed the podium, and they quieted down. Her body shook, but she refused to show it. Her legs were barely holding her up. However, her voice was steady as she looked out at the packed room eagerly waiting for every scandalous detail.

"My name is Tate Carlisle. I believe many of you have forgotten that I am a human being based on the type of questions you are asking. I'm going to give a brief statement, and I'll answer respectful questions only. That picture was taken on a private beach while I was in long-term relationship with my former agent, Fitz Houlihan. We were blackmailed with the picture and paid off the person who had taken it two years ago. Apparently not all copies were destroyed, and I'm not surprised. Since the release of this image, which I am not ashamed of, I

have been called all sorts of vile names. Why? Simply because I had sex with someone I loved at the time? I'll make this simple. This invasion of my privacy changes nothing. I am still the press secretary, and I will do my job regardless of what salacious things are said about me. I am proud to serve this country, and I will be proud doing so for the rest of my time at the White House. Thank you. Questions?"

Hands shot up, people yelled, and Tate almost wobbled off her heels. For the next five minutes, she answered only the questions that had any journalistic value. Yes, the president supported her in her job. Yes, she believes there are problems with respecting people's right to privacy. The resort was in the Caribbean, and a fisherman took the photo. She was with Fitz for years until he broke up with her when she was fired from BBN. And yes, Fitz now represents Claudia Hughes. That timely question came from Flint Scott, who leaned against the wall with his man-bun and an old-fashioned notepad.

Flint raised his hand again, and Tate called on him immediately. "Brent Eller from Tinselgossip.com told me that an anonymous source sent the picture, and when he looked into Fitz Houlihan, the man identified in the photo, he discovered rumors that Ms. Hughes is now in a relationship with Mr. Houlihan. It also appears that their relationship started immediately after your firing — an unjust firing, my sources within BBN say — which was pushed for by Ms. Hughes." People

turned to look at the reporter from BBN as if he could respond for Claudia.

Tate suppressed the desire to pump her fist in the air. Bless Flint and his research. "Is there a question, Mr. Scott?"

Flint looked up from his notebook. "Yes, do you believe Ms. Hughes had you fired so she could enter a personal and professional relationship with Mr. Houlihan, who is commonly known to refuse to represent competing clients?"

Tate looked shocked. "No, I can't believe that. Claudia was a mentor to me at BBN and has been one of my role models through my journalistic career. No more questions, thank you."

Tate walked away from the podium praying she didn't shake out of her heels and fall on her face. That was easily one of the hardest things she ever had to do. She felt slightly guilty at manipulating the press just the way Claudia had been manipulating the people. But soon it would be over. Soon they'd have the advantage on *Mollia Domini* through the power of the truth. Whatever Tate had to go through to achieve that end, it would be worth it.

CHAPTER THIRTEEN

"Valeria is gone," Alex said as he rushed into the bar.

Lizzy turned off the television. Poor Tate. She handled herself beautifully, but now she would be useless to the group since the media would be focusing on her continually.

"What do you mean, gone?" Dalton asked from where his arm had been around Lizzy as they watched Tate's press conference.

"I mean she's gone gone. Like, not coming back. All her electronics have been shut off and were waiting at her apartment with a note. Here." Alex shoved a piece of paper at Lizzy.

If I make it back, I'll have answers. If not, then I failed. Don't come looking for me. It could jeopardize everything if you do.

"Great. Tate has basically become useless and Valeria is gone. Our team is falling apart," Lizzy sighed as Dalton hugged her.

"It'll be all right. You have me, and we did just fine on our own. I won't leave you. I promise."

Lizzy closed her eyes. How did he know that was what she was afraid of?

"Dude," Alex said, looking at his phone. "We might have lost Valeria, but we have a new Secret Service guy. Crew is picking him up now. The president wants us to meet in two hours."

"This morning? Before the Fourth of July celebration? We'll be seen," Lizzy worried.

"We're to meet in the tunnels. Humphrey will lead us to the meeting site," Alex said.

"At this rate, I'll never get the fingerprints done," Lizzy groaned.

"Come on, let's get ready. We'll need to leave well in advance with all the holiday traffic."

Lizzy let Dalton lead her back home. She couldn't help the feeling of despair, and she hated it. They needed a win badly, but today they'd suffered two blows. "Dalton, I want you to start surveillance on Epps as soon as our meeting is over. I'll get to work on the fingerprints. It's going to take a while to gather and log them all before running them against the partial we have. It's a real long shot," Lizzy worried.

"But we've done more with less. We have a plan, and we'll stick to it. I'm glad that this new guy is joining us today. The president and Tate will be under fire constantly now. Now, come here," Dalton said with a smirk as he closed the door to her house. "I know of a way to turn that frown upside down."

Lizzy laughed and then gasped as Dalton pushed up her skirt and knelt in front of her. Her hands speared his hair as his tongue—"Oh fuck," Lizzy groaned, tightening her grasp on Dalton's hair.

Dalton stood up and dragged her past a yipping Dave and upstairs. And by the time Lizzy and Dalton left for DC, she had a big smile on her lips.

★   ★   ★

"Crew Dixon?" Brock asked a man in a flight uniform who met him at Andrews Air Force Base.

"Brock Loyde?" the man asked in return.

"That's me."

"Then I'm your ride. We have a meeting soon. I'll take you straight there."

Brock followed the pilot to a pickup truck and tossed his bags in the back before getting in. "What can you tell me about this meeting?"

"You'll meet the group. I'm not really part of the day-to-day stuff. I just know about it and am on hand if needed."

"Elizabeth James is the leader, is that correct?" Brock asked. He had memorized everything Humphrey had told him.

"Yes, but her friends call her Lizzy," Crew told him before describing the rest of the team. "And then of course you know Valeria."

"How is she?" Brock would find out soon. He was nervous about seeing Val after all these years.

"Intense."

Brock chuckled. "She always has been. Can you tell me what you know about the mission so far?"

Crew nodded as he sped toward DC. "Humphrey said to bring you up to speed. Here's all I know."

Brock listened to some of what Humphrey had told him and some that Humphrey had not. As they entered DC, Crew maneuvered through traffic to a hotel near the White House.

"There are tunnels leading into the White House from The Knox. Humphrey will meet us and take us to some meeting room in the tunnels. The White House is too busy to meet there today," Crew explained.

"How is the president going to get away unseen?" Brock asked, thinking of the Secret Service that should be with him almost constantly.

"The tunnels lead to the residence, and he can order Secret Service to stay downstairs. He's cleared the floor of his staff for a private phone call. No one will bother him for about twenty minutes."

Brock got out of the truck when Crew did. They entered the hotel and used a biometric keypad hidden behind an old painting to gain entrance to the secret tunnels in the basement. Humphrey was already waiting for them. "Brock, good, good. Glad you're here. There have been a lot of developments. Hurry, the others are waiting."

Brock and Crew followed Humphrey's bald head through a series of tunnels. He finally stopped at a door and knocked. It was opened by a man with *military* written all over him. "You must be Dalton Cage."

"And you must be Brock Loyde. Welcome. This is Lizzy James, our team leader. And this is Tate Carlisle, our inside source at the White House. And lastly, this is Alex Santos, our tech man."

Brock looked from Lizzy to Tate to Alex. No president. And no Valeria. "Where's Val?"

Lizzy stepped forward. "She's disappeared. You know her better than we do. What do you think?"

Lizzy handed him a piece of paper and he instantly recognized Valeria's handwriting. He handed the paper back and felt the eyes of the entire team on him. "It's Val. She's always been the lone wolf type. Whatever she's doing, it's dangerous and she has a high chance of getting caught, which is why she has cut all ties with you. If she does get caught, then nothing will lead back to you."

Brock didn't like it, and clearly the rest of the group didn't either. "Has Crew filled you in?" Lizzy asked.

"Yes." Brock looked at Crew and saw him stiffen as Lizzy stood close to Dalton. Well, that sure complicated things.

The door opened and the president walked in. "Brock," he said, holding out his hand. "So glad you could make it. Call me Birch. Are we just waiting for Valeria?"

The president stepped over to Tate as she explained the situation. If he thought a relationship between Lizzy and Dalton with a jealous Crew thrown in was complicated, then a relationship between Tate and the president was a freaking nightmare. These things always had a way of coming out, no matter how tightly the Secret Service tried to protect the president.

By the looks Lizzy was giving the two, he wasn't the only one worried about the relationship. "What's

going on with you guys?" Lizzy asked brusquely.

"What's going on with you and Dalton?" Tate shot back.

"We're sleeping together, but we both know a relationship is impossible. You two on the other hand," Lizzy answered bluntly.

The way Tate turned red and the president stood ramrod straight as if he would physically defend Tate told everyone in the room exactly what the relationship was.

"Fucking great," Lizzy groaned.

"This changes nothing," Birch said.

"No, this changes everything. Your judgment already nearly cost us our cover because you sent us flying into the hotel over fears that Tate might be in danger. I hate to say this, but Valeria was right. Tate, you're our weak link. You're out," Lizzy said without a trace of remorse in her voice.

"You can't do that. I'm in charge here," Birch said, coming toe to toe with Lizzy.

"No, you aren't. I am. And Tate's already impaired your judgment, and that was before you slept with her. Now I can't trust your judgment. I can't risk this group being sent into another dangerous situation just to protect Tate."

"And you would leave Dalton if you had to."

"Yes," both Dalton and Lizzy said at the same time.

"But you don't even know what I've learned," Tate said, sounding more pissed off than Brock thought possible.

"And what have you learned?" Lizzy asked

with a sigh.

"I have a way to take Claudia out of use for *Mollia Domini*."

Lizzy's eyebrow rose. "And how do you know that?"

"There's video of her sleeping with Peter, Birch's head Secret Service agent, and then reporting on information he passed to her. So, Brock will replace Peter and Claudia will lose her inside source. Then you all know about the photo that was released today?" Everyone nodded. They'd all seen it. "I released it. I'm using Brent Eller and Flint Scott, anonymously of course, to put the information I want out to the public."

Lizzy shook her head. "Wait, why on earth would you bring so much scrutiny to yourself?"

"Because Alex didn't just get video of Claudia and Peter. He has footage of Claudia and Fitz that expressly says she got me fired in order for Fitz to represent her. What happens when Claudia asks the president about me after bashing me for days only to have Tinselgossip.com release video proving that Claudia is manipulating everything? Flint already asked me about it at the press conference," Tate said as she started pacing around the small room.

"And Claudia will be completely discredited, thus throwing everything she's reported on into question and leaving *Mollia Domini* without a face to push their propaganda. You did all this on your own?" Lizzy asked.

"Yes, and I know Claudia. The first thing she'll do is head right to her handler to complain about the

tables being turned on her."

"And we'll have a chance to nab the next in line who we can then question to finally find out who might be in the inner circle. If this person isn't in there already." Lizzy shook her head. "I'm sorry for not trusting you, Tate. That's great work. You're sacrificing yourself to take down two or more *Mollia Domini*. I'll back off you and Birch as long as your judgment is unclouded. You get Birch ready for that interview. I take it you have a detailed plan?"

"I do."

"Good. Dalton is on Epps. Brock, you need to take over for Peter, but there needs to be a reason. He can't know that we know he's the leak," Lizzy ordered.

"I'll take care of Peter," Humphrey said. "Yeah, I got it. Brock, be ready. It won't take long. Then walk right in through the employee entrance. And Alex, make sure Brock is the only name on the short list for the job who is available." Before Brock could say okay, Humphrey was scuttling out the door.

"And I'll start on the fingerprints," Lizzy said as the door closed behind Humphrey.

"What do you want me to do?" Crew asked.

"I want you with the president," Lizzy answered.

"I'm honoring military all day today. Crew can be my guest of honor. Just get into a dress uniform and that should do it," Birch told him.

"Got it. Where should I meet you?" Crew asked.

"Give me an hour and come to the gate. Your name will be on the list."

Crew took off and Dalton stepped forward. "Alex, I need a press pass or something that will get me into any area with Senator Epps."

"No problem, dude. Give me fifteen minutes. I just got to do this thing for the Hump man."

Brock rolled his eyes as the young man hurried from the room. "How many times was he going to say *dude*?"

"Every time he speaks," Lizzy answered.

"I didn't mean to say that out loud," Brock said, embarrassed at being caught.

"We all ask that question," Dalton told him as everyone nodded.

"I have to get back to the White House and add Crew into my speech. Tate will be with me all day," Birch told them.

"Tate, can I have a word?" Lizzy asked as she pulled Tate away. The room was small, and it was easy to hear Lizzy apologizing again. Brock was somewhat comforted in the fact that their team leader could own up to mistakes. Brock also saw her hand off a small gun to Tate. Now, that might not be the best idea.

Tate nodded and the women came back to the group. "A gun?" Birch asked just what Brock was thinking.

"Tate's not the best with hand-to-hand, but she's a good shot. Has an Olympic medal to prove it," Lizzy defended. "And if she's with you, then she won't have to go through a metal detector. It's just an added layer of protection because if *Mollia Domini* has any idea what we're up to, they'll have

no problem taking us out—especially Tate. The elevator attack, the house ransacking . . . they think she knows something. They just aren't sure of it, and that's the only thing keeping her alive right now."

CHAPTER FOURTEEN

Tate and Birch hurried back through the tunnels to the White House. Within minutes of hanging up the phone that had just been sitting on the president's desk in his private study, it rang again.

"Yes?" Birch asked. "He has? Is he all right? Okay, just let me know who my new lead agent is."

Tate waited for Birch to explain, but he just shook his head. "Well, what happened?"

"Apparently Humphrey somehow tripped Peter going down the stairs and Peter is at the hospital with a broken leg. He'll be off active duty for months."

Tate felt her mouth drop. "Humphrey broke Peter's leg? No way."

"I sure did. And I don't feel bad about it at all," Humphrey said, coming into the room.

"What, did you shove him down the stairs?" Birch asked, wide-eyed.

"Ye of little faith. I used fishing line. And as soon as Peter tumbled, I put the line in my pocket before anyone could see it. I even called the doctor for him. But now we need you visible. You need to thank the military at the White House before your speech on the South Lawn to kick off the military

BBQ picnic. Then you're welcoming guests for this evening's reception starting at seven tonight. You'll be at the reception from seven until nine, with fireworks following shortly after dinner is completed. Guests will move to the South Lawn to watch the fireworks at the Mall and then move back inside for dancing until eleven," Humphrey said as if he hadn't just broken a guy's leg.

"Humphrey, can we get Tate something to wear to both events?"

"I can—" Tate started to say.

Birch held up his hand. "You're not leaving the White House until I know you're safe."

"I'll get right on it."

Humphrey hurried out, and Birch went to meet with the Marines and other service members who were stationed at the White House and were guests for the day's festivities. Tate walked back to her room. She stepped up to the window and regretted it the instant she did. Protesters in front of the White House held signs that said things like *Whore of the White House* and *Keep our children safe from Tate*. Tears rolled down her cheeks. Pain squeezed her heart as she read more and more signs. And at the end, these people who hated her enough because of one picture to protest her would never know she was saving all their lives and freedoms. Or maybe she should just let *Mollia Domini* win. Then these people wouldn't have the right to protest.

Tate turned her phone on and went to sit on the couch. She would not look on social media. She would not let people who are so filled with such

hate that they only feel good about themselves if they were tearing other people down destroy her. Instead, she answered emails and deleted all media requests except one. Flint Scott said he was onto something and wanted to meet with her at Lancy's.

Tate replied that she could meet him tomorrow evening, but the entire meeting and everything said in it must remain confidential. As she set down her phone, she heard a ring. But this time it was the phone that only one person had the number to.

"Hello, Brent," Tate answered in her best valley girl impersonation.

"I have the information you want. Your story has almost broken my servers."

"Good. I'll text you the upload instructions. And I have an even bigger story for you."

"What is it?" Brent asked, trying to temper his excitement.

"You'll have to wait and see. I'd add some reinforcements to your server if I were you."

"It would be easier if you just told me who you are and what you have. I'll protect your identity."

"I know you would. When I send this second story to you, how long will it take to get it up?"

"I'll have to vet it first."

"You already have. It involves everyone you just looked into."

"Video?"

"Yes," Tate answered.

"Thirty minutes to verify the video is unedited and to write the story that accompanies it."

"Timing is everything, Brent. It has to be thirty

minutes and not a minute sooner or later. Can you promise me that?"

"What are you involved in?" Brent asked instead.

"I just want to wake people up to the realities of the world. Promise me, or you don't get the file. I have another reporter I can trust with it," Tate threatened.

"I promise."

"You'll get it Monday at four forty-five your time. Happy Fourth of July."

Tate hung up as Humphrey knocked on her door. "I hope these clothes are all right. And I got you a little something in the box, too."

"Thank you, Humphrey."

Humphrey shoved his glasses up his nose. "How are you doing?"

"It's going to be a long couple of days. I can't wait until Monday night."

"You have to hang on until then." Humphrey sent her a smile and placed the clothes and the box on her bed before leaving. Three days of constant harassment. She could do it. She looked back out the window. *Fire the slut* was being chanted. Tears pressed against her eyes as her heart began to pound. Anxiety threatened to crush her. No, she could do this. She did this to herself. She knew it would be hard. Tate took a deep breath and reminded herself that putting her life on the line was for a greater good. It would expose Claudia as the hypocrite she was. It would show the people currently demanding her head on a spike that it was

Claudia who was trying to hurt them, not Tate. She just hoped they'd listen because she was doing this all for them.

★   ★   ★

Birch walked down the long hallway filled with military. He thanked each one as he shook their hands. He felt Brock standing slightly behind him and for the first time, felt that he didn't need to watch his own back. The trouble was it wasn't his back he was worried about. It was Tate's. She hadn't said anything, but this morning after she'd checked her email and had seen the morning news, she had withdrawn into herself.

When Birch made his way to the end of the line of military, the director of the Secret Service was standing there waiting for him. "I need a word, sir," she said.

"Yes?" Birch said, resigned to the fact it would be bad news. After all, the director didn't need to see him most times. It was usually the head of the presidential protection division or the intelligence division.

"You have on your agenda that Miss Carlisle will be attending the Fourth of July picnic. Is that still the plan?" she asked.

"Yes. She'll be down shortly for it. Why?" Birch asked, not really wanting to hear the answer.

"Today's threat report is in. There have been credible reports against Miss Carlisle and yourself for employing her. I don't think it's a good idea for

her to attend."

Birch stared down the woman he wasn't completely sure he could trust. "Are you saying you and your agents can't keep us safe?"

"No, sir. I'm just saying—"

"You're just saying that you don't want to do the extra work to keep her safe. The White House has had some of the most hated people in the world visit before and they were all protected. If you can't or don't want to do the job, then I'll be happy to find someone who can."

Birch saw her jaw work in irritation. She'd been a Mitchell appointment, and they had not meshed well since he took over the presidency. "That won't be necessary. I'll assign more agents to the event."

Birch wanted to tell her that's what she should have done in the first place, but instead he walked past her to his office. "Brock, a word."

Birch opened the door to his office and shut it behind Brock, the only agent he knew he could trust. "Did they fill you in on the threat assessment?"

"Yes, sir."

"What's your take on it?"

"My take is *Mollia Domini* is using the photo to rile up citizens in hopes that the people will do their dirty work from them. I think Tate is probably in their gray area, and they won't mind if someone takes her out just so they don't have to worry about her. I read some of the threats. They're nasty, but BBN and some of the papers have been saying worse. A couple of BBN's reporters, especially Claudia Hughes, have been using social media to

post memes of Tate along with making her address and other personal information available. I suggest we ask her to turn over her phone and give me access to her email so I can monitor for those who go beyond the regular hate speech into defamation and stalker. It's really sad. They think they have a right to go after her because she's somehow done them a wrong," Brock explained.

Birch let out a sound of frustration. "Regular hate speech," he said, shaking his head. "I remember a time if I said something rude, even if it was just speaking to myself and my mother heard me, lord help me. Respect, manners, civility. They were drilled into me as a boy. Anyway, I want men you trust on her. Right now, she may be more of a target than I am."

"I'll take care of it," Brock promised.

★　★　★

It was scary how fast Alex had printed the press pass out of the trunk of his beat-up car. A few strokes of the keys and Dalton was on every VIP all-access press list. He'd made a quick stop at the camera store and picked up a professional camera with a microphone attachment.

"Press pass," a guard ordered as Dalton approached the gate reserved for the media to enter in for the South Lawn BBQ.

Dalton handed him his identification as another guard searched his bags. When he was cleared, he walked through a metal detector and was then

patted down. "Excuse me, where is the VIP room?" Dalton asked one of the guards.

"Show your badge to that guard, and he'll show you where to go."

Dalton looked to where he was pointing. Two guards stood by the base of the steps leading to the portico. Dalton headed their way. "Hey, I'm heading to the VIP room."

"Up the steps. People are gathering in the Blue Room and on the portico, but I need to see your pass," one of the guards said as the other talked with a woman Dalton recognized as a senator. "Okay, you're all set."

Dalton thanked him and headed up the steps after the senator. It was a warm day but not overly hot for July. The portico overlooking the South Lawn was filled with politicians mingling with some of the more famous journalists and celebrities attending the event. Dalton headed toward some photographers and nodded his hello before using his camera to scope the area and find Senator Epps. Bingo, inside the Blue Room, talking to Sandra Cummings.

Dalton examined his camera to record and made sure his microphone was on before slinging the camera over his neck and walking into the Blue Room. As he went to get a drink, he moved the camera to face Senator Epps and the secretary of state, sitting next to a refreshment table.

They ignored Dalton as he got a drink and looked over the finger food. Epps gestured wildly with his hands, and his voice went from unheard to

a harsh whisper. "That's wrong and you know it."

"I don't care what kind of intelligence you think you have, Martin. I can guarantee you it's nowhere near as reliable as mine," Sandra hissed.

"I'm warning you, Sandra. I'm doing this with or without you," Senator Epps threatened as he turned his back on the secretary of state and stormed from the Blue Room through the opened jib door and disappeared from sight onto the portico.

Dalton picked up a drink and slowly followed. He took a position on the far side of the portico and watched an obviously aggravated Senator Epps talking to Thurmond Culpepper, the secretary of state's top aide.

Slowly making his way closer to Epps, Dalton kept his eyes on the streams of military families now making their way onto the South Lawn. This time Epps didn't seem as worried about keeping his voice down.

"If you thought that Blackhawk being shot down in Syria was bad, just wait," Epps said as he poked Thurmond in his thin chest.

"Senator Epps, please. There are some things that are better left to those with the clearances to know how to handle them. I'm sure the secretary will do the right thing," Thurmond said, rubbing the spot Epps had poked.

"Get this straight, you little shit. If you don't listen to me, then I'll make sure you two go down in flames — one way or another."

Epps turned and disappeared back into the White House as Sandra came out to join Thurmond.

"Is he still insisting everything must be done his way?"

"He threatened us if we didn't," Thurmond said with a shake of his head before taking a drink. "He mentioned Syria."

Sandra's hand fisted, and then she forcibly relaxed it. "That bastard. If he's behind . . . Oh my god. I can't believe it. The president brought *her*!"

Dalton turned as the crowd grew silent. President Stratton and Tate walked out onto the portico with Secret Service hovering nearby. A couple staunch allies stepped forward to greet them as others began to lean their heads together and trade gossip. Tate stood with her hands clasped as she looked out at the lawn with a serene and completely forced smile on her face. At that moment, Dalton realized Tate was the strongest person on the portico.

CHAPTER FIFTEEN

Alex's fingers flew over his keyboard. He had known something was going on when the dark boards he frequented had gone quiet. It had taken days, but he'd found out why they went quiet: they had moved.

Gaining access had taken all his skills as a hacker, and he was pretty sure his identity was already known since someone referred to him as Leavenworth. However, he also knew the identities of several of the people in there as well. One in particular he was interested in. Rock Star was the screen name for Penny Stark, who lived in London.

Over the years, the members on the dark boards hacked everyone. It was a game of sorts to test your abilities. Alex had been anonymous except for five people who had gotten through his protections. In return, he'd worked and worked until he had discovered their identities. Two were from the US, one was from China, one was from London, and the final one was from someplace Alex had never identified beyond being close to Hong Kong, possibly Taiwan.

It was after reaching out to them that he found the new dark boards. These boards were limited to

people everyone knew. At the most, twenty-five people from around the world were present on this hidden site. Alex eventually gained access and was scrolling the posts. Everyone from Canada to Australia and everywhere in between was talking about what was going on. Someone had hacked the previous dark site and was monitoring it.

Alex typed: *Does anyone have any government contacts? I think something is going on.* There was a missing bomb out there, and he wanted to find it.

Rock Star responded: *I don't have contacts, but I've come across some news from chatter.*

Alex asked: *Chatter?*

Rock Star answered: *Someone tried to hack the London Stock Exchange Group.*

Dark Surfer, a hacker from Australia, added on the post: *There has been a break-in at a government facility in Sydney. No one is talking, but something big was stolen.*

火龍, or what Alex had learned was Chinese for *Fire Dragon*, added: *There's been an increased military presence in Shanghai.*

Rock Star responded: *It's why we moved. Something big is going on. There's nothing about it on the news, and our governments are not speaking either. What do you know?*

Alex stared at the computer. When it came down to it, he didn't know whom he could trust. A group of hackers, even if they were hacking for noble reasons, were still criminals like him. How did he know that they weren't associated with *Mollia Domini*?

Alex: *Our media isn't reporting anything either.*

Alex took a breath. He'd test the waters: *I heard chatter about some group, though. I don't know anything more than some group is working hard to stay dark. I wonder if they may be affecting things.*

Nothing. No one typed anything and Alex was worried he'd blown his cover.

Finally the response came through from Rock Star: *I thought I was the only one.*

The others responded: *Me too.*

Fire Dragon finally asked: *So, how do we find out who they are?*

That was the question. At least Alex had help now. He just had to walk a fine line of giving enough information for people to go on, but not enough to break his confidentiality with the president and put his team in jeopardy.

★   ★   ★

"Move!" Lizzy shouted at the long line of traffic not listening to her. She'd left the group over an hour before and was moving at a slow crawl out of the city. There had been an accident on the bridge to complicate all of the traffic for the Fourth of July celebrations. She'd be lucky to make it home by nightfall. At least that's what it felt like to her as she put her car in Park and tried to take a calming breath. She hated traffic.

Lizzy's phone pinged with a notification. She picked it up, happy for a distraction. It was a NEWS ALERT from *The Washington Leader*. Lizzy read the

headline and cursed.

She tried Tate first, but her phone went to voicemail. She tried Dalton next, but his did the same thing. She sent an urgent message on the secure messaging system. *Jeff Sargent just spilled his story. I'm stuck in traffic. If he's not dead already, he will be soon.*

A second later, her phone rang. It was Humphrey. "We're shutting your road down so we can get you out. I see you're on the Capital Beltway, but where are you exactly?"

"I'm looking at the parking for the outlets at the National Harbor." Lizzy looked at the packed shopping areas and almost broke out in hives at the thought of all those people crammed together.

"Can you get to the Oxon Hill Bike Trail?"

Lizzy looked around. "No problem. Traffic's at a standstill."

"We're shutting the road down so it won't move until we're ready for it to. Get out of your car and head over to the trail. Crew will touch down in the field near the parking area. He's lifting off now."

"Don't you think Marine One will be a little noticeable?" Lizzy yelled as she started jogging down the interstate toward the bike trail.

"He, um, borrowed a media helicopter nearby."

"Please tell me it was BBN's," Lizzy chuckled as she crawled over the guardrail.

"It was. He'll leave it on top of some nearby building after wiping it down when you two are done."

"Thank you, Humphrey. How is Tate doing?"

Humphrey sighed. "It's hard to watch, Lizzy. I don't know how she's doing it. Some military men are hitting on her. Some wives are openly calling her names. The media is taking every opportunity to question her, using the most vulgar questions possible. All the while, half the politicians are going after Birch for keeping her on staff. But Tate has kept her head up even though it's probably taking a mental toll."

"Tell her to stay strong. I'll let you know when I'm done."

Lizzy hung up and waited for Crew to arrive. She pulled up the article and read.

It's my duty as a reporter and a news editor to tell the truth and report the news. However, I have failed at that duty recently out of fear. I refuse to be fearful any longer. My job has transitioned from reporter to salesman. Pressure to sell advertising, to sell the products of our parent company, and to sell the fear that has you opening the paper every day. Because of this, you, the readers, have no ability to identify the propaganda to get you to buy more insurance or to turn against a rival company.

My reporter, Joel Davidson, had a story he wanted to run and was killed before he could. I know Joel, and while I have no direct evidence, I will guarantee Joel did not murder his wife and commit suicide. Instead, I believe

the person who deleted his article killed him to prevent it from being published.

What article could be worth killing someone over? One that has an FBI source reporting a missing chemical bomb that links back to former FBI Agent Phylicia Claymore. That's what. An article that alleges Phylicia Claymore wasn't acting alone in her treasonous activities. An article that alludes to a conspiracy to harm you, the American people, for a power grab.

I had thought it impossible that someone was telling lies to the American people until I was told by corporate to publish a piece of fake news about President Stratton or lose my job. The email from corporate is pictured below. I had thought it was impossible that a group could be stealing bombs from the FBI and working with FBI agents to commit genocide until I came home from a funeral to find my house bugged and myself followed. Tell me, why would that happen unless there is truth in Joel's story? Joel was a reporter who didn't care what he had to do to break a real story in order to keep America safe. And in his honor, I'm defying all orders from corporate and those who have been threatening me, and I am publishing Joel's story.

The sounds of helicopter blades sliced through

the air and tore Lizzy away from the screen. She took a screen shot of the story. She was sure it wouldn't be up much longer. Just like she was sure Jeff Sargent wouldn't be alive much longer.

She looked up to see a bright blue helicopter descending. Lizzy leaped in the second she could and put the headphones on so she could talk to Crew as he flew in the direction of Jeff's house.

"Thank you for getting me," Lizzy said as they flew over stopped traffic and into the suburbs.

"Anytime. I grabbed some rappelling rope from Marine One in case you need it," Crew said with a motion to the back of the helicopter.

Lizzy moved to hook up the rope and put on the gloves just in case she needed to make a quick exit. She looked over at Crew flying. His cocky attitude was kept in check. He was no-nonsense and the perfect professional. His dark skin seemed to glow in the sunlight as he handled the helicopter with precision. After all, he was one of the best pilots in the country.

"You haven't been around much the last couple of days. How are you doing?" Lizzy asked.

"Fine. It's a lot to come to grips with, you know?" Crew didn't take his eyes off the sky as he answered her.

"I do know. Look, I know things didn't work out between us like you had hoped, but I am glad you're part of the team."

Crew finally looked at her and gave her a nod of his chin. "I was an ass. I didn't have any claim to you, even if my grandpa thought I did. But if I'm

going to lose my what-might-have-been, at least it's to someone that I can respect and someone who's so in love with you that I feel bad I even tried to get in the middle of it all."

Lizzy sputtered. There was that word again. Why was everyone saying it? "Dalton doesn't love me, but thank you. I didn't mean for it to happen, and it seems silly to even focus on it when we have all of this going on. I feel as if a clock is counting down, and we're almost out of time."

"Love is never silly. And it's completely obvious you both love each other." Crew laughed and looked back at her again. "Never took the two of you as cowards of the heart." His face grew serious again. "I feel it, too. That time is running out. And I can't do anything about it. I don't know how to investigate like you do. I feel I'm just watching the world implode."

They sat silently for a minute, each lost in the severity of the circumstances few people knew about. Crew leaned forward, and Lizzy turned to see what he was looking at. "What is it?"

"That house with the garage door opening. That's Jeff's house." Crew moved the helicopter into a slanted approach so they could look into the garage as they went to land. But the second they started to land, a dark blue SUV shot out from the garage.

Crew jerked the helicopter up to avoid hitting the SUV and Lizzy reached for her gun. A woman was gagged and bound on the floor in the backseat of the vehicle. In the front passenger seat, she saw

who she guessed was Jeff. She couldn't see his face, but she could see that his hands were bound to the door.

"Who's driving?" Lizzy asked, grabbing a pair of binoculars.

"Give me a second." Crew maneuvered the helicopter so Lizzy could see in.

"I don't know him. But I'd be willing to bet he's Dan's replacement. We need to stop that car. Can you do that?" Lizzy asked.

Crew grinned at her. "You wouldn't believe what I can do in a helicopter." He sent her a wink before pulling up into the sky. "This helicopter's max speed is 112 miles per hour. We need to get him before he can get out of this suburban maze."

Crew pushed the helicopter ahead of the SUV. He waited for it to slow down and take a turn and then Crew dropped fast. Lizzy yanked the rappelling glove from her right hand and pulled her gun as Crew hovered feet from the ground in front of the oncoming car.

"I don't think he's going to stop," Crew told her calmly as he held the helicopter steady.

"Let's see if I can help with that." Lizzy opened the sliding window and shot at the driver. The driver stepped on the gas. He was a man who made her shiver when he looked at her. Instead, he barely moved as Lizzy's shots grew closer to him. The man was ice cold in his handling of the car. Lizzy saw Jeff's eyes grow wide. Tape covered his mouth as his tied arms were hidden from view.

"I gotta pull up," Crew said in a calm voice. At

the last second, he pulled the helicopter up as the SUV raced under them. "I can try hitting him with the landing gear, but honestly, I don't think that will scare him. He didn't take his eyes off me as he headed right at us."

"Can you get me next to him?" Lizzy asked as she reloaded her gun.

"Negative. The street is too narrow for the blades."

Lizzy pulled on her rappelling glove. "Then get me on top of him."

"Are you sure?" Crew asked as he followed above the SUV.

"Yes. If I hit wrong, I could take out the Sargents. And I don't want to wreck the car and risk them that way either. I need to get my hands on this guy."

Lizzy pulled the headset off, ending the discussion as she moved to open the door. Crew slowly lowered them as close as he could get to the roof and Lizzy stepped onto the landing gear, holding onto the rappelling rope she'd secured. She watched as the roof came closer and closer, but then the driver took a hard right, tearing into a driveway, through a fence, and onto another street.

She held on tight as Crew followed. Her body swayed out from the helicopter, but Lizzy just kept her eye on the SUV that was picking up speed through the connected neighborhoods.

Crew kept up and again began to lower the helicopter closer to the roof. Not waiting to try to jump onto the car's roof, Lizzy slid down the rope.

She stopped herself just like Dalton had taught her at the end of the rope. She dangled there as Crew maneuvered into position. Lizzy looked ahead and saw the street ending. The man would be turning either right or left. If Lizzy didn't jump now, she risked him making it onto a straight road where he could potentially lose the helicopter.

Lizzy took a deep breath and let go. Her feet hit the roof and she let her body fall flat. She gripped the side of the roof with her fingers and the other side with her toes as she stretched out across the roof. The SUV turned sharply, and Lizzy battled the momentum that threatened to throw her from the roof. As the car straightened out, Lizzy moved toward the driver's door only to be stopped by bullets ripping through the roof.

"Shit," she grunted as she rolled to the other side. She was reaching for her gun when the driver slammed on the brakes.

The breath was stolen from her lungs as Lizzy flew forward off the roof. Time seemed to be suspended as she flew off. She tucked herself into a ball and felt her hip slam into the hood of the car before she bounced off and landed hard on the pavement. Air was forced from her lungs. Pain shot up the entire left side of her body.

Lizzy tried to blink her eyes open, but her body fought it. When she managed to finally crack an eye open, she saw the door to the SUV slowly open before her eyes closed again.

CHAPTER SIXTEEN

"Have you heard anything yet?" Birch asked as he leaned in close to Humphrey at the picnic. "No."

The one word was enough to worry Birch. That one word conveyed the fear and worry Humphrey had about Lizzy and Crew.

Tate smiled and took another bite of hamburger. She chatted easily with the other people on their blanket, but by the looks she kept sending him, Birch knew she was worried, too. They all were. It had been over thirty minutes since Crew left the party, and they hadn't heard a thing from him.

"The article is offline. It was taken down five minutes after it went up, but I grabbed a screen shot. Alex tried the writer's house, but there was no answer," Humphrey whispered.

Birch nodded. When Tate looked at him, he gave a barely perceptible shake of his head. Tate lost a little color but kept the smile plastered on her face. Like him, she was starting to crack, but only a force of will kept them holding it together. They refused to let these bastards win by showing that they were hurting.

★   ★   ★

Crew knew how to push a helicopter. When Lizzy went flying from the hood, Crew had reacted instantly. He'd spun around so he could see the front of the SUV. The door opened, and Crew dropped the helicopter fast. He hovered a foot or two off the ground between Lizzy's still body and the SUV.

The man started at him, his eyes never leaving Crew's. Crew didn't wait to see what he would do. Crew's window was already open, and while he wasn't the best shot with his left hand, it would be enough to keep this asshole away from Lizzy.

Crew fired and the man ducked behind the open door. The second Crew paused in his firing, the man was up and returning fire. "Dammit," Crew cursed as a bullet pinged off a blade. The man wasn't aiming for Crew. He was trying to disable the helicopter.

The sound of someone slamming against the side of the helicopter had Crew turning quickly, ready to fire on a second enemy. Instead, he found Lizzy shaking the haze from her head. Blood ran down her arm from road rash. Her hair was windblown and streaked with blood. And she was pissed.

"Give me your gun," she yelled as she used the helicopter to steady herself.

Crew reloaded his gun and handed it out the window to her. One of his hands instinctively went to cup his balls because the look on her face said

she'd happily cut them off anyone who crossed her right now. Thank goodness that look was directed at the man coming around the side of the SUV door. Poor dumb bastard—Crew almost felt sorry for him.

Lizzy didn't bother talking. She didn't ask any questions. Instead, she straightened up and walked toward the man, not even flinching when he fired off a couple shots at her. A shiver ran through Crew. This wasn't the Lizzy he knew from the bar or the one his grandfather loved as if she were his own granddaughter. This woman was tough as steel, deadly, and didn't have a flicker of emotion in her.

Crew watched as Lizzy raised both arms and fired. The man leapt behind the door, and Lizzy pushed her advantage by charging. She ran with a hitch in her gait. It was the only sign that she'd been hurt when she'd been flung from the top of the car. When the man rose to fire his gun, it was too late. Lizzy slammed the door on him, knocking him to the ground. Crew swallowed hard as he watched her pull the door back and slam it against the man again.

Crew flew higher and looked down at the scene. Lizzy was bleeding and breathing heavily. The man was not moving. His head seemed to take the brunt of the hits. Lizzy motioned for Crew to come closer.

"Return the helicopter and take my car back home. Call the team and have someone meet me where I held Phylicia for questioning." Crew nodded as Lizzy handed him her car keys. "And, Crew, thanks for your help."

"Glad to be of assistance," he yelled over the

noise of the propellers.

Crew lifted the helicopter and again felt for his balls just to reassure himself they were still there. He was never going to get on Lizzy's bad side again. Thank goodness he'd apologized for his behavior. He was man enough to admit tears might be involved if he had to apologize now after seeing her in action.

Lizzy turned from Crew's departure and let out a shaky breath. She was hurting badly. She reached into her pocket and pulled out a switchblade. She opened it and walked around to Jeff's door. He looked at her wide-eyed and pale-faced. When she approached him, he shook his head and tried to pull away from her, his muffled voice begging her not to hurt them.

"I'm not going to hurt you. I'm here to rescue you," Lizzy said as kindly as the pain she was enduring let her.

Jeff didn't look as if he believed her and pulled away from her again.

Lizzy rolled her eyes. "Fine, have it your way." Lizzy slammed the door and opened the back door. Mrs. Sargent's blue eyes were wide with terror. "I'm here to rescue you. Do you believe me?" Mrs. Sargent nodded and Lizzy ripped the tape from her mouth.

"Who are you?" Mrs. Sargent asked as Lizzy moved to slash the zip ties on her hands and legs.

"Just a person who knew you needed help. Now, Mrs. Sargent, I need your help."

"Of course. Can you let my husband go?" she asked as she wriggled from the backseat.

"I will in a minute. But before all these people start coming out of their houses, we need to get out of here. Come help me toss this guy in the trunk." Jeff let loose with a string of muffled yells, but Mrs. Sargent followed Lizzy anyway.

"Oh my," she gasped when she looked down at the man who had kidnapped her. "Is he . . . dead?"

Lizzy put her fingers to his neck. "Not yet. Grab his legs."

Mrs. Sargent bent down and grabbed his legs. She and Lizzy moved him to the tailgate and hefted him inside. "Maybe we should bind his legs then? I'd hate for him to pop back to life and kill us. It happens in movies all the time."

"Do you have anything to tie him up with?" Lizzy asked.

"He tossed the tape in the back with me. Hold on, I'll get it." A second later, Mrs. Sargent, her mouth red from the tape being ripped off, helped Lizzy tie his hands and feet together. "Here, I use this to hide my purchases at the mall, but it'll work now, too, I guess," she said as she pulled a cover over him.

"Thank you. Let's go."

Lizzy walked to the driver's side and got in. She handed her knife to Mrs. Sargent and drove off. "You can free your husband now."

God, her head hurt. Her vision wasn't completely there and her side hurt so much that her leg shook as she pressed on the gas. She had a bit of

a drive to the abandoned warehouse she had used to interrogate Phylicia Claymore, and she wanted to make it there before she passed out.

Jeff grabbed the knife from his wife once he was freed and pointed it at Lizzy. She took a deep calming breath as his wife scolded him. "Jeff, I have a gun. Put the knife down."

Jeff looked down to Lizzy's left hand that rested on her lap with her gun pointed right at him and set down the knife. "Who are you?"

"I told you. I'm here to help."

"You know who that was?"

Lizzy tried to shake her head but groaned instead. "No. I just know where he comes from. I've killed others like him."

"Where are you taking us?" he asked.

"Someplace safe. You and your wife are safe now even though you were a dumbass and posted that article. You have no idea what you've done."

Jeff gasped. "I knew it! I knew there was more to Joel's story, and I bet . . . I bet that bitch set me up."

Lizzy reined in her temper because she had a pretty good idea who he was talking about. "Who's the bitch you think set you up?"

Headless of the warning in her voice, Jeff answered quickly. "Tate Carlisle. She's the president's press secretary, and the only other person who knows I had this information."

"I'll tell you this once. If I weren't driving, I'd kick your ass. Tate's the only reason you're alive right now. Show some damn respect," Lizzy ground out between clenched teeth.

"Wait," Jeff said, his reporter instincts kicking in. "You know Tate? And you know what I wrote about. So it's real. There really is someone or a group out there trying to . . . well, trying to do what?"

"Sorry, I'm not some exclusive. Now let's get something straight. You and your wife are alive because of us. You're the one who broke your word to Tate to not say anything, and then you blame her. I think you owe her a big apology. For now, you will go where we tell you. You will not get on the news or on social media. You will not call anyone, and you will not email anyone. You and your wife will be completely off the grid until we come get you. Do you understand?"

"Where are we going?" Mrs. Sargent asked, cutting off whatever her husband was about to say.

"I'm thinking Africa. Ever wanted to go on a safari? Or how about the summer in a remote cabin in Canada? The point being, you need to stay the hell away from everything you've ever known. Do you understand the consequences if you don't? Not only will you two be killed, but you'll be tortured first. I have to have your promise that you will stay put—a promise you actually intend to keep this time." Lizzy stared at Jeff, but it was his wife who answered.

"Canada sounds lovely. Jeff has always said he wanted to write a book. A cabin in the woods sounds perfect for him to write. Doesn't it, Jeff?"

"It does," Jeff said slowly. "And thank you. It's hard to fight years of journalistic instinct for a story.

But I will. You have my word."

"I hope it's a better word than you gave Tate. You've put her in enough danger already."

Jeff nodded as the suburbs gave way to rolling hills. "I was being followed, and I lost it. I found the bugs. I saw people outside my house and my work. It was clear someone had been at my desk and gone through my files. I just went off. I'm sorry. I never thought of Tate being the one in danger. I thought she was the one trying to cover for the government."

"Now you know better. Do any of you have any electronic devices — cell phones, workout bracelets, anything that transmits a signal?" Lizzy asked.

Jeff handed her his cell and his wife handed her a workout tracker. Lizzy slowed as they crossed a good-sized stream. It wasn't a river, but it would do. She tossed the devices into the water and then sped off. She just hoped backup wouldn't be too far behind because she felt her body weakening.

★   ★   ★

Tate saw Humphrey hang up the phone. She walked over with a smile on her face as Humphrey and Birch stopped to pose for photos with various celebrities, families, and politicians.

"Doesn't your face hurt?" Humphrey asked once they were alone.

"The pain is the only thing stopping me from crying," Tate said, widening her smile. "I've been called every name in the book today, and I don't know how much longer I can take it."

"You're giving a Herculean effort. If I didn't know you so well, I would think nothing was bothering you." Humphrey dropped his voice. "I heard from Crew. Lizzy got to the Sargents in time. Apparently it was a sight to behold. Crew said something about Lizzy jumping from a helicopter and being thrown from a roof of a moving car. She's pretty banged up but is taking them to an extraction site."

"I wish I was strong like Lizzy or Valeria," Tate said sadly.

"But you are. Do you think they'd have held up like you have today? There's all different kinds of strong, Tate. And from where I stand, you're just as strong as they are," Humphrey said, giving her hand an encouraging squeeze.

When Birch looked over, worry for her was clear in his eyes. She smiled back at him—a real smile this time. He'd fight everyone here for her if she let him. His belief in her gave her the strength to continue through the day. She gave him the thumbs-up sign, and he visibly relaxed. How was it only one o'clock in the afternoon? Tate took a deep breath. She was strong. She held the power. She released the image. She had a plan. She would cut off *Mollia Domini's* line of communication to the public. The more Tate repeated it, the taller she stood. She could do this. She had to do this. It wasn't about her. It was about the entire country.

CHAPTER SEVENTEEN

"**D**ude, you look like you've been run over by a car," Alex said as he handed Lizzy a new cell phone. Her other one had been smashed when she'd been thrown off the roof of the SUV.

"Close," Lizzy snarked back. "The Sargents need new identities and a cabin in Canada—a place fit to write a book. And romantic," Lizzy said. Jeff was a typical reporter, but Mrs. Sargent had found a soft spot within Lizzy.

"No problem-o," Alex said, firing up the portable printing press he kept in his trunk. "Private jet?"

"Definitely. And make them Canadian citizens so we can just drop them into the country without having to worry about immigration issues," Lizzy said. The image of Jeff screaming as he was pushed out of a plane brought a smile to her face.

"I'm on it," Alex said as he left to take pictures of the Sargents.

Lizzy got to work on the car. She stripped and scraped all VIN numbers off and burned the license plate and anything with any possible identification on it. An hour later, Lizzy's vision had gotten better, but her headache was getting worse as she put the

SUV into Drive and placed a cinderblock on the gas pedal. The SUV accelerated before leaping into the Potomac and sinking out of sight.

"Miss? Ma'am? Goodness, I don't know what to call you," Mrs. Sargent laughed. "Is it okay to give you a hug?"

"Of course." Lizzy smiled as she was wrapped in a motherly hug. It felt so good that Lizzy was afraid she'd never want to let go.

"Thank you for saving us. For giving us a beautiful place to live. And for giving us new identities. I always thought Iris was a pretty name, so that suits me well. I don't know what you're up against. Jeff told me his theory but whatever it is, it's evil. You swooped in from the sky like an angel. So every night I will send a prayer to my own angel. I wish you the strength and the goodness to defeat what you're up against."

"Thank you, Iris," Lizzy said as she swelled with pride. She had someone praying for her. And right now she needed all the help she could get.

Mrs. Sargent, now Iris Sallies, walked back to her husband as Alex approached. "I got them all set. Do I need to take you with me?"

"No. I have someone coming to pick us up," Lizzy said, looking to where the man was tied up. He had begun to groan about ten minutes earlier. However, his eyes had yet to open.

"Okay. Are you sure it's safe to leave you here?" Alex asked. "Oh, right. You're you. Got it. I'm taking the Sargents to an airport in West Virginia. I'll be back this evening."

Lizzy surprised herself by reaching out to Alex and wrapping him in a hug. "Thank you."

"Dude," Alex said, his cheeks bright with a blush as he walked to his car and drove off with the Sargents.

It didn't take much longer for the sound of another engine to reach her. Lizzy turned from where she was watching the river flowing out to the ocean to see the old 4Runner bounce into view.

The big SUV came to a stop, the door opened, and a prosthetic leg came into view first as Jason Wolski got out. The man was a giant—all muscles, broad shoulders, and pain. He'd just buried his wife because of his involvement with Lizzy, and she was surprised he agreed to come.

"Got another one for me?" Jason's deep voice boomed off the abandoned building.

"Hi, Jason. Thank you for coming. I know how hard—"

"I'm glad you called," he said, cutting her off. His face was covered in what might become a beard, but now just looked as if he hadn't bothered to shave since Michelle was killed by Phylicia during her ill-fated attempt of escaping the Wolskis' farm. "I need to be doing something."

Lizzy didn't hug him, though she wanted to. Everything about his posture said he didn't want any sympathy. She remembered the feeling. The feelings of despair didn't disappear simply because she found out her fiancé had faked his death.

"This is an assassin/all-round handy man for *Mollia Domini*. I need a ride close to Quantico and

then I need you to take him to your farm if you're willing," Lizzy said as she whispered a quiet thanks for strong men. Jason easily slung the man over his shoulder.

"You got it." Jason dropped the man in the back and made sure he was securely bound before covering him with a tarp. "What do you want me to do with him?"

Lizzy got in the front with Jason. "Whatever you want. I just want to know what he knows. If you don't feel like doing—"

"Nope, I'm good. I'll call if I get anything."

"Then you'll need this." Lizzy set a phone in the cup holder. "It's secure. Our numbers are in it. Only use this phone if you need to contact us. Destroy it if you think it's been compromised and we'll get you a new one. Welcome to the group."

"Got it," Jason grunted, putting the SUV in gear and driving off.

★ ★ ★

Dalton moved silently through the White House. The VIPs were restricted to the middle of the first floor, which was swarmed by Secret Service and Marines. People were coming and going from the Red and Green rooms that surrounded the oval-shaped Blue Room and all had views of the South Lawn.

The Cross Hall was filled with people milling from room to room, but it was the Entrance Hall that Dalton was interested in. A minute before, Senator

Epps had brushed back his graying hair, looked around the Blue Room, and then slowly strolled out into the hallway. Instead of going to a neighboring room, he made a beeline for the entrance area.

Dalton followed at a distance. Epps looked around once again before going out the front door of the White House. He disappeared off the North Portico and Dalton hurried to a window to see where he was going. Pretending to take in the artwork so the agents and Marines wouldn't be suspicious, Dalton looked outside and saw that Epps wasn't leaving. He was meeting someone.

A car had pulled up to the left of the covered entrance. Epps was leaning through an open window, talking to the driver. He looked frustrated as he shook his head at the driver. A minute later, the car took off and Epps turned back to the White House.

Dalton strode out of the Entrance Hall before Epps returned. He needed to find out who was in that car. He pulled out his phone and saw the flurry of notifications. Shit, he'd had it on silent so no one would notice him. A phone going off at the wrong time was a perfect way to get noticed.

One of the notifications was for a missed call. He pulled up his call log and saw that Lizzy had phoned him — no message. Whenever anyone left a message on the secure messaging system, an exclamation point appeared on Dalton's screen. He pulled up the secure messaging and felt the blood drain from his face as he read. Jeff Sargent was in trouble. Lizzy was going after him. Crew was

assisting. And then there was the message from Crew. *Lizzy injured. Sargents are secure. She needs evacuation and help at place Phylicia was taken. Suspect in custody.*

Dalton scrolled down and saw that Alex had responded. Then, nothing else appeared on the list. Dalton called Lizzy's phone, but the number was disconnected. Dalton hurried from the hall out of the Blue Room and onto the South Portico. He scanned the crowd until he found Tate. She was still plastering that damn smile as she talked to people. Humphrey was at the bottom of the stairs, talking to a couple of congressmen, and when he looked up, he gave a barely perceptible shake of his head. No, Dalton couldn't talk to them. There could be no public contact between them.

Epps walked past and Dalton was left with only one choice—do his job. He entered a message, *Status Update,* and then followed Epps. All the while his heart was pounding for information on Lizzy. They had said their relationship wouldn't interfere with their work, but Dalton knew better. He loved her. There was no way his feelings wouldn't interfere. He knew his job, and he'd do it. That didn't mean he wouldn't be worried sick until he heard from her.

Dalton checked his phone every five minutes. Finally, as he watched Epps and the committee head for national intelligence talking, he received the notification on his phone. He pulled up the system and looked around. Humphrey was similarly on his phone, as was Tate, their faces all set to show impassiveness.

*Old phone destroyed. This is my new number.
I'm all right. Banged up from being tossed off
the roof of an SUV. Jason is with me. He's
driving me back to Quantico so I can get
cleaned up. Crew is returning the helicopter
he borrowed and then bringing me my car.
Humphrey, you can open the interstate now.
Jason will take the suspect to his farm. He's
connected via a phone Alex gave him. He'll
notify us if he learns anything. Alex is
transporting the Sargents out of the country.
Mission accomplished.*

Dalton wanted to sigh with relief. Instead, he
closed his eyes for a brief second. When he opened
them, he saw that Epps was agitated. His hand
movements were stiff and aggressive before he
leaned forward with his finger pointed in the face of
the congressman. Epps stormed off a minute later. It
appeared he was having a very bad day.

Tate didn't know how, but as she stood surrounded
by people, she felt utterly alone. Birch touched her
arm to get her attention and she flinched. "Sorry, I
didn't mean to startle you," Birch said softly. "I'm
good here. You've withstood everything they've
thrown at you. Why don't you go back upstairs and
relax before tonight? I'll be up in about an hour."

Relief made Tate almost weak-kneed. "Okay. I
think I've given them all the gossip they need." Tate

turned to leave, and her two guards followed her. She kept a smile on her face as she climbed up the stairs to the portico. She made her way through the Blue Room, waving and talking to people on her way.

Tate walked past Sandra and Thurmond and almost stopped when she heard Thurmond gleefully say, "Now we know how she got on the news. She screwed the most powerful Hollywood agent, who probably called in a favor. And now we know how she got her job as press secretary, too. I'm sure it was handy there was no wife to dupe. What a joke," he snickered.

Tate sucked in her breath and kept walking. She would not cry. Not in front of any of these people.

Finally. Tate collapsed on her bed and kicked off her shoes. Now she could cry. Her guards had checked the residence, and after declaring it clear, had gone to wait at the bottom of the exits. As soon as Tate took a shaky breath to allow the tears to come, she heard some of the staff walking around. She needed privacy. She needed peace, if even for just a couple of minutes.

Tate peered around her door, and the second the hall was clear, she darted for the stairs leading to the third floor. She strolled around looking at the small bedrooms, the larger suites, a workout room, and what she really came for — the solarium. She entered the room and sounds of talking coming from the linen room disappeared. When Tate closed the door, she found the peace she was searching for.

The room had a large rectangular window directly in front of her with two equal-sized windows at a slight angle to each side. This was the true escape for those living in the White House. Extended family would stay on the third floor when they came to visit, plus there was a billiards room as well. But it was this room that Tate had wanted to see. It was filled with Birch. Not the president, not even the Birch from the second floor, but the real Birch. An Army blanket was flung over an overstuffed leather chair with an ottoman. It was clear Birch liked to sit there to watch football on the large television. Books were scattered on the table and the couches were made for comfort, not for display.

The sun shone through the windows and Tate could see lounge chairs outside on the promenade. If she desired, she could walk around to the greenhouse or simply sunbathe. But it was the leather chair and the Army blanket that smelled of Birch she wanted. Tate sank into the chair. She wrapped the blanket around her and felt her body finally relax. Her muscles ached from standing tense all afternoon. The relief allowed the tears to finally fall. And as she cried, Tate finally drifted off to sleep.

CHAPTER EIGHTEEN

B irch thanked man and woman after man and woman for their service. He was glad to see some people from when he'd been deployed and to meet some of the heroes who had sacrificed a great deal keeping the United States safe. That didn't mean he wasn't relieved when Humphrey came and told him it was time to go.

"We need a private word," Humphrey said softly in between Birch posing for pictures.

Birch nodded and Humphrey did his best to get the president out of the Blue Room and up to the second floor as quickly as possible. In the Treaty Room, Birch yanked his tie loose as Humphrey looked around before closing and locking the door.

"I have an update. The day has been very full, and it's not even three yet. I hope tonight is more peaceful." Humphrey filled him in on Jeff Sargent and how Lizzy was doing. Birch was surprised Jason was helping again but understood he probably needed a purpose right now.

After Birch signed the paperwork he needed to and dealt with emails that required his attention, he was ready to see Tate. Humphrey took the stack of papers off to his office and Birch walked down the

hall to the room where Tate was staying. He knocked softly, but there was no answer. He opened it quietly, but found it empty. "Tate?"

"Excuse me, sir?" one of the butlers said from behind him.

"Yes?"

"The young lady is in the solarium. Is there anything you will be needing?"

Birch was about to say no, but then thought better of it. "Yes. Will you send up a tray of finger food? It's been a long day, and I don't think either of us really ate."

"Perhaps the lady has a favorite food that will help her feel better after a long day? My wife personally loves truffles," the older man in his tux said with a slight bow of his head.

"That would be perfect, Gene. Thank you for suggesting that." Birch took off for the third floor, knowing in a matter of ten minutes Gene would be back with food and some chocolates for Tate.

While the staff had been generally ignored during President Mitchell's short time at the White House, Birch had found many of them to be great people. His being single had made things interesting for them, but they'd adapted well even though he still hadn't picked a china pattern. The idea of asking Tate to do that for him excited him. Before they could do that, they had to make it through the next couple of days.

Birch walked down the small hall to the solarium. When he got inside, Tate looked so small wrapped in his blanket. Her eyes were closed, and

there were dried tearstains down her face where she had cried herself to sleep. His heart ached for her. It had taken every iota of control he had not to simply carry her off in his arms today. He heard the protesters, he heard the remarks others made to her, and he remembered exactly who made them. There would be reckoning among those who had so boldly decried her as a whore, as if times since *The Scarlet Letter* hadn't changed. For now, though, there was something he could do.

Birch slipped his arms under and around her. Tate opened her eyes in surprise as he lifted her up enough for him to take a seat on the chair and place her on his lap. He adjusted her so that he cradled her in his arms and hugged her to him.

"Birch!" she squeaked as his hand traveled under the blanket to palm her flat stomach.

"I've missed you," he whispered against the side of her head before kissing her temple.

"I was with you most of the day."

"Not like this. I missed this," Birch said, moving his hand to cup her breast. "Did you miss me?"

Tate smiled and Birch felt as if he had accomplished a great feat. "Hmm, I don't know. Maybe you should remind me a little more."

"Minx," Birch whispered as his fingers traced her nipple through the lace bra at the same time he kissed her. She opened for him, and he took his time savoring the taste of her.

The sound of a throat clearing sent Tate jumping, but Birch used his arm to keep her tight against him.

"I have a food tray, sir," Gene said as he rolled a trolley over to where they were sitting. "And for you, ma'am." Gene lifted a silver dome containing a huge piece of what looked to be a chocolate truffle pie with a side of raspberry drizzle.

Birch chuckled as he felt Tate's stomach growl at the sight.

"You're a lifesaver, Gene. Thank you." Birch smiled up at his butler.

"How did you know that was exactly what I wanted?" Tate asked, her eyes wide with a mixture of gratitude and surprise.

"A man never reveals his secrets. I have cleared the third floor for the next hour, sir. I also have your tuxedo laid out. Ma'am, is there anything you need assistance with in your preparations for the ball?"

"No, thank you," Tate said, getting the full White House treatment. It was the first time she'd met any of the residential staff.

"Gene, are you working tonight?" Birch asked.

"Yes, sir. Until midnight."

"Wonderful. I hope you don't mind staying alone a bit tonight, but I trust your impeccable discretion."

"No problem at all, sir. What do you need?"

"Will you make sure the rest of the residential staff knows that they can leave at eight thirty so they can watch the fireworks. And will you please inform them that the Queen's Room is off limits?" Birch knew Gene would move mountains to get things done. He was incredible, and he made sure the butler knew how much his hard work was

appreciated.

"Of course. I'll personally take over the Queen's Room services if you're comfortable with that, ma'am?" Gene asked Tate.

"Yes, thank you. But you don't have to go through any trouble for me."

"It's no trouble at all," Gene smiled before taking his leave. "I'll see you tonight, sir. Have a very enjoyable evening."

Birch leaned over and handed Tate the plate of truffle pie. "You've been eyeing this since Gene showed it to you," Birch chuckled.

"They all know we're . . . well, we're whatever we are," Tate said before taking a bite of the pie. Her eyes rolled back in her head in pleasure, and she made the sexiest little moan that had Birch growing hard.

"That we are sleeping together? Yes, they probably all know. But Gene will make sure there's no evidence of it. No one will be around to confirm the suspicions," Birch said as he watched her take another bite.

"Did you ever ask him about *Mollia Domini*?" Tate asked.

"No."

"I bet he heard the Mitchells talking, and we know they were part of it. Everyone forgets the staff," Tate concluded in between bites. "This is so good."

"You have a point. I'll talk to him. But first I have one hour without interruption, and I'm going to use every second of it." Birch snuggled her tight

against him as his hand moved back under her shirt. Only this time, he didn't stop at her stomach. Tate took the last bite of the pie and groaned as he cupped her breast.

"I've always heard chocolate was better than sex, but I didn't believe it until I had this pie," Tate sighed as she licked the fork.

Birch smiled against her neck as he took the fork from her hand. He pulled her shirt off, tossing it on the floor next to the chair before spinning Tate around until she faced him. He pushed her legs apart so she could straddle him. Birch's hands cupped her breasts as he leaned forward. "Challenge accepted," Birch said a second before tracing her nipple with his tongue.

Birch felt Tate's head fall back as her fingers speared his hair, holding him to her. He let one hand slip under her skirt as she ground against him. Soon Tate was all his, and the chocolate pie was a distant memory.

★　★　★

The guests for the Fourth of July Ball were a mix of the who's who of politics and those who thought they were in politics, like several actors and singers. It was filled with many who didn't mind the steep price tag to get into the event supporting the National Archives.

"Sir, could I get a picture of you and the lady?" Dalton asked a man he didn't recognize. The woman was Kerra Ruby, who was wearing the most

inappropriate dress for the elegant evening, although the American flag nipple pasties were a nice touch. Dalton stood by the entrance to the ball snapping pictures and generally eavesdropping to make sure he had identities of all possible *Mollia Domini* insiders.

"Sure," the man wrapped his arm around Kerra who pushed her breasts out, angled her head, sucked in her cheeks, and kind of smiled. The man identified himself and Dalton wrote down the name.

Next an old man with a very young woman in a skin-tight dress stopped to pose. Bertie Geofferies and his wife, Vivian. Bertie put his hand on her stomach where there was a slight bulge.

"Mr. Geofferies, are you about to become a father again?" Dalton asked as he snapped the picture along with the rest of the press who were corralled in a line.

"I sure am. Viv and I are very blessed. And Rue couldn't be happier to have a new brother or sister," he said of his forty-three-year-old son. Dalton was sure Rupert "Rue" Geofferies VII was thrilled to no longer be the sole heir to the Geofferies fortune. Vivian smiled lovingly at her husband, and Dalton had to applaud her acting. She was about to pass off Trip Kameron's child as a Geofferies heir.

Over the next thirty minutes, everyone from Hollywood's "it couple" to Senator Epps and his wife came through. Sandra Cummings was with her assistant, Thurmond. FBI Director Kirby and his wife were next. A pop singer brought her agent, Fitz Houlihan. As the line began to dwindle down,

Sebastian Abel appeared right behind Trip Kameron. This was a reality show waiting to happen.

Sebastian only paused a half a second when he saw Dalton before heading into the dining room. Dalton put away his camera and flashed his VIP pass along with a dinner ticket to the guards, who then let him out of the press section.

Once inside, he found his table. He was seated with other no-names in the back of the room, but he'd asked for that so he could observe the entire room. Geofferies was staring daggers at Sebastian, who was flirting with Geofferies's wife. Trip was happy to sit back and let the pop star Fitz came with fling herself all over him while Fitz was looking for someone.

Epps was making his way over to Sandra when the double doors opened and the president entered with Tate Carlisle walking in behind him. The room erupted in whispers, the general consensus being Tate slept her way into the job as everyone tried to guess if they were a couple. Epps stopped his progression toward Sandra and went back to his table as Birch made his way to the front of the room.

Tate scanned the crowd, and Dalton noticed the second she found Fitz. Her face hardened, and her hand fisted quickly before all emotion was wiped from her face. She took a seat opposite the president as he stood and gave a speech about the importance of preserving history.

Soon waiters poured from the kitchens, and dinner was served. Dalton watched Sebastian and

Geofferies, seated at neighboring tables. Sebastian
would regularly lean over to whisper something to
Vivian that had her laughing, and Dalton was
worried Geofferies might have a heart attack,
judging by how red his face became.

Trip seemed not to have a care in the world that
multiple women he was sleeping with were in the
same room. And more surprising was that
Geofferies didn't seem to know about Trip. He was
more annoyed with Sebastian. Mixed in were the
whispered conversations FBI Director Kirby and
Sandra Cummings were having and the angry looks
Epps kept sending their way. There was so much
going on he wished Lizzy were there to help.

Tate heard the whispers when she entered. She
ignored them and looked around the room. But
when she saw Fitz, she almost faltered. People were
looking between them as if they would break out
into dramatics at any second. Instead of feeling
cowed by their whispers and stares, she grew
angrier with each passing minute. No one was
whispering about Fitz. No one was calling him a
whore for having sex on a private beach. No one
was telling him to quit his job.

The entrees were cleared, and dessert was set
down. She blinked as she saw a piece of chocolate
truffle pie instead of the tarts everyone else was
eating. Her eyes shot to Birch, and she smiled.

Birch winked and then turned to the secretary of

state. "Sandra, I want to set up a meeting with China. We need to lay down the law once and for all about the South China Sea."

"I'm handling it, sir," Sandra said with a tight smile.

"And now I am." Birch turned to Humphrey. "I want a face-to-face with the leaders from the area in two weeks. I'll talk to them all individually on Monday to get their agreement to join me. Can you set that all up for me?"

"Of course," Humphrey replied, ignoring the daggers Sandra was sending them.

"Sir, I have been working with China—" Sandra started.

"Yes, and you'll be part of the discussion. But we need stability, and we need it soon. But now what we have to do is mingle," Birch said as he looked to Tate and Humphrey. Getting the hint, they both stood, along with Sandra.

"I'll send over my notes on Monday," Sandra said as she moved to stand by Birch. Tate saw Birch thank Sandra and then the two went off to the neighboring table. Humphrey moved to her side.

"Ready to face the wolves?" Humphrey whispered as a smile played on his lips as if they were joking about something rather than telling the truth.

"Fitz is here."

"I know. I saw his name on the guest list. I'm sorry I didn't tell you."

"It's okay. I might as well face him so everyone can get over the suspense."

"We'll work our way back to him."

Tate let Humphrey do the talking as she greeted Senator Epps's wife. Epps was clipped in his statements but didn't tear her down. Instead, he seemed as if his mind were someplace else, and he didn't want to talk to them.

"That was painful," Humphrey said, leading them to the table where Sebastian sat. They stopped between Sebastian and Vivian.

"Hello. Is everyone enjoying the festivities?" Humphrey asked with a big grin on his face.

Sebastian smiled up at him and again Tate was struck by what an attractive man he was. His gray eyes took her in, and he looked both dark and sinfully handsome in a tuxedo with his black hair. "Miss Carlisle," he said, ignoring Humphrey, "how is my best friend doing? Tell him I'm mad he hasn't stopped to see me yet."

"Face it, Abel," Geofferies said from his table, "you're not as important as you think you are."

Sebastian's grin turned lethal, and his expression went from seductive to menacing in a blink of his eye. "And what would you know about importance, Bertie? Your tech company hasn't come out with a new product in over a year. The stocks on your hotels have fallen ten percent while mine have grown. But, I shouldn't say any more. My mother taught me to respect my elders. Now, Miss Carlisle, how are you holding up?"

"I saw that photo," Vivian said, joining the conversation as her husband looked fit to be tied. "It wasn't like it was a sex tape."

Tate blinked. She guessed that was support. "Thank you, Mrs. Geofferies." Tate turned to her husband. "Mr. Geofferies, I have to thank you for growing my retirement fund. I invested in your holding, and it's done very well."

"Please, call me Bertie. I believe in my investments, and I'm glad they've been able to help you. Some of us aren't obsessed with ourselves to the point of forgetting to help people."

"And that's what we're here for tonight, to help preserve our history for the people," Tate said, smiling as she shot a warning glare to Sebastian to behave himself. But as Tate and Humphrey made their way to another table, she couldn't help but hear Bertie's last remark.

"Better hang on, Abel. I'm working on something now that will take your company down. You'll be begging for investors by the end of the year."

Tate leaned over to Humphrey, "I knew they were rivals, but I had no idea it was so personal."

"Oh yes. Sebastian has told Birch numerous times that Bertie is out to destroy him. It's all because Sebastian came into the marketplace and followed the outline for success that Bertie paved. Only Sebastian did it better. He adapted to the new times and foresaw what was needed now and in the future. It's a bitter rivalry and one that will continue, I'm afraid. Bertie has been grooming his son to take over for him after he dies. Rue is Thurmond, just with real power and money behind him."

"That thought will give me nightmares," Tate

joked before turning to greet the next guest
Humphrey deemed important enough to schmooze
with.

CHAPTER NINETEEN

Lizzy poured drinks at the bar while a local band Valeria had hired right before she disappeared, played. She and Alex worked nonstop as the bar filled to capacity. She joked that her injuries were the result of Alex trying to teach her how to ride a motorcycle. The story was laughed about around the bar as she served drinks.

The door was propped open and Lizzy's eyes were drawn to the man who walked in—Crew. The man who had saved her butt earlier that day and who had also seen the other side of Lizzy. He came over and patted his grandfather, Buzz, on the back before taking a seat next to him. Lizzy headed their way.

"I'm telling you my grandson will be here when you're ready for a husband," Snip said. Everyone else groaned.

"Grandpa, you have to stop trying to hook me up with someone who already has a boyfriend," Flint Scott said with an apologetic look to Tate.

"Besides, when she's ready to settle down, it'll be with my Crew," Buzz said as Crew almost choked on his beer.

"Pops, who said anything about marriage?"

"Yeah, flyboy isn't mature enough for that," Flint shot over the heads of the two old men.

Lizzy sighed. Some things never changed.

"Where is my girl?" Buzz said with a waggle of his bushy eyebrows.

"Valeria?" Snip said with a bit of Latin flare. "I think you are referring to *my* girl."

As the two battled over which man Valeria liked the most, Lizzy just shook her head and filled another order. She was setting the mugs on the bar for Alex when Flint caught her attention.

"Sorry about my grandfather. I know you're with Dalton. I was actually wondering if I could ask you a question."

"Sure," Lizzy said, leaning against the bar.

"What do you know about Tate Carlisle?"

Lizzy didn't have to pretend to be surprised. "Well, she's Tucker's sister. He's with the FBI here in Quantico, and that's how I met her. She's very nice. Down to earth. Why? Are you wanting to date her?"

Flint shook his head. "No, just curious. I'm meeting her tomorrow for an interview and wanted to know what kind of person she was."

"You mean, is she honest?" Lizzy asked.

"Yeah," Flint said as he flipped his long hair into a messy bun.

"As far as I know she is. She's easy to talk to. We usually talk girl stuff, but she's never seemed gossipy or anything. I know it's not much. I can say I consider her a friend."

"That's exactly what I was wondering. Thank you. And hey, where is Valeria?"

"She's visiting family," Lizzy smiled as she reached for a new order ticket to fill.

Flint went back to his grandfather, and Lizzy caught up on orders. She went to fill a round of tequila shots and realized she was low on tequila. After sending them off with Alex, she hurried to the storage area. When she stepped inside, she felt someone behind her. She whirled around ready to fight but stopped when she saw it was Crew.

He shot her his trademark grin. "I hate to tell you, but I don't think we can date."

Lizzy crossed her arms over her chest as Crew leaned against the beaded door. "And why is that?"

"I don't date women who can kill me." Crew's grin slipped. "Seriously, how are you?"

"I'm okay. I had someone clean up the wounds for me," she said, thinking of how Jason had tended her after they tied up the man in the horse stall.

"I swear my heart stopped when you flew off the roof. I just kept thinking how Dalton would kill me if something happened to you. I know he's busy tonight. I want you to let me walk you home."

"Thanks for worrying about me. I can walk home myself. You don't have to do that," Lizzy said, reaching for the new bottle of tequila.

"I know. I'd feel better if you let me." Crew let out a deep breath. "I want, no need, to be useful."

"I understand the feeling. All right, you can walk me home."

Lizzy waited for Crew to leave. He seemed to be carrying the weight of the world on his shoulders. He had just realized how big this mission was. How

dangerous. How imperative it was for them to win. She knew the feeling well.

★   ★   ★

Birch slipped his hand to the small of Tate's back. She flinched and took a step away from him. He gritted his teeth together as she moved closer to Humphrey. He knew why she did it, but that didn't mean he didn't hate it. He'd heard the rumors about how she got this job because she was sleeping with him. It wasn't like he could stand up and tell them the truth. So he let her walk away.

She was beautiful in a sapphire-blue sequined gown tonight. Birch felt almost primal in his need to publicly claim her as his, but as president he couldn't. He was hampered by rules, public opinion, and responsibility to his party unless. . . Birch looked around at the people filing onto the portico. A thought nagged at him, and he put it away for later. Right now, he was going to fight the tradition of backing away from scandal for image's sake and stand by the woman he was quickly falling in love with.

Humphrey was standing next to Tate at a baluster and Birch stepped behind them. He was close enough for Tate's bottom to brush his hip. He smiled as she stiffened.

"Birch, people will talk," she whispered up to him.

Birch leaned down, putting his lips to her ear. "Sweetheart, they're already talking."

The phone in his pocket vibrated, and he saw that Humphrey similarly pulled his phone out. Birch looked down at the secure message. It was from a number he didn't recognize so it had to be Jason's.

Humphrey turned to talk to them. "Jason found out the man is from South Africa. He has links to a large bank there."

"Which one?" Birch asked, putting away his phone.

"Davenport Bank."

Tate whistled. "I did a story on them. That isn't a normal bank. It's based out of England, but South Africa is where a lot of questionable activity goes on. Bribes, illegal loans, improper investment . . . all to make the bank richer. I did a story on it for BBN. A story that Claudia stole and sanitized."

"Strange link to Claudia, don't you think?" Birch asked.

"I see conspiracy everywhere," Tate admitted.

"Did Jason learn anything else?" Birch asked Humphrey as the first firework exploded.

"Not yet."

Birch leaned forward again. "Did you meet with Kerra Ruby?"

Tate shook her head.

Humphrey held up his phone again, and Birch leaned forward. Kerra had posted a picture of her and him. Underneath, Birch read where they had a great talk about turning the slumping economy around. However, she felt he still wasn't invested in saving people's jobs.

"What the fu—"

"Shh!" Tate cut him off as Birch lowered his voice.

"That never happened. She just said 'selfie' and that was it. I was hoping you could rule her out of *Mollia Domini*, but this. . . Tate cocked her head. "What?"

"I've heard that exact language before." Tate almost jumped as another firework lit the sky. "I need to get to my office. Now."

"Take Brock with you," Birch said, feeling Tate's sense of urgency.

Tate nodded and took off. Humphrey shrugged. "We need to resolve the Fitz issue. Now may be a good time."

Birch looked around and found Fitz at the other end of the portico. "Bring him over."

Humphrey meandered off as to not draw attention. Birch took a deep breath. Tate didn't love Fitz anymore. Birch knew that. She had told him it was casual, and he believed her. It still didn't mean he liked the idea of this asshole being with her.

A minute later, Fitz stood arrogantly next to Birch. "You requested an audience?"

Birch rethought his stance on making a scene by punching Fitz. Instead, he smiled the smile he held for terrorists when he knew he'd broken them. "I don't request anything. I'm the president. I order."

Fitz looked amused. "What, are you going to throw me in jail because I don't come kiss the ring?"

Birch shook his head and slapped Fitz on the back. "No, but it would be a shame if the IRS had to freeze your accounts while they investigated you for

213

tax fraud."

Fitz's amused look faded. Instead, he looked pissed. "And if I follow your orders, what do I get?"

"Aren't you going to ask what I want?" Birch asked with a hint of his own smirk.

"It's irrelevant, isn't it? The important thing is Fitz. What does Fitz get?"

"What does Fitz want?" Birch tried not to laugh as they both spoke about the man standing in front of him in the third person.

"I want a contract with you signed — in perpetuity — naming me as your agent."

"No."

"Then no deal," Fitz shrugged.

"How about this?" Birch turned to face Fitz fully. "You smile and pose with Tate for some of those photographers. You don't upset her. You treat her with respect. You pretend you're old friends having a laugh. And then I won't turn you over to the IRS . . . or worse."

Fitz's jaw worked as he ground his teeth. "Fine. After all, maybe we can renew our relationship. Tate was always good in bed." Tate appeared and Fitz seemed to smile even bigger. "There's my girl."

"Stuff it up your ass, Fitz," Tate said, holding a piece of paper. "Or better yet, Brock, can I borrow your gun?"

Birch chuckled. "You have some kind of effect on women, Fitz. Humphrey, go find a photographer or two and casually point them this direction if they aren't already. Tate, smile and pretend it's nice to see Fitz."

Birch saw a couple of other photographers move in and snap some pictures as Tate laughed. Birch stepped out of the frame, and he had to give it to Fitz. He knew how to spin a picture. He had his hand on her arm, and they laughed as if sharing a private joke.

"Mr. Houlihan, are you upset about your picture with Miss Carlisle being released?" a reporter asked.

"Of course. It's a complete invasion of privacy. Tate and I shared a beautiful relationship and are still friends."

Tate and Fitz posed for a couple more photos and suddenly the pop star was there. It was like a moth attracted to an electric blue zapper. She saw the lights and couldn't stop herself from going to them. Tate politely excused herself and rejoined Birch and Humphrey.

"I know why the post sounded familiar. Look, these are the talking points Harriet gave me on my first day."

Birch looked down at the paper and, there in bold, read about a slumping economy and saving jobs. The only difference is Kerra added one word — *not* — before the jobs language. "She's part of it."

Humphrey stared at the paper and back to Kerra. "Does that mean it's not Claudia? Trip said — "

"Shit, Trip probably doesn't even remember what he said. But this proves it's Kerra," Tate said excitedly. "I can't wait to tell Lizzy."

"Wait," Birch said as he paused to think. "Claudia is still an issue. We've seen the videos. We know she's spinning the stories. We need to pull her

stories and compare her reports to the talking points Harriet gave you. I can guarantee I've never seen those before."

"Me either," Humphrey said, reading over her shoulder.

Tate nodded. She would take care of that. People started to head back into the White House. Birch took the paper and handed it to Humphrey. "Can you hold this while we dance?"

"Dance?" Tate said as she suddenly stopped walking.

"Yes. We have to open the ball."

"Then dance with someone else. They'll talk."

Birch shook his head. "I don't care, Tate. I want to dance with you, so I am. For the next three minutes, I am no longer the president. I'm just a man who is dancing with the woman he loves."

Tate opened and then closed her mouth. He saw her eyes grow wet as she blinked quickly. "I love you, too, Birch."

His heart pounded, and the guilt he expected to feel was absent. His wife would have loved Tate, and something about that made Birch know the risk of putting himself first over public opinion was worth it. There would be no polls asking what the people thought of the President of the United States dating. There would be no questions to focus groups to see what their response was, as so many did while playing the game of politics. Tate was more important than politics.

Birch walked into the ballroom as the band started the opening song. The dance floor cleared as

he slipped his hand around Tate's waist, and she put her hand in his. The music claimed him as he looked down at her smiling face. Her violet eyes were dark with emotion. There was nothing in his touch that told the world he loved the woman in his arms. It was all in their eyes and hearts. The room fell away, and for a few brief moments, he was just a man taking a chance on love.

CHAPTER TWENTY

"**I** can't stand it anymore," Epps growled to Kirby. The two men stood in the back of the ballroom as the guests watched Birch and Tate dance. Dalton stood in the shadows by the literature on the National Archives.

"Patience, Martin," Kirby hissed. "Or you will ruin everything. Now stop talking to me in public."

Kirby walked off and Epps's hands clenched at his side. He took a deep breath and asked his wife to dance as other couples took to the floor.

Dalton pulled out his phone and sent Lizzy a text. There was something in the way Birch was looking at Tate that caused him to miss Lizzy. His phone vibrated a minute later, and he read her text. She was safe, back at the bar. She'd told people she'd tried to ride a motorcycle. *When will you be home?* Home. Being with his unit of PJs had been his home for more years than he could remember. Six? Seven? Hell, it was probably closer to a decade. But at some point in the last week, he'd stopped thinking of his black site in the middle of hostile territory as home. Home was with Lizzy in the small house in Quantico with a little fluff ball of a dog.

Epps was their guy. He didn't know how Epps

had been cleared the last time, but there was enough on his camera that he wouldn't be getting away again. There were too many unanswered questions that Epps appeared to have the answer to. Furthermore, with a bomb missing, Kirby's not notifying Birch about it, and their overheard conversations, Dalton was pretty sure Epps and Kirby were working together.

The Washington Leader had yanked the story and replaced it with a statement that Jeff was mentally ill and was on a leave of absence while he sought professional help. The story seemed so far-fetched that hardly anyone mentioned it that night. The mission was coming to a head. Dalton felt it in his bones. When Epps and his wife left the dance floor and the White House shortly afterward, Dalton headed home.

★ ★ ★

"I'm going to kill her," Lizzy hissed to Alex as she wiped sweat from her forehead. It was almost midnight and the bar had only picked up in activity. "Have you found anything about where Valeria has gone?"

"Not a thing. She's completely off the grid." Alex picked up a tray of beers with one hand and hiked up his sagging shorts with the other.

"Not only would it be helpful to have her on the missions, she's left me high and dry at the bar as well. Let me know when you find her, and you'd better find her."

"Dude, do you want me looking for Val or taking prints from the folders. I can only do so much, and every time I get ready to run some prints you call me away. Come rescue me. Get a private plane. I need a new phone . . . for the hundredth time," Alex snapped.

Lizzy took a deep breath. "You haven't done anything wrong. I just feel as if we're so close to getting answers but having to maintain a cover is wearing me down. It means things move slower. I'm sorry, Alex."

Alex sent her a half smile. "I know. I miss being cussed out in a language I don't understand, too."

"It feels like our family isn't together. I just can't help but feel she needs us."

"You know what I need?" the deep voice said.

"Dalton!" Lizzy cried in relief.

"Dude," Alex sighed happily before taking off with the full tray.

Lizzy watched as Dalton walked around the bar, and before she knew it, he was standing behind her. He placed a soft kiss on her neck, and she leaned back onto him, ignoring the shouts for orders for just a second longer.

"Let's get to work so I can get you home. I've been thinking about you all evening," Dalton whispered before diving into the orders waiting to be filled.

Tate couldn't catch her breath. They'd danced the

first dance together, and it was the most romantic moment of her life. He loved her. But just as fast as the excitement came, it went. Birch wasn't just Birch, he was the president. A president didn't date. He'd be crucified for taking time away from running the country to have a personal life. Re-election would be impossible.

Tate couldn't do that to Birch. If Birch wasn't in office, then their group wouldn't exist and *Mollia Domini* would flourish. Tate watched as Birch danced with Sandra. It was the hardest thing to do, but she had to walk away. There were more important things than her heart right now. Until *Mollia Domini* was dismantled, she couldn't risk Birch having a political misstep. And having an affair with his press secretary wasn't a misstep; it was something so much bigger.

Tate took one last look at the man she loved before turning around and slipping from the crowd. Her heart broke as she thought of Birch's reaction. She would have to tell him they had to wait. It would be hard, but until *Mollia Domini* was destroyed everything had to be completely professional between them. He would understand. She would make sure of it.

"Ma'am?" Brock asked, coming to walk next to her.

"Tate, please."

"Where are you going, Tate?" Brock asked, following her out to the hallway to the grand staircase.

"Home."

"I'll see you to the residence."

Tate shook her head. "No, I'm going to my home."

Tate made her way up to the residence with Brock right behind her. "Does the president know?"

"He will," Tate said, walking into the Treaty Room and picking up a piece of paper. She began her note. She explained her reasoning and hoped he'd understand that she was doing this not just for his election, but so they still had enough power and sway to take down *Mollia Domini*. No matter how much it came to power figures versus power figures, the public would play the biggest role. They just didn't realize it yet. And if they didn't believe in or didn't trust Birch, then *Mollia Domini* could still live for another day.

"Then I'm coming with you," Brock announced as he followed her to her room. Tate threw her clothes into her bag, and in minutes was ready to go.

"Just make sure he gets this," she said, handing him the letter.

"Ma'am? Can I be of assistance?" Gene said from the door. He looked concerned about the bag she held in her hand.

"Yes," Brock answered for her. "Give this to the president the second he comes upstairs. I'm accompanying Miss Carlisle home."

"Of course," Gene said, taking the note. "Ma'am."

Tate smiled at him and gave him a hug. "Thank you for being my hero today."

Tate hurried from the room before she changed

her mind and ran into Birch's arms.

The drive home was made in complete silence.
When they pulled up to her house, she swallowed as
fear shot through her. *WHORE* was scrawled on her
garage door in red spray paint.

"I'm taking you back to the White House,"
Brock said, but Tate already had the door open.

"It'll be fine. It's not as if I haven't heard it
before." Tate pulled out her keys and opened the
front door. She looked around. It was clean. Brock
checked the entire house with Tate following behind
him. The people she had hired did a great job.
Everything broken was simply gone. The house was
set up a little differently, but it was still home.

"I can crash on the couch," Brock said as he took
a seat.

"You don't have to do this."

Brock smiled softly. He was a good man.
"You're a friend of Val's. She'll kill me if I don't take
care of you."

Tate gave a little laugh. "I don't think Val likes
me very much."

"Is she hard on you?"

Tate almost rolled her eyes. "That's a massive
understatement."

"It just means she believes in you. She always
pushes harder on those she sees something in than
everyone else. It's her way."

Tate kicked off her heels and took a seat in the
one remaining chair in the room. The other had been
smashed. "What happened between you two? She

said it was just a distance thing after you went into the service and she went with the DEA."

Brock shrugged. "Basically. We never stopped loving each other, though. We realized we both were each other's number two. For her, the DEA came first. For me, the Secret Service came first. It shouldn't be that way when you're deeply in love."

"Do you miss her?" Tate asked softly as her mind went to Birch.

"Sometimes. She was my best friend as well. But we both know we made the right decision. Not all couples are like us. If you love him —"

Tate shook her head. "No, we're exactly like you. The country and *Mollia Domini's* defeat must come first."

Tate loved Birch with all her heart. But as Brock said, sometimes there were things that were even more important than love. Tate climbed into bed and turned off the light.

She didn't know whether she was dreaming or not when she heard a crash. She sat up and screamed as she tried to figure out what was going on.

"Stay there!" she heard Brock yell. It was no dream.

Tate looked around her room. It was empty except for the sound of glass breaking again. It echoed in the house as tires spun on the pavement outside. She heard the front door slam behind her as Brock raced out into the street.

Then, from the darkness of her closet, a shadow emerged. Tate opened her mouth to scream, but the

gun pointed at her stopped her as he put a finger to his lips to indicate she needed to be silent.

"*Hola*, Miss Carlisle," the man said with a Latin accent. His tan skin and dark hair made her think he'd just come from a beach in Mexico.

He wasn't tall, probably close to Tate's five feet eight inches. But he was strong. The muscles on his arms were three times the size of Tate's and covered in tattoos. He stepped closer and ran a hand over her cheek. "I don't mean to scare you, but I need some answers for my boss. And you'll answer them for me, *sí*?"

Tate nodded as her body shook. "Do you know Valeria McGregor?"

Tate couldn't stop the shock from showing on her face. This wasn't about *Mollia Domini*?

"I can see you do," he said softly as he continued to stroke her face as if he were trying to calm a wild animal. "Who is she?"

"She's a waitress at a bar I go to. Why would you—?" The hand tightened on her face, pushing her cheeks into her teeth. Tate winced.

"I'll ask the questions. You be the good *chica* and answer them." Tate nodded, and he relaxed his grip.

"She's a waitress. Where?"

"Lancy's."

"How do you know her?"

"I meet my brother there for drinks," Tate said, sticking to the story they'd all agreed on. "He tried to pick her up one time. That's the first time I met her."

"Did it work? Is she a whore like you are?"

Tate's eyes snapped to his in anger, and she spat in his face. She was as surprised as he was, but he reacted quicker. The hand across her cheek sent her falling back onto the bed. The shock robbed her breath for a moment as the prickles of pain throbbed.

"What do you know about her being part of the DEA?"

"I don't know what you're talking about," Tate said as tears began to fall. She tried to catch her breath but couldn't. She was failing the lessons Val had taught her, but she would never fail Valeria. She'd protect her until this man killed her.

"Does she still work for them?" he asked, fisting his hand in Tate's hair and pulling her upright.

Tate sobbed harder. "I swear I don't know what you're talking about. At the bar, she always says mean things about the DEA trainees. I . . . I don't understand," she stuttered. "Why are you asking me? I hardly know her. She just works at a bar I go to."

"What does she say?"

Tate folded in on herself, but he yanked her head up. "I don't know. She says it in Spanish."

"Then how do you know it's mean?"

"She narrows her eyes and it's . . . I don't know, but it's just not nice. Um, it's something like *chinga tu cabra*," Tate pronounced very poorly.

The man chuckled softly, the meaning coming through in translation. "Has she ever sold you drugs?" the man asked as he resumed his gentle stroking of her cheek.

"I'm so sorry. I don't do drugs." Tate flinched, expecting to be hit. Instead, the man smiled and raised the gun inches from her head.

"You've been very helpful."

"Why did you ask me?"

"Because she told us to. Now, close your eyes."

She closed her eyes tight. At least she didn't give Valeria up.

"Tate? It's okay to come out now," Brock called as he walked through the front door.

Tate screamed. If she were going to die, then hopefully Brock could catch the man. She waited for the bullet to tear through her skull, but instead she heard her door crash open. Tate opened her eyes.

"What is it?" Brock asked.

Tate blinked. Where was he? Tate's head spun as she took in her room. There was no evidence the man had ever been there except for the slight flutter of the curtains covering the French doors leading to the patio.

CHAPTER TWENTY-ONE

B irch paced his bedroom. Humphrey was the
one talking about running for president during
the next election, but that was years away, and Birch
hadn't said a thing about it. For Tate to leave
now . . . Birch took a deep breath, but it didn't help
as he reread the letter she had left for him.

"Fuck!" he yelled, sending his glass flying
against the bulletproof window. He was a prisoner
in his own house.

He heard footsteps racing up the hall. "Sir!"

Birch turned when the night agent crashed into
the room with his gun drawn.

"Abrams, we're going out," Birch snapped,
storming out of the room.

"What? Out where? Now?" Special Agent Jim
Abrams sputtered in confusion. It was two in the
morning, after all.

"Yes, now. And we're taking your car."

"But, sir," Abram said, racing to catch up with
Birch.

"But nothing. Where are you parked?"

"At least take the Beast," Abrams begged,
referring to the armored limo.

Birch looked to the man in his mid-thirties. He

looked back worriedly at him. "No, I don't want anyone to know I'm gone. If they see the Beast leaving, they can follow me." Birch turned back and jogged into his room. He was already wearing his workout gear. He grabbed a baseball cap and slid it low over his brow. No one would look twice. "Let's go."

"But—"

"But nothing. I'm the president and I say we're going. Now."

"Yes, sir," Abrams said nervously, leading Birch past the Uniformed Division guards whose job is to guard the White House from any threat presented. What they didn't expect was the president rushing past them into the parking lot in the middle of the night.

"Mr. President?"

Birch smiled at the guard. "I'm good. Agent Abrams is following my orders. I'll be back soon. Tell the gate."

"This is me," Abrams said, pointing at the sports car.

"I knew I liked you, Abrams. You want to let me drive?"

"You know I can't let you do that, sir. I'm already breaking so many rules."

Birch felt sorry for the young agent, but he did miss driving. As vice president and now president, he hadn't driven on a public road since the campaign started.

The drive to Tate's house was uneventful. It also

gave Birch a taste of freedom. Things were going to change now that he knew he could flex his presidential power to leave the White House. He even ignored the undercover car that had trailed them to Tate's house. He knew Abrams sent a message to the other agent on duty. Whatever made them feel better about him walking out was fine.

"Agent Loyde is here. You may want to make him aware of our presence. Is that window broken?" Birch asked as he stared at the large rectangular window that looked as if it was missing glass.

"Yes, sir," Abrams said, putting his hand on his gun and taking in the entire street as he called Brock. "It's Abrams. I'm outside with the president. He wants to see Miss Carlisle. Is the site secure?"

Birch was running short on patience and seeing the broken window wasn't helping. What had happened? Was Tate safe?

"We can go in. There was an incident, but it's secure now," Abrams said as the other agent parked his generic black SUV a block away and stepped out with his hand on an M-16. So much for remaining inconspicuous. Birch shook his head and went up the steps. The front door opened and Brock was standing there armed as he looked past Birch to take in the neighborhood.

"Where's Tate?"

"Couch," Brock said, nodding toward the living room.

Tate was sound asleep on the couch, but her brow was furrowed. It was clear she wasn't sleeping peacefully. "What happened?" Birch whispered.

"Well, you saw the graffiti, I'm sure. But then as we were going to sleep, someone threw a brick through the window. I headed outside to secure the front lawn and try to get a description. While I was out, a Hispanic male suspect came in through her bedroom door and held a gun to her." Brock stopped talking and looked at Abrams. "Abrams, will you do a lap around back for me? I was going to walk the perimeter now for safety."

"Of course," Abrams said, heading out the front door.

Brock waited a second and then lowered his voice. "The man wanted to know about Valeria. He said that Valeria told him that Tate knew her and could vouch for her. He asked about her being part of the DEA, her interaction with DEA trainees, and if she'd ever sold drugs to Tate. I'm worried. Val would never send someone to check on her background unless she was in deep and needed to prove her cover. The first rule of going undercover is keeping as close to the truth as you can so you don't mess up your background."

"What do you think she's doing?" Birch asked.

"Look at the pieces: Hispanic, knowing her history with the DEA . . . it has to be something about why she was fired from the DEA that she thinks may relate to *Mollia Domini*. I just can't believe she would put Tate in this position," Brock said as they looked down at an exhausted Tate.

"I would think she would send someone to Lizzy who has experience lying," Birch said, fighting the urge to draw Tate into his arms.

Brock nodded, but then stopped. "Maybe that's why she sent them to Tate. Tate has no law enforcement background, nothing to make anyone suspicious of her working for an agency. They would have looked Lizzy up and seen her FBI record. If they wanted to see if Val was out of the game, then Tate's the exact person to go to—a complete innocent in the world of drugs and federal agency work."

"I hope so. I want this over so badly. Are you worried about her?" Birch asked, looking away from Tate and toward Brock.

"Yeah, I am. I may not be dating Valeria anymore, but I'll always love her. And whatever she's in right now, it's some deep shit." Brock looked away from Birch and down at Tate. "I'll give you a minute alone."

Birch watched Brock move out the front door and close it behind him. Birch went and knelt in front of the couch. He used his finger to push a long blonde curl from her face. "Sweetheart?"

Tate blinked her eyes open when Birch gently shook her shoulder. "Birch! What are you doing here?"

"You leave me a letter about it being better for me if you left, and you're surprised to see me? I couldn't sleep without you. You're already a part of me."

Tate sat up and looked at him so sadly it hurt Birch's heart. "I'm so tainted, Birch. Being around me will hurt you, and I couldn't stand that. You have to be our president. You have to be able to run

the group to take down *Mollia Domini*. If you're not
in office, then who is going to stop them?"

"Oh, Tate, I will. We're closing in on them.
Don't you feel it? It's like when I was in the Army. It
would be nothing for long periods. Hints of chatter
here and there, but then I'd get a feeling that ran
down my spine when I saw a bit of intercepted
information or when someone from a village would
step forward. And I would know it. I would know
we had them. I have the same feeling. Two days,
Tate. Just hold on for two days. I need you now
more than ever, and you need me, too," Birch said,
finally taking Tate in his arms as she tried to choke
back a sob.

"I can hear them all the time calling me names.
It's only been a day, and I already feel completely
helpless against them. The names they call me . . .
There's a site telling me I should kill myself. It
makes me forget I put myself in this position. They
make me forget I did nothing wrong. They make me
want to run off alone and hide. I hear the names
they call me in my head even when I'm all alone."
Tears streamed down Tate's face as Birch held her
close to him.

"Then let's fight back. Come back to the White
House with me. Stay there with me. You have your
team looking into Epps and Harriet. Throw yourself
into that work. I have to have you with me. I have to
know you're safe. Tate, I love you. I know that it's
the last thing we should be thinking about during
this whole mess, but it's the light amidst all this
darkness for me. You're my light. You're my love.

Stay with me, please."

Tate cried harder, but when she looked up at him she was smiling. "How can we have this hope, this love, in the middle of this nightmare?"

"I don't know. But we do and *Mollia Domini* can't take that away from us. Come home with me, Tate," Birch asked quietly as he held his breath.

"I love you, Birch. I was just trying to protect you," Tate said, pulling away from his chest.

"I know, sweetheart. But we are stronger together. Will you come with me?" Birch asked, standing up and holding out his hand.

"Always." Tate placed her hand in his, and Birch never felt better. He was invincible with Tate by his side.

All too soon, they were back at the White House. Back to their headquarters and back to their bubble of safety that sometimes seemed like a prison to Birch. But as Birch looked into Tate's eyes as he slowly made love to her, he decided that a life mandated by rules didn't seem as oppressive with her in his bed with him.

★ ★ ★

No matter how amazing it was waking up naked in Birch's arms, Tate knew the rest of the day wouldn't be so great. And she was right. Her team had texted her that morning that Fitz was trying to get an appointment with her.

"What is it?" Birch asked. It was still dark out, but that didn't matter. Neither of their work lives

stopped for something as annoying as sleep.

"Fitz wants an appointment to discuss marketing for the Claudia interview," Tate sighed as she responded to her team to set the appointment for right before lunch. "I'm going through all the information Brent Eller sent me and trying to find what I can dig up on Epps. Dalton is sure he's *Mollia Domini*'s source on the Hill. Thank goodness we found out about Peter. Having someone close to you like a Secret Service agent telling *Mollia Domini* what you're up to is bad news. What are your plans?" Tate asked, as she slid from the bed and started to get dressed.

"Lots of meetings and phone calls," Birch sighed.

They were quiet for a minute as Tate thought about the mission. "Do you think Claudia is reporting to Epps, and he's the one behind all of this?"

"No, even Epps doesn't have the power to pull this off. They have to be funded by someone with deep pockets, or a group of people with deep pockets. I think we have an idea Harriet and Phylicia were controlling Dan March and Bram Smit, and that they were reporting to Epps. I think Epps is reporting to someone even bigger."

"And we know Kerra Ruby had some connection to Harriet or at least to the talking points. And I'm pretty sure Claudia is on it, too. I know we don't have direct evidence. I'm going to work on that today. She just has to be part of this. But I still think Trip is the one pulling their strings. And Trip

definitely has the right kind of money and contacts to pull this off," Tate said as she brushed her hair.

Birch thought for a moment before shaking his head. "Maybe, but Trip is as dumb as shit. He only thinks of himself, and he even told Lizzy he'd been asked to join. With the drugs she had him on, I don't think he could lie about it."

"Then who are Kerra and Claudia getting their orders from?" Tate wondered. She felt as if she were missing a key part. "We have foreign governments in on the politics, we have people on the Hill, in the White House, and in all government agencies doing *Mollia Domini*'s bidding. We also know the media is controlled the same way. They've been using Claudia on BBN to spread their lies to the people nationally, so who is the Claudia of international reporting? And we have Kerra shaping pop culture—" Tate stopped talking as her mind raced forward.

"I gotta go. I have an idea." Tate smiled. Damn, Lizzy was right. It was a web, and a web interconnects, and she had the key to finding the connections.

"Go? What—"

Tate kissed Birch into silence. "My mind. I just can't. I'll talk to you soon," Tate said clumsily as she raced out of the residence, leaving Birch looking confused. She got like this when she had a lead for a story. Her brain was too busy working on the details to talk it out.

Tate pulled her phone out and dialed. "Dude, it's like six in the morning," Alex said sleepily as

Tate ran through the White House and into the West Wing.

"Search the talking points I'm sending you with all of the international news outlets," Tate said as she slammed the door to her office, leaving the lone night worker staring at her in surprise.

"What?" Alex questioned.

"Just do it! I'm emailing you now," Tate said quickly.

"I'm supposed to be working on prints. You know, the main lead we have," Alex grumbled. "Every time I try to get to work—"

"I know, but this is a big lead, too. Can you do it?"

"Dude." Alex said it all with that one word. "But, Lizzy—"

"Tell Lizzy to call me if she gets on you. This is big, Alex. They're all using the same talking points. Kerra Ruby posted last night on social media. It sounded familiar. It was because it was from off-the-books talking points Harriet had given me when she was trying to control the White House's responses to the media," Tate responded. "I'll email it now. Just do it, Alex!"

Tate hung up and snapped a picture of the document Harriet had given her and sent it to Alex. Birch was right, it was a tingle down her spine, and she felt it now. She was onto something—something big.

CHAPTER TWENTY-TWO

The problem with doing research on the computer was that you were on the Internet. And when you are on the Internet, it's nearly impossible to prevent yourself from looking up your public profiles. Tate took a deep breath and typed her name into the search bar and hit Enter.

She'd been feeling good until she did that. Her office wasn't far from Birch's and he'd checked on her twice already. Even if it was just for a quick kiss, it meant the world to her. She'd been entering the snippets from Harriet's notes into search engines and finding speeches from governors, senators, and members of Congress over the past three weeks discussing one or all of the talking points Harriet had highlighted. One focused on the economy and the other laid suspicion on the president for his foreign affairs policy. The only difference in their speech compared to Harriet's: the word *not* had been added. President Stratton is *not* helping the economy with his jobs program. President Stratton is *not* helping the country with his foreign agenda.

Tate had gathered the names and then moved onto social media. She'd searched hashtags and found Kerra Ruby posts, those of Kerra Ruby

followers, and at least fifteen other celebrities spouting the same message, almost to the word, as if it were a script. Action stars, reality stars, singers, and models were all involved. Now Tate just needed to find out what they all had in common. Unfortunately, she saw one thing, and that was how she got sucked into the rabbit hole of searching her own name. All of them had been bashing her.

"Miss Carlisle? Miss Carlisle?"

Tate finally turned to her secretary. "Um, sorry. What is it?"

"Mr. Houlihan is here for his appointment."

Tate let out a breath. "Put him in the conference room. I'll be there in a minute."

Her secretary closed the door and Tate looked back at the screen, her good mood evaporated. Tate snapped a picture of her notes and sent it to the group with her findings before taking the paper and shredding it. She couldn't do anything right. They were right. She felt worthless.

Tate shoved away from her desk and with heavy feet made her way to the conference room. She smelled Fitz before she saw him. His signature power scent lingered in the hallway. Tate opened the door and didn't even bother trying to fake it.

"What do you want, Fitz?"

"What's wrong, baby girl?" Fitz asked, hurrying over to her.

Tate tried to shake it off. "The press is getting to me. That's all."

"I have been thinking about that. If I were to represent you again, the press would stop talking. I

bet even Claudia would stop reporting it. It's not news if we're a team again."

Tate cocked her head and really looked at Fitz all shined up. "You never represent people in competing fields. You told me that's what made you so powerful when it came time for negotiations."

"But you're not in a competing field. I've thought about it since I ran into you at BBN. This could be really good for you. I have a strong network connection to BBN that could save your reputation. Plus, I already have interest from Stanworth Motion Pictures and their publishing company. I pitched George Stanworth the idea of a tell-all after you're out of office in a couple of years, and he's ready to offer you a seven-figure book deal with his publishing company and a right of first refusal for Stanworth Motion Pictures to turn that book into a movie," Fitz said eagerly.

"Why do you think I'll be out of a job in a couple of years?" Tate asked, taking it all in.

Fitz looked at her as if she were stupid. "Everyone in the know knows that Stratton is out. There's talk about someone running against him in the primary. When was the last time a seated president had opposition in the primary? That is, if he makes it through without being impeached for something. I'm telling you, Stratton is out. You need to be getting all you can from this."

"Is that why you wanted to see me? I thought this had to do with Claudia's interview?"

"Yeah . . . I lied. I want you back. Tell me what to do."

Tate shook her head. "Fitz, I'm the biggest controversy in the media right now."

"Exactly. You are a hot item, and I can sell that. I can get you on every news outlet, every TV talk show, and every late-night show. I can force Stanworth into a two million dollar advance if he wants your story. Come on, baby girl, you know we're good together," Fitz said in that seductive crooning voice that had once turned her on but now made her want to punch him in the face.

"It's all so much. Give me a couple of days to think about it." Tate took a deep breath. "I guess with your connection to BBN you are in with the Stanworths? I heard it's a real soap opera over there. George's kids, Helena and Auden, are fighting each other and George's new wife, whom I believe is his granddaughter's age, right? All for power of the company."

"Yeah, but it won't happen. George won't give up power without a fight."

"Isn't he in his nineties?" Tate asked with surprise.

"I guess being married to a twenty-five-year-old keeps you young." Fitz chuckled before turning serious. "Personally, I like my women to be real women and not fresh off the college cheerleading team. You're looking good, Tate. I have missed you."

Tate wanted to scream at him. He was the one who blew it with her. He was the one who fucked Claudia and ditched Tate as both a girlfriend and a client. Instead of yelling, Tate just smiled. "Thank

you, Fitzie. I'm glad things are going well for you, business wise."

"They are. They've really turned around this past year. Even before we split. You know how hard I was working and how badly I was scraping my way up to the top. I've finally reached it, and I've got to say the view from the top is excellent. I'm working with everyone from the Stanworth family to Bertie Geofferies to Trip Kameron to Sebastian Abel. And I've picked up a ton of new clients."

Tate smiled. No matter what, there had been a lot of good memories between them. "I'm happy for you. I'll think about what you said and get back to you. And I'm sure I'll see you soon."

"I have to fly to LA to negotiate a deal for one of my new clients — the pop singer I brought to the party. But I'll be around."

Tate nodded and opened the door. Her secretary immediately joined them to show Fitz out. As Tate headed back to her office, all thoughts of Fitz vanished. She had a lead to follow.

★ ★ ★

Lizzy tapped her fingers on the bar in frustration. She was pissed off. First Dalton left to follow Epps. Then Tate commandeered Alex. And now Buzz and Snip had interrupted her right before she could get the prints out to start running them herself. At this pace, they were never going to get done.

"Come on, girlie. Take a pair of old men out for a walk," Snip said, holding the front door of Lancy's

open. They never wanted to go on a walk. They always wanted free beer.

"Okay," Lizzy said slowly as she turned to the old men. She'd just have to wait to go upstairs and get to work on the fingerprints.

The trio headed to the park by the river just as they had the night they told her about her father's involvement investigating *Mollia Domini* — not that Buzz and Snip knew about the group. The familiar actions and looks sent her stomach flipping. Something was wrong.

They chatted about their grandsons, about the bar, and about the weather until they were standing next to the moving water. "What is it?" Lizzy asked as soon as she was sure they were safely away from anyone.

Buzz and Snip shared a look, and it was Buzz who took a deep breath and started. "We know you're involved in whatever got your father killed. We haven't asked, but kept an eye on things from a distance. No one ever pays us any mind. We're just two old farts drinking beer."

Lizzy didn't say anything. She couldn't admit to being in the shadow group by order of the president.

"So far, we've figured Dalton and Valeria are your muscle, Tate's your insider, and, well, we can't figure out what the hell Alex is," Buzz said, keeping his gaze locked with hers.

Snip shook his head. "If he says *dude* one more time, I'll hog-tie him and shave his head."

Buzz rolled his eyes before turning to Snip. "If

anyone needs a haircut, it's your grandson. Every time I see that bun, I want to cut it off."

Lizzy smirked as the two men fell into familiar bickering. "Gentlemen, you brought me here for a reason?"

Snip smacked Buzz as they stopped arguing and turned back to her. "Well," Buzz started again, "this morning we decided to go fishing, and well . . ."

Lizzy stared at him.

"Okay, we were going to raid the bar for a couple of beers to take with us when we went fishing. Every liquor store is closed," Snip defended.

"Anyway," Buzz said, staring daggers at Snip for snitching on them, "we were sitting in the car looking for the key to Lancy's when the door opened and a man walked out. I thought it was Alex with his hair pulled back, but it wasn't. It was some Latin man, probably around thirty-four to thirty-eight years old. When we put on our glasses, we saw he was shorter and thicker than Alex."

Lizzy pursed her lips. She'd been in the bar that morning, but she hadn't swept it for bugs. She was getting complacent. Alex had already left when she'd arrived. Luckily all the evidence they had was still hidden in the attic.

"What time this morning?" Lizzy asked.

"Five-thirty," Snip answered.

Alex had still been there at that time. Lizzy looked at her watch. It was almost one in the afternoon. "What the hell took you two so long to tell me?"

Buzz and Snip looked sheepishly at each other

before Snip handed over the bag he was carrying. "Fish?"

Lizzy called Alex and verified that he had been at the bar that morning and hadn't seen anyone. Lizzy was hoping it was a friend of Alex's, but she knew that wasn't the case. She hung up and headed back to the bar when her phone rang.

"I'm not in a good mood," Lizzy snapped.

"I'm afraid this won't help," Humphrey's slightly nasally voice said on the other end of the call. "Someone broke into Tate's house last night and held a gun to her head while asking about Valeria."

"What the hell? And again, why am I only hearing about this now?" Lizzy yelled.

"Brock is sleeping and Birch has been in meetings all morning. I just found out. Tate told me he was a Latin man around five foot eight and muscular. Probably around her age."

That stopped Lizzy. "What time?"

"Huh?"

"What time was he at Tate's? Oh, screw this." Lizzy hung up on Humphrey and called Tate.

"Yes," Tate answered with a snap.

"What the fuck are you doing, Tate? You get attacked and don't bother to call me?" Lizzy felt her blood pressure skyrocketing. Her control on the situation was slipping. As team leader, if anything went wrong . . .

"Didn't Humphrey call you?" Tate asked. Her voice was lined with anger, which only made

Lizzy's temper rise.

"I don't want to hear from Humphrey almost twelve hours after it happens. You should have called me the second it was safe. We are a team, and I'm in charge. Just because you're fucking Birch doesn't mean you don't have to report to me. Am I clear?" Lizzy said with a tight restraint on her temper.

"But I'm onto something," Tate defended.

"I am, too, but apparently you don't care since you took Alex this morning when you knew I needed his help on these fingerprints. You know, the one solid fucking lead we have?"

"That's what I'm trying to tell you!" Tate practically shouted. "I have multiple leads. I've identified over twenty celebrities, like Kerra Ruby, who are getting their marching orders from *Mollia Domini*. I have to meet Flint at the bar tonight. I'll bring everything with me. You'll be proud of me, Lizzy. I promise."

Some of the air went out of Lizzy's anger. "Tate, this isn't about being proud of you. This is about being a team. And I can't do my job as team leader when everyone is running off in different directions without telling me. First Valeria and now you. Speaking of which, I had a visitor at the bar around five-thirty this morning. Latin male in his mid-thirties, approximately five foot eight and muscular." Tate gasped on the other end of the line. "I'm taking a guess that description sounds familiar?"

Lizzy listened as Tate relayed the events of the

night. Her mind was systematically detailing the facts and filing them away. "Valeria is involved with drugs. She said she thought *Hermanos de Sangre* owned the originating bank in Mexico. Do you think she went to that bank?" Lizzy asked, but continued without waiting for an answer. "It was smart of her to give your name."

"Is it because I don't have any agency ties?" Tate asked. "Because we both know she doesn't think highly of me."

"Stop feeling sorry for yourself, Tate. You wouldn't be part of the team if you weren't talented. Your talent is dealing with the press and looking into stories. And Val obviously trusted you enough to give your name as someone who could vouch for her being out of the DEA."

"I just can't believe she gave them her real name," Tate said, voicing the same concern Lizzy had.

"I hope she gave it, and it wasn't found out while undercover. We just need to trust that Val knows what she's doing. She'll get an earful when she gets back. I guarantee that much," Lizzy said, lightening up a little on Tate. She could feel the stress Tate was under and knew enough that her point had been made. Tate needed her support now. "So, what can I do to help?"

Tate let out a relieved sigh. "Can you just let me borrow Alex for the rest of the day? He's in my hotel room, and I'm heading over there in a minute to meet with him. I'll come to Lancy's as soon as I can to explain everything."

"Okay," Lizzy said, staring at her father's bar from across the street. "I have to go over the bar with a fine-tooth comb before it's clear."

Lizzy hung up and walked across the street with the fish Snip and Buzz caught slung over her shoulder in a cooler bag. It was going to be a very long day.

CHAPTER TWENTY-THREE

Tate rushed into Lancy's with a full briefcase. She looked around and saw Lizzy behind the bar, talking to Buzz and Snip. "Hey, Lizzy. Is my brother here yet?" Tate asked, making sure to keep her cover. Her excuse for frequenting the bar was Tucker, whom she knew didn't get out of work for another hour. Lizzy smiled at her as the two old men turned to look at her. Buzz winked, and Tate got the feeling she was missing out on something. "I'm going to be meeting Flint here in an hour," Tate said instead of asking what the wink meant.

Snip nodded. "He mentioned that to me. He's a good boy, that one. You could do worse, like if you dated that one's grandson. Wild is what he is."

Tate shook her head as the two instantly fell into bickering.

"Hey," Lizzy said, rapping on the gleaming wood bar top. "Cover me for a bit. I need to show Tate this new dress I got."

"Sure thing, boss," Snip said, sending her another wink.

"Free beer?" Buzz asked with a sly grin.

Lizzy rolled her eyes. "It won't take long. Two free beers each and that's it."

"Deal," the old men said as they used the bar top to help them stand.

"Come on. It's so cute. I was thinking about wearing it if Dalton ever takes me someplace fancy." Lizzy lead the way to the storage closet. "It's not clean out there. It is here, though. It took me hours, but I combed the place from top to bottom. I'll make Alex do it, too, when he gets here, which should be soon, right?"

"Yes. He was just packing up when I left."

Lizzy let out a sigh and closed her eyes for a second. "Your visitor left six bugs in the bar. Two were on table centerpieces. Two are around the bar area. And two were behind the bar. They are high tech, very expensive bugs. And they are different from the ones that were here when my dad was alive."

"He wants to find out about Valeria? Or did Valeria tell him about us?" Tate asked, keeping her voice low.

"It's okay, Tate. We can talk freely in here. It appears he didn't bother bugging my storage areas. This one and the one in the basement are clear. None of my bottles have been moved and none of the motion sensors were triggered. I think he's checking out Val's story. The question is, how can we help?"

"What do you mean?"

"I wonder what we should say so the bugs pick us up. I left them active for now. It'll take a week or so of setup to get them out. I'll start with the centerpieces. Say they look outdated and to throw them away and so on until I have a clean house

again," Lizzy explained.

"Maybe have me sit at a table with someone and talk about Val?" Tate suggested.

"Exactly. Buzz or Snip could do it. You could sit at the bar next to them. There's one close by that should pick you up," Lizzy said. "The trouble is what to say. I can have Buzz ask where Val is."

"Do they know?" Tate asked. She couldn't believe Lizzy would trust two gossiping old men with their group.

"They're the ones who told me about my morning visitor. And they see a lot more than I thought. They've been watching the comings and goings since WWII. And they knew my father was involved in something. They're the ones who warned me something was going on. I trust them, but I will keep them in the dark as much as possible. I'll bribe them with beer as a distraction," Lizzy smiled. "Now, what did you find?"

"Oh, my gosh, Lizzy, so much. We knew it wasn't isolated to us in the States, but I found so many people all over the world whose job is to sway the public by just repeating the same messages over and over." Tate reached into her bag and pulled out sheets and sheets of paper. "Here are all the ones I found on social media. These are just celebrities and such. Then I translated the talking points Harriet had given me when she was trying to corrupt me to her side of thinking into the main global languages and found all these."

Lizzy's eyes got larger as she starting flipping through them. "It's just as interesting to see who is

not here — like Trip. And Vivian Geofferies. We really can cross them off the list." Lizzy paused. "Wow, he's on here? He's like the biggest action star in the world."

"I know!" Tate exclaimed. "And look at this. Three princesses who are always front and center at fashion shows and gossip rags. But then Alex . . . wow, he found a lot, too," Tate rushed. "I'm getting ahead of myself. I'm just excited. I was going to have my team run Claudia though Harriet's talking points. But I don't know who we can trust, so I had Alex do it. Not only does Claudia match ninety percent of Harriet's anti-Stratton talking points, so do all these politicians and journalists." Tate handed over the file.

"These are all USA?" Lizzy asked, quickly flipping through the pictures and the quotes.

"Yes. Alex is going to do the best he can internationally tonight after the bar closes," Tate said, waiting for Lizzy to find what she had.

"Senator Epps —"

"Exactly," Tate said with a smug smile.

Tate sat at the bar watching Lizzy pass a note to Buzz. He read it and slowly slid it over to Snip. With a nod of their heads, they turned to Lizzy.

"Lizzy, bring us two beers will ya, dear?"

"Sure thing," Lizzy called out.

Tate watched Lizzy pour two beers as Buzz and Snip continued to talk. Buzz pulled out his lighter and burned the napkin, tossed the sputtering flames into the beer Lizzy placed on the bar top and looked

sadly at the loss of his drink.

"Hey, where's that cute bartender of yours?" Snip asked.

"Dalton is off for a couple days," Lizzy smiled as the men practically rolled their eyes at her.

"Not him. I'm talking about Val. I want her to date my grandson," Snip smiled.

"Now I'm hurt. I thought you wanted me to date your grandson."

"At this point, I'll take anyone," Snip huffed.

"I'm sorry, but Val kind of ditched me. Left us in a real pinch." Lizzy let the annoyance show in her voice. Tate knew that wasn't made up. They all felt that way. Val should have trusted them with her mission.

"Think she went back to the DEA?" Buzz asked.

Lizzy snorted. "God no. She hates them with a passion. I actually fear it's something worse. I caught her trying to sell some drugs out of the bar right before she took off. I was going to give her a chance to straighten up, but she left instead. Sadly, your grandson will need you to pimp him to someone else. The MP's daughter is easy, just ask Crew," Lizzy laughed before leaving the two men to instantly leap on that morsel.

Lizzy looked to Tate and the two nodded. The way the men were now going at their grandsons, they appeared completely oblivious to the bug. After all, what was a bug compared to the bomb Lizzy just dropped. Tate almost felt sorry for Crew. His grandfather was going to rake him over the coals for this. The cocky pilot needed to be knocked down a

peg or two.

The bar door opened, and Tate saw Flint walk in. He was just under six feet with a runner's build. He was younger than Tate, not that early thirties were much different from mid-thirties, but he carried himself as if he were much wiser. His dark blond hair was pulled back in his signature man-bun. Tate glanced over at the two old men and saw Buzz was making scissors gestures with his fingers in Flint's direction.

Tate stood up and walked over to him. With a tilt of her head, she indicated they should go back outside. Once the door closed, she smiled. "It's so nice out. Lizzy said there's a great park at the end of the block with picnic tables. Let's talk there."

They didn't speak until they reached the picnic area next to the river. The night was hot and muggy, but a breeze came off the river enough to flutter Tate's hair as they sat down.

Flint pulled out a notepad and pen from his satchel and took a deep breath. "I think you've looked into me. You know I'm reputable. You know I tell the whole story and follow through with leads."

"Yes," Tate said slowly.

"I've been investigating a story, and I would like your input. Anonymously, of course," Flint said seriously. He seemed so different from the slightly egotistical hipster she knew from the bar.

"It depends. You know I can't share classified information. That would be treason."

"Will you hear me out?" Flint asked. Tate

nodded and Flint set down the notepad. "I got into journalism to tell the stories no one wanted to tell, but ones the people should hear. I've exposed corruption, abuse, and injustice. But I have never come across something like this before."

"Like what?" Tate asked, trying to control her breathing.

"A story that leads me to turn against my own profession." Flint stopped and studied her. Tate tried not to show any emotion as he took in her hands, the muscles of her face, and her eyes.

"Go on," Tate said.

"Claudia Hughes and all of BBN is purposely reporting false stories in an effort to sway public opinion for some kind of self-fulfilling prophecy," Flint said, keeping his eyes locked on hers. "But you know that, don't you?"

"Well, I know the stories she's done on the president's involvement with Prince Noah and Zambia are inaccurate," Tate said, taking in Flint's reaction as much as he was taking in hers.

"And you know she had BBN fire you, right? Come on, Tate. You can trust me," Flint said softly as to not scare her.

"Why don't you tell me the whole story you're working on, and I'll see if I can help," Tate said instead. She knew Flint wouldn't tell her everything, but a baseline of what he had found would be good.

"I have evidence that Fitz and Claudia are in a relationship. Furthermore, I have evidence that Fitz has used his connection with Claudia to climb the ranks of the Fourth Estate Media Trust owned by the

Stanworth family. He's now the go-to agent when hiring actors for upcoming projects, actors who happen to have the exact same ideology as Claudia Hughes. Do you see the connection between them all?" Flint asked, drilling her with his eyes.

Puzzle pieces clicked together. It had been staring at her this entire time. "George Stanworth," she gasped.

"What I want to know," Flint said calmly as if trying to keep her focused, "is why George Stanworth is trying to discredit President Stratton? Do you know?"

Tate took a wobbly breath. Flint was even better that she had thought. She didn't think he would uncover more than she had.

"But then," Flint said when he figured Tate wasn't going to answer, "I thought why Stratton? Why not Mitchell? They are both in the same party, not that I've seen any indication that political parties even play a part in this. Do you know what does?"

Tate nodded. "Power."

"Exactly. When I looked into President Mitchell, I found out why they're attacking Stratton. President Mitchell used the same language as Claudia Hughes when he spoke to the public. President Mitchell was a traitor."

Tate had known President Mitchell was a traitor. What she didn't know until now was the talking points Harriet had given her hadn't come from Claudia, but from President Mitchell himself. President Mitchell had set the country on a collision course with total economic collapse. "Why?"

Tate snapped her eyes back to Flint's. She hadn't meant to say that out loud. "That's what I'm wondering, and I think you have a pretty good idea."

Shit. Tate needed Lizzy. She didn't know what to say. She didn't know what to do. Tate shot off the bench and started pacing. Flint just watched her. When she used Flint to get their side of the stories out to the public, she didn't expect Flint would turn around and use her for the story of a lifetime.

"You just want a good story. Is that it?" Tate asked.

"Of course, but you know even better than I do what is going on. I find it interesting the president isn't fighting back—" Flint paused, his eyes flying to hers. "Son of a bitch. It was you."

"Me what?" Tate stopped pacing and looked confusingly at Flint.

"You are the one emailing me the inside information I needed to start this investigation," Flint said, surprised yet completely sure of himself.

"I thought I saw a light. What are y'all doing down here?"

Tate spun to see Crew walking through the park toward them. He was eyeing them curiously. "Pops said he saw you all head out of the bar. Did I interrupt a date?" Tate saw the disapproving look on his face. As if he had any right to judge.

"So you decided to follow us?" Flint asked suspiciously.

"Hell no. I just had to escape the bar. Pops leapt on me for sleeping with Hannah, so it was more of a

tactical retreat," Crew said, sending a wink to them.

Tate moved over and wrapped her arms around Crew. Pulling him in for a hug, she whispered, "Flint has new leads, and he knows I'm involved. Tell Lizzy and see how she wants me to handle this."

Crew's smile faded. "I'll leave you to it."

Crew turned to leave but Tate stopped him. "The bar is bugged," she whispered before letting him go this time.

"Tate," Flint called her attention back to him. "You don't have to get help. I promise, I'm not going to hurt you. I'm not going to expose you. I only want to expose the truth, which is what I think you're trying to do as well."

"What did you want to ask me?" Tate asked, not acknowledging she had sent the emails to him.

"I want to know how you became aware of this . . . movement. It's certainly well past the point of conspiracy. I want to know how much information you have, what the president knows, and what's being planned to handle it. And lastly, I want to know how deep it goes. From my investigation, it certainly doesn't stop with Claudia or even George Stanworth."

Tate swallowed and took a seat on the bench. "You do realize that if what you say is true, you may be in danger?"

"I do. But I've had two assassination attempts on my life for stories I've written. I don't scare easily."

That surprised Tate. She'd had fallouts from her

own stories before — stalkers and threatening letters, but never an assassin. "What stories?"

"One on human trafficking through Mexico and one on how ISIS is funded." Flint stopped and looked up the street. "You told Crew to get my grandfather?" Flint asked with surprise and horror.

"No, I —" Tate looked up the street and saw Crew, Lizzy, and Snip heading toward them. "Where's Buzz?"

"You can't say anything about my story, Tate. You know how critical it is to keep the investigation secret. If George Stanworth finds out about this, he'll —"

"Try and have you killed is my guess," Tate finished for him.

"Flint," Lizzy said, stopping in front of them. "I hear you've done some good work."

"Dammit, Tate," Flint hissed a second before Snip slapped him upside the head.

"You don't talk to women like that," Snip said before shooing Flint over so he could sit on the bench next to his grandson.

"Flint," Lizzy said kindly yet in complete command of the situation. "Tate didn't turn on you. She's giving you the story of a lifetime."

Tate saw Flint look among them all. "Wait, you all know what's going on?"

"Not all of it. And Tate says you found something very important. In cases like these, so there's no confusion, we should start at the very beginning. Go ahead, Snip."

Tate sat back and listened. Even she hadn't

heard the role Snip and Buzz had played in bringing Lizzy into the case. She saw Lizzy tear up and look off at the water for a moment when Snip told of her dad's death. "And then we saw this Latin man exit the bar this morning and Lizzy here said she found bugs. That's why Tate brought you out here."

"Thanks, Snip. Want to go help Buzz for a little while?"

Snip opened his mouth, but Lizzy smiled first and held up two fingers.

"Fine, two beers each. We deserve more."

"You've probably had more if you've been sneaking into the bar to steal beer before your fishing trips."

"Humph." Snip didn't answer, but slowly got up and turned to his grandson. "Protect these ladies, Flint."

Flint nodded and watched his grandfather slowly head back to the bar. "That's not a lot to go on," he said, turning to Lizzy and Tate. "And what does Rotorhead know?"

Lizzy put her hand on Crew's arm to silence him. "I don't want Buzz and Snip involved any further than they already are, so I have deliberately kept them in the dark as much as possible. Now Flint, are you ready for the whole story?"

CHAPTER TWENTY-FOUR

Flint set down his pen and took a deep breath. "Shit," he said slowly.

"That about sums it up," Tate said. "Did Birch give authorization to bring Flint in?"

"Yes," Lizzy told her as she kept her eyes on Flint for his reaction.

"That's not fair. He didn't have to find Humphrey snoring and drooling on his couch," Tate complained, trying to lighten the mood. It was hard to do when you just realized you were standing smack in the middle of an international power grab.

"Prince Noah, the African rebels, President Mitchell, and now a stack of other high-ranking politicians and royalty all involved," Flint said, ignoring Tate's attempt to lighten the mood. "Celebrities, a media magnate, an FBI higher-up, three assassins, and a missing bomb."

"More or less." Lizzy wasn't trying to break the tension. "You can walk away right now. I'm sure Jeff Sargent wished he had. We won't think less of you if you do."

"Fuck that. I *will* think less of you." Crew crossed his arms and narrowed his eyes at Flint.

"And you released the photo of yourself and

Fitz to discredit Claudia?" Flint asked Tate even though Lizzy had already told him about the play.

"Yes. I'll send the videos to Brent Eller right before Claudia's special runs. As she's bashing me and reading from the talking points you identified, her downfall will spread like wildfire before she even knows it's happening. I'll give it ten minutes on Tinselgossip.com before smaller news outlets pick it up and fifteen minutes before the main media markets run with the story. Maybe thirty minutes if they actually try to verify the story. Nowadays that doesn't seem a priority." Tate crossed her arms and waited for Flint to respond. She saw his mind working overtime as he stared down at his notes.

"What do you want me to do?" Flint asked, looking up at Lizzy.

"I want you to continue doing exactly what you're doing now. I want you to report the truth. I just can't allow you to report about us and our mission. Think about it this way: If *Mollia Domini* were a wall that you needed to tear down, you would need to slowly chisel out the foundation until it collapses. Otherwise, you'd need many big swings to destroy everything. And that's something we simply don't have. We've captured both foreign and domestic assassins. We've nabbed both foreign and domestic operatives. But they are all on the outer edges of the spider's web. They're all the blocks sitting on the top half of the wall. We can push them off the wall, but the wall doesn't crumble," Lizzy explained.

"But if we take out the bottom, or kill the spider

in your web analogy, then the rest doesn't matter as the wall will crumble and the web will fall apart." Flint took a deep breath. "I don't like being hampered or told what I can write about."

"We're not telling you what you can or cannot write about *topically*. I'm just saying you never mention us or even the president's resistance right now. When the spider is killed and the wall tumbles, you get the exclusive story and all the evidence we've gathered. You'll be the one who exposes the truth. You just have to swear that you'll never identify us now or anytime in the future. No evidence, no notes, nothing can ever be found. Everything with our names must be destroyed. And no, putting it in a safety deposit box does not count as being destroyed. Or—" Lizzy shrugged her shoulders.

"Or what?" Flint asked.

"Or I'll kill you. I'd hate to do that to you. I'd hate to do that to Snip. But I have to protect this team. And I think you already know that."

Flint nodded. "Here's what I have found that I think will help you."

Tate sat back and listened as Flint told Lizzy about George Stanworth and the reach of his media empire. As Lizzy and Crew listened, Tate thought about the web. George would tell Claudia what to do just as Phylicia had told Dan. He was a higher-up, but the difference in power between someone like George Stanworth and Phylicia or even Harriet Hills was staggering.

"That's great information. And lines up exactly

with what Tate has found," Lizzy said, drawing Tate out of her thoughts.

"He's bigger," Tate sputtered as she stood back up so she could resume pacing. She thought best that way.

"What?' Lizzy asked, turning to watch her.

"George Stanworth is the closest to the spider we've ever gotten. Could he be the spider?" Tate asked as she stopped and looked at their confused faces before resuming her pacing. "Follow along. The edge of the web, the biggest circle with the littlest minions. Dan March, all these actors and singers, Bram, the guy you just caught trying to kill the Sargents . . . they're the outermost circle of the web. The ring above them, a little smaller and a little closer to the spider, are people like Phylicia and Harriet. We know they were both receiving orders from someone another ring up. But compare Phylicia and Harriet to George Stanworth." Tate held her hands out, palms up, as if weighing them.

"Damn, you're right. George isn't a middleman. He already has power, wealth, and influence. So where does he fit?" Lizzy asked, jumping off the bench as she too began to pace. "And Epps. Epps could be equal to Stanworth with the power they wield. Those two could be upper management, as it were, though it's entirely possible Stanworth is the spider. I need to know everything on Stanworth right away."

"But Epps—" Tate started to say.

"Don't worry about Epps. Dalton is on him. I want you to coordinate with Flint. If he has a story

for Monday night to help discredit Claudia, then
that's the best thing to focus on right now while I'll
have Alex work on Stanworth," Lizzy ordered. The
look on her face told Tate there was to be no
argument.

"Okay," Flint said, turning to Tate. "What do
you have on Claudia?"

Tate pulled out her bag as Crew and Lizzy
headed back to the bar. She showed Flint everything
Brent Eller had sent her, along with the videos Alex
had copied from her device. As the night went by,
her phone rang, interrupting Flint's furious
scribbling.

"Are you okay?"

Tate smiled as she heard Birch on the other end
of the phone. "Yes. I'm with Flint."

"Lizzy told me he's joining us. Humphrey
approves. Our group is growing."

"Is that good or bad?" Tate asked when she
heard something in his voice that sounded like
uncertainty.

"I don't know yet. It's more people to help, but
more people who could talk." She heard Birch take a
long breath in. "Sorry, it's just been a long day. And
I miss having you in my bed. When are you coming
home?"

"I was going to stay at the hotel tonight," Tate
told him as she looked at her watch: one in the
morning.

"No, you're not. Stay with me. I'll wait up."

Tate smiled into the phone. "I'll be there in an
hour then."

Tate hung up and found Flint looking at her. "The president?"

Tate blushed as an answer.

"I'm almost done. It's a rough draft of my article that will be posted soon after the videos are on Tinselgossip. What do you think?" Flint pushed the notepad across the table.

Tate moved so that the yellow glow of the lamppost shone on the paper. As she read, she was transported into the words and into the story. "This is amazing. You're a fantastic writer. You lay out the evidence piece by piece and show how the evidence connects to Claudia. You say it concisely, and it's easy to understand. This will ruin not only Claudia, but also BBN. I think it's good you don't mention Stanworth directly. At least not yet."

"The next piece will be on social media, and I'll expose a good number of the names you've found in the entertainment industry with their posts. I have a feeling you'll want to save the politicians for when you bring down Senator Epps. Is that correct?" Flint asked, putting away his notepad.

"Yes. I'll call on you during press conferences also to clue other reporters in that some of their colleagues are being manipulated and they better jump off that boat or they'll go down with BBN. Open and close your hand when it's in the air if it's important that you're the first person that needs to be called on. Tuesday, right before lunch, I'll hold my conference and address Claudia's downfall."

"Thank you," Flint said as they stood up. "I'm glad you trusted me with this. We, as people of the

world, have gotten too compliant with the news. It's less work to just believe everything we read than to challenge it. Yet when the free press was started in this country, it was their job to hold people of power accountable. I don't know when that shifted to the media being the ones with the power, but it's time the people took a stand."

"They will, starting Monday night."

Tate and Flint walked quietly to their parked cars. Tate headed out of town before opening up her car on the highway. At one in the morning, traffic would be minimal. A few headlights were scattered along the highway in both directions as she drove closer and closer to DC.

In her mind, she practiced the speech she would give Tuesday. She decided to show the hurt and pain she'd lived through in just a few days. And she planned to take Claudia down. Fitz would be collateral damage, but it wasn't like he was completely innocent.

Headlights filled her rearview mirror, causing Tate to squint at the sudden blindness. Tate looked in her side mirror to see the car, but it was too late. The car hit her at a high rate of speed from behind. Tate felt the scream shooting up from deep inside but didn't have time to open her mouth to let it out.

Her car began to swerve as the driver behind her pressed on the gas, sending her spinning before flying by her. Tate clutched the steering wheel, fighting to regain control as the car shot off the road. She knew she was going to crash. She battled the

wheel, attempting to navigate the out-of-control car from hitting one of the trees lining the highway a good twenty yards from the road.

Time slowed. The accident seemed to go on forever but Tate felt as if molasses was slowing her movements. By the time she wrenched the wheel to the left to avoid hitting some of the shrubs, it was too late to miss the sloping hillside. Her front passenger tire rode up the side of the hill. She stopped breathing as the car seemed to freeze for a brief second before rolling over. The airbags slammed into her, causing Tate to go blind as the car rolled over. Her face was on fire and the air smelled from the powder expelled with the airbags.

The roof crumpled as it slammed into the ground. Tate instinctively tried to duck but was pinned to the seat by the seatbelt and the airbags. The force of the hit expelled all the air from her lungs as she frantically clawed at the airbag in her face. Claustrophobia she never knew she had hit hard and fast. Tate felt as if her heart would explode as she fought to free herself.

The belt was cutting into her neck as she hung upside down, but she felt no pain. Her body shook with a combination of fear and adrenaline as her trembling hands found the latch. Tate pulled her seatbelt from the latch and fell head first onto the roof of her car. That one action allowed her to take a breath of air.

Tate reached for the door. She stopped and sniffed—gas. Frantic, she grasped for the door handle—locked! Tate shoved aside the airbag

curtain and froze. Two legs in suit pants stood
outside the window. A split second later, it looked
like it began to rain and the stench of gas grew. Tate
scrambled back against the passenger door.
Someone was out there trying to kill her.

Her bag. She needed her bag. Everything in her
car was now sitting in the middle of the roof. She
shoved aside a sweatshirt and some books to find
her bag. She flung it over her neck and pulled out
the gun Lizzy had encouraged her to carry before
crawling to the passenger door. Tate had to get clear
of the car before she could fire her gun. She knew it
would be too risky and likely ignite a fire inside the
car.

Tate tried the passenger door. Locked. She tried
to unlock it—nothing. Tate looked around
frantically until her eyes saw the dual metal prongs
of the headrest. Tate grabbed the headrest and
yanked it free from the seat. She scooted to the side
window and looked up at the seal holding the
window in place. She shoved the prong of the
headrest into the seal a couple of inches and then
pulled the headrest as hard as she could toward her.
The opposite side of the glass shattered and Tate
shoved her way through the now broken window.
She felt the glass cutting into her hands and knees as
her skirt was shoved practically up to her waist,
allowing her to move more freely.

The overpowering smell of fumes made her eyes
water as she crawled through the gas-soaked grass
before collapsing on the hillside. Tate dragged in a
lungful of clean air, looking around for the man's

legs she had seen earlier.

"Ta-a-ate," she heard him sing from somewhere in the darkness surrounding her car. She saw him stand up from the other side of the car. He had been peering in to find her.

"There you are," he smiled. "I'm sorry we had to meet again like this. We had so much potential. But then I followed you to Lancy's. What a dive, by the way."

Tate's throat constricted as her hand wiped the gas off on the grass before closing around the gun lying hidden in the uncut grass as the man strode forward.

"And you know what I saw when I parked my car? I saw you and a famous investigative journalist having quite the *tête-à-tête*. I was about to see what you were talking about when suddenly the door to the bar opened and the owner came out with someone who is clearly military and some old man. I looked into the owner. She's FBI."

"Former," Tate corrected as he continued his advance upon her.

"That may be, but what does a *former* FBI agent, a military man, an old man, the president's slut, and a journalist have in common? And what would keep them holed up in a park that is situated perfectly by the water so your conversation can't be overheard?" He took a deep breath. "It really got me thinking, Tate. And I think this is where you need to make a decision."

"And that is?" Tate asked as she kept her eyes locked on his while her finger skimmed over the

gun looking for the safety.

"You have a choice." He came to stand a few feet in front of her and looked down at her. He held up one finger. "One, you can die right now. Or two, you can join me. We can be partners in all ways. We'll drive back to DC while I call my friend to arrange a little accident for everyone you were talking to tonight."

"You can't kill them!" Tate gasped.

He chuckled. "Of course I won't kill them. We have people for that. You, I might have to make an exception for, though, since I caught you red-handed. You either join me, or I'll drag you back to the car and light it."

"I'll never join *Mollia Domini*!" Tate swore.

His eyebrows rose. "I was right. You do know about us. Tate, you're not stupid. We have money. We have power. And we have the ability to make all your dreams come true. You want to take over Claudia's spot? Fine. I can make that happen now. I'm that powerful. Claudia is a hireling, but I've moved up. I've proven myself to be a great recruiter. We'd be unstoppable together, Tate."

"Why? Why is *Mollia Domini* even doing the things they are doing?" Tate asked, her hand closing around the grip of the gun. She tried to pay attention to the man in front of her, but she knew what she was going to have to do. Shooting a person was an entirely different thing from shooting a target.

"Laws, regulations, PC bullshit . . . I could go on and on. And then the people go and elect do-

gooders who are more concerned with making everyone feel special than doing what needs to be done. We get things done all over the world. We've brought people together. Just look at how low Stratton's approval ratings are. We've joined forces with the people who will do whatever it takes to come out on top. It's the law of nature; only the strongest survive. And you're strong, Tate. You'd be an asset to us, and we never let our own down. We do whatever it takes to win."

"You believe George Stanworth will help you? You believe he'll do everything possible to make you more powerful? You're an idiot if you think he'd let anyone challenge him in terms of power. Just look at how you think about Claudia. She's disposable and so are you."

"My, you really have learned a lot about us. Who told you?"

"You're not as smart as you think. We know about Claudia Hughes, Kerra Ruby, George Stanworth, Dan March, Bram Smit, Phylicia Claymore, Harriet Hills, Prince Noah, and so many more. How about I make you a deal? You drop your gun and come with me. You tell us everything about the entire organization, and we'll let you live," Tate suggested. She kept her eyes locked on his and watched as he processed all she knew.

"I'm sorry, Tate, but you know too much," he said, his voice disjointed from the man she knew.

Tate saw him raise the gun. She waited to see if the raised hand would shake and then she'd know he could be reasoned with. But it didn't. He held it

steady and aimed for her chest.

"Goodbye, Fitz."

Tate moved so quickly that Fitz never knew it was coming. It only took one shot. Fitz fell slowly to his knees as blood ran from his heart. His eyes blinked in surprise as his mouth fell open a second before he fell face first onto the ground.

Tate fought the urge to drop her gun. Instead, she inched forward and reached for Fitz's neck. There was no pulse. Tate watched as traffic continued to pass every now and then. They were lost in the shadows of the night, far enough off the highway that headlights didn't reach them.

Her whole body shook as she crawled back to the car. Tate didn't know if she could stand. Her teeth clattered together, her vision wouldn't focus, and she felt so cold.

Tate slid partially through the broken window and began to search for her cell phone. It took a couple of minutes, which felt like hours, for her to find it. And when she did she was shaking so badly she couldn't dial. She used voice command to call Dalton. Lizzy was the leader, yes, but this situation called for Dalton's particular talents.

"Tate? What is it?" Dalton asked, sounding as if she hadn't just woken him.

"Fffff . . . Fitz just tried to kill me."

Dalton didn't exclaim. He didn't ask about Fitz. He calmly asked her location and if there were any injuries.

"I'm c-c-covered in gas," Tate stuttered before telling him where she was. It was hard since she

wasn't entirely sure, and she didn't want to risk getting any closer to the highway. But they could track the GPS on her watch to find her.

"We're on our way. Hide in the woods until we get there, okay?"

Tate nodded instead of answering even though Dalton wouldn't be able to see it. The line went dead anyway. Dalton was the epitome of efficiency. He would be there soon and then she'd be safe. Tate grabbed her sweatshirt from the car. She crawled to the safety of the woods and sat staring down at Fitz's body. She kept her eyes on him and the gun by her side as she pulled off her gas-soaked skirt and shirt. She used leaves to wipe down her body. The gas had probably evaporated, but she couldn't get the fear of being burned alive out of her head. She scrubbed and scrubbed until her skin was red. Tate slipped on the sweatshirt, drew her knees to her chest, and stretched the hem of the sweatshirt over her legs to keep warm. She would keep her eyes on Fitz until Dalton arrived just in case he wasn't dead.

CHAPTER TWENTY-FIVE

Birch lay in bed watching a movie as he waited for Tate to arrive. He looked at his watch. She should be getting there soon. He had gone into the family kitchen and made an old family treat for Tate, an after-midnight snack for when they were curled up in bed together.

His phone rang, and he smiled as he saw her name. "Hey, sweetheart. Are you almost home?"

"Killed him."

Birch shot up in bed. "Are you safe? Are you hurt? What happened?"

As Tate told him, he felt his whole body come alive with energy. He had to get to her. "I'm on my way," Birch said, already stepping into running shoes.

"No. Dalton is on his way."

Birch knew it was better this way, but that didn't mean he liked it. Again he felt completely useless. "No. I'm coming to get you. That way Dalton can take care of things there and I can take care of you. I'll be there soon. Hang on, Tate."

"I l-l-love you," Tate stammered.

"I love you, too, sweetheart. I'm coming. You'll be in my arms before you know it."

Birch reluctantly hung up the phone, then called Crew.

"Yeah?" Crew answered sleepily.

"I need a helicopter pickup now."

"Turski is on duty tonight, sir."

"Well, your commander-in-fucking-chief is telling you to get your ass to the White House immediately. Tate's been attacked."

Birch didn't wait for Crew's answer. He knew pilots had strict rules on when they could fly. They had to be alcohol-free and fully rested when it was their time on call. But right now he'd didn't care. It was the fastest way to get to Tate.

The White House phone rang, and Birch snatched it up as he bent to tie his shoes. "Mr. President, this is HMX-1 Commander Johnson. Marine pilot Crew Dixon has informed me that you have requested immediate use—"

"Yes, and I want Dixon. Now."

"With all due respect, Mr. President. Dixon is not the pilot on call tonight. We have procedures—"

"And as I told Dixon, I'm your Commander-in-Chief and I am ordering Crew Dixon to the White House immediately. It's a matter of national security for which you have not been cleared, but Dixon has. Do you understand?"

"Yes, sir," the commander said reluctantly.

Ten minutes later, Birch was standing outside waiting for Crew. Abrams stood nervously by on the night shift. He didn't like that Birch hadn't told him what the emergency was. All Birch would say was

that it was a matter of national security.

After Birch had put on his shoes, he'd called Dalton. It was Lizzy who answered and explained what they knew. Tate had had to kill Fitz. Lizzy was handling logistics as Dalton drove. His heart hurt for Tate, and all he wanted to do was get to her so he could see for himself that she was safe.

Birch looked up and saw the lights of Marine One. He turned to Abrams. "Crap. I forgot my briefcase in my room. Can you go get it? It's in my closet. It has papers I need for this emergency meeting."

"Yes sir." Abrams took off at a jog as the helicopter landed. Birch walked on board without a second thought of ditching his agent.

"Let's go. And kill the GPS," Birch said, sliding into the copilot's seat instead of the back.

"You got it." Crew flipped some switches, and they were airborne before Abrams made it back. "Now, can you tell me what's going on?"

"Tate shot her ex-boyfriend and manager, Fitz Houlihan. She's along the side of the interstate, hidden from the road. She sounds as if she's in shock."

"My commander said this was a national security issue," Crew hedged.

"I'd bet my election that it is. Lizzy said they'd had a breakthrough tonight with *Mollia Domini*."

"Yeah, I was there. But what would Fitz have to do with . . . shit. I got it. He's the intermediary," Crew said, turning to Birch.

"I think you better explain. Remember I wasn't

there, but I know Flint Scott was onto something."

"Flint and Tate. They figured so much out."

Birch listened, but the short time it took to get to the interstate was only enough time for the summary. It was enough, though, to get Birch's blood pumping even more than it was.

"Can you see them?" Crew asked.

Birch grabbed a pair of night-vision binoculars and began to scan the side of the road as they flew. There, huddled in the trees, was a figure. "Right here!"

"Let's hope traffic stops for us," Crew said, eyeing the few cars driving so late at night. Slowly, Crew began to lower the helicopter as Birch strained to see Tate in the shadows of the trees some distance off the road.

"Stay inside, sir," Crew told him as they touched down. "I'll tell any civilians that it's a training exercise."

Birch watched as Crew climbed out of the helicopter. So far no one came their way. The blades were still turning as Crew ran toward the treeline. Birch turned when he saw headlights. The van pulled to a stop and Birch looked nervously to the trees. He looked back as the doors to the van opened and let out a sigh of relief when he saw Dalton and Lizzy get out.

Birch opened the window as Dalton jogged forward while Lizzy sprinted for the trees. "We put up flares and a *Road Closed* sign about a mile back. Didn't have time to stop the other side, though. I'll take Fitz's body and dispose of it while Lizzy gets

rid of the car."

"Crew said George Stanworth, that blowhard, is part of *Mollia Domini*."

"That's what Lizzy says. Here they are."

Birch turned and saw Lizzy holding a blanket around Tate as Crew kept his arm around her waist for support. Birch couldn't wait anymore. He jumped from the helicopter and ran for Tate.

"Sweetheart, you're safe. You're safe." Crew relinquished his hold as Birch wrapped his arms around Tate. Until that moment, she'd seemed as if she were in a complete daze. But then the dam broke and huge sobs wracked her body.

"I killed him. He was in *Mollia Domini,* and he said if I didn't join them, he'd have *Mollia Domini* kill Crew, Lizzy, Snip, and Flint. I couldn't let him tell anyone about us."

Birch rested his head on hers as she clung to him.

"He . . . he . . ." Tate pulled back and looked at the group as she sucked in big gulps of air. "He climbed the ranks and got his orders from George Stanworth. Fitz's job was to control Claudia, Kerra, and the rest of Hollywood. His body . . . I shot him."

"We'll take care of it. You did the right thing. I know it's hard. You know I've been there, and I'm so sorry that you had to do this. You were very brave." Lizzy hugged Tate, but Birch refused to let go of her all the way. "I got the car. I'll meet you at our spot," Lizzy said to Dalton.

"Wait," Birch said. "They came after the woman I love. Did Fitz tell anyone about us?" Birch asked.

Tate shook her head. "He said he would. He was trying to recruit me first."

"*Mollia Domini* has no idea we're onto them. We played with them a little when you got rid of Phylicia's body. Now I want to make a statement." Birch told them his plans. Tate's eyes widened, Dalton smiled, and Lizzy nodded her agreement.

"By Monday night, we'll have delivered the first wave of our attack, and they'll never see it coming," Tate said, keeping her side pressed against his. "But now I really want a bath."

Birch sat in the back of the helicopter on the sofa with Tate in his arms all the way to the White House. Abrams was standing with his hands on his hips looking pissed. Birch stepped out with Tate's hand in his. She was a fright, but Birch tried to conceal her as best as possible with blankets wrapped around her body and over her head like a cloak.

"National security meeting?" Abrams said with anger in his voice.

Birch pressed on Tate's back to indicate she should go inside without him. "Don't forget who I am. And don't forget you have no power to stop me from doing my job. If you have a problem with that, then you can be reassigned. And not that I owe any explanation to you, but that had everything to do with national security."

Birch left Abrams trailing after him as he caught up to Tate. "Come on, sweetheart."

Birch helped her upstairs and into the privacy of

the residence. He turned the shower on until the glass panels were steamed with heat. Then he turned to help Tate undress. As he unhooked her bra, he fought the automatic reaction his body had to seeing her naked.

"Take your shower, and I'll make you some hot chocolate."

Tate shook her head. "Don't leave me."

"Okay. I'll be right in." Birch watched as she stepped into the shower and took a deep breath. He looked down at the growing tent in his pants. "One, two, three." He had to get control of himself before he entered the shower.

"Are you coming?" Tate called out.

Birch almost groaned aloud as he tore off his shorts, tossed his shirt to the ground, and stepped into the shower.

Tate was on him the second the door closed. She wrapped her arms around his waist, her breasts pushed into his chest, and she laid her head against his heart. "Thank you for coming to get me. I followed orders and called Dalton, but I couldn't stand not having you there with me. I would have fallen apart completely if I had to help clean the scene."

Birch just held her close for a full minute. "Let's get you cleaned up. Turn around and I'll wash your hair."

Tate turned, pressing her ass against his erection as he shampooed the horrors of the night away. Next he washed every inch of her. His hands slid over her breasts, down the slope of her hips, and he

knelt to run the soap along her long legs. Tate's head fell back as she moved just enough to give Birch access to her center.

"Tate?" Birch asked, unsure what she was offering.

"Kiss me, please. Wash away all the memories," Tate whispered.

Birch looked up from where he knelt. Tate looked back at him, her eyes pleading and her nipples hard. Birch reached around her, running his hand softly over her ass before pulling her to him. He buried his head between her thighs and kissed her deeply. Tate moaned loudly, and he felt her grab onto his shoulder. She arched into him, and he gave her everything she asked for. When she cried out his name, Birch stood up and turned off the water.

"We've only begun," he whispered, kissing her as he picked her up. He stepped out of the shower and placed her, soaking wet, on one side of the bed. Grabbing a condom as fast as he could, Birch listened to every sound Tate made as he thrust inside her, making sure to give her exactly what she needed.

By the time Birch and Tate snuggled into bed, her eyes were heavy, and she fell asleep on his chest without a single line of worry on her face. Birch held her to him, feeling her heartbeat against his side as he looked down at her lowered lashes. There was a shift inside him. He knew with certainty he wanted Tate beside him for the rest of his life. He didn't care if it cost him the presidency. He would do whatever it took to show her how much she meant to him.

The sense of urgency he'd felt upon finding out Tate was in danger slowly faded. Instead, as Birch finally fell asleep, he planned his courtship with military precision. And it would start with a dinner date.

CHAPTER TWENTY-SIX

D alton was tired of following Senator Martin
Epps. He either went to his Moose Tribe at
night or out on a dinner date with his wife.
Otherwise he was at his home or most likely at his
office. And unfortunately, Dalton couldn't find a
way to go unseen in the Capitol Complex, especially
with its being late on a Sunday afternoon. There
weren't many people strolling the halls of the
Russell Senate Office Building.

It itched at him. Dalton wasn't used to
surveillance. He was used to action. He was used to
running into dangerous situations, not sitting back
in the shadows, waiting for something to happen.
But as the hours ticked by and the sun's hot rays
turned into a warm late afternoon glow, Dalton
continued to stay in the shadows.

Tate and Birch sat across from each other at the table
in the Solarium on the third floor of the White
House. She sat back listening to Birch practice his
talking points with Claudia for later that afternoon.
They kept the conversation light and discussed

having to decorate the residence on his own and the fact that he still hadn't picked out a china pattern — all duties that had previously fallen on the First Lady. Birch talked about the history and the honor of living at the White House before Tate sprung a tough question on him.

"And what it is like working from home?" Tate asked with a light laugh as if she were Claudia.

"The commute is great," Birch joked back.

"What do you say to those who think you shouldn't have someone like Tate Carlisle — your personally selected press secretary currently embroiled in scandal over a picture showing an intimate relationship — not only working with you, but also a frequent visitor to your residence?"

Tate kept her face impassive as she noted Birch's face turning a shade red and his hands clenching.

"You can't do that. She'll smell blood," Tate sighed.

"What did I do?" Birch asked with frustration. Tate had been nitpicking everything he'd said and done for the past two hours.

"You clenched your hands, your eyes narrowed a fraction, and your cheeks are a little flushed. You need to think of puppies and kittens when she asks about me. Keep your entire body relaxed," Tate instructed. "Let's go again."

★　★　★

Lizzy's gloved hands worked the powder as she dusted for latent prints on the folders from the

meeting at the White House the other day. She had rows of cards with each person in attendance lined up waiting for the tape with the prints to be applied. As she brushed off the excess dust, exposing a clear fingerprint for Senator Martin Epps, she slowly set down her brush and reached for the tape.

"Is that Epps's?" Alex asked, his face inches from hers.

"Yes," Lizzy said, pulling the tape slowly off the print and pressing it to the card, then repeated the steps on the rest of Epps's fingerprints. It took time, but she was able to get a complete print for every finger.

Letting out a breath, she handed the card to Alex. "Scan it and compare it to the partial from the rock that we found. If Epps was the one leaving the orders for Phylicia, then we can take him down tonight."

Alex took the card and scanned it. Lizzy watched as the fingerprints appeared on the screen on the left while the partial print was visible on the right side. The software began an analysis as lines connected. Lizzy leaned forward holding her breath. Every fingertip, every ridge, every nuance of the print was analyzed and compared to the partial print she'd recovered weeks earlier.

"Dude," Alex said slowly, turning to look at Lizzy when the results flashed across the screen.

Dalton was impatient. Epps was holed up in his

office and Birch's interview would be starting soon. He felt as if he were the one teetering on the edge of a cliff. He either fell off into nothingness or soared across to the answers, waiting on the other side. It was so close he could almost reach out and touch the answer to solve all this.

Dalton leaned forward as his phone rang — Jason.

"Hey man, did you find anything out?" Dalton asked his former mentor.

"Yeah. The man's name is Hugo. His mother was a diplomat. His father was an actor. His mother retired from the Swedish government when she married. They moved to L.A. and Hugo was born and grew up in the States. After college, he worked for the Swedish government for a couple years before coming back to the States and taking a security job at one of the movie studios. Then he started a bodyguard business for some of the actors he made connections with."

"Which studio?" Dalton asked.

"Stanworth Motion Pictures," Jason responded.

"Of course," Dalton said, connecting another dot. He filled Jason in on what they'd found and Tate's killing of Fitz.

"That lines up with what Hugo told me. He doesn't know much beyond Fitz being his handler. But there is something I need to tell you." Jason sounded worried, and Dalton held the phone closer to his ear to make sure he didn't miss a single word.

"What happened?"

"He tried to attack me when I entered this

afternoon. I was going to try to learn more about his time in Sweden. He had taken a strip of his pant leg off. I didn't notice and when I walked in, he kicked out my prosthetic. I fell to my knees and he was behind me with the fabric around my neck. I was close to blacking out when I took my knife and sliced blindly behind me. I hit his femoral artery. I tried to save him so you could question him. I'm sorry, I messed up." Dalton heard the guilt in Jason's voice.

"Jason, you got more information out of him than we thought. He attacked you. I would rather you killed him than he killed you. If I ever get married, someone will have to be my best man, and I would like it if you were around for that."

What the hell? Dalton paused and didn't even hear Jason's response. Who the hell was talking about marriage? He'd never thought of marriage, never mind who the best man would be.

"I'm happy for you, Dalton," Jason said, bringing Dalton back to the conversation completely freaked out. "Lizzy's a great woman. It's about time you got married."

Dalton heard the sadness in his voice. They'd just buried his wife, and Dalton brought up marriage. What the hell was wrong with him? He needed to shoot something—and fast. Dalton almost jumped out of his seat when the door opened to the Russell Senate Building and Senator Epps stepped out.

"Nothing's set in stone. It just popped into my head. Besides, who'd marry me? But look, Jason, the

guy I'm following is leaving. I need to go. Good work today." Dalton asked suddenly, "Are you busy tonight?"

"No, what do you need?"

"Want to take a trip?" Dalton asked with a smile. Birch was going to love this.

"Sure. Where to?"

"L.A. and bring the body."

★　★　★

Birch straightened his tie as he sat on the chair in the library. Claudia Hughes was surrounded by makeup crews as she discussed their upcoming interview. Cameras were in place and ready to capture the moment. The managing editor, Larry Wilkinson, was off to the side talking to Tate. He couldn't believe how calm she looked. It wasn't as if in twenty minutes she wouldn't start the first crack in the foundation of *Mollia Domini* with the press of a button.

Humphrey kept close to Birch's side answering any of the questions the crew or Claudia had. Birch eyed Claudia. She was dressed in a patriotic blue suit that seemed ironic, considering who she was in league with.

Humphrey looked down at his phone and excused himself. Claudia shooed the makeup artists off and smiled at him. "Thank you so much for choosing me to do this interview." Her hand came to rest on his knee.

Birch smiled warmly and shifted so her hand fell

off. "Of course. I got the questions you want to ask, and I'm good with them. Do you need to know anything before we begin?"

Claudia shook her head. "I have all I need." She looked off to the side and saw Tate and Larry smiling as they talked. "How's it working with Tate? You know, she used to work at BBN with us. We sure miss her there."

"I bet you do. She's the best journalist out there." Birch looked down and brushed an invisible piece of fuzz from his suit coat as Claudia slowly registered the insult.

"I heard she was your date to the Fourth of July Ball. I bet that caused quite a stir! But Tate's such a sweet girl. You couldn't have picked better."

Birch smiled back, neither confirming nor denying Claudia's statement.

"Mr. President," Humphrey said quietly as he approached Birch. "I'm so sorry to interrupt. This won't take but a minute."

Birch unhooked his microphone and stood up. He placed the microphone and pack on the chair before turning to Claudia, who wasn't all too pleased that he remembered to remove the microphone. "Please excuse me, Miss Hughes."

Birch strolled out of the room with Humphrey and into the soft yellow Vermeil Room across the hall. "Yes?"

"Dalton just called. Jason got information from the hostage. He's a dual citizen, American and Swedish. He worked security for Stanworth Motion Pictures before going out on his own. He took his

orders from Fitz."

"Took? As in past tense?"

Humphrey nodded his little bald head. "He attacked Jason. Jason won. That's why Dalton called. Jason can transport Fitz and Hugo to L.A. right now for us."

Birch let a slow smile creep along his face. "That will make a statement. Make sure Brent Eller is tipped off—anonymously, of course."

"Good. Jason is already headed for Mr. Abel's private jet. I'll have Alex grab Fitz and meet him there."

"Sebastian is going to love this." Birch chuckled.

"Lizzy has instructed me to keep Mr. Abel in the dark about all activities."

Birch stopped laughing. "What? Why?"

Humphrey looked slightly uncomfortable. His bow tie bobbed as he swallowed hard. "It seems Mr. Abel's name has come up in the investigation where it shouldn't. And he asked Lizzy to do some things that were slightly off the books. She did it because it helped the group. But she's cut him out of all future missions until they can clear him in the investigation."

Birch felt the blood drain from his face. Sebastian was his best friend. The only man he could trust until recently. "That has to be wrong."

"I'm sure Lizzy can explain it to you better."

"Mr. President? They're ready for you," Tate called from the doorway.

Birch spun around and walked toward her when he saw she was alone. Dropping his voice, he

asked, "Did you know Lizzy is keeping Sebastian in the dark?"

Tate looked guilty as she nodded. "Um, payments made to and from subsidiaries of SA Tech through the bank in Mexico gave us cause for concern. It's a bank owned by a cartel and was used to pay off Phylicia."

Well, shit. That wasn't what Birch was expecting. He took a deep breath. "Okay. We'll talk about it later. Humphrey, have the group meet here tonight after the bar closes. I think we will have a lot to talk about. Now, let me play nice for one last time."

Birch walked through the door and into the library. It was a comfortable room that he enjoyed spending time in. It's why he chose it for the interview setting. It was relaxed, just like him. At least that was the appearance he wanted to give.

Claudia smiled as a crew member hurried to reattach the microphone. "Is everything okay?"

"Yes," Birch said with a casual smile in return. "Just an everyday occurrence around here. There's always something that needs to be handled. Are you ready to get started?"

Claudia gave a nod to Larry, who set the ball rolling. The camera light turned red and Birch relaxed back in his chair.

"I am Claudia Hughes and this is the *Claudia Hughes News Hour* brought to you from the library of the White House. I'm spending tonight with President Stratton for his first exclusive interview since he was sworn into office." Claudia turned to

face Birch. "Thank you for having me in your home, President Stratton."

"A pleasure, Miss Hughes."

★　★　★

Dalton watched as Epps walked down Delaware Avenue, past his car, and into the park directly behind the office building. He didn't go to the more popular Upper or Lower Senate Park, but kept to this side of Delaware Avenue until he turned into the park just past C Street.

Dalton got out of the car and strolled after Epps. The park in question had two main walking paths that ran catty-corner, forming an X. There was a circular area in the middle where the two paths crossed. Dalton began a slow jog, running down C Street, and saw Epps walking toward the middle of the park. Dalton cut into the park, jogging through the grass and trees past Epps. He reached the circle and took a deep breath, stretching as if he were out for his evening jog. He didn't see anyone until he turned toward the far end of the path Epps was on. A man was walking toward him.

Dalton couldn't see who it was, but the man slowed when he saw Dalton. Dalton did one last stretch and then turned to go down another path, away from the center of the park.

Stopping as soon as he could, he ducked off the path and circled around behind the man he'd seen. From his spot in the trees he made his way closer, tree by tree. The two men stood in the center,

looking toward the senate building. Dalton stopped behind the nearest tree large enough to support his weight and silently pulled himself up. The full leaves of summer hid him from view as the man did a slow circle. Dalton waited as the man's face slowly came into view — FBI Director Kirby.

"I saw a jogger," Kirby said, looking for Dalton.

"Well, he's not here now," Epps hissed. "We don't have much time. I think I'm being followed."

"We shouldn't be here," Kirby said, sounding angry.

"We have a problem, and we have to solve it," Epps reminded him before they both slowly looked around once more. Dalton tried to creep farther out on the limb, but the branch moved. He froze as both men looked toward the tree.

They looked long and hard, but then a squirrel darted down the trunk and the two men relaxed.

"Do you have any leads on the bomb?" Epps asked. Dalton almost fell out of the tree at the mention of the missing bomb.

Kirby shook his head. "Fucking Phylicia Claymore. I was pressured by Mitchell to assign her to that position. I knew she was trouble, but I owed him for my appointment. I never should have played politics."

"It's not your fault, but we have to find it before they can use it."

They? Dalton held on tight with his left hand as he angled his ear toward them and cupped it with his right hand. He was confused. He thought Epps and Kirby had the bomb.

"My contacts in border control tell me the tunnel that *Hermanos de Sangre* use has been seeing increased activity. I'm worried about an attack on that front as well as whatever Phylicia has put into motion before she was killed," Kirby told Epps as he maintained a constant vigilant eye on the park.

"I'm getting stalled on the political front. I was denied permission to travel to Africa. I was told there was a hold for now on entering the country where Phylicia was found. I'm afraid someone is on to us," Epps said, looking nervous again.

Oh, someone was onto them all right. Dalton didn't know what they were up to, but right now he couldn't decide if they were assisting *Mollia Domini* or resisting them. One thing was clear. The time for observation was over.

CHAPTER TWENTY-SEVEN

Tate knew it was coming. The questions had been growing steadily hostile. Claudia had been nice at first. She asked Birch to tell about being the first vice president sworn into the White House since Lyndon Johnson was sworn in as our thirty-sixth president hours after the assassination of President Kennedy. She asked about the Mitchell family and what President Mitchell meant to Birch.

Tate had almost cheered as she stood next to Humphrey when Birch clearly stated he and Mitchell were complete opposites, but he'd been honored and humbled to serve as his vice president. They talked about living in the White House, the perks and downfalls of living the job every minute of the day, and what he does as a way to relax. But then Claudia started hinting at the failing economy.

"Should you relax when the economy is so unstable? The latest reports state that the dollar is on the verge of a complete collapse, which will grind our economy to a halt. Riots, complete financial ruin, people weren't even allowed to pull their money from the banks . . . and you're relaxing at night, living the bachelor life?"

Tate had sucked in a breath apparently loud

enough for Claudia to hear. Claudia shot a smirk to Tate, and Humphrey had to put a restraining hand on her arm.

"I'd like to hear your sources on that information, Miss Hughes," Birch stated with a clear challenge to his voice. "Because the dollar has shown no signs of weakening. In fact, our stock market is strong and overseas trading is on the rise. I've just negotiated three trade deals to benefit American's ability to purchase necessities from foreign countries at a lower price by encouraging foreign investment in America."

Claudia smiled and Tate shivered. "You know I cannot reveal my sources. You would be violating my first amendment rights. Are you advocating the stripping of American rights, Mr. President?"

Birch cocked his head to the side slightly as he looked at Claudia. "No," he said easily, "I'm simply calling attention to the fact that you have no evidence that the economy is in trouble. I, however, can cite study after study as to the stability of our economy. So, let's make sure we stick to the facts, Miss Hughes."

"And the facts are you are too busy being involved in a romantic relationship with your press secretary, Tate Carlisle, to see the crumbling of the economy right in front of your face. Americans are angry, and they are scared. And instead of taking steps to keep their hard-earned money safe, you talk of limiting constitutional rights and focus on supporting a scandalous woman who should have been fired for such immorality as shown in this

photograph." Claudia paused for a second. In edits, this would allow them time to put the photo of Tate up on the screen. "Are you or are you not dating a woman who was fired from her previous job and who has earned quite the bad reputation for, let's just call it, her personal life?"

Tate saw Birch relax. He didn't get angry. But Tate gripped Humphrey's hand so tightly that tears formed in his eyes.

"Yes, I am dating Miss Carlisle," Birch said easily. The world swam in front of Tate's eyes. This wasn't part of the script. "And I'm ashamed of the cruelty perpetrated against a woman by some members of the media and people hiding behind social media. I find the way she has conducted herself with strength, class, and honor during such a vile invasion of privacy as being beyond question. How can you turn against one of your own sex for sharing an intimate act with a man she loved at the time? Are you saying every woman who has engaged in the act of making love has a bad reputation? I sure hope you are not guilty of, according to you, such immoral acts. Instead, the talk should be about such issues as supporting female small-business owners and equal pay, but instead you're focusing on tearing another woman down over her personal life. That doesn't make sense to me."

Tate felt tears prick against her own eyes. Birch had just told the entire world she was his girlfriend while viciously tearing Claudia apart.

"And no self-respecting man would allow you

to call the woman he loved such a disrespectful
name."

Tate lost her battle to the tears. They fell silently
down her cheeks as she clasped her hands over her
heart. She didn't even realize a camera had panned
over to capture her. She didn't hear the makeup
artists claiming it was the most romantic knight-in-
shining-armor moment they'd ever seen. All she saw
was the love on Birch's face as he smiled
encouragingly to her.

"I will say this, Miss Hughes. After seeing the
horrific way Tate has been treated, I am encouraging
Congress to finally pass a federal cyberbullying law.
No woman, man, or child of any race, religion,
gender, or sexual orientation should feel that they
are not safe being the person they are for fear of
online bullies. It's time to stop letting hate and fear
poison us — hatred of a woman who has done
nothing to any of you, fear about this ridiculous
notion that the economy is on the verge of collapse,
and poison from people clearly pushing their own
agendas. The American people will see through the
lies and manipulation. I have faith in them even if
you do not."

Across the room, Tate saw Larry nod his head.
She leaned over to Humphrey. "We need to make
sure the tape is handed directly to Larry. We'll have
a word with him and remind him of the agreement
that the broadcast is required to show unedited
audio of the president. His complete answers must
be included even if they try to limit the impact by
placing graphs or stock video clips over him while

he talks."

All Humphrey could do was nod as he watched Claudia sputter.

Birch took control of the interview from then on. He talked about the great responsibility he faced as president. He talked about his hopes and dreams for the country and its citizens. He talked, for the first time, as if he were president. Sure, he'd had press conferences, but right now he was wearing the presidency to perfection. Power, confidence, and compassion rolled off him as he spoke about his hopes for the upcoming year. Claudia on the other hand, was reduced to simply nodding her head.

The producer gave the wrap-up signal, and Claudia turned a fake and somewhat wobbly smile toward the second camera. "What an amazing conversation with the President of the United States. Thank you, President Stratton. I'm Claudia Hughes and this has been *The Claudia Hughes News Hour*. We'll see you tomorrow when I'll be speaking with actor Kerra Ruby on her new role in this summer's blockbuster."

Claudia turned and held out her hand for Birch who shook it as Claudia provided small talk for ten seconds of airtime while the credits rolled.

"And cut," the producer called. "Thanks, everyone."

The crew swarmed Claudia and Birch, taking off microphones and removing strategically placed lighting. Tate took off across the library for Larry with Humphrey straight on her heels.

"Mr. Wilkinson," Humphrey called out as Larry

worked on shutting down some of the equipment. "I'm sure you're aware this interview has been recorded for historical purposes by the White House. As per our agreement, we will not air such footage. However, I want your personal guarantee that you, and only you, will remain in control of the digital files for this interview."

"Larry, you know how important it is that this interview is shown in full," Tate said softly.

"I do. Why do you think I'm over here doing a crew job?" Larry said, keeping his head down as he worked. "I'll be contacting you when I lose my job. But it needs to be aired."

"Thank you. You always have a place on my team here. You're the best there is at your job, Larry."

Larry nodded and took off out the door with equipment under each arm.

"Will he do it?" Humphrey asked.

"Definitely. He knows a good story when it's presented. I do feel we need to check in on him. I think he'll get a pass after tonight's surprise. But just in case, let's have Brock check him tonight after our meeting and then someone else from the team tomorrow. I want to make sure he's not threatened like Jeff was."

Claudia stormed out a second later. She didn't stop to say anything to Tate, and Tate didn't care. She was just anxious to get Birch to herself. He'd put his election at risk to admit he was dating her. Polls, surveys, and interviews of citizens should all have taken place before he made it public. Tate smiled at

him as he went around the room shaking hands and taking pictures with all of the crew and productions staff. He finally made it over to her and stopped.

He looked at her, and Tate smiled with tears in her eyes again. The amount of love and the emotions running through her was overwhelming. "I love you."

"I love you, too." Birch bent his head and placed an achingly sweet kiss on her lips. "Now, let's go home." He winked.

Tate laughed as Birch placed his hand at the small of her back and they walked from the room. Relief, love, and a sense of peace filled her. Even if she didn't release the video of Claudia, the damage was done.

"I'm telling you, Epps is somehow involved," Dalton said into the phone as he watched Epps head inside his house. "We need to talk to him. I'd do it myself, but with the wife there it would be better if it were the two of us."

He heard Lizzy sigh on the other end of the phone. "Okay. I need a break from collecting all these fingerprints. Alex can use the time to catch up on scanning and running the ones I've done so far. I have the vice president's and most of the cabinet. I still have secretaries of education, veterans affairs, and housing to run. But they're not high on my list of suspects. I have to tell you something. In this meeting, Senator Epps and a couple of other

congressmen and women were there to begin the meeting with a report of some sort. I ran their prints. None of them matched the partial from the rock."

Dalton felt his brow knit. "Epps's fingerprint didn't match? Maybe the print of the rock was of another finger of his."

"Nope," Lizzy said over the phone. "I had a good five fingerprint from Epps. They are not even close to matching. I don't know how Epps is involved, but I do know he's not the one leaving orders for others to carry out."

"Then we really need to have a talk with him." Dalton looked at the house. What did Senator Martin Epps know?

It took Lizzy over an hour to get there. It was closing in on seven, and in his excitement over the interview, the president had asked them to be at the White House to watch the interview and subsequent fallout from the email Brent Eller was going to get in forty-five minutes instead of later that night. Brent, to his credit as a hard-nosed journalist in his past, had insisted on verifying the video before airing it. Humphrey had said the interview went well, but Humphrey was known to be the king of understatements.

Dalton snapped his head to the window when he heard someone tap the glass. Lizzy grinned back from under a ball cap pulled down so far he couldn't see her face. He opened the door and got out shaking his head.

"I totally got you," Lizzy smiled. "And don't

you think it's risky having your car on the same street as Epps?"

"I switched the plate with a house around the corner with the same make car. I'll return them when we're done here." Dalton filled her in as they walked toward the house.

"How are we going to do this?" Lizzy asked.

"When he entered his garage, I cloned the door with my opener." Dalton pressed the button and the garage door opened. They kept their heads down and put black masks on the second they were off the street.

"I told you I heard the door," Senator Epps called to his wife as he opened the door leading into the house.

Dalton moved so fast that Epps didn't see it. His hand closed around Epps's wrist as he yanked him into the garage. Lizzy closed the door and headed inside. From the garage, Dalton heard Mrs. Epps scream again. He should send her flowers or something for the number of times they scared her.

Epps struggled, but one punch to his jaw had his head snapping back and his knees buckling. "What do you want? I'll give you everything, just leave my wife alone."

"It's good to see you again, Senator."

The senator's eyes bugged. "I signed up at the Freemasons just like you told me to last time you broke into my house. I swear."

"I don't give a shit about that. I want to know about the stolen bomb you and FBI Kirby were talking about."

Epps was quiet for a moment. Then he stoically lifted his gaze to Dalton's. "I've been expecting you. Are you going to kill me?"

"Now, why would I do that?" Dalton wondered.

"Because I know about the bomb, and I'm trying to expose whoever you are as the traitor you are."

That got Dalton's attention. "You're telling me Kirby didn't steal the bomb and destroy the biometric evidence proving genocide by the rebel leader?"

Epps gasped. "How did you know about that? Wait, who are you?"

"I'm the good guy, and Senator Epps, I'm beginning to think that you are, too."

Epps nodded. "I am. Kirby came to me with what happened at Quantico."

"Why you?" Dalton asked.

"Because I'd come to him with concerns about the past president and his staff. I was worried they were giving classified information to foreign leaders and rebels. They would say something in private like, 'China could blow up any ship in the South China Sea and they would have the right to do so' and then suddenly there were ships being blown up a couple months later. Then they used it as a reason to give in to China."

"What have you found?"

Epps shook his head. "I need to know who you are. I can't just tell you what I know."

"Epps, you're making me think I shouldn't hurt you and then you go and say something like that. Look, I know Phylicia Claymore orchestrated the

theft of the bomb and that Harriet Hills ordered a mercenary to wreak havoc in the South China Sea. Now you tell me what you know."

Dalton hoped his instincts were right or he'd have to kill Epps after telling him so much.

"I knew it. President Mitchell defeated me, and everyone ignored me as being bitter when I brought my concerns to them. I knew something wasn't right. Something happened in Syria. Do you know about it?"

Dalton nodded. He knew about it intimately.

"It was supposedly a diplomatic mission, but what in reality, it was a payoff. I don't have proof, but Thurmond Culpepper, do you know who he is?" Dalton nodded again. "He gave this lackey a case that couldn't be opened. I saw the kid try to open it, but it was locked. Thurmond said the informant had the key. Now, how in the hell is that possible? Well, I was leaving a meeting with the secretary of state, and I may have hung around a bit."

"You were eavesdropping," Dalton stated.

"Yes. I heard Thurmond send this kid to Syria to collect an ISIS leader with five million in the bag. Where did that money come from? Taxpayers? This kid was as green as could be. I knew there would be trouble. It was just luck that I was in a meeting with Sandra when Thurmond came in the next day and whispered in her ear. The meeting ended abruptly, and I was shown out."

"But you didn't leave?"

"No. I heard Sandra on the phone with some military commander. She told the rescue team to

stand down. She refused to allow the military to go in and rescue the team after their helicopter had been shot down. They did anyway, and now that kid is gone. I mean, nowhere on the face of the earth can I find him."

Dalton felt his breathing pick up. Sandra Cummings, the secretary of state, had issued him to stand down from the rescue. "What were you threatening Thurmond with at the Fourth of July party?"

"Who *are* you?" Epps asked again with amazement. Dalton didn't answer. "Fine, I was going to go public with the helicopter and the missing bomb like that reporter did, who subsequently can't be found either. I thought maybe Sandra had told Phylicia to steal the bomb. I had guessed it was Phylicia after her body was found in Africa. Frankly, I'm surprised I'm still alive. A lot of people have been disappearing."

"Some, and some are just not wanting to be found. Senator, I need you to trust me. Can you do that?"

"Um, I don't know," Epps answered honestly. "Who are you?"

"I need you to back off because I'll need you to bring all the evidence to Congress, and I can't have you looking like an eavesdropping, bitter loser when you do. You understand the situation. It needs to be you as the face of the cleanup to make sure the correct message gets through. I'll be in touch, Senator Epps. Now let's get you back inside."

Dalton walked Epps inside and collected Lizzy

before walking out the front door. They didn't say anything until they were back in Dalton's car. "Sandra Cummings issued my stand-down order during the Blackhawk rescue."

"Sandra Cummings?" Lizzy blew out a breath as Dalton drove her to the house where he had swapped plates. "I'll have Alex run her prints. Could it be her? Could we have found the person in charge of Washington politics for *Mollia Domini*?"

"I sure hope so. Either way she'll pay for leaving men behind and getting my team suspended for doing our jobs."

Lizzy leaned over the console and placed a soft kiss on his lips. "I can feel it. The first crack and tonight the second crack. *Mollia Domini* is falling."

"You know they won't go down without a fight."

Lizzy smiled slyly. "I'm always up for a good fight. Especially when I have you by my side." Lizzy kissed him deeper this time. "I'll see you at the tunnels."

CHAPTER TWENTY-EIGHT

T ate watched in silence as the interview on BBN went from good to worse. She heard Lizzy gasp when Claudia called her reputation into question and as Birch lambasted Claudia for her behavior. An email came through. Larry had just been fired. She'd make sure he'd have a job by the end of the week.

"It's time," Tate said, her voice slightly worried. Brent Eller had once upon a time been a tough-as-nails reporter. But after years of trudging the trenches only to be told to write fluff pieces that ten other reporters were working on, he had quit and founded Tinselgossip.com. Did he pay for stories? Yes. Did he feel sleazy? Yes. Was he still a damn good reporter? Yes. And that was why Tate was nervous to see what he did with the videos she sent.

Birch turned down the volume on Claudia and turned up her competitor as Humphrey brought up Tinselgossip.com on one of the other screens in the office.

CLAUDIA HUGHES'S HYPOCRISY MAKES BIAS EVIDENT – WHAT'S HER AGENDA? was written in huge caps across the top of the webpage. The room let out a collective breath as they read a story written by Tinselgossip's own Brent Eller. It would go down as

one of the best pieces of journalism Tate had ever read about rogue reporters pushing their personal agendas and the need for true independent journalism. Ten minutes later, BBN's competitor broke into the middle of a live interview to show the video. Within twenty minutes, every major news network was live with the breaking story. Larry emailed again—he had his job back, and Claudia Hughes was the one being thrown out.

"Dude!" Alex burst in as Humphrey finished reading Flint Scott's journalistic masterpiece complete with screen shots and comparisons of one hundred politicians and celebrities from around the world, including a clip of Claudia Hughes saying the exact same thing, effectively cutting off *Mollia Domini*'s ability to influence the public. Flint's story was already being picked up by the media as reporters flashed screen shots and wondered for the first time if President Stratton was being set up to fail. The reality of a conspiracy began to sink in on everyone.

"I know! It's great and you did it!" Tate said, hugging Alex.

"Dude, not that. I mean, I *am* great. But I got a match to the partial print."

"Who?" Dalton asked quickly.

"Sandra Cummings."

"What?" Birch and Humphrey said at the same time, both standing up in surprise.

"It's positive. It's her."

"I thought so," Dalton said, smiling. "I can't wait for some payback."

"Payback?" Birch asked.

"I talked to Epps. He and Kirby are working together to try to find out what's going on. They don't know about *Mollia Domini*, but Epps has the skill of eavesdropping. He told me right before I arrived here that Sandra was the one who ordered the Blackhawk to Syria with a suitcase filled with five million dollars. And she's the one who ordered my team to stand down."

"Find her," Birch snapped. Humphrey hurried to the phone and called.

"She's not answering her cell," he told them as he pulled up his phone and scrolled through the numbers before dialing again. "She's not answering her home."

"Call Thurmond," Dalton suggested.

Humphrey located the number and dialed. "Thurmond, Orville here. I need Secretary Cummings immediately. I see. When? What for? Return date? Fine. I expect you in my office tomorrow morning at eight sharp." Humphrey slammed the phone. "She's in the wind."

"What?" the group said in surprise.

"Her flight apparently just took off. Thurmond says it's some kind of family emergency."

Birch ground out between his teeth. "Lizzy, Dalton, find her and drag her back to me."

"Thurmond didn't make the travel plans, and as far as I know, Sandra doesn't have much family besides a son in California."

"Check all the flights. Do whatever it takes to find her." Birch slammed his hand on the desk as

reporter after reporter began tearing down every story Claudia had reported.

Humphrey and Tate's phones were ringing nonstop. Tate shared a look with Humphrey and the two stepped out in the hall. "As much as I want to unravel the web more and find Sandra, we still need to do our jobs. I'm calling in my staff. We need to set things right with Birch's image and his politics. I'm afraid we're going to be too busy for the next couple of days to help them."

"Ah, but we are helping them." Humphrey smiled at her and shoved up his glasses with his finger. "I'll call my staff in as well. Go tell Birch. We'll gather in the Roosevelt Room."

Humphrey was already calling his staff as he walked out of the residence and headed for the West Wing. Tate pulled up her contacts and sent a brief text to her staff before talking to Birch.

The room was full of activity as Tate closed the door. Alex was on his laptop. Birch and Brock stood by his desk in deep discussion. Dalton and Lizzy were talking animatedly in front of the bank of televisions.

"Birch, I have to go. Humphrey and I are pulling the staff together. We're fielding so many calls. I'm sorry I can't stay."

Birch wrapped her in his arms and kissed her. "You were fantastic. You and Alex saved us. I'll be down in a little bit."

A knock sounded at the door and everyone froze. Birch tightened his grip on her as his eyes shot to Dalton, Lizzy, and Alex. He didn't need to say

anything. They were already slipping into hiding.

"Yes?" Birch called out.

Gene opened the door and Agent Abrams walked in. "My shift just started, sir. I didn't know what the plan was after—" Abrams gestured to the television. "I can't believe it."

"Tate is on her way to the press offices. Humphrey is heading that way, too. I'll be down in a bit. Can you walk Tate down and check with the Uniformed Division to see what's happening outside after this breaking news? By then I should have a handle on this situation."

"Yes, sir. Ma'am?" Abrams stepped back and Birch gave Tate one quick kiss before letting her go.

"I'll see you soon."

Tate left the room with Abrams trailing after her. She heard Gene asking if there was anything Birch needed and then closed the door when he'd been dismissed. Tate hadn't even realized the butler had been there. However, as she looked around, she noticed there were a couple of staff members still on the floor. No wonder Birch had been so paranoid about keeping the door closed.

"Found something," Alex said, drawing Birch's attention from the door Tate had just exited. "The only flights that left this area around the time of our call to Thurmond are these."

A list of twelve flights displayed on the screen. Paris, London, Los Angeles, New York City, Dallas, Rio, Mexico City, St. Thomas, Atlanta, Minneapolis, Jacksonville, and Salt Lake City.

"How can you narrow it down?" Dalton asked as he looked up at the list.

"I'm running the names of all the passengers who checked in on those flights right now," Alex said, sitting back as his computer worked.

"Shouldn't you have just searched her name first?" Lizzy asked.

Alex snorted. "Dude. You think I'm like an amateur or something? I already did that. There's not a single Sandra Cummings in the entire country flying right now. She used a fake name. I'm pulling up all the tickets of Caucasian female passengers within eight years of Sandra's age and matching her height and weight."

His computer finished and a list of seven names appeared on the screen. "Wow," Lizzy whistled. "We can work with that."

"Dude." Alex rolled his eyes as if Lizzy had just insulted him. Apparently she had because less than five minutes later they had pictures of all seven women. "Bingo. Number five, Sally Coleman. Destination: Bucharest, Romania, with a connecting flight in London. She arrives tomorrow afternoon."

"Let's go," Dalton was already standing up. "We can take another of Sebastian's planes."

Birch shook his head. "No. Fly military. Do you still have your cover from when you were in the South China Sea?"

"Yes, but flying private—" Lizzy started to argue.

"Save what money we can. Something is off with Sebastian. Until I find out what it is, I want you

off the grid as much as possible," Birch instructed.

"Let's get our uniforms," Dalton sighed.

"You better hurry. You can leave from Andrews in two hours. I'm getting you all lined up. You'll be about ten hours behind Sandra. Good luck," Alex said as his fingers flew over the keyboard. He shoved his shaggy hair out of his eyes and redoubled his efforts.

Lizzy and Dalton nodded. "Be safe," Birch called out as Brock checked the hall before slipping them out. A sinking feeling settled in his stomach. It was hard sending people he'd begun to think of as his only friends into danger.

Brock returned just as Alex shut the laptop. "I got their travel all set up and just sent them their info. I have to get back to the bar. The two old geezers are watching it, and they've probably drunk half the beer themselves. This double life is exhausting."

Tell him about it. Birch was tired of pretending he didn't know what was going on. He wanted to look *Mollia Domini* in the eye and tell them he was coming for them. Birch let out a deep breath and closed his eyes as Brock made sure Alex left unseen. If Birch couldn't challenge them, then what Jason was doing would have to do for now.

Birch let out a harsh breath and picked up the phone. Brock returned and at least now there was something Birch could control. "Brock, tomorrow I want to go on a date with Tate. A real, honest-to-goodness date someplace outside of the White House."

There was a knock on the door. "Come in," Birch called out as Brock shook his head. Gene walked in and stood quietly, waiting to speak.

"A date? Tomorrow? We need more time to plan," Brock told him.

"No. I know every president before me has gone out for lunch on the spur of the moment. You're lucky, I'm giving you a heads-up to plan a dinner date." Birch smiled at Brock, who didn't smile back before turning to Gene. "Gene, can you order enough pizza for the entire chief of staff's and press secretary's staff and have it sent to the West Wing? They're going to be at it all night."

"Sure thing. Maybe some caffeinated beverages as well?" Gene suggested.

"Perfect. Thanks, Gene," Birch said before turning back to Brock. "How about Gimiagano's?" Birch asked. Tate loved Italian and that was his favorite hole-in-the-wall place to eat.

The door closed as Gene left and Brock pulled up the restaurant on his phone. "This is good. It's not a hot spot. And with it being slightly out of downtown, there's less foot traffic we have to worry about. I'll put a team together."

"Let's walk down to the West Wing and see how the team's doing, and you can plan what you need for tomorrow." As Birch headed to the West Wing, his mood was buoyed. Things were finally going their way.

It was almost early morning when Tate finally rested her head on Birch's chest. They lay entwined in bed simply enjoying the quiet. There was something relaxing about feeling the person next to you in bed. Tate's hand absently roamed the plains of his chest and abs as his hand stroked her back. That night had been successful beyond all belief. The team had prepared a statement that Tate had released after Birch signed off on it. Request for media interviews and passes to the next day's press conference went through the roof. More and more stories were appearing that showed the press was slowly connecting the dots the team was laying out for them.

Flint had called her, stating he was gathering even more information now that other journalists were going public with stories they had wanted to follow but had been pressured to abandon. Journalists were tracking down each person Flint had outed. Tinselgossip.com ambushed Kerra Ruby coming out of dinner at a posh L.A. restaurant. She'd stammered about making a difference. Another Hollywood action hero was hiding behind his manager and had reportedly hired the top PR spin doctors in the world to help him out of the mess.

In hours, downloads for certain movies and music slowed so substantially for the artists named that some had already come out and begged for forgiveness. They placed the blame on their agent or their PR company, which reporters dug into, finding that the PR company in common with these stars

was JES Public Relations in Hollywood and New York City. Jill E. Sage, the ex-wife of Fitz Houlihan, owned JES. Unlike most exes, Jill and Fitz were still partners in every way. Socially they were each other's dates if need be and bed partners when they wanted. Professionally, JES Public Relations recommended Fitz as an agent for its clients and vice versa. By morning, Tate guessed JES would be closing its doors temporarily as they attempted to spin the story. But like all of Hollywood, you let the scandal die down and then reinvent yourself. No one truly disappears.

Birch stroked his hand down Tate's bare back, and she snuggled in closer. "I wanted to ask you something."

"Hmm?" Tate murmured as she ran her fingers over his chest.

"Would you go on a date with me tomorrow? Say eight o'clock?" Birch asked.

"You mean, doing what we're doing now?" Tate teased.

Birch shook his head as he looked down at her. "No. A real date. In public. You and me and a small team of Secret Service," he said with a smirk and a little bit of nervousness.

Tate grinned against his chest before pushing up on her elbows and looking him in the eye. "I'd love to. But aren't you worried about, well, everything?" The thoughts of what the media would say about a president dating his scandalous press secretary would give her nightmares.

Birch stroked his fingers lightly over her back.

"I'm no longer afraid. I don't want to live my life according to a poll. I love you, Tate. I know our situation won't be easy, and it won't be private, but I'll do whatever it takes to make it as normal as possible so we can see where this goes."

Tate pulled herself closer against him. In a time of darkness, what they shared was her light. "Then you have a date."

Tate laughed as Birch pumped his hand into the air before rolling her over onto her back. The searing kiss he placed on her lips, however, was no laughing matter. They were each other's salvation. And as their tongues caressed and his hand moved to cup her breast, Tate put aside all the worry of the future for just one moment.

"Mmm. You think I'll get a goodnight kiss even if you have to pay for dinner?" Birch asked as he looked down at her. "I have no idea if my credit card still works." His finger gently pushed back a lock of hair from her face.

"If I had a dime for every time a man tried to get out of paying for a date because he was president, I'd . . ." Tate paused and cracked up at the look in Birch's eyes. "Well, I'd have a dime."

Tate's phone rang at the same time Birch's did. They rolled their eyes as they answered. Her deputy was talking so fast Tate could hardly understand him. "Okay, I'll look. Thanks. Now get some rest before the morning chaos."

Tate hung up at the same time Birch did. "That was Humphrey. Something about Tinselgossip.com."

"Me too," Tate said, pulling up the site on her phone. She blinked when she saw it. Then tears began to form.

Birch smiled and squeezed her to him. "I could have already told them it was true love."

Brent Eller had followed up on his piece about Claudia with an insider scoop on the love story of the president and the press secretary. The makeup artists had told him what had happened during the Claudia interview. There was a picture of Tate silently crying as her actions were called into question, and there was a picture of Birch hugging her as if she were the most important thing in the world. Then there was a picture of the gentle kiss they shared as well. She read that the witnesses said the president was brave and protective of his love. Tate was described as elegance and intelligence mixed in one beautiful package. References to Camelot were made and Tate stopped reading. She didn't need a fairy tale. She had the real thing.

★   ★   ★

Valeria looked at the man across the table from her. There were more guns than people at the table. The house was a large stucco mansion. It was a bright and cheery yellow on the outside, but the inside was dark. Twelve men sat in the large, deep-brown leather chairs placed around the clunky, thick, wooden farm table. Twelve men and her.

She sat at one end of the table. The head of the house sat at the other. A young woman set down

plates of food, but the man never took his eyes off her. And when he reached for his gun instead of his fork, Valeria knew she'd overstayed her welcome.

THE END

Other Books by Kathleen Brooks

The Forever Bluegrass Series is off to a great start and will continue for many more books. I will start a new series later in 2016, so stay connected with me for more information. If you haven't signed up for new release notification, then now is the time to do it:

kathleen-brooks.com/new-release-notifications

Bluegrass Series
Bluegrass State of Mind
Risky Shot
Dead Heat

Bluegrass Brothers Series
Bluegrass Undercover
Rising Storm
Secret Santa, A Bluegrass Novella
Acquiring Trouble
Relentless Pursuit
Secrets Collide
Final Vow

Bluegrass Singles

All Hung Up
Bluegrass Dawn
The Perfect Gift
The Keeneston Roses

Forever Bluegrass Series

Forever Entangled
Forever Hidden
Forever Betrayed
Forever Driven
Forever Secret
Forever Concealed – coming September 2017

Women of Power Series

Chosen for Power
Built for Power
Fashioned for Power
Destined for Power

Web of Lies Series

Whispered Lies
Rogue Lies
Shattered Lies – coming October 2017

About the Author

Kathleen Brooks is a New York Times, Wall Street Journal, and USA Today bestselling author. Kathleen's stories are romantic suspense featuring strong female heroines, humor, and happily-ever-afters. Her Bluegrass Series and follow-up Bluegrass Brothers Series feature small town charm with quirky characters that have captured the hearts of readers around the world.

Kathleen is an animal lover who supports rescue organizations and other non-profit organizations such as Friends and Vets Helping Pets whose goals are to protect and save our four-legged family members.

Email Notice of New Releases:

kathleen-brooks.com/new-release-notifications

Kathleen's Website:

kathleen-brooks.com

Facebook Page:

facebook.com/KathleenBrooksAuthor

Twitter:

twitter.com/BluegrassBrooks

Goodreads:

goodreads.com/author/show/5101707.Kathleen_Brooks

You Choose Stories: Superman
is published by Stone Arch Books,
A Capstone Imprint
1710 Roe Crest Drive
North Mankato, Minnesota 56003
www.mycapstone.com

STAR39712

Cataloging-in-Publication Data is available
on the Library of Congress website.
ISBN: 978-1-4965-5825-1 (library binding)
ISBN: 978-1-4965-5830-5 (paperback)
ISBN: 978-1-4965-5836-7 (eBook)

Summary: Darkseid is back! He's stolen Superman's
Fortress of Solitude, and plans to take over the Earth!
It's up to Superman to fight Darkseid's Parademon army
and protect Metropolis. But will the Man of Steel be
able to defeat one of his most dangerous and powerful
enemies? Only you can help Superman defeat Darkseid
before he conquers the world!

Printed in the United States of America.
010830S18

SUPERMAN™

APOKOLIPS INVASION

Superman created by
Jerry Siegel and Joe Shuster
by special arrangement with the Jerry Siegel Family

written by
Matthew K. Manning

illustrated by
Dario Brizuela

STONE ARCH BOOKS
a capstone imprint

←YOU CHOOSE→

SUPERMAN

Darkseid is back! He's invading Earth
with his Parademon army, and this time he's
making sure that Superman won't interfere.
How is Superman going to defeat his most
powerful and dangerous enemy? Only YOU
can help him. With your help, the Man of
Steel can put a stop to Darkseid's plans in
Apokolips Invasion!

Follow the directions at the bottom
of each page. The choices YOU make will
change the outcome of the story. After you
finish one path, go back and read the others
for more Superman adventures!

The weather is much colder than usual in the Arctic. As a dark figure makes his way through the night, he doesn't feel the cold wind on his face. He doesn't even feel the bite of the icy waters as he dives into the freezing lake.

When he bursts out of the water, moonlight shines on the bold S-shield on his chest and his red cape. The freezing cold air doesn't bother him. He is Superman, the Man of Steel. He can't remember the last time he was cold.

Superman hasn't visited his secret Arctic base, the Fortress of Solitude, in several weeks. So when he emerges from the lake entrance, he wonders if he somehow got the location wrong. Superman looks up and sees a star-filled night sky. However, there should be a thick layer of ice above his head. There should also be chambers filled with Kryptonian technology, an intergalactic zoo, and trophies from his many adventures. But none of those things are here — only a flat plain of snow and ice.

Turn the page.

Superman doesn't have the location wrong. The Fortress of Solitude is missing!

Superman scans the ground with his X-ray vision. He sees nothing out of the ordinary, so he scans for other types of energy. That's when he notices small amounts of strange radiation floating in the air.

Most scientists would have no idea what could create such radiation. But Superman recognizes it instantly. It's left behind from a device called a Boom Tube. It is the preferred method of travel for the powerful New Gods.

"Apokolips," Superman says out loud, breaking the silence of the cold air. He narrows his eyes. He knows that planet well. It's the homeworld of the powerful tyrant named Darkseid.

Turn the page.

Superman's boots lift off the ice as he raises his arms. He shoots into the sky like a rocket. His red cape waves dramatically behind him in the wind. Superman balls his hands into fists as he breaks the sound barrier, leaving a thunderclap in his wake. If Darkseid has stolen the Fortress of Solitude, he has no time to waste. The hideout isn't just Superman's home away from home. It also houses a large supply of Kryptonite and some of the most dangerous weapons in the galaxy. They are weapons that should never fall into the wrong hands.

And there are no hands more dangerous than those of Darkseid.

No sooner does Superman touch down in Metropolis than he hears a familiar sound.

BOOM!

Superman's super-vision sees the sky light up with the same radiation he saw in the Arctic. A Boom Tube has opened over his city.

Even before the Man of Steel's lightning-fast reflexes can kick in, hundreds of dark shapes cloud the Tube's circular entrance. An entire army of Parademons fills the sky above Metropolis. Each of the flying alien soldiers carries a laser rifle in its hands. They are ready for battle.

Their chanting words echo in the air. They simply say, "Darkseid IS."

If Superman fights the Parademons, turn to page 12.
If Superman flies through the Boom Tube, turn to page 14.
If Superman flees downtown, turn to page 16.

There is no choice in Superman's mind. He has to stay and defend his adopted city. Superman flies up toward the Boom Tube. A Parademon dives at him, its snarling jaws slobbering as it fires its laser rifle.

FZZZZAP!

Superman dodges the blast, swooping upward in one motion. He makes a fist with his right hand and smashes it into the Parademon's jaw. The animal-like soldier falls from the sky and crashes onto a nearby rooftop. Superman continues on. He punches his way through a swarm of nearly identical creatures, armed with identical weapons.

But there are too many of them. No matter how many Parademons Superman takes out, three more seem to fly out of the still-open Boom Tube. Fighting them is like trying to stop a waterfall with a sponge.

One by one the creatures latch onto him until the Man of Steel is completely covered. He looks like a thriving mass of wings, claws, sharp teeth, and armor. The Parademons continue to pile on him even as he barely manages to hover in the air.

Suddenly, the creatures shoot off in every direction. Superman has thrown them off in a huge burst of strength. But more Parademons continue to attack. It won't be long before he's overcome once more. Superman needs a plan.

If Superman allows the Parademons to take him hostage, turn to page 18.

If Superman scans his surroundings for information, turn to page 25.

Superman knows there is only one being who could be responsible for this attack on Metropolis. The tyrant from Apokolips who rules with an iron fist — Darkseid. Superman hates to leave Metropolis alone and unguarded. But he knows that the only way to save his adopted planet is to cut off this attack at the source.

Superman clenches his jaw and prepares for the battle to come. Then he flies through the Boom Tube above him.

BOOM!

The effect of the Boom Tube hits Superman harder than he expects. He falls to the ground, hundreds of feet below.

A few moments later, Superman opens his eyes. He's dazed and it takes him a minute to remember where he is. He's lying on the side of a dirty alleyway. The road twists through a series of rundown metal structures. The only people he sees scurry away into the shadows. They don't want to be a part of what they've just seen.

Superman knows this place. He's been here before. It's the Armagetto, the filthy, rundown home for most of the people of Apokolips.

"Psst . . ." says a voice from the closest structure. The person is trying to be quiet, but Superman could hear his voice even if he simply mouthed the words. "In here!"

If Superman follows the voice, turn to page 21.
If Superman is suspicious of the voice, turn to page 27.

The sky over Metropolis looks like a living mass of wings, fangs, and claws. There are hundreds of Parademons flying out of the Boom Tube. Superman knows he's no match for a horde this size. He needs to gain some distance and see how widespread this problem really is.

In a flash of red and blue, he flies toward the furthest point of downtown Metropolis. Seeing no Parademons, Superman crouches down, then uses his powerful legs to shoot into the sky.

Hovering high above the city, Superman can now see what the Parademons are up to. The majority of the winged aliens are gathering near the Daily Planet Building. In the air above the building, the alien soldiers seem to be putting together some sort of large device.

Using his telescopic vision, Superman immediately recognizes the technology. It's Kryptonian. What's worse, at the center of the device is a familiar green glow. Before Superman can react, the Parademons activate the machine.

The entire sky over Metropolis quickly turns an eerie shade of green. Superman suddenly feels weak. It's clear what has happened. The sky has been contaminated with Kryptonite!

If Superman leaves the city, turn to page 23.
If Superman heads underground, turn to page 29.

Dozens of Parademons charge Superman. But instead of raising his fists and preparing for a fight, the hero lowers himself to the rooftop of a nearby skyscraper. While his face appears ready to do battle, Superman does not fight back. He merely lands on the roof and places his arms at his sides.

The first Parademon tackles him in less than a second. But Superman remains unmoved. A second Parademon grabs him, followed by a third.

Superman is soon covered in Parademons. He lets their combined weight pull him down. The red and blue of his uniform disappear under the yellow and green armor of the Apokolips warriors.

"That's enough," says a grating voice from across the roof. Superman knows who it is. He recognized the strange heartbeat the second he set foot through the Boom Tube. Unlike a normal heart, this one seems to ooze rather than thump or beat. It fits the robed man's personality perfectly.

Superman feels himself being lifted to his feet. He sees two Parademons carrying large high-tech shackles and lets them bind his hands. He wants to see this man with the oozing heart. He wants to see Darkseid's henchman face to face and have words with this man they call Desaad.

Turn to page 32.

Superman stands up and makes his way to where the man is whispering to him. The man is an older citizen of Apokolips. He puts his arm around Superman to help steady him. His attempt at helping the weakened Man of Steel doesn't go unnoticed. Superman smiles at the man as they enter the rusted metal structure the man calls home.

"You'll be safe in here," says the man in a raspy voice. "Well, as safe as one can hope to be on Apokolips."

"Thank you," says Superman. "I'm . . . the Boom Tube . . . it must have affected me more than I thought."

Turn the page.

"No," says the man. "I doubt it's just the Boom Tube."

The man helps Superman into a rickety chair before heading to a small circular disc on the wall. The disc looks like a hubcap or a garbage can lid. But when the man touches it, it begins to spin in a circle. Its center slowly opens until the disc becomes a metal ring outlining a simple window.

"Look," says the man. "Up in the sky."

Superman does as he's told. The Apokolips sky is its usual red hue, but there's something different now. The clouds appear to be a sickly green shade.

"Is that . . . Kryptonite?" Superman whispers. But the old man doesn't answer. There's a knock at the door.

If Superman tells the man to open the door, turn to page 34.
If Superman hides, turn to page 52.

Superman knows he can't waste any time. Kryptonite is a radioactive rock from his home planet. It's the only thing known to weaken him. And Darkseid's Parademons have successfully polluted the air over Metropolis with the dangerous substance. If Superman is going to survive, he needs to get out of Metropolis fast. He needs to leave before his powers are completely drained.

Superman lands on the sidewalk. His legs feel surprisingly weak. He narrows his eyes. Just leaving the city is going to take every ounce of strength he has.

Turn the page.

Superman is surprised at how slow he's moving. As he rushes to leave the city, he still travels at a speed impossible for even the best track athletes. But to Superman, it seems he's moving at a snail's pace. He likely breathed in some of the Kryptonite in the air.

If this were a normal day, Superman would retreat to his Fortress of Solitude. There he could regroup and plan a way to end Darkseid's attack. But the evil godlike tyrant has already stolen Superman's sanctuary. Superman's home . . . and his home away from home . . . have been taken away from him. The Man of Steel's mind races almost as quickly as his feet. Where does he go now?

If Superman heads to Smallville, turn to page 36.

If Superman travels to the Justice League Watchtower, turn to page 55.

Before the Parademons can regroup, Superman scans the area with his telescopic vision. The Parademons that aren't attacking him seem to be focused on various tasks. Some are swarming around the Daily Planet Building. Others huddle in packs near the Galaxy Communications building. Superman can tell they are constructing something on each skyscraper. And if they're following Darkseid's orders, whatever they're building can't be good.

As the Parademons begin to attack him again, Superman flies toward the Daily Planet Building.

Turn the page.

The Parademons on the *Daily Planet's* rooftop are huddled around the building's famous rooftop globe. They seem to be altering it, outfitting it with alien technology. Superman recognizes the machinery right away. It's too advanced to be anything from Earth. And it's not from Apokolips either. It's Kryptonian technology from Superman's own home planet.

But Krypton was destroyed when Superman was just a baby. There is only one place Darkseid could have gotten this machinery — the Fortress of Solitude. Superman's jaw clenches in anger. But before he can act, he hears a shout from inside the *Daily Planet*. It's Lois Lane's voice.

"Superman, help!" she screams.

If Superman goes to help Lois, turn to page 68.
If Superman attacks the Parademons, turn to page 86.

Superman hears a voice calling to him from the shadows. He uses his super-vision to see the man standing by a rickety building.

"This way," says the man.

Superman stands up. He feels weaker than normal. The Boom Tube must have taken more out of him than he realized. But he's not so weak that he needs to put another person in danger. Or worse, fall into the trap of one of Darkseid's lackeys.

"Go back inside," Superman says instead.

The man rushes out to him. Superman can see the fear in his eyes. The man offers him a torn, brown robe.

"For a disguise," says the man. "So . . . so Darkseid can't find you."

Turn the page.

Superman takes the brown robe and thanks the man. He feels a tinge of guilt for not trusting this stranger. But this is Apokolips. He can't afford to trust anyone.

Draping the rough brown fabric over himself, Superman continues down the alley. At the end of the backstreet, the Man of Steel sees a group of other similarly dressed peasants gathering. There is a man standing on a monument in front of them. The stone statue is of Darkseid. Its rocky face matches the tyrant's own perfectly. No one notices Superman as he steps forward to mingle with the crowd.

"This oppression has gone on long enough!" the man standing next to the statue is saying. "The time has come to rally our forces and to —"

But he doesn't finish his speech. Darkseid's son Kalibak has stepped into the town square.

If Superman attacks Kalibak directly, turn to page 71.
If Superman stays hidden among the crowd, turn to page 89.

Kryptonite is one of the only substances in the galaxy that can harm the Man of Steel. Even the smallest piece can cause him extreme pain and weakness. The thought of the air above Metropolis filled with the stuff is overwhelming. Superman knows he has to get away.

He looks over his shoulder and sees a manhole. Using his super-speed, Superman quickly rushes over to the manhole and rips the cover from the street. He quickly drops down into the sewer, feeling his boots splash into the murky water. Most people would have a hard time seeing in this dark and shadowy tunnel. But it's not a problem for Superman.

Turn the page.

Superman's vision adjusts instantly. He rushes forward through the tunnel. He wants to put as much room between himself and the Kryptonite-filled surface as possible. He soon finds a metal ladder leading deeper into the city's underground. He ignores the ladder, and instead simply leaps down the steep drop. He stops himself in midair right before splashing into a huge pool of filthy water.

Superman looks around the dimly lit chamber and hovers over to a connecting tunnel. The long metal passageway is dry. He lands on its dirty floor. The surface seems to have been untouched for many years. In front of him the tunnel splits in two directions. One tunnel leads back up toward the Daily Planet and Darkseid's Kryptonite engine. The other leads away from Metropolis toward the countryside.

If Superman leaves the city, turn to page 48.
If Superman heads uptown, turn to page 73.

"Desaad," Superman says, locking eyes with the figure in the purple robe.

"Superman," Desaad replies. "You can stop pretending to be weakened. I know what you're up to."

"And what's that?" Superman asks, even though he knows the answer.

"You're curious as to why we're here," says Desaad. "You're waiting for me to tell you all about our plan."

"Well, go ahead," says Superman. "You know you want to."

"How about I do you one better?" says Desaad. "How about I show you?"

Focused on Desaad, Superman didn't notice what the Parademons were up to. Aside from those that attacked him, the other Parademons all seem focused on individual tasks.

Superman looks to his left. A group of Parademons are grouped on top of the Daily Planet Building. It's where Superman works while disguised as mild-mannered reporter Clark Kent. Superman looks to his right. Even more Parademons are huddled on the roof of the Galaxy Communications building.

To the Man of Steel, the swarming aliens look like bees, crawling around their various hives. And like bees, the Parademons are certainly up to something. There is a plan to their chaos.

Turn to page 38.

"Open the door," says Superman. He musters his strength and gets to his feet.

The old man's face turns paler than before. He goes slowly to open the front door. Behind the door stands one of Darkseid's elite soldiers. He's dressed like a musketeer from stories Superman read as a child. Although he wears a smile on his face, the man is anything but friendly.

"Kanto," Superman says.

"I see you got our invitation," says the man at the door. "Tell me, what do you think of our new weather project? We couldn't have done it without the wonders stored in your precious Fortress of Solitude."

The man called Kanto opens his mouth again. But before he can speak, Superman rushes across the small room!

WHUNK!

With a devastating uppercut, Superman knocks Kanto flat on his back — unconscious. Superman peers out the door. Six Parademons stand facing him, their laser guns pointed at Superman's head. But the Man of Steel used his last ounce of strength to deal with Kanto. He isn't ready for this type of battle.

"Out the back!" yells the old man from behind Superman.

Superman slams the door shut as best he can and then limps after the old man.

Turn to page 42.

Metropolis is Superman's home, and the Fortress of Solitude is his home away from home. But there's one other place the Man of Steel once called home — the tiny country town of Smallville, Kansas.

After leaving Metropolis, Superman takes a second to get his breath. Then, steadying himself, he uses all the strength he has left to launch into the air. He flies slower than normal, but still lands at the Kent farm in just a few minutes. He's far away from Metropolis now. He can finally breathe deeply. The fresh country air smells sweet, and it cleans out the traces of Kryptonite still lingering in his lungs. It will only be a matter of minutes before Superman has his strength back completely.

"Clark!" comes a voice from the small farmhouse behind Superman.

The Man of Steel turns to see his mother, Martha Kent, rushing out to greet him. Her face is full of worry. Behind her is Superman's father, Jonathan. He looks just as concerned.

"We saw the news, son," Jonathan says as Martha hugs Superman. The force of her embrace takes Superman off guard. "We're glad you're okay."

"I'm fine, Pa," says Superman, sounding more like his alter ego — Clark Kent. "I just need to collect myself for a second before heading back out."

"I'm glad you came," says Martha. "This doesn't look like something you can just punch your way out of."

Turn to page 45.

Desaad approaches Superman and grips the chain between the hi-tech shackles binding his hands. He takes a moment to smile at his captive. "Come along," says Desaad. "There's much to show you and very little time to do it."

Superman follows Desaad across the rooftop. He decides to play along for now. Before he can take action, Superman needs to understand Desaad's plan. Luckily, Desaad seems more than happy to tell him all about it.

Standing on the ledge of the skyscraper, Superman looks out at the Daily Planet Building.

"Look closely now," says Desaad, pointing to his swarming Parademons.

Superman uses his telescopic vision to better inspect the Daily Planet Building. Bit by bit, the Parademons seem to be changing the outside. They're attaching electronic panels to the building. Some are busy wiring sections together. Some are busy ripping out stone and glass, letting the debris fall to the street below.

Turn the page.

"That . . . that's Kryptonian technology," says Superman.

"Ah," says Desaad with a laugh. "You're starting to understand now. Our lord and master, Darkseid, has plans for this city. For this entire world, really."

"You're using tech from my Fortress to . . . what, create some sort of satellite towers?" Superman says.

"The short answer is yes," says Desaad. "Darkseid will broadcast a frequency to make your fellow Earthlings as obedient as his Parademons. All will be ready and willing to do as the lord master requests."

The shackles binding Superman's hands snap, falling to the rooftop at his feet.

"Yes," says Desaad through yellow, crooked teeth. "It's time to act, isn't it?"

Superman grabs Desaad by the purple cloth of his robe and lifts him easily. Desaad's feet dangle over the side of the skyscraper.

"And you would be successful, I'm sure, if I hadn't stalled for so much time," says Desaad.

Superman's head feels light and woozy.

"For you see, the towers are finished and operational," says Desaad. "And that buzzing you feel in your brain? That's the frequency. That's Darkseid's will taking over your own."

"I . . ." says Superman. But he can't say another word. He freezes in place.

"Now put me down," says Desaad.

Superman has no choice but to obey.

"Oh, won't this be fun," Desaad says with an evil grin.

THE END

To follow another path, turn to page 11.

Superman and the old man stumble out onto another Armagetto back alley. The Man of Steel looks up to the sky. The clouds maintain their green, Kryptonite-tinged hue. The atmosphere must be completely laced with the radioactive material. Superman can't remember when he last felt this weak. Only Kryptonite, rock from the core of his exploded home planet, has this effect on him.

"I need to get back to Earth," Superman says, as he puts all of his weight on a piece of scrap metal in the street. "Rushing here, unprepared . . . it was a mistake."

"Well, at least you still maintain your keen intellect," booms a voice behind Superman.

Superman notices the shadow before he sees the impressive figure casting it. As the Man of Steel turns around, the figure begins to laugh.

"Ha!" the imposing figure says from lips that look as if they are chiseled from stone. "This was all much too easy."

The large man standing before Superman has come here alone. He is not backed by an army of Parademons as Kanto was. This man needs no help. This man needs only his own superior strength and nearly indestructible form. The one standing in front of Superman is the notorious ruler known as Darkseid.

Superman locks eyes with the dark god.

Turn the page.

Aside from The Flash, his ally in the Justice League, Superman is the fastest person he knows. But the Kryptonite-filled air has slowed his reflexes. As he lunges for Darkseid, his movements are painfully slow to the dark god.

Darkseid merely puts out his palm. He effortlessly catches Superman's fist. Then he delivers a punch of his own to Superman's face. The Man of Steel falls to the ground, unconscious and broken. Darkseid looks down at his opponent. He seems disappointed that the fight is over so soon.

"Darkseid IS," says the old man standing near his dwelling. He kneels to his ruler.

"Yes," says Darkseid in a gravely voice. "Darkseid most certainly IS."

THE END

To follow another path, turn to page 11.

"Who's doing this?" asks Martha. "It's . . . it's Kryptonite, isn't it?"

"It's a powerful being called Darkseid," says Superman. "He's trying to conquer the Earth like he did his own planet. The Kryptonite is just his first strike to weaken us." Clark pauses. He grinds his teeth in anger. "To weaken *me*," he grates.

Martha puts her arm around her adopted son as Jonathan pats him on the back. The three walk toward the farmhouse.

"He's got technology that can just alter the air like that?" says Jonathan. "That's beyond anything I've seen."

"It's Kryptonian, Pa," says Superman. "My people used this type of technology to purify the air near their cities and . . ."

Superman freezes in place.

Turn the page.

It's all so simple. Superman just needed a break from the action . . . a moment to think straight. He knows this technology. It's from his Fortress of Solitude after all. All he needs is a way to communicate with it.

Superman looks away from the Kents' house. He uses his telescopic vision to look beyond Kansas and hundreds of towns and suburbs. There, in the Metropolis neighborhood called Suicide Slum, Darkseid has set up a home base. He has teleported Superman's own Fortress of Solitude right to the edge of the battlefield.

Pausing only to hug his parents, Superman takes off into the air. Flying at full speed, he's back in Metropolis within seconds.

CRASH!

Superman breaks through the wall of his Fortress of Solitude. He only has seconds before the Kryptonite in the air takes its toll on him. He flies past dozens of Parademons into the Fortress' monitor room. He begins typing on the computer, faster than human eyes can see.

Within moments, the Kryptonian machines in Metropolis come to a halt. In another second, they begin to hum again, but the engines are pumping in reverse now. Superman is using the technology to suck the Kryptonite out of the air.

Suddenly, Superman feels a shooting pain in his back. He turns to see the hulking figure of Darkseid standing over him.

Turn to page 60.

Heading back toward the Daily Planet Building doesn't make sense. A direct attack on Darkseid's forces in the Kryptonite-laced atmosphere would be suicide for Superman. He turns toward the tunnel heading to the countryside outside of Metropolis.

It takes him longer than he expects, but Superman is soon outside the city limits. He uses his X-ray vision to look above him through the dense layers of earth and tunnel. He's reached the end of the sewer system, and all he sees on the surface is a factory and a few parking lots.

At the end of the tunnel is a ladder. Superman decides to conserve his energy and climbs the ladder instead of flying. But for some reason, he still feels weaker than usual.

When he gets to the top, Superman pushes a manhole cover out of his way. It seems heavier than it should be. He steps out of the sewer and into the daylight. But there's no sun to greet him. Instead, all he sees is the sickly green color of a Kryptonite sky.

"There's more than one engine," says a voice to his side.

Superman turns to see Darkseid. The towering New God's rocklike features are twisted into a wicked smile.

"If you're wondering how the Kryptonite has spread so far, that's your answer," says Darkseid. "You had quite a lot of it in your Fortress. I thought, why not make multiple engines?"

Turn the page.

Superman makes a fist and sprints at Darkseid. But he's too weak. His hand feels like it shatters when he punches the dark god in the stomach. Darkseid is unmoved. Superman crumbles to the ground.

"You disappoint me," says Darkseid. With that, the tyrant's eyes begin to glow. His powerful Omega Beams shoot from his eyes, creating a red zigzag through the air until they hit Superman.

ZZZOT!

Superman lurches forward in pain. And then he simply disappears. Where he has gone, or if he even exists any longer, only Darkseid knows.

Darkseid's grin widens. There is no longer a Superman. Only Darkseid remains. Only Darkseid IS.

THE END

To follow another path, turn to page 11.

The old man locks eyes with Superman. The knocking at the door continues.

"You can't be here!" whispers the man. Superman only nods in response. The Man of Steel scans the room with his X-ray vision. He notices a secret chamber located behind a metal bookcase. Without being offered the room, Superman limps over toward it. He pushes the bookshelf out of the way, and then disappears behind it.

The old man watches Superman slide the bookshelf back into place. Then he finally opens the front door.

"Yes?" says the man.

In front of him stands a soldier in fancy clothing. His yellow beret hat slants to one side, shading his eyes. There is no mistaking Darkseid's elite soldier, Kanto.

"Kneel, worm," says Kanto. He smiles despite the cruelty in his voice.

"Yes, master," says the old man. "Of course."

"A man was spotted outside your dwelling," says Kanto. "He was wearing clothes from another world."

"Another world?" says the old man, trying his best to sound surprised.

"Perhaps you saw him," says Kanto. "He was dressed in a red cape."

"No, master," says the old man. He keeps his eyes focused on the ground. Even a casual glance upwards could enrage the cruel soldier in front of him.

"Of course there would be a substantial reward," says Kanto.

"I've not seen him, my lord," says the old man without pause.

Turn the page.

In the back room, Superman listens intently. Suddenly he hears something behind him. It's a familiar sound to the Man of Steel . . . a heartbeat.

Superman turns to see a young woman, her face full of fear. "It's okay," Superman whispers.

"I know of you," whispers the woman. "Everyone in Armagetto knows of the Superman."

Without another word, she signals for Superman to follow her. He takes a look through the door with his X-ray vision, watching Kanto leave. The old man is safe. Superman turns and follows the woman out the back door of the home.

Turn to page 62.

Now safely outside Metropolis and across the river, Superman looks back at his city. The green color in the sky seems to be expanding. At this rate, the Kryptonite will soon spread to the neighboring suburbs and rural areas. It won't be long for the green sky to cover all of North America.

Superman straightens up as best he can. He feels weak. It's as if he hasn't eaten for days. He presses a button on his utility belt. This was exactly the type of situation that inspired Superman to join the Justice League in the first place.

Superman's body glows, and then he turns a brilliant white color. Suddenly, the Man of Steel disappears.

Turn the page.

The Justice League is a team of the Earth's mightiest heroes. In fact, it is more than that. Several of its members come from far distant planets. They aren't just the Earth's protectors, but the galaxy's as well. Unfortunately for Superman, no one is present at the Justice League's Watchtower at the moment. But Superman knew this going in. Green Lantern had an emergency out of the solar system, and he recruited the majority of the team to help him.

But the Watchtower will serve Superman well. As a satellite floating in space, the Watchtower has exactly what he needs: a place away from Metropolis to plan his next move.

Superman walks across the control center to the large windows overlooking Earth. Through the empty void of space, Superman sees his glowing adopted planet. But Earth isn't its familiar blue self. Much of it is glowing green, as if the Kryptonite sky has almost covered the entire planet.

The situation is worse than Superman thought. Metropolis must not be the only city with Darkseid's Kryptonite generator. Darkseid's Parademons must have set up similar machines in locations across the globe. Not only would the skies weaken Superman, but they would also slowly kill the Earth's citizens. Kryptonite is radioactive. That means the people of Earth will slowly grow sick and die. There would be few, if any, survivors.

Turn to page 65.

Superman stands in place as the melted lead pours over his body. He doesn't feel the scalding heat. His mind remains on the job. As he continues to melt the pipe, he takes a deep breath. His head, and soon his entire body is coated in the liquid metal.

"What is this?" Darkseid says. Superman can barely see him through the dripping metal. Darkseid has dropped down into the sewers to finish him off. The Man of Steel doesn't answer, he simply bends his knees, and then rockets back up to the surface.

Just the few minutes free from the Kryptonite-tainted air helped Superman regain some strength. It's enough to try one more attempt at flying. And one more attempt is all he's going to get.

The quickly cooling lead is working. It protects Superman from the radioactive Kryptonite. Superman has just enough strength to fly up to the Kryptonite engine.

He can still feel pain through the lead, but Superman doesn't stop. He blasts his body through the engine as if it were paper. Then he spins around, and with every bit of strength he can muster, he blows the air left in his lungs as hard as he can. Slowly, the sky above Metropolis begins to lose its green shade.

By the time Superman lands on the street, Darkseid has vanished. Superman didn't hear the Boom Tube, but the tyrant and his Parademons are gone. Superman's powers would return soon, and apparently Darkseid was in no mood for a fair fight.

Seeing a bench nearby, Superman limps over to it and sits down. He would find Darkseid soon enough. But for now, the Man of Steel needs to rest.

THE END

To follow another path, turn to page 11.

Darkseid punches the Man of Steel. The pain shoots through Superman's entire body. The Kryptonite has weakened him, but Darkseid doesn't have the same problem. The dark god is at full strength, and Superman can feel it in every powerful blow.

"Do you think you've won?" Darkseid says, punching Superman again. The Man of Steel's face feels as soft as a pillow to the super-strong tyrant.

"Not yet," says Superman, taking another of Darkseid's punches, this one to his gut.

Darkseid smiles in reply, and then punches Superman again. But this time, Darkseid feels pain in his fist.

Turn to page 104.

The walk is long and difficult. Superman has a hard time understanding the weakness in his legs. He's used to feeling strength in his muscles, where now there is none.

Nevertheless, he follows the woman. After they've walked at least an hour, she stops.

"There," she says, pointing to a large structure that looks like a castle. "They have the technology inside."

"Technology? What technology?" Superman says in a weak voice.

"You call it the . . . Boom Tube," the woman replies.

Superman nods to her.

"What is this place?" he asks.

"This is the resistance," says the woman. "We are the ones fighting against Darkseid and his minions."

"I didn't know there were . . . people like that . . . here," says Superman weakly.

"There are such people everywhere," says the woman.

Suddenly a shadow falls across her face. Superman looks up. Two Parademons are flying above. The soldiers haven't noticed them yet, and Superman means to keep it that way. He pulls the woman into the shadows of a nearby building.

"Go," she says. "The resistance will help you."

There is a part of Superman that believes this might be a trap. Part of him doubts the woman's intentions. But he has no choice but to trust her.

Turn the page.

Superman limps forward through the shadows. At the base of the castle-like structure, he sees a tunnel. He continues on, bracing himself for any possibility. He walks into a chamber and sees an older man holding a Mother Box. The object has the power to open a Boom Tube and send Superman back to Earth.

The man doesn't even seem surprised. "Let's get you home," says the older man.

"I'll come back," says Superman, feeling weaker than ever. "I'll . . . I'll save all of you."

BOOM!

The Boom Tube opens in front of Superman. But the Man of Steel does not enter it. Superman collapses to the ground. He's too weak to move.

"I'll save you," Superman says as he closes his eyes, falling unconscious.

But he doesn't. He doesn't save anyone.

THE END

To follow another path, turn to page 11.

Superman looks at the Earth through the Watchtower's thick glass. He thinks of Krypton, the planet where he was born. The planet he never knew. The Man of Steel clenches his jaw. He refuses to simply sit by and watch another planet die. He turns and quickly walks to the Watchtower's monitors.

Just being away from the Kryptonite-tainted air helps Superman feel renewed strength. He feels his powers coming back to him. His muscles harden and regain their strength. But most importantly, Superman can think clearly once more. The technology that powers Darkseid's Kryptonite engines was stolen from his own Fortress of Solitude. Superman knows that tech better than anyone in the galaxy.

Turn the page.

To put that much Kryptonite into the
atmosphere requires a massive power source.
When Superman saw the Parademons
constructing the Kryptonite engine, he noticed
that the device wasn't very large. That meant
the engines were powered by another source.

Superman types furiously on the
Watchtower's control panel. The monitor in
front of him finally reacts.

PING!

The Justice League's computer has located
the source of the engines' power. It's a large
space vessel hovering on the opposite side of
Earth. Darkseid has taken every precaution.
He's using the Earth itself to hide his spaceship
from the Watchtower!

Superman takes a deep breath of the filtered
air inside the Watchtower. Then, like a missile,
he shoots from the satellite's airlock. He soars
around the Earth and collides with Darkseid's
ship. He darts through the ship's interior,
destroying every piece of technology he finds.

Finally, he punches his way into the engine room. With a giant burst of his powerful heat vision, Superman fries the entire chamber. Then he retreats back into space as the ship explodes.

BOOM!

Superman looks back to the wreckage of Darkseid's spaceship. But there is nothing there. The entire vessel has disappeared thanks to another Boom Tube. Down below, Earth's skies begin to lose their greenish hue. Without their power source, the Kryptonite engines are exploding one by one.

Superman narrows his eyes. Earth is safe from Darkseid this time, but for how long?

THE END

To follow another path, turn to page 11.

With no hesitation, Superman flies down to the *Daily Planet's* newsroom. The room is full of familiar faces, but none more familiar than Lois Lane, the newspaper's top reporter. At the moment she is busy punching a Parademon square in the face.

The Parademon recoils. Then it raises its laser blaster. As it fires, Superman uses a burst of super-speed to put himself between the laser blast and Lois. The shot collides with his chest. Superman doesn't even flinch. Instead, he pulls his arm back, balling his hand into a fist.

POW!

In the next instant, the Parademon is sent flying through one of the *Daily Planet's* windows.

"They're everywhere," Lois says, locking eyes with Superman. Superman turns his head to face the rest of the crowded newsroom. As the employees attempt to flee, Superman counts at least twelve Parademons terrorizing his friends. His eyes narrow.

FZZZZZZZ!

Superman blasts one of the Parademons with his heat vision. Then he flies toward another, slamming the creature's back with both of his fists. As the Parademons rush him, Superman takes them out one by one. A well-placed punch sends one flying. A powerful kick sends another crashing into the wall. Still another is crumpled by a blast of Superman's powerful breath.

In less than a minute, the fight is over. Superman stands over a pile of unconscious alien warriors. And he doesn't look happy.

Turn to page 75.

"No loitering!" Kalibak yells.

Superman has regained some of his strength. He has seen enough. Throwing his robe off, he flies toward the brute in a flash.

"Uggh!" is all Kalibak can say as Superman's two fists strike the brute.

Superman stands above him, looking down at his fallen foe.

"Where's your father?" he asks. Superman's eyes glow red with heat vision.

"Kryptonian scum," Kalibak says through gritted teeth.

But that doesn't answer Superman's question. His eyes grow hotter.

"He's in his fortress," the speaker calls from behind Superman. "Where else would he be?"

Turn the page.

Superman turns to look at the leader of the rebel crowd. The man still stands next to Darkseid's statue. "We can help you," the leader says.

"No," says Superman. "I'm not going to risk any more innocent lives."

"Hrragh!" Kalibak yells as he grabs Superman's leg. With strength rivaling the Man of Steel's, Kalibak hurls Superman back over the crowd into a rusty metal structure.

CRASH!

The building topples down onto Superman. The crowd goes from screaming to silence as it turns to watch Kalibak get back on his feet.

Turn to page 79.

Superman lifts up off his feet and leans forward. He flies straight ahead through the tunnel that leads back toward the Daily Planet Building. Some of the walls down in the sewer are made of lead or coated in lead paint. That means Superman can't see through them with his X-ray vision. But he can see well enough to know that he's moving in the right direction.

It takes less than a minute for Superman to reach his destination. He looks up, and while his view is partially blocked, his X-ray vision can see the Daily Planet Building. He can also make out Darkseid's Kryptonite engine floating in the sky above. All he has to do now is think of a plan.

Turn the page.

Down in the sewer, the Man of Steel is safe from the Kryptonite-filled atmosphere. But the second he reaches the Metropolis street, he's sure the air will affect him. He'll only have a matter of seconds to reach the machine and shut it down. Even for Superman, that act seems impossible.

Suddenly the Man of Steel has no more time to think. With his X-ray vision, he sees a construction worker being attacked by a Parademon. The man is struggling against the monstrous creature high up on a half-finished building. The man slips off a steel beam, and the smiling Parademon just watches him fall.

If ever there was a job for Superman, this is it.

Turn to page 82.

Superman looks up using his X-ray vision. There are hundreds of Parademons outside. They have constructed some kind of signal device on both the rooftops of the Daily Planet and Galaxy Communications buildings. But the Man of Steel knows this technology too well.

He has seen hours of hologram projections of Kryptonian technology in his Fortress of Solitude. Superman is the one person on the planet who knows how to use it.

In less than a heartbeat, Superman flies to the Daily Planet's rooftop. As the Parademons fly toward him, he prepares himself. He'll be ready for them this time.

Turn the page.

THOOM!

Superman claps his hands together with incredible power. His clap is like thunder. The wave of sound and air knocks the Parademons off their feet. Some simply fall over, while others topple off the rooftop to the ground below. The Man of Steel realizes this is only a temporary setback for them. He has to move quickly.

In a blur of blue and red, he rips off a panel on the side of the Kryptonian machine. His hands move faster than the eye can see.

Just as another group of Parademons are about to attack, Superman finishes his task. He presses a button on the machine, and it whines to life. The Parademons behind him suddenly freeze in their tracks. The hordes in the sky pause as well. Their eyes look blank. Their mouths hang open. Superman has taken Darkseid's technology and turned it against the dark god's army.

"Hmm," booms a rumbling voice above the Man of Steel.

Superman looks up and sees a stonelike giant of a man. Darkseid is standing in an open Boom Tube hovering high in the air.

"You should know this is not a defeat," says Darkseid. "This is only a setback until I return in full force."

"I'll be here," says Superman as the Boom Tube disappears, taking its mad god with it. He looks around the sky at the hundreds of Parademons. "And so will your army," Superman says with a smile.

Superman again scans the air over the city.

Well, that seems to settle things, he thinks. *But I'll need to rebuild the Fortress of Solitude. While I'm at it, it looks like I'll have to expand the intergalactic zoo as well.*

THE END

To follow another path, turn to page 11.

A pair of red eyes glows in the rubble. Through the dust and smoke, Superman steps forward. Kalibak is not the one he wants to fight. But he has no choice now.

"You want to meet my father?" Kalibak yells at Superman from across the square. The citizens of Armagetto scatter and take whatever cover they can find. Most rush into the shoddy metal structures that pass as homes on Apokolips. Soon the battlefield is cleared. Aside from a few Parademon soldiers, only Superman and Kalibak remain on the street. "You want to face *him*?" Kalibak shouts. "You don't even deserve to fight me!"

"We'll see," says Superman, hovering up into the air.

Turn the page.

Kalibak leaps at Superman. The son of Darkseid raises his beta club above his head as he jumps. Superman catches the golden weapon just inches from his face. Then he spins, sending Kalibak crashing into the same rubble pile Superman just emerged from.

Superman lands near the fallen structure. He looks at Kalibak. The fight is already taken out of the beast-like man. Kalibak looks as if he can't even keep his eyes open.

"That's always been his problem," says a voice like gravel scraping against itself. "He thinks with his fists."

The Man of Steel doesn't have to turn around to know who is speaking. It's Darkseid. He is perhaps the most powerful being Superman has ever faced.

"Why the attack in Metropolis?" Superman demands, turning to face his enemy.

"Why does one ever fight, if not to test one's theories?" asks Darkseid.

Superman then notices a man standing behind the dark god. It's Desaad, Darkseid's right-hand lackey. He's holding a large, silver weapon. It looks like some sort of huge gun, and appears almost too heavy for him.

Superman recognizes the technology immediately. It's Kryptonian. It looks as if it was pieced together from equipment stolen from his Fortress of Solitude.

Turn to page 103.

Superman doesn't give it a second thought. He doesn't pause to think about his own safety. He doesn't worry about the Kryptonite in the air. He only thinks about the man who is falling to his death. Superman is not about to let that happen.

With his two fists out in front of him, Superman crashes through layer upon layer of underground tunnels. He smashes through lead, steel, and stone until he has flown all the way to the surface. Chunks of concrete fly in every direction as Superman bursts through the sidewalk. Looking up, he flies directly toward the falling man.

The Man of Steel relaxes his arms. When he catches the falling man, he's not like steel at all. Years of living on Earth have taught Superman how fragile humans can be. When he catches the construction worker, it's as if he has fallen into a pool of water.

Superman sets the man down on the sidewalk. Although he holds his breath, Superman knows that the Kryptonite air will affect him anyway. He has only a few seconds left before he becomes as vulnerable as the man he just saved.

With all his strength, Superman crouches down, and then shoots off into the green sky.

Turn to page 85.

Like a streak of red and blue light, Superman rockets toward the Kryptonite engine. Every foot closer brings greater pain and weakness. But Superman ignores it. He continues to climb higher and higher into the green air.

Parademons rush at him, but Superman easily knocks them to the side. He continues to climb higher and higher.

The Kryptonite engine is almost in reach. Superman tightens his fists. The engine is only a few feet above his head, but the Man of Steel can't go any further.

He swings his fist, but misses the engine by only a few inches.

Then Superman falls.

Turn to page 92.

In a fit of rage, Superman sends out a burst of heat vision in the direction of the Parademons. The aliens scatter. A few unlucky Parademons are struck by the super-heated beam and are knocked off the *Daily Planet's* rooftop.

Superman swoops over to the rooftop. In a flurry of super-speed, he punches, kicks, and sweeps away the remaining Parademons. Many are sent flying over the edge to fall to the sidewalk below.

This attack on the *Daily Planet* is too personal. Earth is Superman's adopted home. And now Darkseid's minions are attacking it with technology from his homeworld of Krypton. Darkseid is pitting Superman's two homes against each other.

Through his anger, Superman doesn't notice the man in the purple cloak approaching. Two obedient Parademons carry him on a platform. Superman is too busy fighting the other Parademon warriors to notice the man in purple smile a sickly grin.

Superman finally turns to see the man in purple. His name is Desaad, Darkseid's loyal right-hand man. His is perhaps the most twisted mind in all of Apokolips. Standing behind Desaad is a Parademon holding a figure that Superman knows all too well. In its arms is the struggling form of Lois Lane!

Turn the page.

"Let her go," Superman says through his gritted teeth.

"And hello to you, too," says Desaad. He grins larger now. His teeth look even more rotten than his haggard face.

"I said —"

"Let her go. Yes," says Desaad. "I heard you. However, I don't think I'll be doing that anytime soon. We have a deal to make, you and I."

"I don't make deals with lunatics like you," says Superman.

"And I don't make deals with alien scum in red capes," says Desaad. "But today, I believe we must both make an exception."

Desaad raises his hand. In it is a small black device. It's a remote control. And it has only one button.

Turn to page 96.

"Silence!" Kalibak yells.

The young man standing on the statue looks at him, and then looks at the people.

"Now, my brothers and sisters," the man says. "We rise up! We take on this barbarian and his Parademon hordes!"

Superman peers out from beneath his robe. The man near the statue is just that, a man. Even if he convinced the people to fight, they'd be no match for the super-strong Kalibak and the Parademons standing behind him. Kalibak is the son of Darkseid, after all.

Turn the page.

"Attack!" shouts the man near the statue.
"Revolt! Fight!"

With a rallying scream, the men and women
in the square turn and rush at Kalibak and his
Parademons. Kalibak's eyes widen. He seems
almost afraid.

Then he leaps toward the leader of the people,
easily bounding over the mob of attackers.
Superman has stood by idly for long enough.
He has to act. He lunges forward into the air.
As gently as possible, Superman tackles the
man near the statue, knocking him away from
Kalibak. Instead of hitting his target, Kalibak
collides with the statue of his father, reducing it
to rubble.

As the rebel leader looks around, confused
by what just happened, Superman turns back to
face Kalibak.

Without saying a word, Superman uses his super-breath to create a powerful gust of wind. It blows Kalibak away from the crumbled statue and into a nearby building. Kalibak's head smashes into one of the building's metal support posts.

"Uuhnng," Kalibak groans, before slumping to the ground unconscious.

Pulling his robe's hood down firmly over his face, Superman gets to his feet. It takes him a few seconds longer, but the rebel leader is soon standing as well. They both look to the crowd. With seeming ease, the crowd has successfully chased away the Parademons. Perhaps Superman has misjudged these rebels. Perhaps they're the key to defeating Darkseid after all.

Turn to page 99.

CRUNCH!

Superman hits the pavement. The force of the impact crushes the street. The shockwave knocks down lampposts, trashcans, and mailboxes for two blocks in every direction.

In the crater created by his fall, Superman weakly moves his head.

"Uuhhnng," he groans weakly.

"I would say that was a valiant attempt," says a deep, gravelly voice. "But I don't like to encourage losers."

Superman feels too weak to move his head. But he knows the man who is talking to him. In fact, the speaker isn't a man at all. He is the dark god known as Darkseid.

Soon Superman can see his enemy. Or rather, he can see his enemy's large boots. Darkseid is standing above the crater, his laughter ringing in Superman's ears.

"Before we begin," says Darkseid, "I'd like to thank you."

Superman hears the villain, but he doesn't understand the meaning of his words.

"If not for your so-called Fortress of Solitude, I would never have gained the Kryptonite needed to alter your city's atmosphere," Darkseid explains. "Nor would I have the technology to create the engine in the sky above you."

Darkseid raises his hands and gestures to the sky. "All of this is only possible — because of you."

Superman moves his lips to reply. But he's too weak to speak. The words don't come. Instead, he simply lies there as Darkseid punches him in the stomach, through the street itself.

Turn to page 95.

Superman crashes through the tunnels below. He keeps falling like a ragdoll until he splashes into a sewer tunnel face first. He looks up. Away from the Kryptonite atmosphere, he has enough strength to use his X-ray vision. On the street above stands Darkseid, preparing to leap into the tunnels after his prey. But Superman's vision is partially blocked. The piping above him must be made of lead. Lead prevents his X-ray vision from working. And it also prevents . . .

Superman's eyes open wide. This could be it. This could be a way to defeat Darkseid.

Mustering all his strength, Superman pushes himself to his feet. Then he looks up and begins to blast the lead pipe above him with his heat vision.

Turn to page 58.

"You see," says Desaad as he raises the remote, "my Parademons have constructed two signal towers. Both are activated by the button on this control."

"Signal towers," Superman repeats suspiciously.

"Yes," says Desaad. "Once activated, they'll reduce the people of your . . . Metropolis . . . to nothing more than mindless bugs, following Darkseid's every command."

"I don't believe you," says Superman.

"You don't have to," says Desaad. "It will happen either way. I'm giving you this one chance. Out of curiosity, more than anything. Leave now with this woman, and never return. Or else suffer the same fate as the people of this city."

Superman doesn't answer. He decides to let his actions speak for him. He flies across the rooftop in an instant. His fist collides with the jaw of the Parademon holding Lois hostage. Then he turns toward Desaad and uses his heat vision to burn the villain's hand.

It all works according to plan. Desaad drops the remote control device. The entire fight takes less than two seconds. But Superman should have ended it in one. Desaad is quicker than Superman believed. He managed to press the button anyway . . .

Turn the page.

A man sits alone inside the Fortress of Solitude. But the man in the chair is not Superman. He's not a hero. He's not Earth's adopted savior. The man in the chair is smiling wickedly.

It has been a year since Darkseid first invaded Metropolis. It only took a few short months to take over the entire world. The Parademons started with North America and worked their way east, conquering every country in their path. After the Earth was his, Darkseid used his Boom Tube technology to return the Fortress of Solitude to its rightful place. He now sits in its control room, watching the monitors that show image after image of a defeated world.

Darkseid likes this Fortress very much. He greatly enjoys his new planet, full of billions of new servants. And he especially enjoys the company of his personal butler, who is approaching at this very moment.

Darkseid smiles as the Man of Steel brings him his dinner.

THE END

To follow another path, turn to page 11.

"Thank you, stranger," says the rebel leader.

"I didn't do anything," says Superman. "I'm just one of . . . one of your people."

The man looks at Superman for a few seconds. "My name is Kencade," he says.

"Kal," Superman says. It's not a lie. Kal-El was Superman's birth name on Krypton.

Kencade steps onto the stone platform where rubble now replaces Darkseid's statue.

"Go home," he says. "Gather your friends. Gather your family. Gather anyone strong enough to hold an axe or a battle staff. We meet back here in one hour. And then we take the fight to Darkseid himself!"

Turn the page.

The cheering is almost deafening. It echoes in Superman's ears as he bides his time. He hides in the shadows near the remains of the statue, making sure Kalibak doesn't wake up.

The hour passes quickly, and soon the square begins to fill again. Men, women, even teenagers all gather, ready to risk their lives for what they believe. But they all look worried. They look prepared for a fight, but still concerned about their safety.

Kencade has brought them this far. But if they are going to defeat Darkseid, they need a rallying cry. So Superman steps out of the shadows. He drops his robes to the ground, revealing his bright red cape and his famous S-shield.

"For freedom!" he yells.

The people of Apokolips might not know Superman's face, but they are familiar with the S symbol on his chest. Immediately they fall in behind him, as Superman keeps pace with Kencade.

The crowd's cheers sound like thunder as they storm the gates of Darkseid's palace. The overwhelmed Parademons attempt to fight, but the people's army seems to gain new members by the second. Soon Darkseid's flying alien army retreats to the air, fleeing in every direction.

When Superman and Kencade lead the throng of people into Darkseid's throne room, they find the tyrant waiting for them. But he is calm. He seems almost relaxed.

Turn the page.

"Well done, Kryptonian," Darkseid says to Superman. "You'll find your Fortress where it belongs. And your Metropolis is untouched. But you'll find me again, at your throat, when you least expect it."

BOOM!

The chamber fills with the sound of Darkseid's Boom Tube. Superman watches his enemy disappear. And then he turns to Kencade.

"Darkseid tried to steal your home," says Kencade. "But we took his."

"No," says Superman. "That's not true. You just took yours back."

Kencade smiles. He says something to Superman. But neither can hear the words. The crowd is cheering too loudly.

THE END

To follow another path, turn to page 11.

"This is all a test," say Darkseid. "Let's see if you fail."

ZZZAPP!!!

Superman feels pain in his chest before it spreads throughout his body. His legs become weak and he soon buckles under his own weight. The laser cannon struck him dead center with a concentrated blast of Kryptonite.

"I think we have our answer," says Darkseid. "It seems that robbing you of your Kryptonian technology was the proper course of action."

Superman tries to get to his feet, but he doesn't have the strength.

He feels shackles snap around his wrists. Then he feels himself lifted into the air by the Parademons. But Superman can't move. He can only listen to Darkseid's laughter echo in the street behind him.

THE END

To follow another path, turn to page 11.

Superman straightens himself back up. Darkseid twists his head a little in curiosity. He wasn't expecting the Man of Steel to get a second wind.

"Impressive," says Darkseid in a voice like thunder.

He punches Superman again. Superman remains unmoved.

"Huh," says Superman, smiling. "Looks like that whole Kryptonite thing has finally worn off."

Darkseid's eyes widen. But he's too slow to react. Superman delivers a powerful uppercut to the tyrant's jaw, knocking him clear off his feet.

WHUMP!

After hitting the floor of the Fortress of Solitude, Darkseid doesn't make another sound. He's unconscious. Superman steadies himself, placing his hand on a nearby ice wall. He's not back to full power yet, but Darkseid didn't need to know that.

BOOM!

Hearing the sound, Superman flies out of the Fortress. He's shocked to see the skies of Metropolis suddenly clear. The Parademons have fled the planet, obviously using another of their Boom Tubes.

BOOM!

Superman hears the sound again. Only this time it comes from inside the Fortress of Solitude. When he returns, Superman isn't surprised to find that Darkseid has escaped as well.

The battle is over, but Superman has no time to relax. People may still need his help. Plus, there's the small matter of carrying his Fortress back to the Arctic. Superman smiles, and then he gets to work.

THE END

To follow another path, turn to page 11.

AUTHOR

The author of the Amazon best-selling hardcover *Batman: A Visual History*, Matthew K. Manning has contributed to many comic books, including *Beware the Batman*, *Spider-Man Unlimited*, *Batman/Teenage Mutant Ninja Turtles Adventures*, *Justice League Adventures*, *Looney Tunes*, and *Scooby Doo, Where Are You?* When not writing comics themselves, Manning often authors books about comics, as well as a series of young reader books starring Superman, Batman, and the Flash for Capstone. He currently resides in Asheville, North Carolina, with his wife, Dorothy, and their two daughters, Lillian and Gwendolyn. Visit him online at www.matthewkmanning.com.

ILLUSTRATOR

Darío Brizuela was born in Buenos Aires, Argentina, in 1977. He enjoys doing illustration work and character design for several companies, including DC Comics, Marvel Comics, Image Comics, IDW Publishing, Titan Publishing, Hasbro, Capstone Publishers, and Disney Publishing Worldwide. Darío's work can be found in a wide range of properties, including *Star Wars Tales*, *Ben 10*, *DC Super Friends*, *Justice League Unlimited*, *Batman: The Brave & The Bold*, *Transformers*, *Teenage Mutant Ninja Turtles*, *Batman 66*, *Wonder Woman 77*, *Teen Titans Go!*, *Scooby Doo! Team Up*, and *DC Super Hero Girls*.

GLOSSARY

Arctic (ARK-tik)—the area near the North Pole; the Arctic is cold and covered with ice

beret (BUH-ray)—a visorless wool cap with a tight headband and a flat top

horde (HORD)—a large group

intellect (IN-tuhl-ekt)—the power of the mind to think, reason, understand, and learn

lackey (LAK-ee)—someone who does menial tasks or runs errands for another

musketeer (muhss-kuh-TIHR)—a soldier who carried a musket

notorious (noh-TOR-ee-uhss)—being well known for doing something bad

oppression (oh-PRESH-uhn)—the treatment of people in a cruel, unjust, and hard way

radiation (ray-dee-AY-shuhn)—tiny particles sent out from radioactive material

shackles (SHAK-uhlz)—a pair of metal cuffs locked around the ankles or wrists of a prisoner

tyrant (TYE-ruhnt)—someone who rules other people in a cruel or unjust way

sanctuary (SANGK-choo-air-ee)—a place of safety or protection

DARKSEID

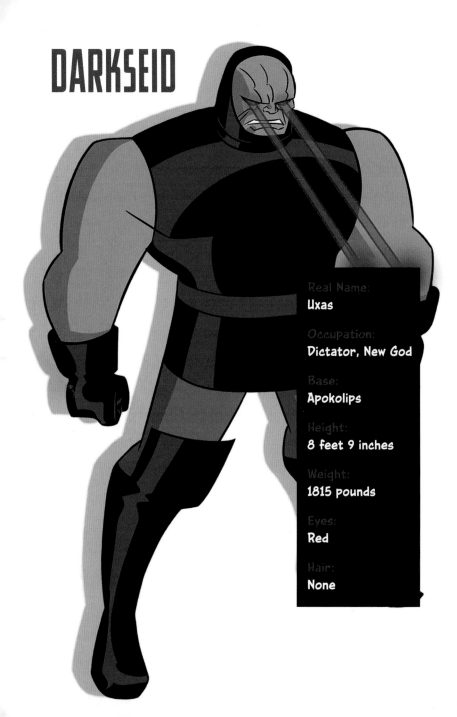

Real Name:
Uxas

Occupation:
Dictator, New God

Base:
Apokolips

Height:
8 feet 9 inches

Weight:
1815 pounds

Eyes:
Red

Hair:
None

Uxas was the son of the King and Queen of Apokolips, and was the second in line to the throne. When he came of age, he killed his older brother, Drax, claiming the throne for himself — as well as the fabled Omega Force. The incredible object transformed Uxas into a rocklike creature, making him nearly impervious to harm. Now, as Darkseid, he rules Apokolips with an iron fist, and aims to take down the Man of Steel, his only true threat. With his unmatched power, Darkseid is nothing less than the most dangerous enemy in the known universe.

- As one of the New Gods, Darkseid's body is not subject to disease or aging. He is considered by most to be immortal.

- Darkseid is nearly invulnerable. However, incredible physical force, like a punch from the Man of Steel, can weaken or even injure Darkseid.

- Injuring Darkseid is difficult enough, but even when he is actually hurt, he's capable of regenerating his body at an incredible pace.

- Darkseid uses his super-strength and endurance to wear down his opponents in battle. He can also shoot Omega Beams, or laserlike blasts, from his eyes (this ability is similar to Superman's own heat vision).

YOU CHOOSE

SUPERMAN

10+ POSSIBLE ENDINGS!